SNOOPY™
PARTY ANIMAL

A PEANUTS™ Collection

CHARLES M. SCHULZ

**Andrews McMeel
Publishing®**

a division of Andrews McMeel Universal

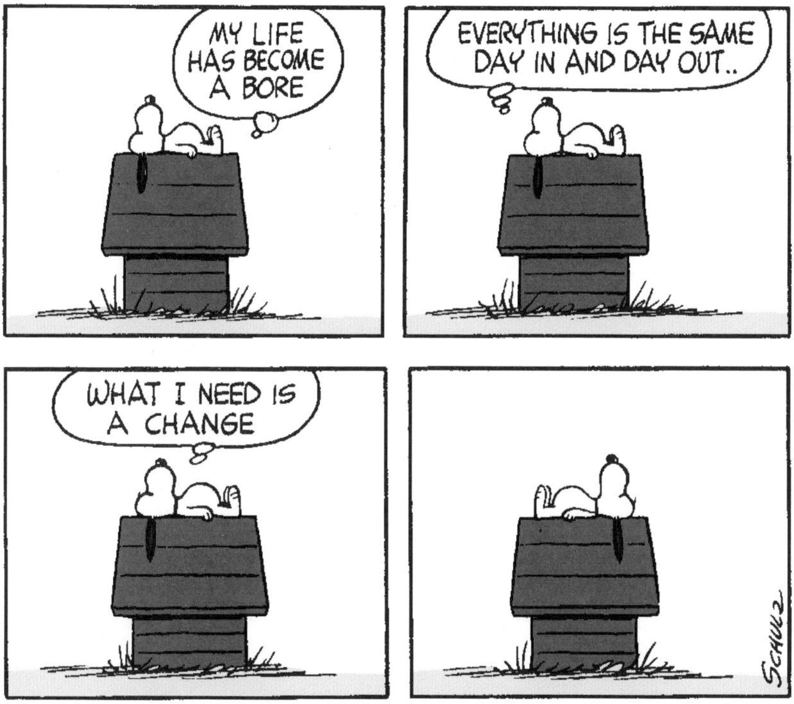
MY LIFE HAS BECOME A BORE
EVERYTHING IS THE SAME DAY IN AND DAY OUT..
WHAT I NEED IS A CHANGE
SCHULZ

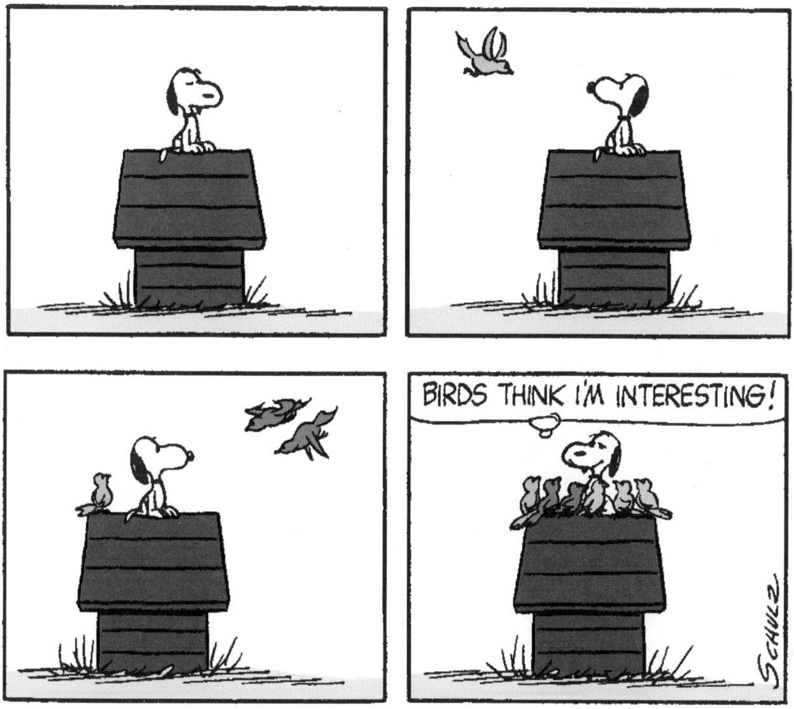
BIRDS THINK I'M INTERESTING!
SCHULZ

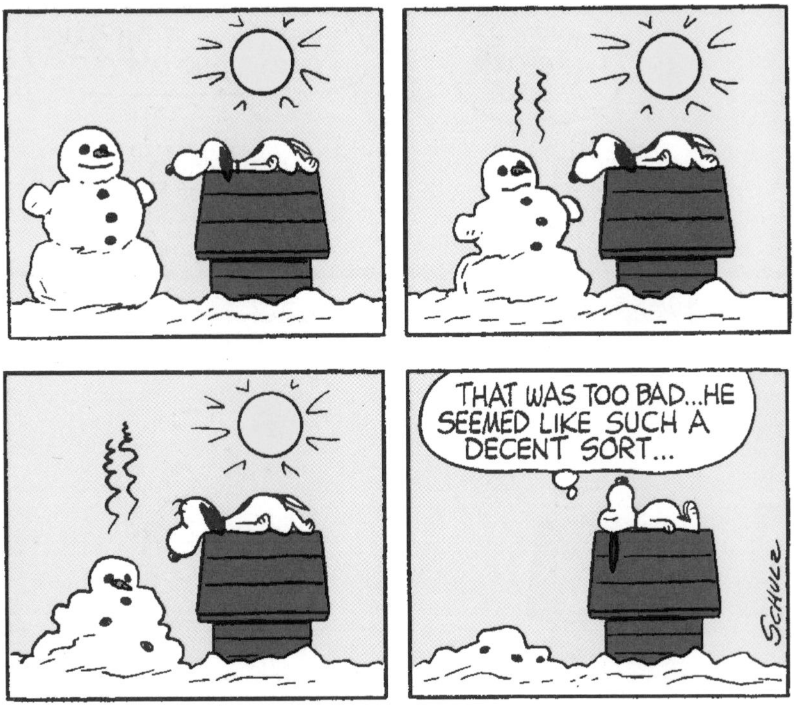
THAT WAS TOO BAD...HE SEEMED LIKE SUCH A DECENT SORT...
SCHULZ

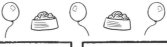

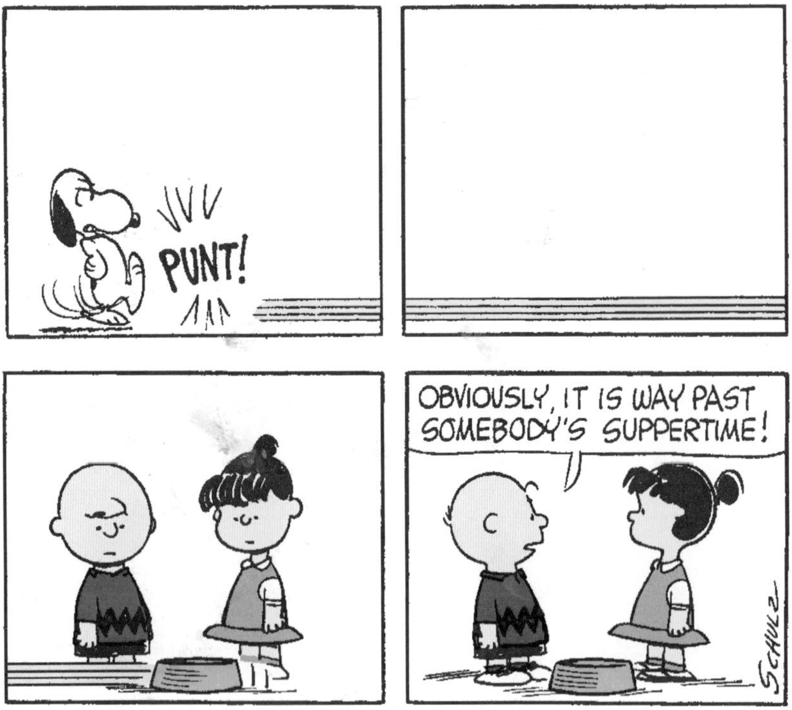
PUNT!
OBVIOUSLY, IT IS WAY PAST SOMEBODY'S SUPPERTIME!
SCHULZ

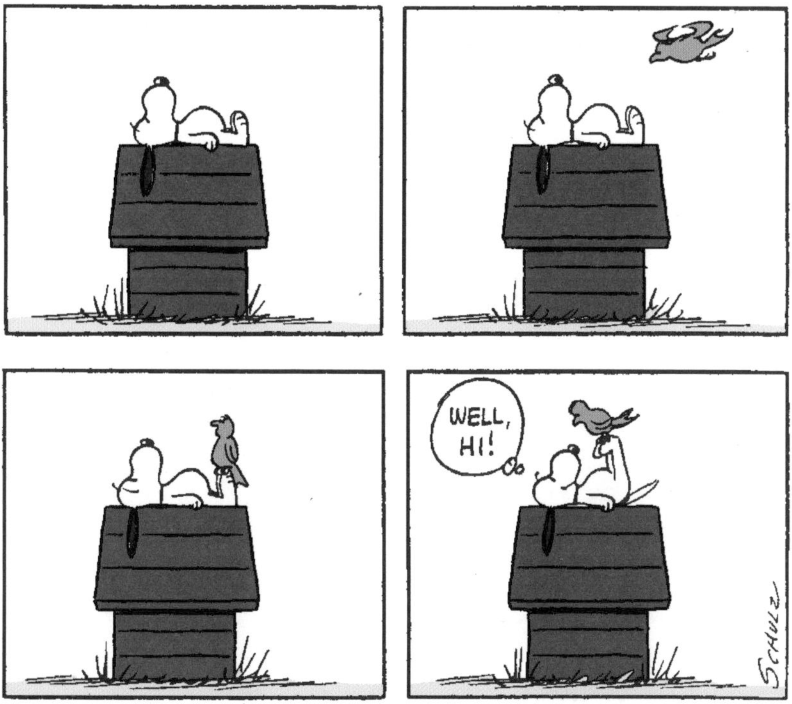
WELL, HI!

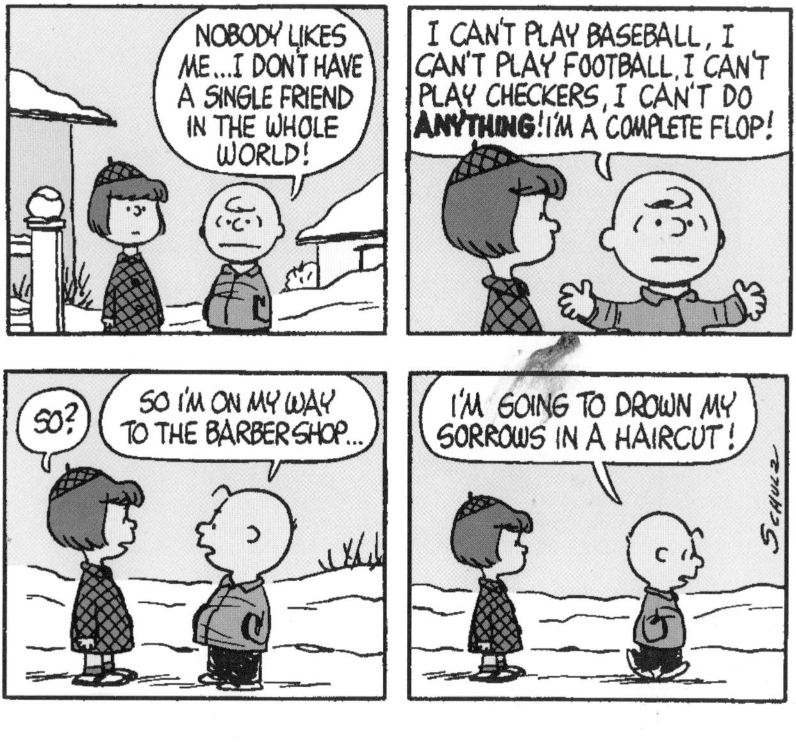
NOBODY LIKES ME...I DON'T HAVE A SINGLE FRIEND IN THE WHOLE WORLD!
I CAN'T PLAY BASEBALL, I CAN'T PLAY FOOTBALL, I CAN'T PLAY CHECKERS, I CAN'T DO ANYTHING! I'M A COMPLETE FLOP!
SO?
SO I'M ON MY WAY TO THE BARBERSHOP...
I'M GOING TO DROWN MY SORROWS IN A HAIRCUT!

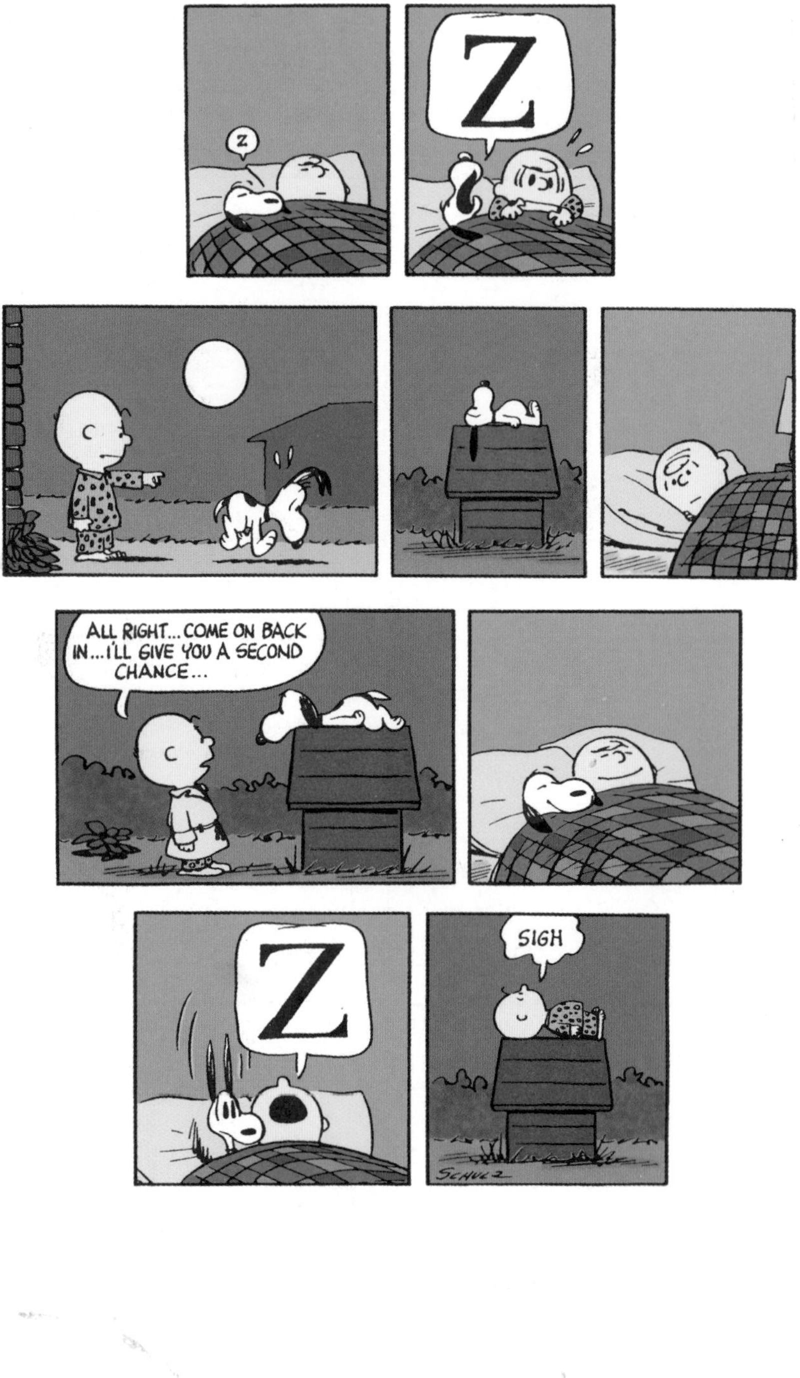
Z
Z
ALL RIGHT... COME ON BACK IN... I'LL GIVE YOU A SECOND CHANCE...
Z
SIGH
SCHULZ

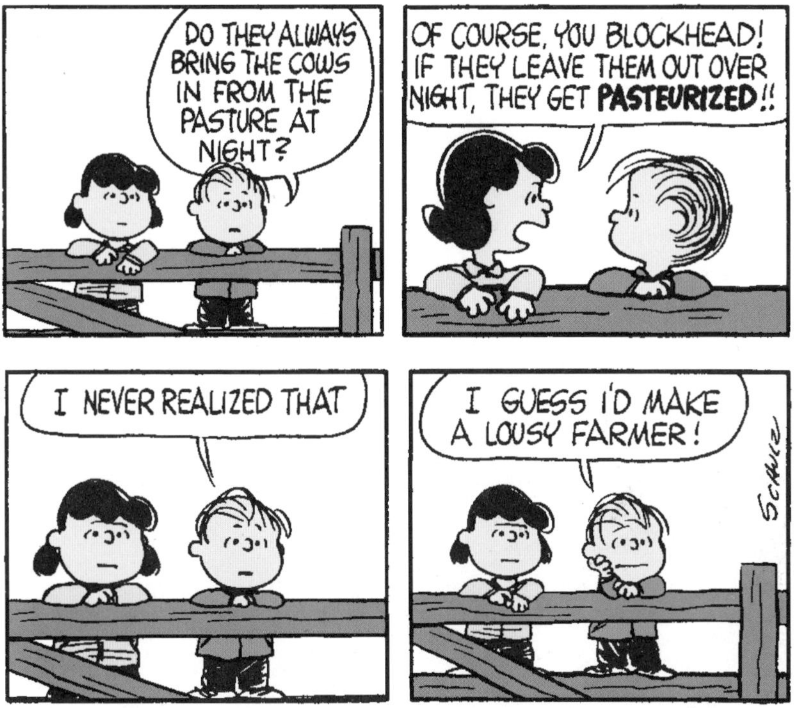
DO THEY ALWAYS BRING THE COWS IN FROM THE PASTURE AT NIGHT?
OF COURSE, YOU BLOCKHEAD! IF THEY LEAVE THEM OUT OVER NIGHT, THEY GET **PASTEURIZED**!!
I NEVER REALIZED THAT
I GUESS I'D MAKE A LOUSY FARMER!
SCHULZ

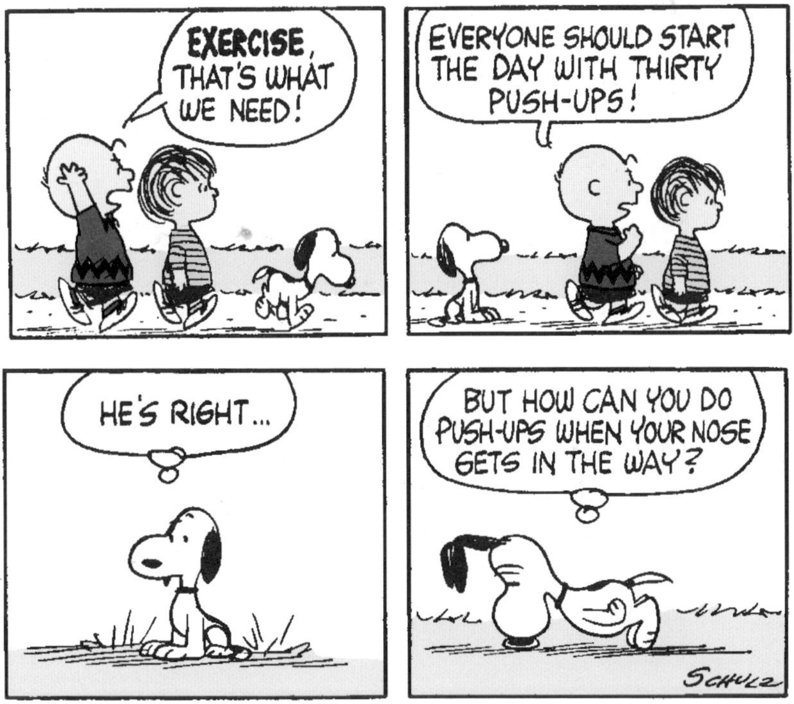
EXERCISE, THAT'S WHAT WE NEED!
EVERYONE SHOULD START THE DAY WITH THIRTY PUSH-UPS!
HE'S RIGHT...
BUT HOW CAN YOU DO PUSH-UPS WHEN YOUR NOSE GETS IN THE WAY?
SCHULZ

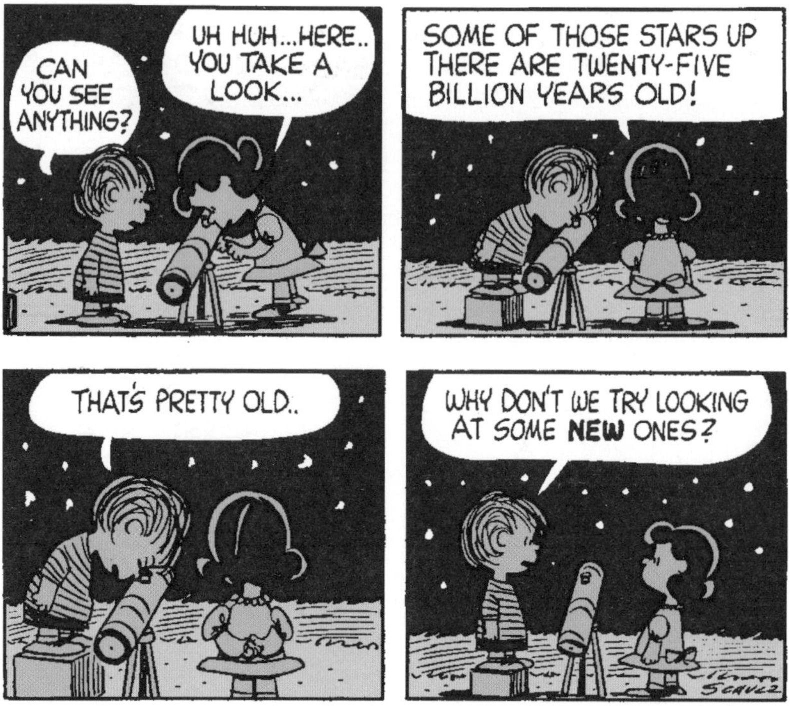
CAN YOU SEE ANYTHING?
UH HUH...HERE.. YOU TAKE A LOOK...
SOME OF THOSE STARS UP THERE ARE TWENTY-FIVE BILLION YEARS OLD!
THAT'S PRETTY OLD..
WHY DON'T WE TRY LOOKING AT SOME **NEW** ONES?

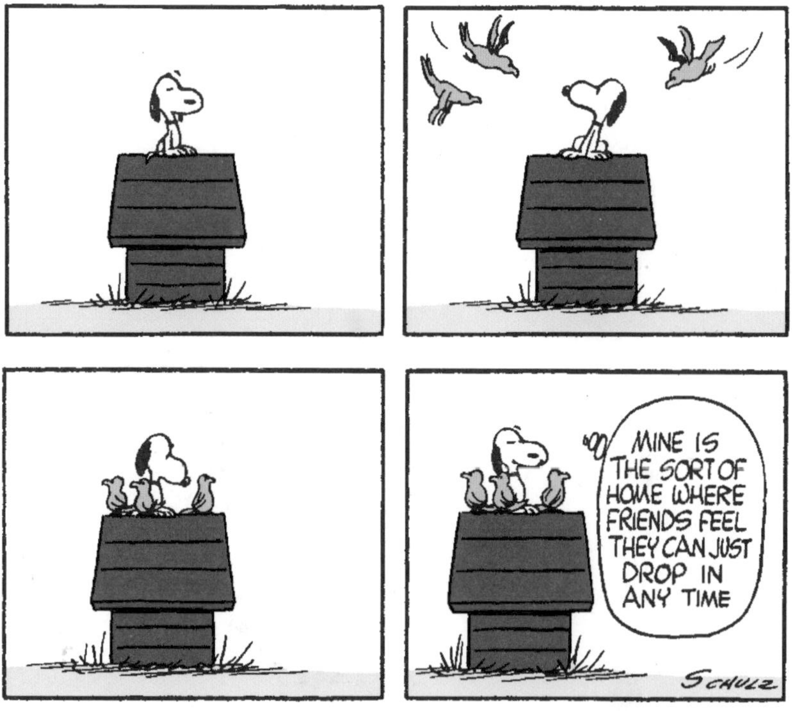
MINE IS THE SORT OF HOME WHERE FRIENDS FEEL THEY CAN JUST DROP IN ANY TIME
SCHULZ

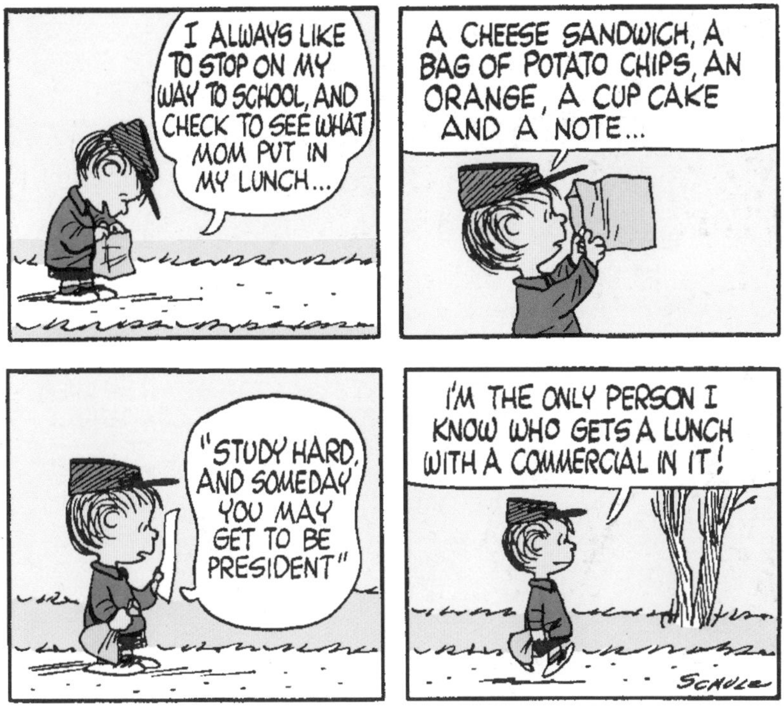
I ALWAYS LIKE TO STOP ON MY WAY TO SCHOOL, AND CHECK TO SEE WHAT MOM PUT IN MY LUNCH...
A CHEESE SANDWICH, A BAG OF POTATO CHIPS, AN ORANGE, A CUP CAKE AND A NOTE...
"STUDY HARD, AND SOMEDAY YOU MAY GET TO BE PRESIDENT"
I'M THE ONLY PERSON I KNOW WHO GETS A LUNCH WITH A COMMERCIAL IN IT!
SCHULZ

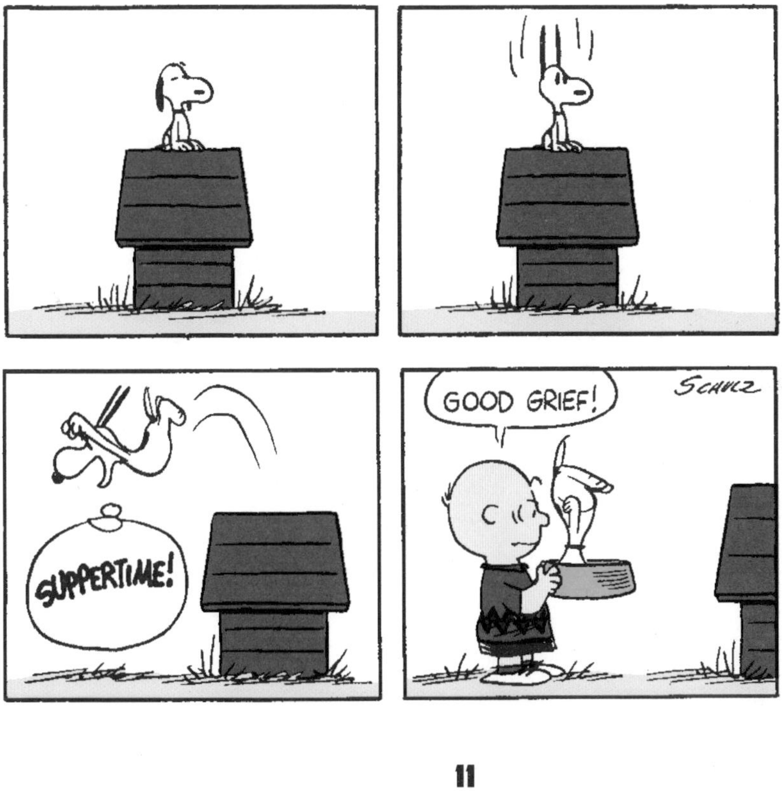
SUPPERTIME!
GOOD GRIEF!
SCHULZ

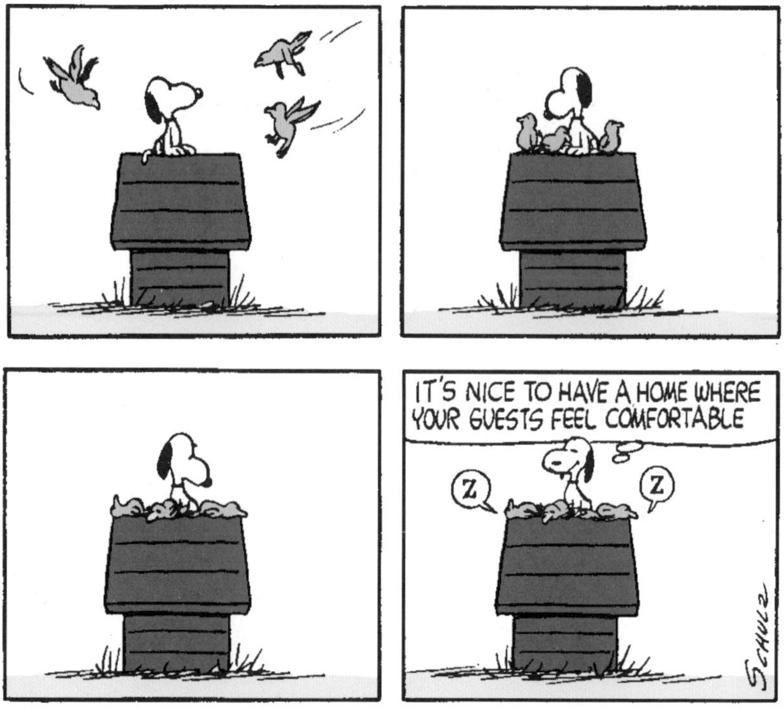
IT'S NICE TO HAVE A HOME WHERE YOUR GUESTS FEEL COMFORTABLE
Z
Z
SCHULZ

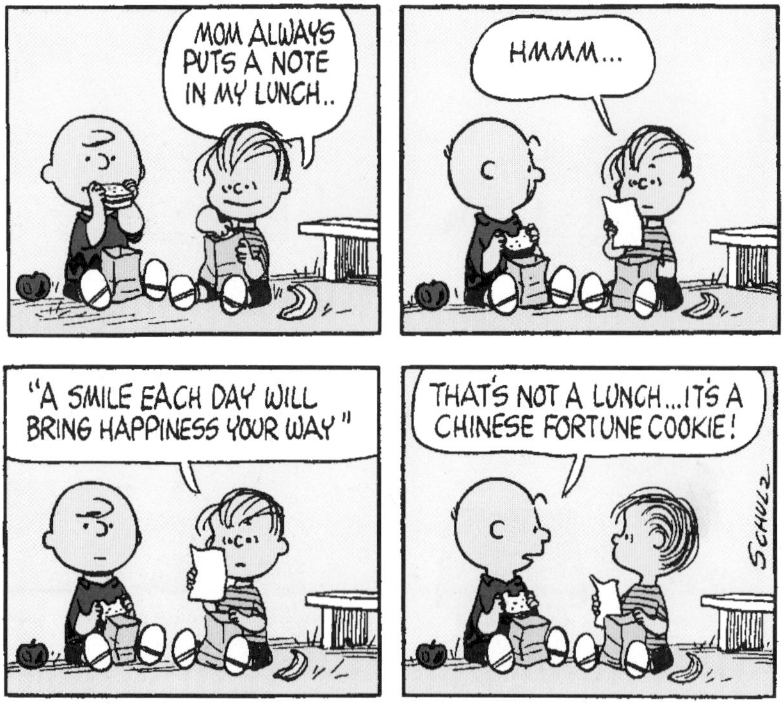
MOM ALWAYS PUTS A NOTE IN MY LUNCH..
HMMM...
"A SMILE EACH DAY WILL BRING HAPPINESS YOUR WAY"
THAT'S NOT A LUNCH...IT'S A CHINESE FORTUNE COOKIE!
SCHULZ

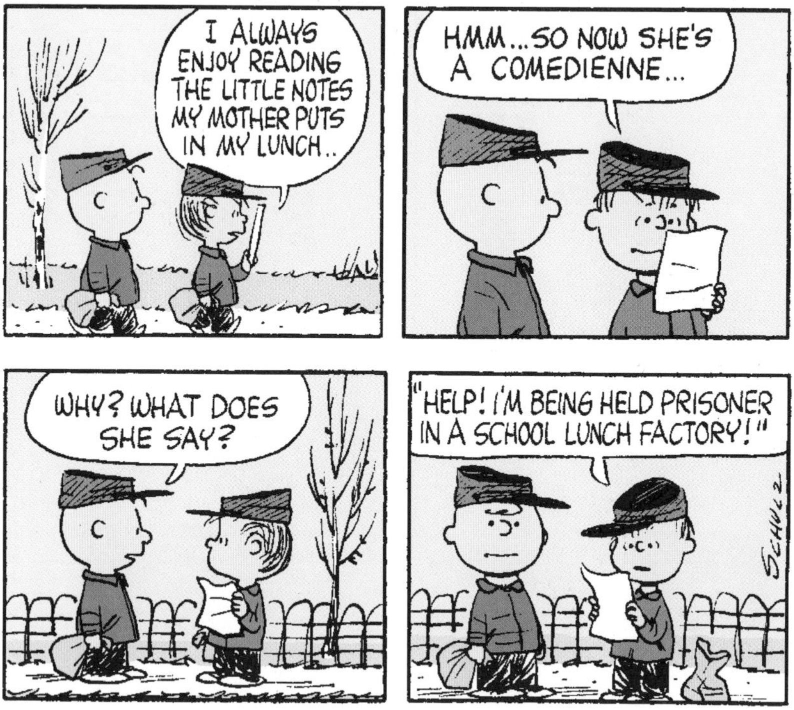
I ALWAYS ENJOY READING THE LITTLE NOTES MY MOTHER PUTS IN MY LUNCH..
HMM...SO NOW SHE'S A COMEDIENNE...
WHY? WHAT DOES SHE SAY?
"HELP! I'M BEING HELD PRISONER IN A SCHOOL LUNCH FACTORY!"
SCHULZ

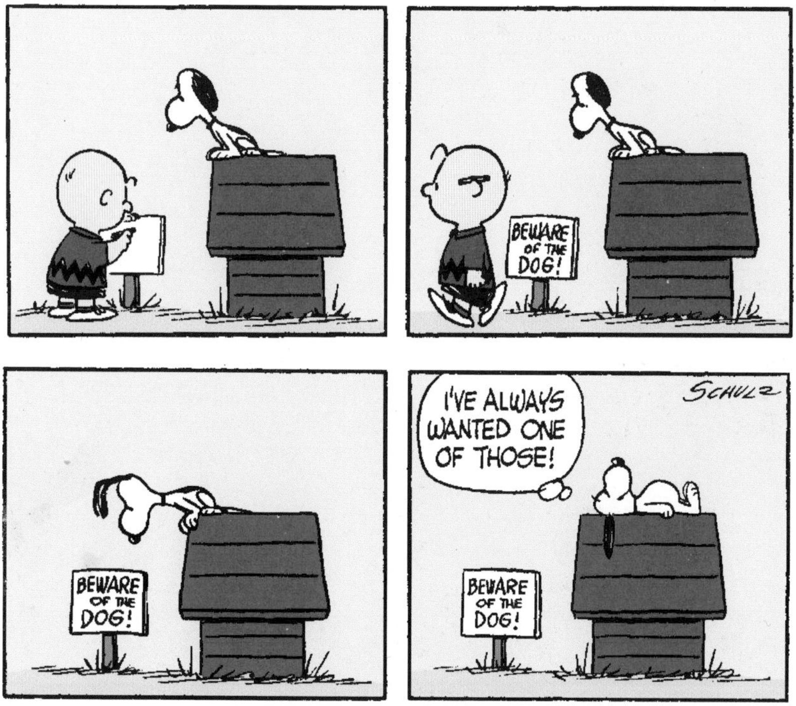
BEWARE OF THE DOG!
BEWARE OF THE DOG!
SCHULZ
I'VE ALWAYS WANTED ONE OF THOSE!
BEWARE OF THE DOG!

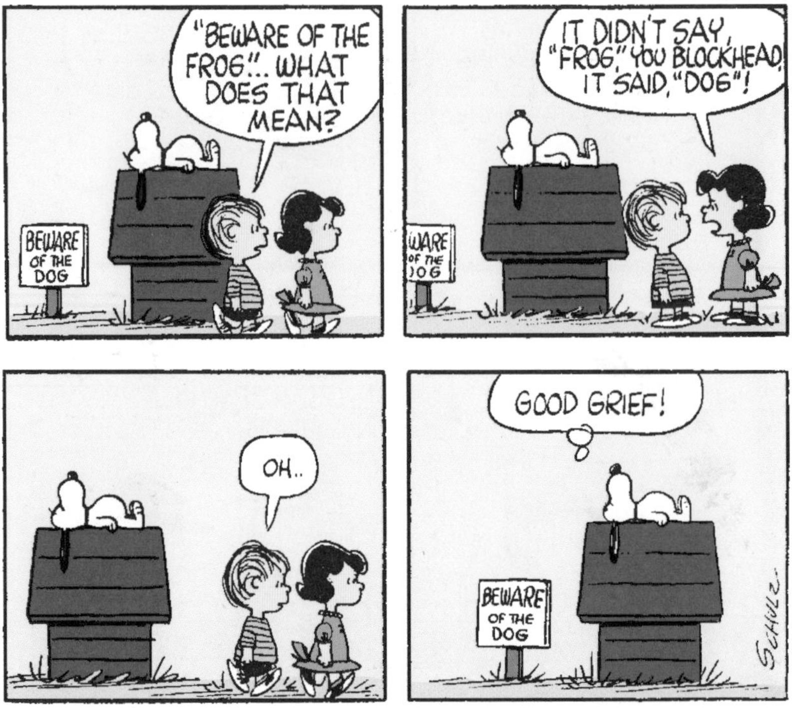
"BEWARE OF THE FROG!".. WHAT DOES THAT MEAN?
BEWARE OF THE DOG
IT DIDN'T SAY, "FROG," YOU BLOCKHEAD! IT SAID, "DOG"!
OH..
GOOD GRIEF!
BEWARE OF THE DOG
SCHULZ

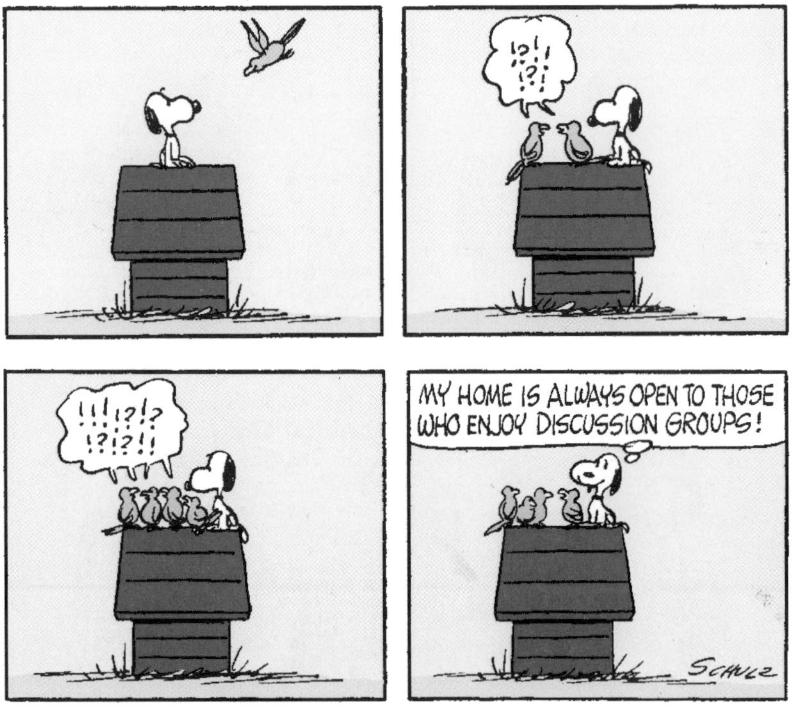
MY HOME IS ALWAYS OPEN TO THOSE WHO ENJOY DISCUSSION GROUPS!
SCHULZ

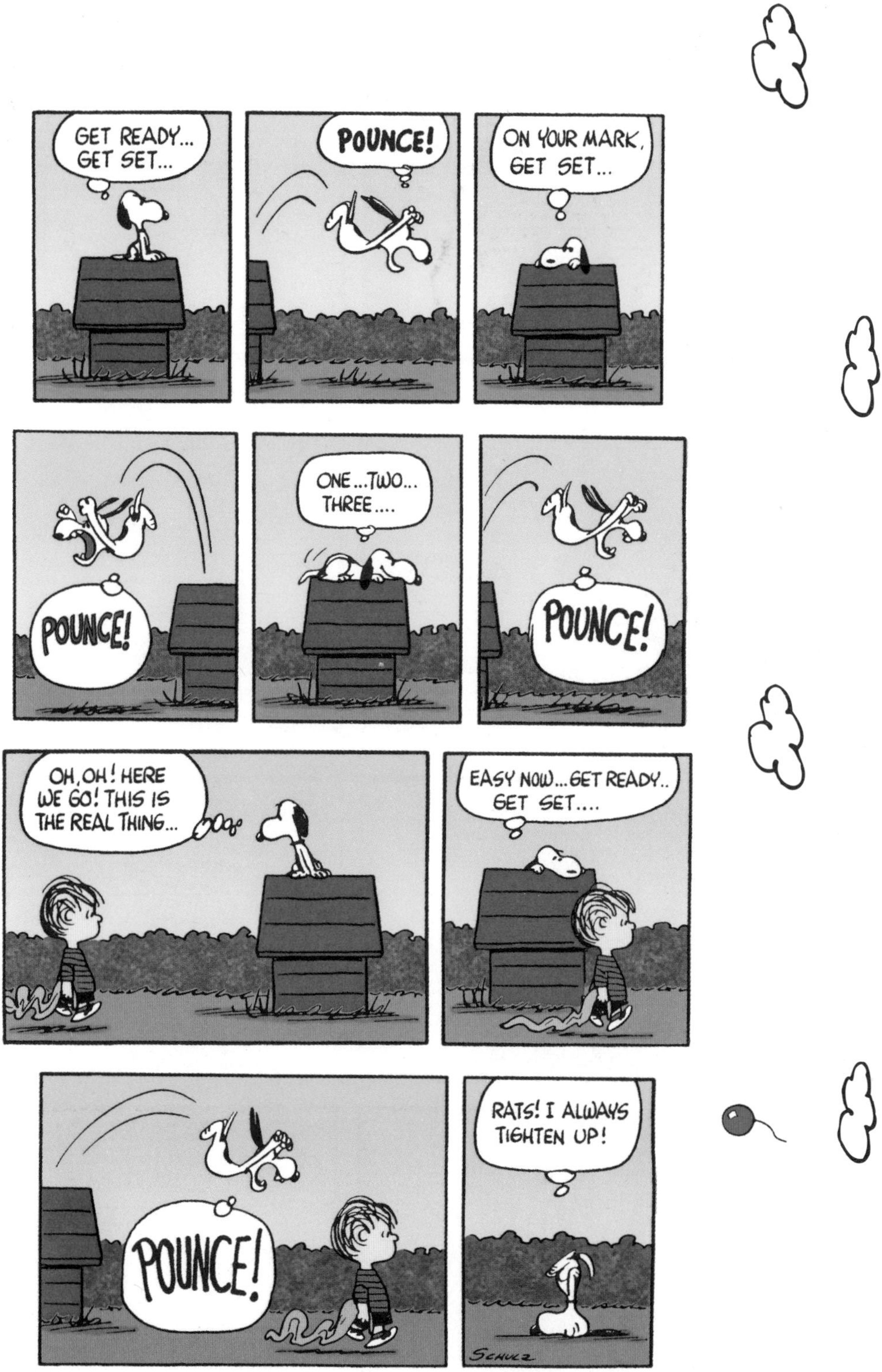
GET READY... GET SET...
POUNCE!
ON YOUR MARK, GET SET...
POUNCE!
ONE...TWO... THREE....
POUNCE!
OH, OH! HERE WE GO! THIS IS THE REAL THING...
EASY NOW...GET READY.. GET SET....
POUNCE!
RATS! I ALWAYS TIGHTEN UP!
SCHULZ

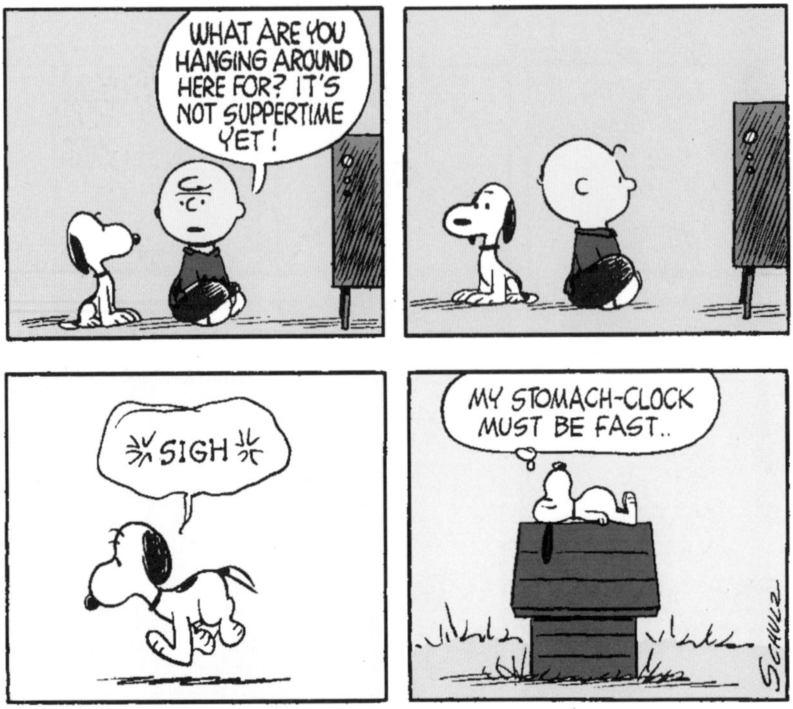
WHAT ARE YOU HANGING AROUND HERE FOR? IT'S NOT SUPPERTIME YET!
SIGH
MY STOMACH-CLOCK MUST BE FAST..
SCHULZ

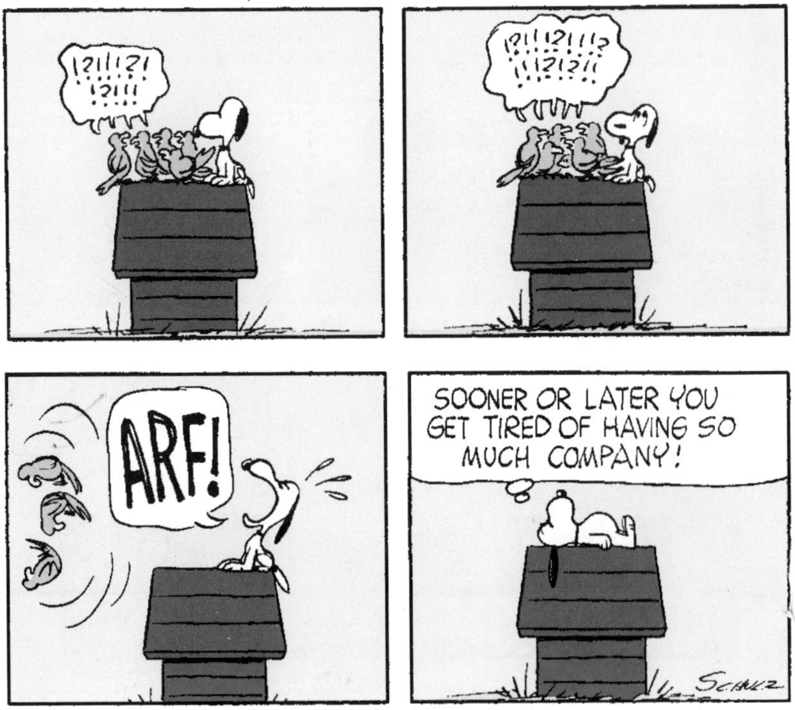
ARF!
SOONER OR LATER YOU GET TIRED OF HAVING SO MUCH COMPANY!
SCHULZ

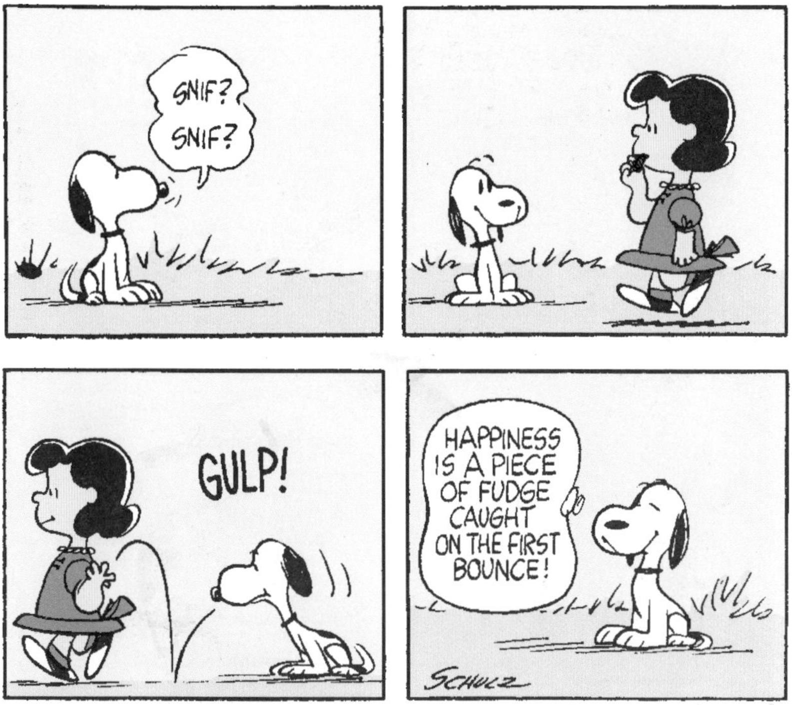
SNIF? SNIF?
GULP!
HAPPINESS IS A PIECE OF FUDGE CAUGHT ON THE FIRST BOUNCE!
SCHULZ

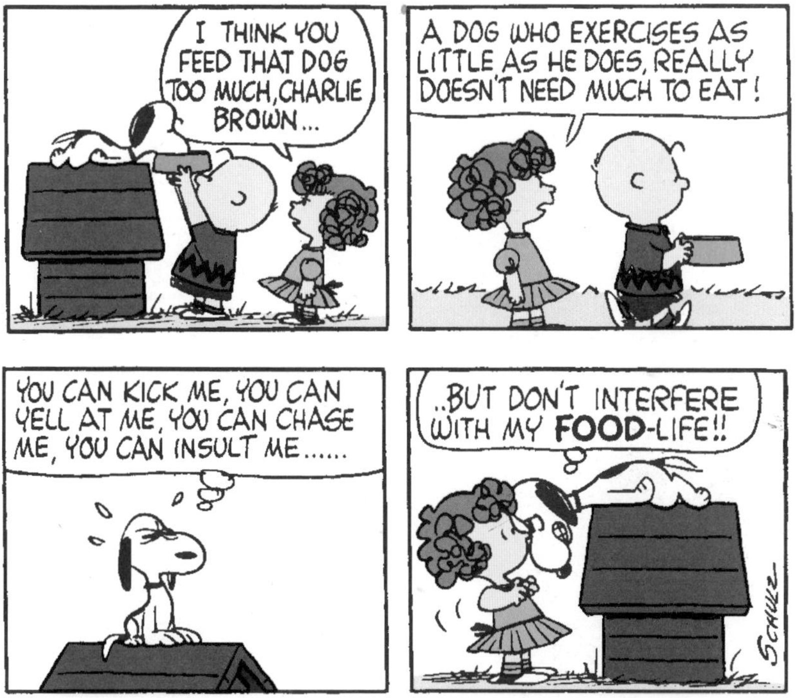
I THINK YOU FEED THAT DOG TOO MUCH, CHARLIE BROWN...
A DOG WHO EXERCISES AS LITTLE AS HE DOES, REALLY DOESN'T NEED MUCH TO EAT!
YOU CAN KICK ME, YOU CAN YELL AT ME, YOU CAN CHASE ME, YOU CAN INSULT ME......
..BUT DON'T INTERFERE WITH MY **FOOD**-LIFE!!
SCHULZ

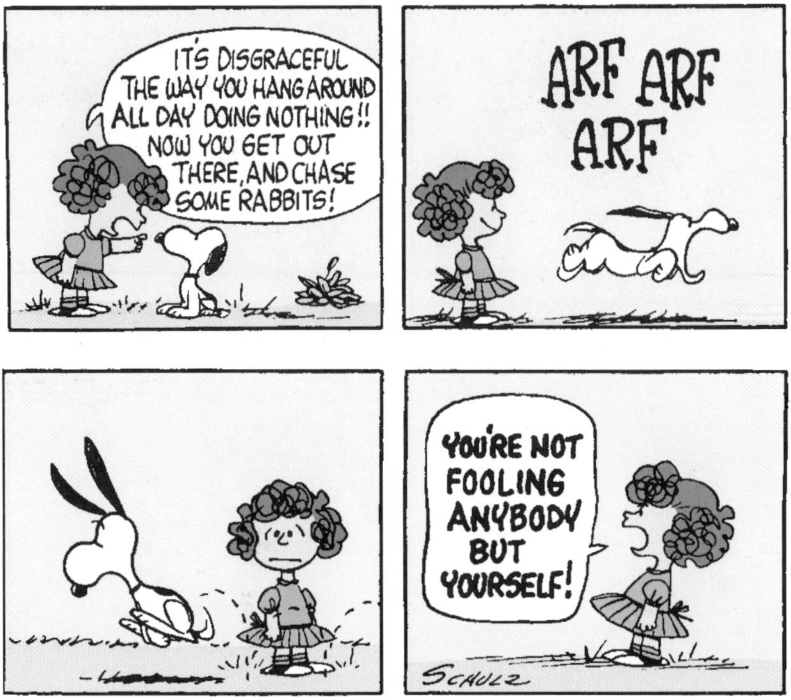
IT'S DISGRACEFUL THE WAY YOU HANG AROUND ALL DAY DOING NOTHING!! NOW YOU GET OUT THERE, AND CHASE SOME RABBITS!
ARF ARF ARF
YOU'RE NOT FOOLING ANYBODY BUT YOURSELF!
SCHULZ

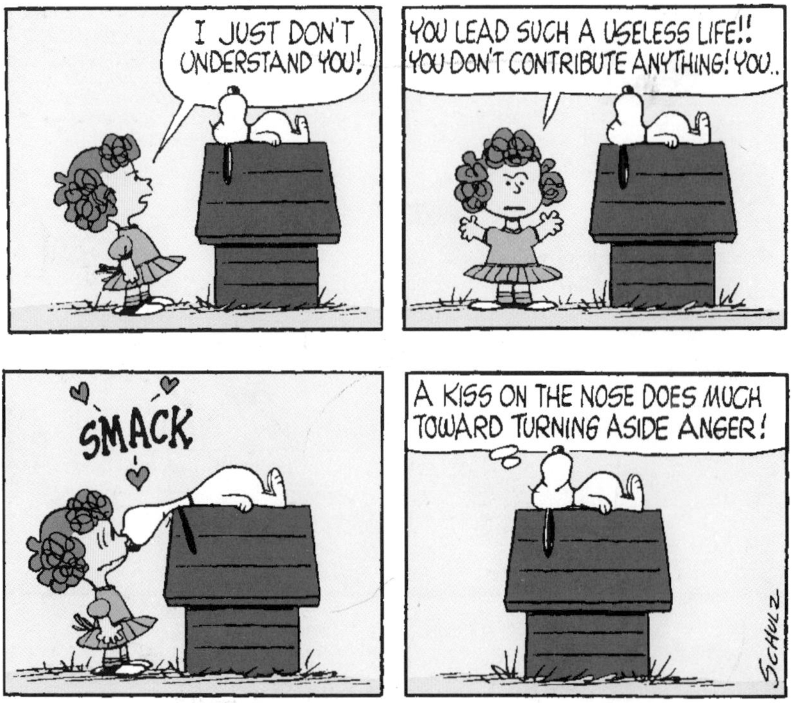
I JUST DON'T UNDERSTAND YOU!
YOU LEAD SUCH A USELESS LIFE!! YOU DON'T CONTRIBUTE ANYTHING! YOU..
SMACK
A KISS ON THE NOSE DOES MUCH TOWARD TURNING ASIDE ANGER!
SCHULZ

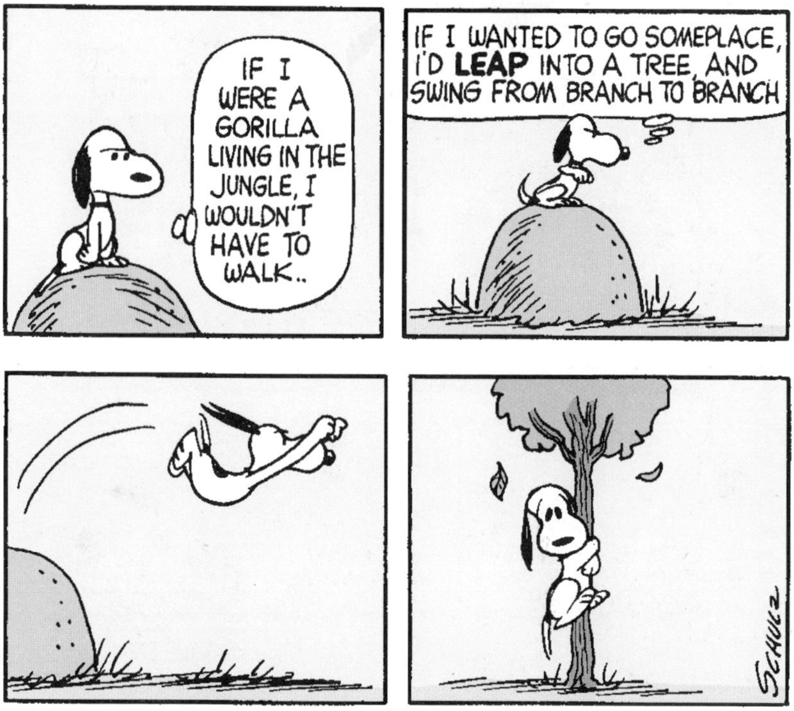
IF I WERE A GORILLA LIVING IN THE JUNGLE, I WOULDN'T HAVE TO WALK..
IF I WANTED TO GO SOMEPLACE, I'D **LEAP** INTO A TREE, AND SWING FROM BRANCH TO BRANCH
SCHULZ

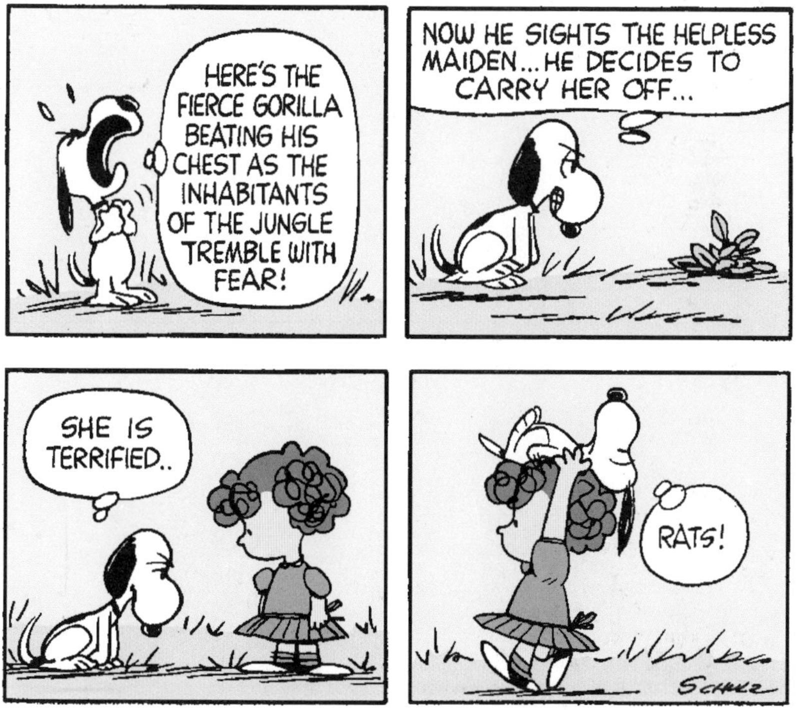
HERE'S THE FIERCE GORILLA BEATING HIS CHEST AS THE INHABITANTS OF THE JUNGLE TREMBLE WITH FEAR!
NOW HE SIGHTS THE HELPLESS MAIDEN...HE DECIDES TO CARRY HER OFF...
SHE IS TERRIFIED..
RATS!
SCHULZ

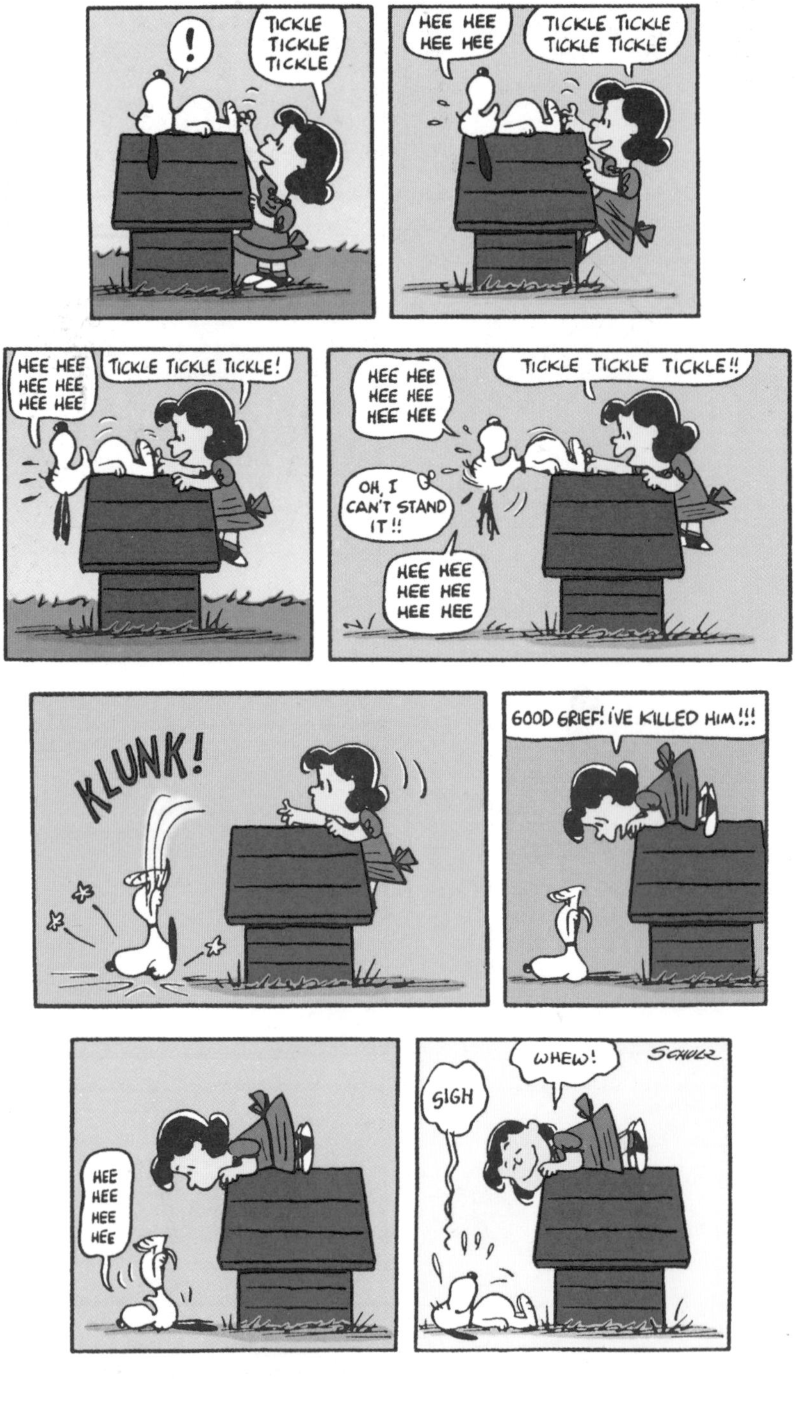
!
TICKLE TICKLE TICKLE
HEE HEE HEE HEE
TICKLE TICKLE TICKLE TICKLE
HEE HEE HEE HEE HEE HEE
TICKLE TICKLE TICKLE!
HEE HEE HEE HEE HEE HEE
TICKLE TICKLE TICKLE!!
OH, I CAN'T STAND IT!!
HEE HEE HEE HEE HEE HEE
KLUNK!
GOOD GRIEF! I'VE KILLED HIM!!!
HEE HEE HEE HEE
SIGH
WHEW!
SCHULZ

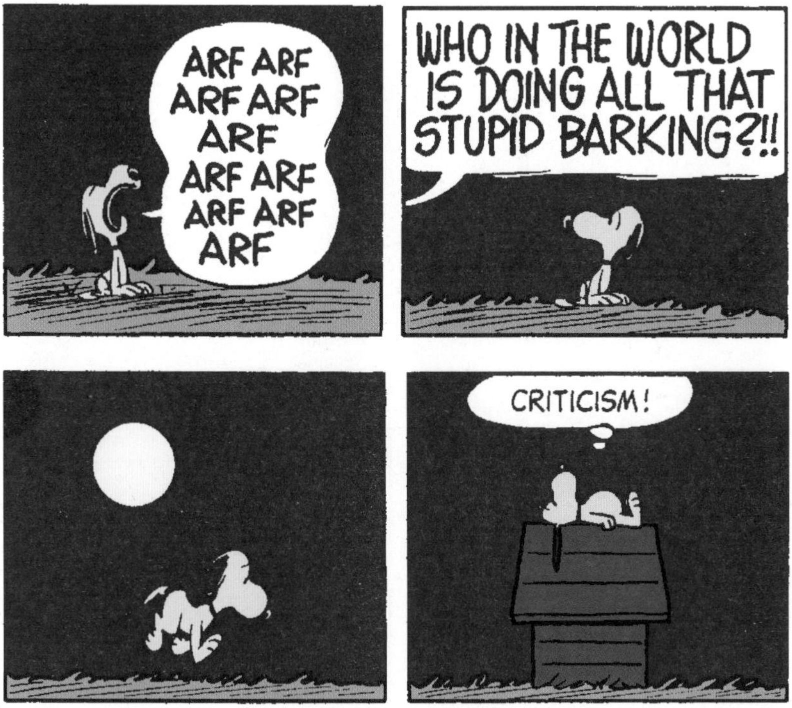
ARF ARF ARF ARF ARF ARF ARF ARF ARF ARF
WHO IN THE WORLD IS DOING ALL THAT STUPID BARKING?!!
CRITICISM!

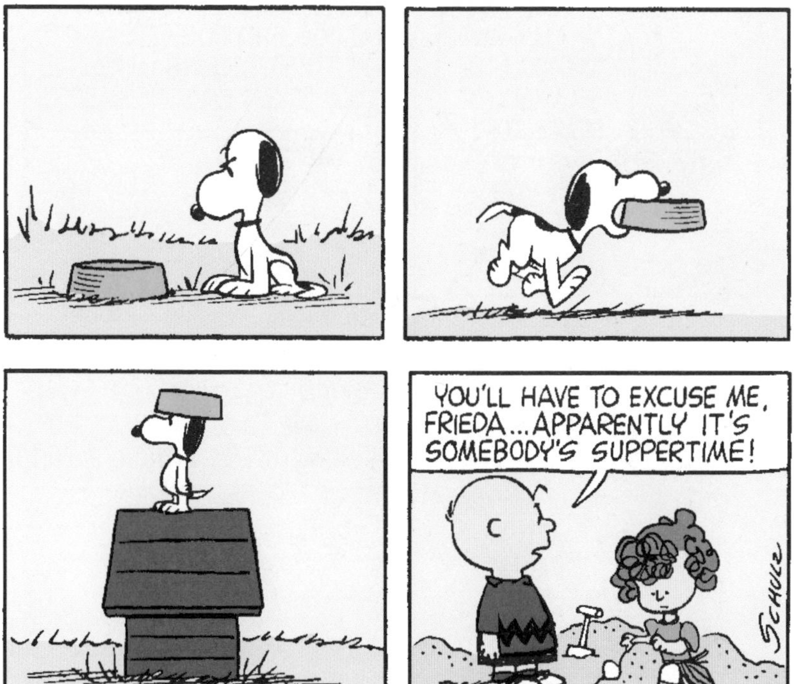
YOU'LL HAVE TO EXCUSE ME, FRIEDA...APPARENTLY IT'S SOMEBODY'S SUPPERTIME!
SCHULZ

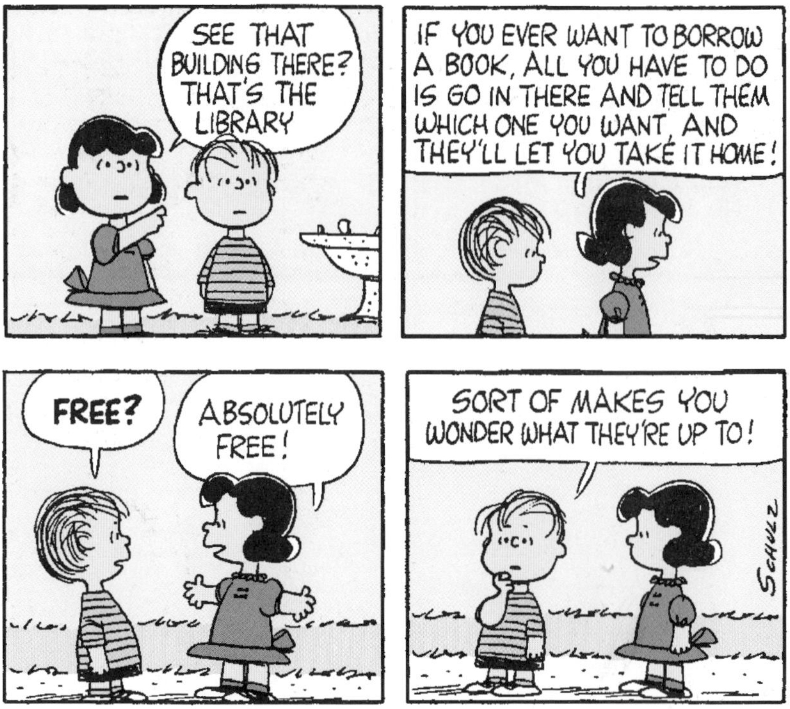
SEE THAT BUILDING THERE? THAT'S THE LIBRARY
IF YOU EVER WANT TO BORROW A BOOK, ALL YOU HAVE TO DO IS GO IN THERE AND TELL THEM WHICH ONE YOU WANT, AND THEY'LL LET YOU TAKE IT HOME!
FREE?
ABSOLUTELY FREE!
SORT OF MAKES YOU WONDER WHAT THEY'RE UP TO!
SCHULZ

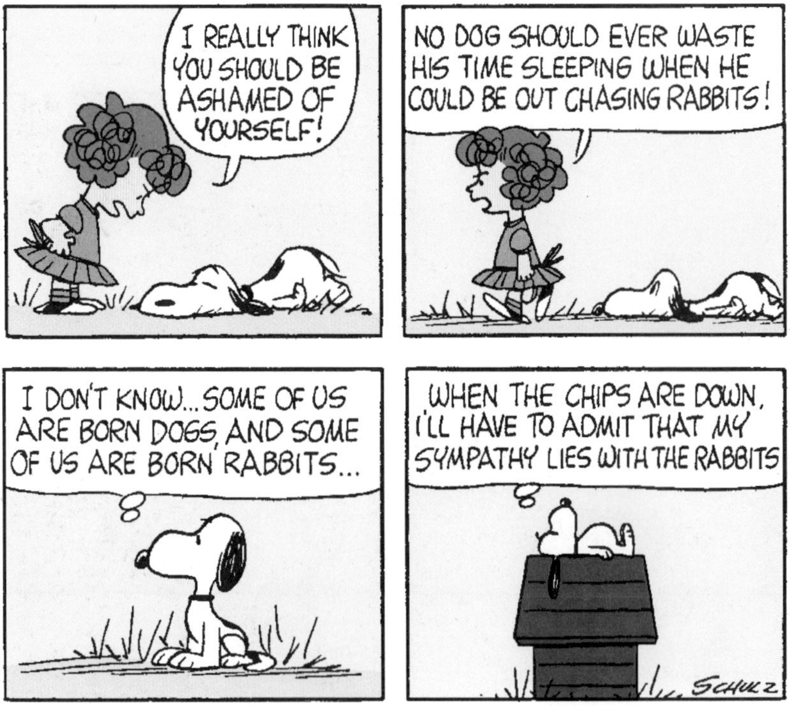
I REALLY THINK YOU SHOULD BE ASHAMED OF YOURSELF!
NO DOG SHOULD EVER WASTE HIS TIME SLEEPING WHEN HE COULD BE OUT CHASING RABBITS!
I DON'T KNOW... SOME OF US ARE BORN DOGS, AND SOME OF US ARE BORN RABBITS...
WHEN THE CHIPS ARE DOWN, I'LL HAVE TO ADMIT THAT MY SYMPATHY LIES WITH THE RABBITS
SCHULZ

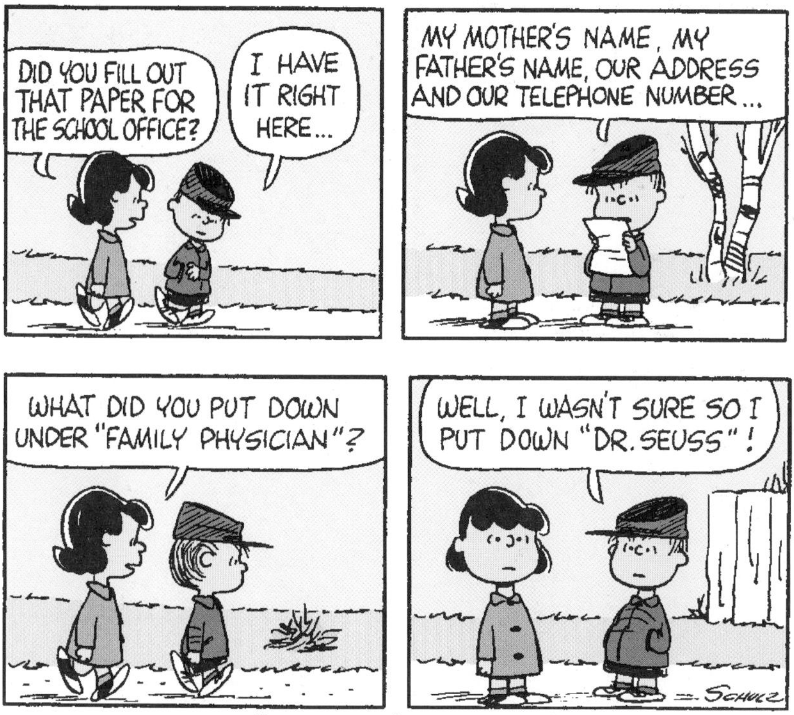
DID YOU FILL OUT THAT PAPER FOR THE SCHOOL OFFICE?
I HAVE IT RIGHT HERE...
MY MOTHER'S NAME, MY FATHER'S NAME, OUR ADDRESS AND OUR TELEPHONE NUMBER...
WHAT DID YOU PUT DOWN UNDER "FAMILY PHYSICIAN"?
WELL, I WASN'T SURE SO I PUT DOWN "DR. SEUSS"!
SCHULZ

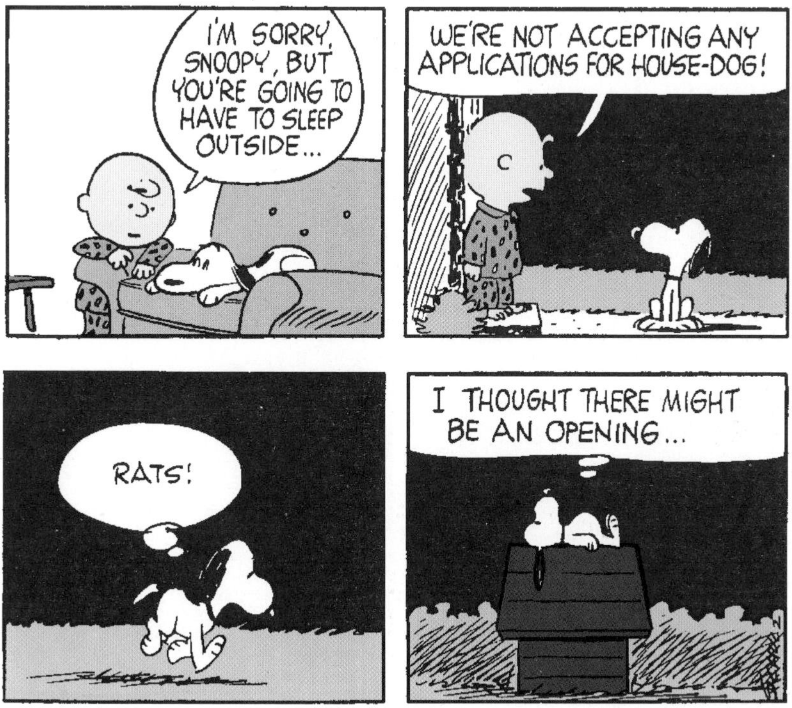
I'M SORRY, SNOOPY, BUT YOU'RE GOING TO HAVE TO SLEEP OUTSIDE...
WE'RE NOT ACCEPTING ANY APPLICATIONS FOR HOUSE-DOG!
RATS!
I THOUGHT THERE MIGHT BE AN OPENING...

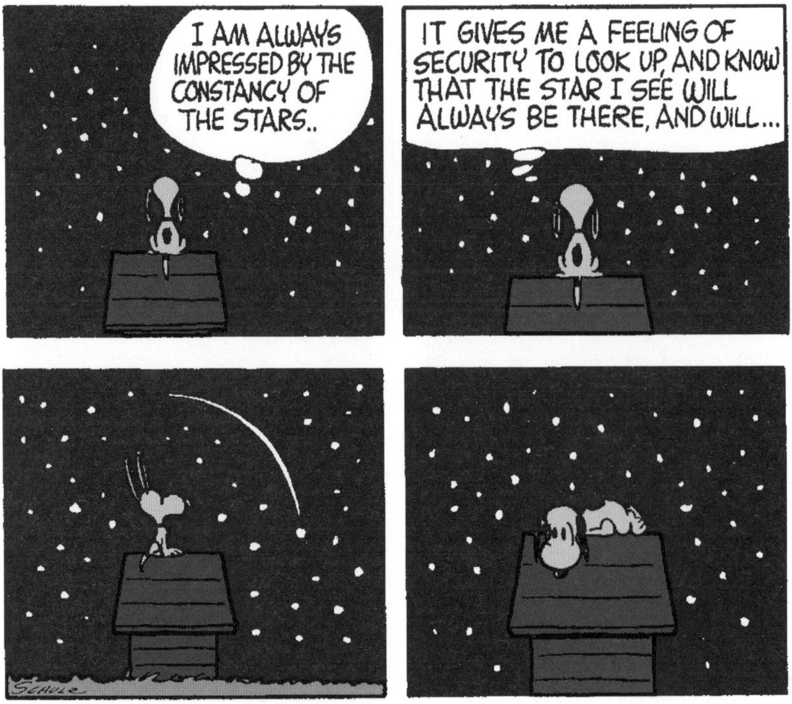
I AM ALWAYS IMPRESSED BY THE CONSTANCY OF THE STARS..
IT GIVES ME A FEELING OF SECURITY TO LOOK UP, AND KNOW THAT THE STAR I SEE WILL ALWAYS BE THERE, AND WILL...
SCHULZ

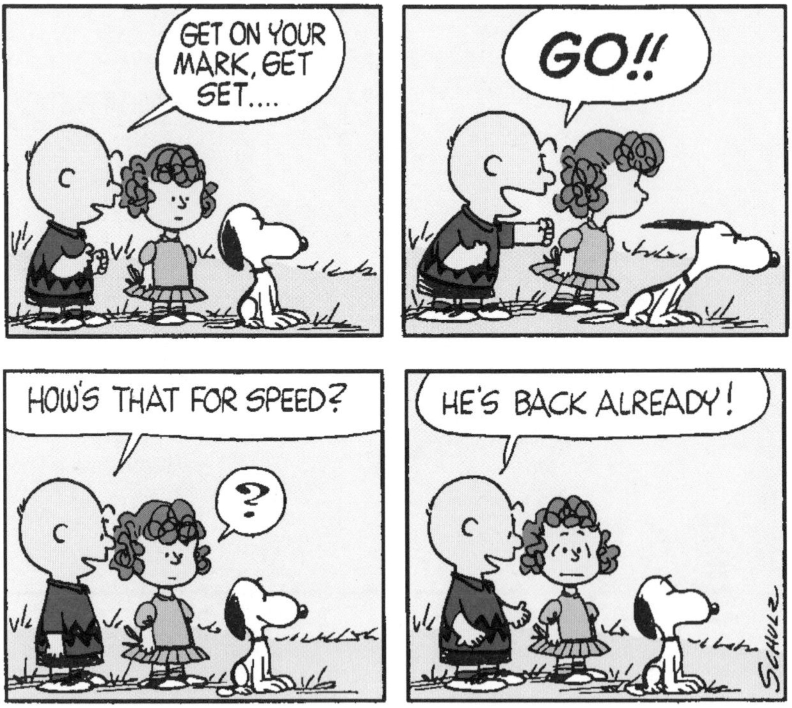
GET ON YOUR MARK, GET SET....
GO!!
HOW'S THAT FOR SPEED?
?
HE'S BACK ALREADY!
SCHULZ

CLOMP!
WHAM!
SCHULZ
SECURITY, LIKE LIBERTY, HAS TO BE WON AND REWON MANY TIMES...
BEAT AGAIN!

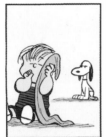

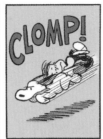

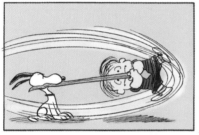

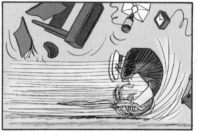

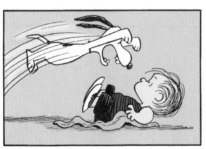

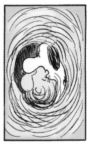

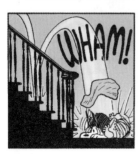

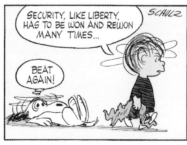

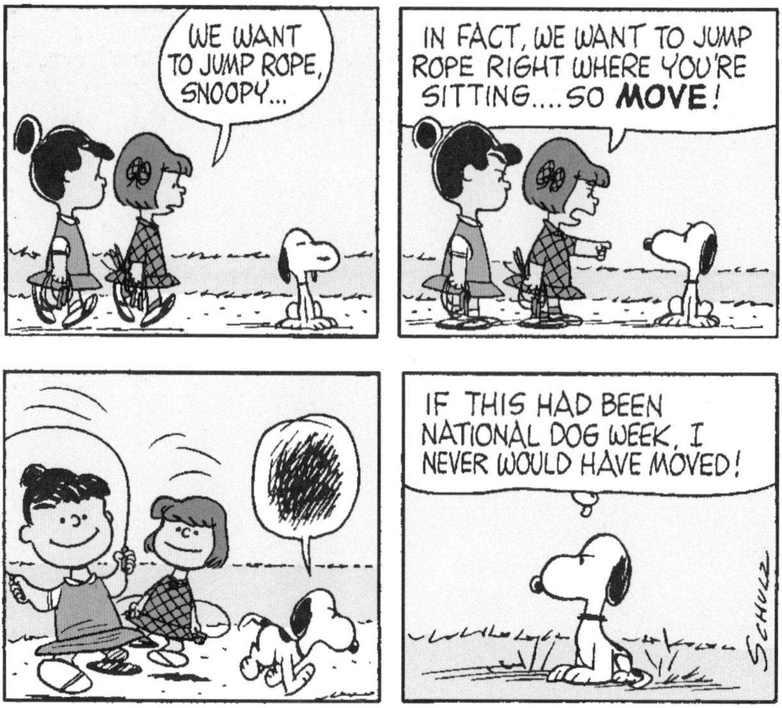
WE WANT TO JUMP ROPE, SNOOPY...
IN FACT, WE WANT TO JUMP ROPE RIGHT WHERE YOU'RE SITTING....SO **MOVE**!
IF THIS HAD BEEN NATIONAL DOG WEEK, I NEVER WOULD HAVE MOVED!
SCHULZ

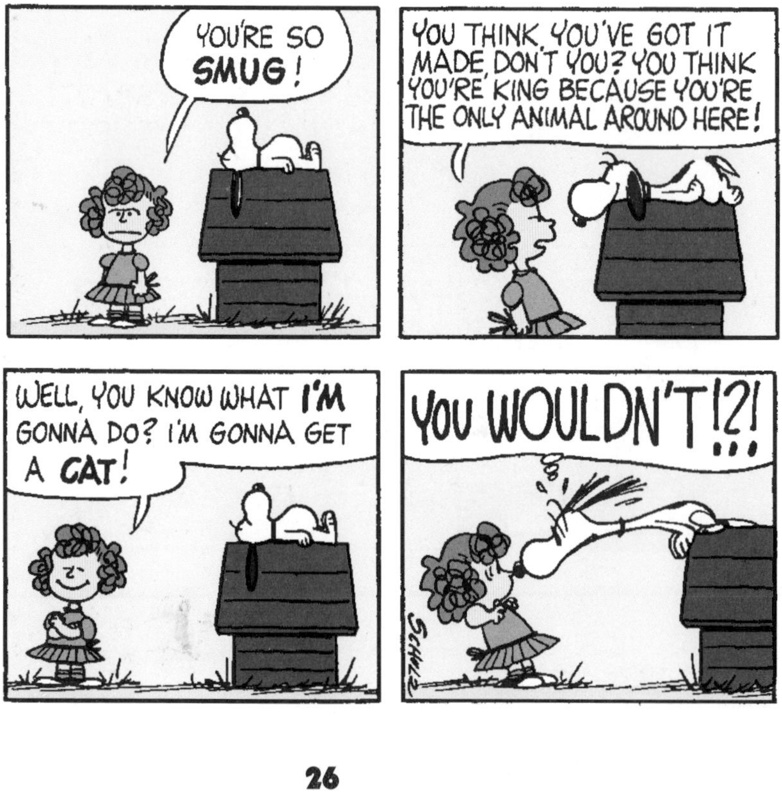
YOU'RE SO **SMUG**!
YOU THINK YOU'VE GOT IT MADE, DON'T YOU? YOU THINK YOU'RE KING BECAUSE YOU'RE THE ONLY ANIMAL AROUND HERE!
WELL, YOU KNOW WHAT **I'M** GONNA DO? I'M GONNA GET A **CAT**!
YOU WOULDN'T!?!
SCHULZ

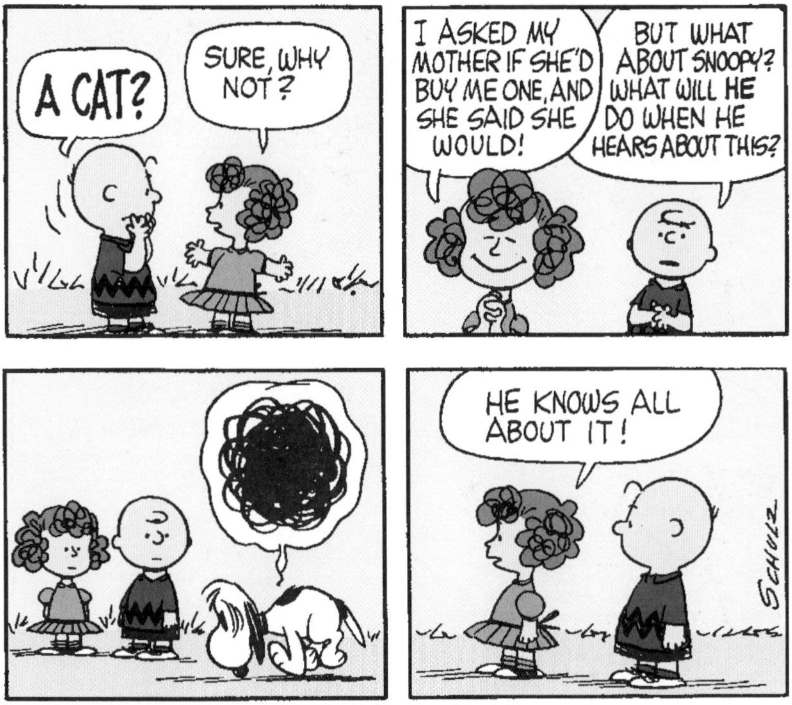
A CAT?
SURE, WHY NOT?
I ASKED MY MOTHER IF SHE'D BUY ME ONE, AND SHE SAID SHE WOULD!
BUT WHAT ABOUT SNOOPY? WHAT WILL HE DO WHEN HE HEARS ABOUT THIS?
HE KNOWS ALL ABOUT IT!
SCHULZ

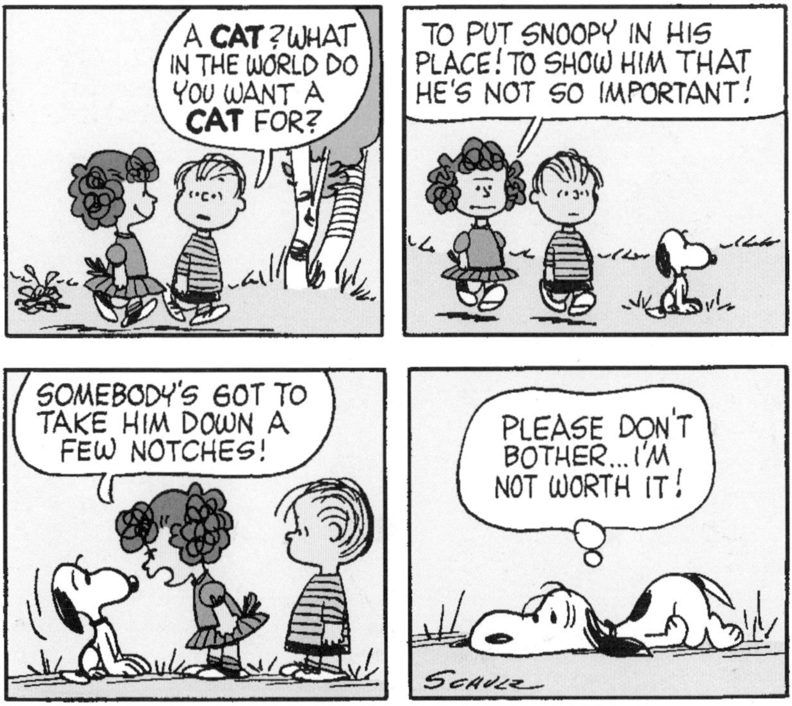
A CAT? WHAT IN THE WORLD DO YOU WANT A CAT FOR?
TO PUT SNOOPY IN HIS PLACE! TO SHOW HIM THAT HE'S NOT SO IMPORTANT!
SOMEBODY'S GOT TO TAKE HIM DOWN A FEW NOTCHES!
PLEASE DON'T BOTHER... I'M NOT WORTH IT!
SCHULZ

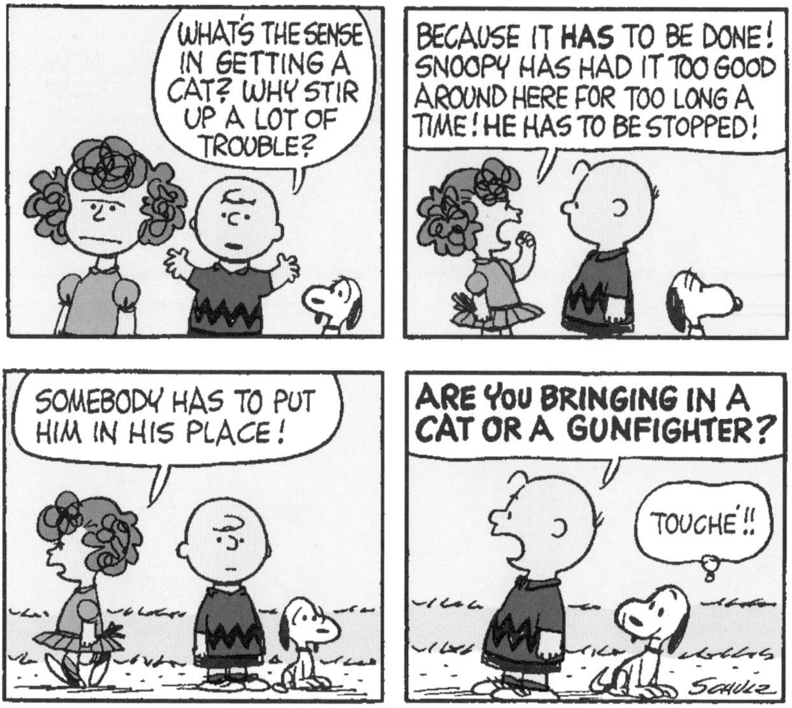
WHAT'S THE SENSE IN GETTING A CAT? WHY STIR UP A LOT OF TROUBLE?
BECAUSE IT **HAS** TO BE DONE! SNOOPY HAS HAD IT TOO GOOD AROUND HERE FOR TOO LONG A TIME! HE HAS TO BE STOPPED!
SOMEBODY HAS TO PUT HIM IN HIS PLACE!
ARE YOU BRINGING IN A CAT OR A GUNFIGHTER?
TOUCHÉ!!
SCHULZ

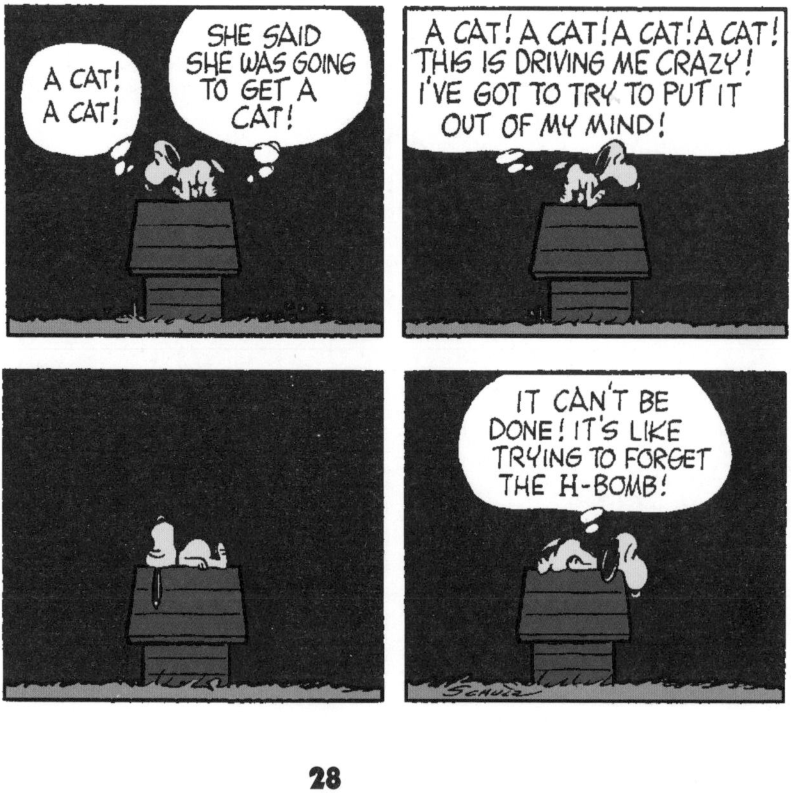
A CAT! A CAT!
SHE SAID SHE WAS GOING TO GET A CAT!
A CAT! A CAT! A CAT! A CAT! THIS IS DRIVING ME CRAZY! I'VE GOT TO TRY TO PUT IT OUT OF MY MIND!
IT CAN'T BE DONE! IT'S LIKE TRYING TO FORGET THE H-BOMB!
SCHULZ

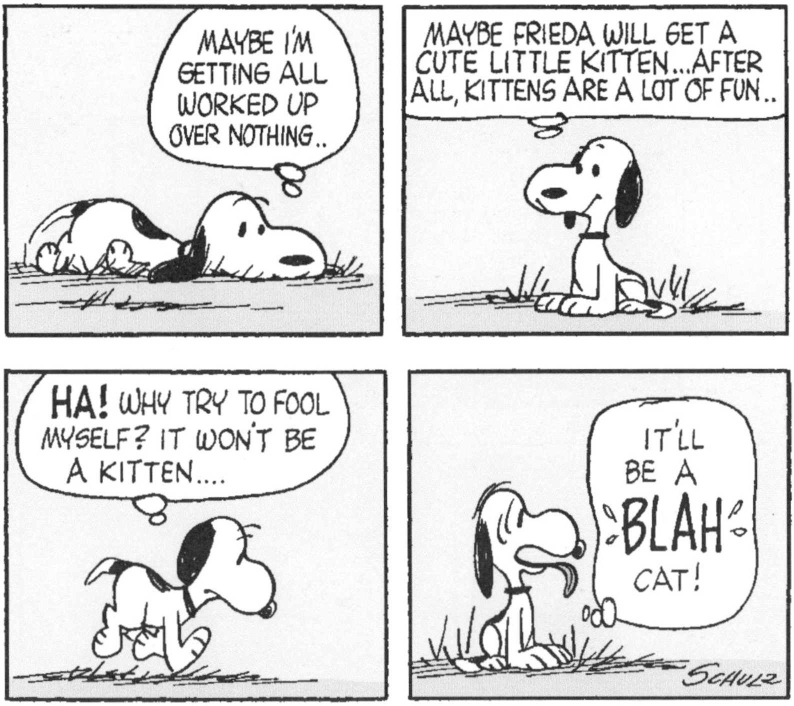
MAYBE I'M GETTING ALL WORKED UP OVER NOTHING..
MAYBE FRIEDA WILL GET A CUTE LITTLE KITTEN...AFTER ALL, KITTENS ARE A LOT OF FUN..
HA! WHY TRY TO FOOL MYSELF? IT WON'T BE A KITTEN....
IT'LL BE A BLAH CAT!
SCHULZ

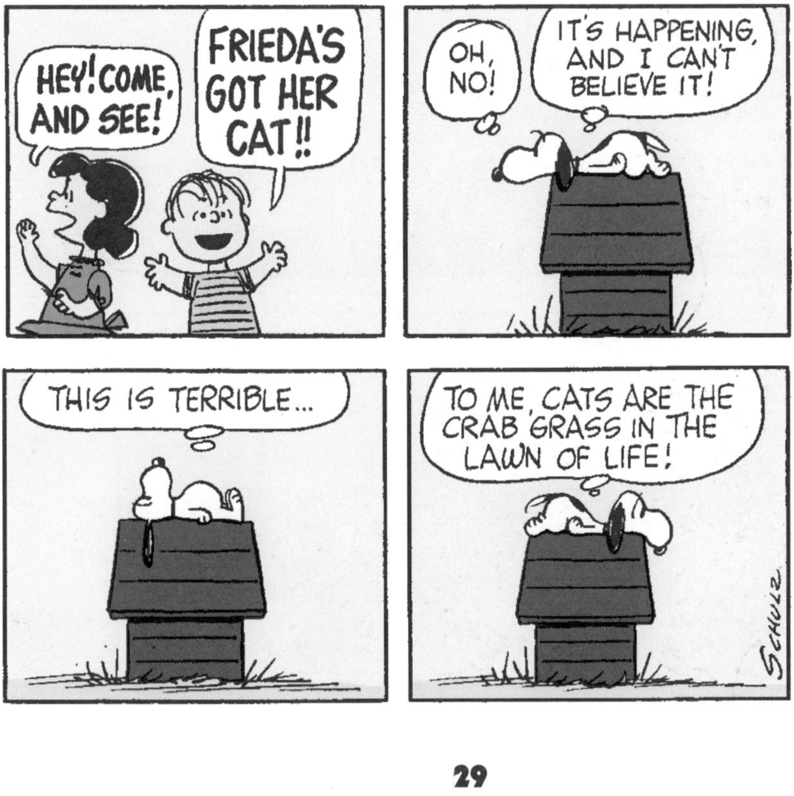
HEY! COME, AND SEE!
FRIEDA'S GOT HER CAT!!
OH, NO!
IT'S HAPPENING, AND I CAN'T BELIEVE IT!
THIS IS TERRIBLE...
TO ME, CATS ARE THE CRAB GRASS IN THE LAWN OF LIFE!
SCHULZ

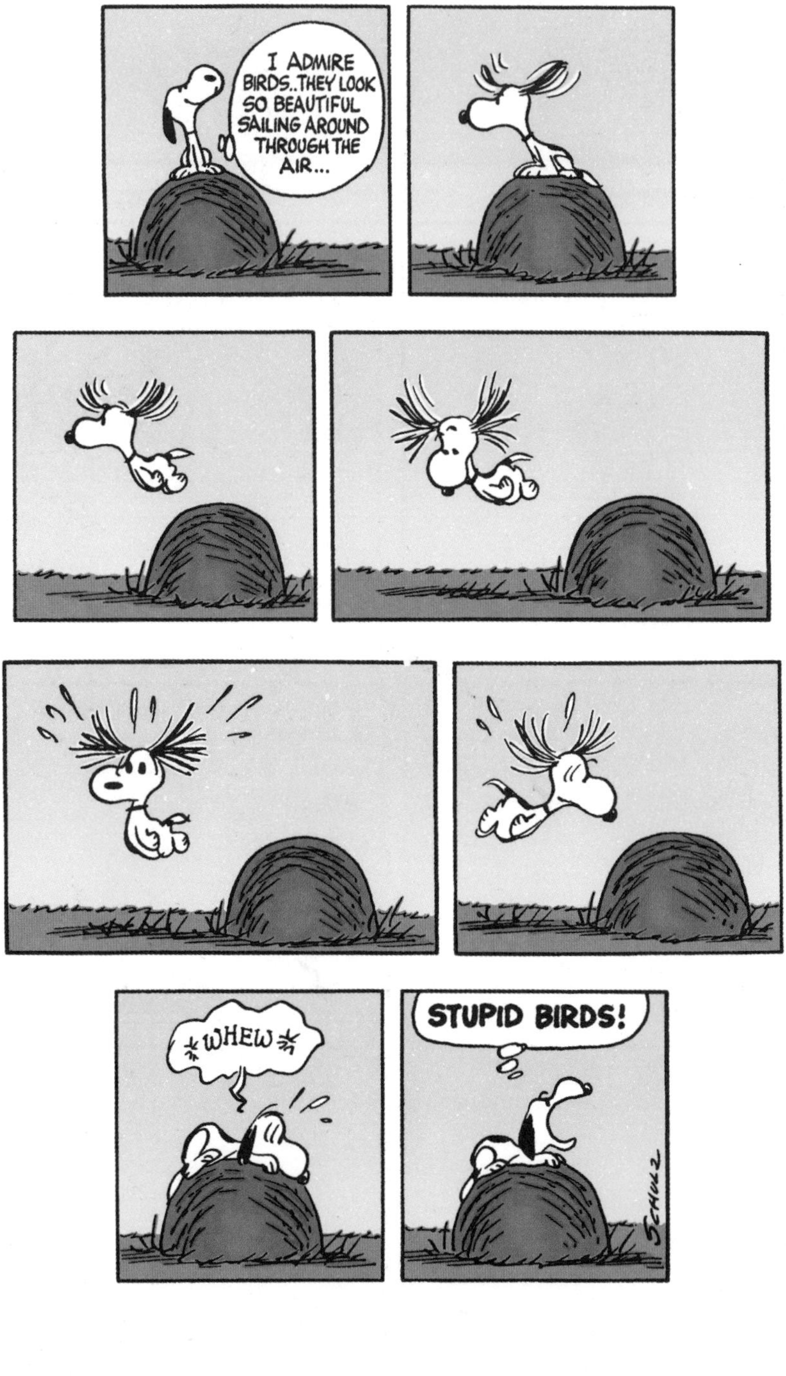
I ADMIRE BIRDS..THEY LOOK SO BEAUTIFUL SAILING AROUND THROUGH THE AIR...
WHEW
STUPID BIRDS!
SCHULZ

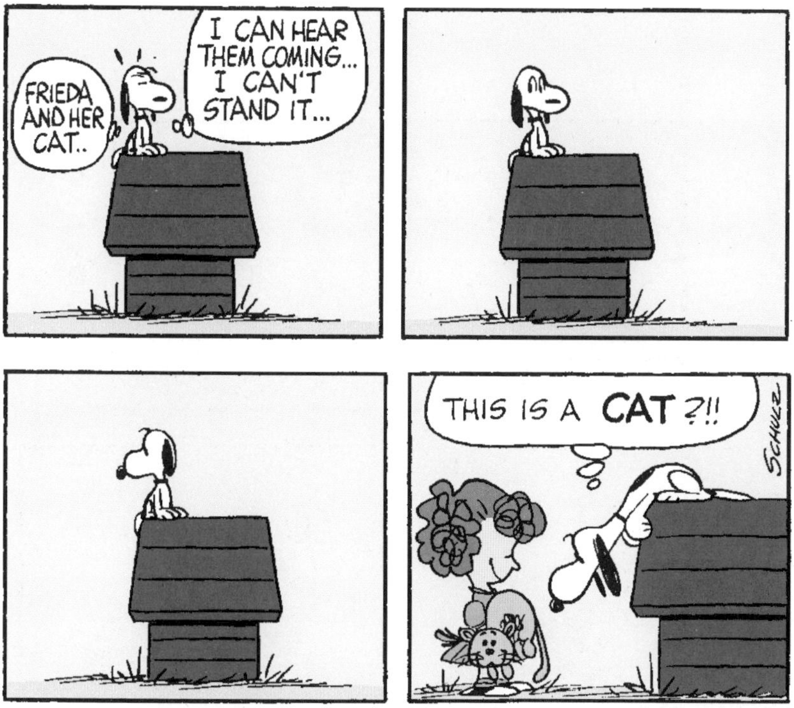
FRIEDA AND HER CAT..
I CAN HEAR THEM COMING... I CAN'T STAND IT...
THIS IS A **CAT**?!!
SCHULZ

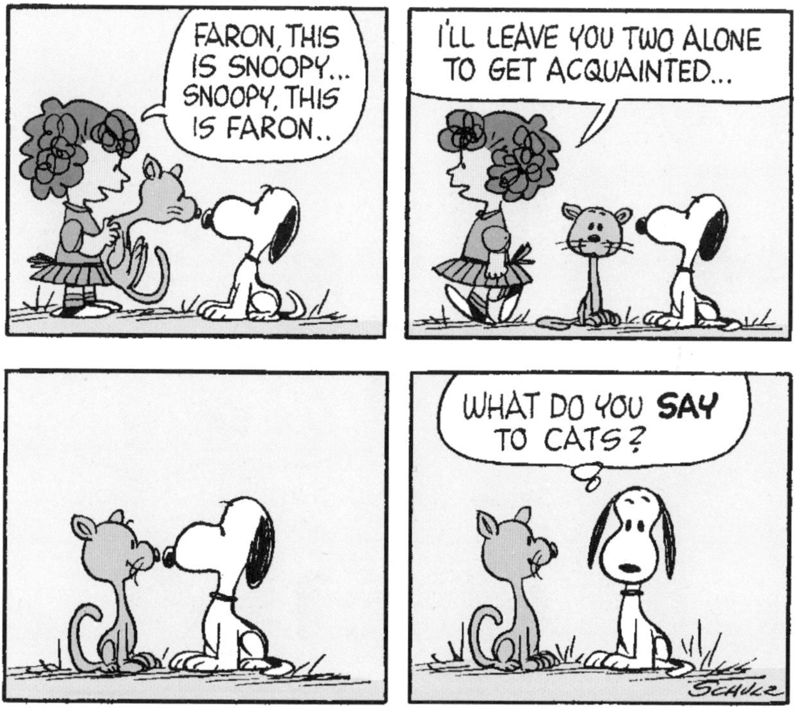
FARON, THIS IS SNOOPY... SNOOPY, THIS IS FARON..
I'LL LEAVE YOU TWO ALONE TO GET ACQUAINTED...
WHAT DO YOU **SAY** TO CATS?
SCHULZ

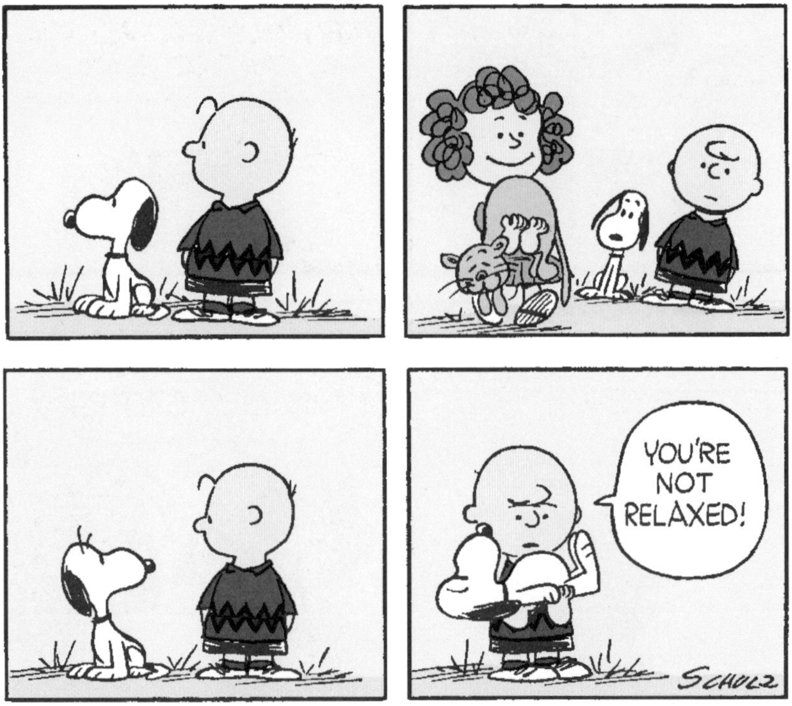
YOU'RE NOT RELAXED!
SCHULZ

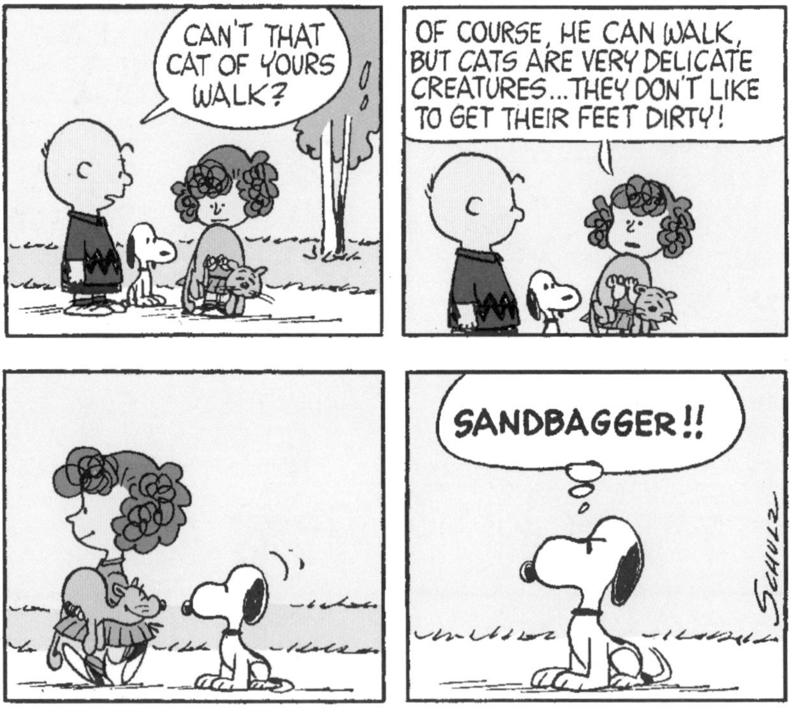
CAN'T THAT CAT OF YOURS WALK?
OF COURSE, HE CAN WALK, BUT CATS ARE VERY DELICATE CREATURES...THEY DON'T LIKE TO GET THEIR FEET DIRTY!
SANDBAGGER!!
SCHULZ

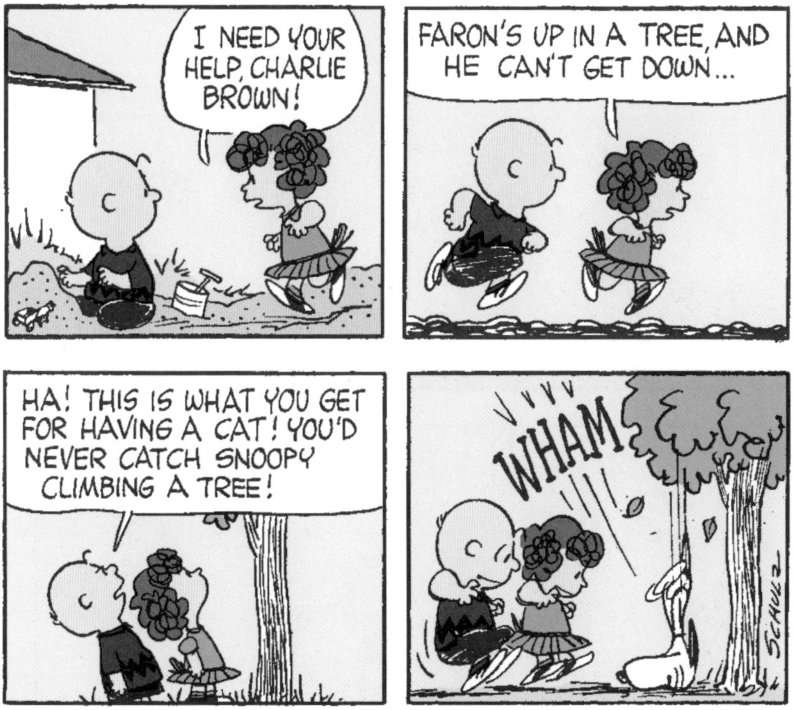
I NEED YOUR HELP, CHARLIE BROWN!
FARON'S UP IN A TREE, AND HE CAN'T GET DOWN...
HA! THIS IS WHAT YOU GET FOR HAVING A CAT! YOU'D NEVER CATCH SNOOPY CLIMBING A TREE!
WHAM
SCHULZ

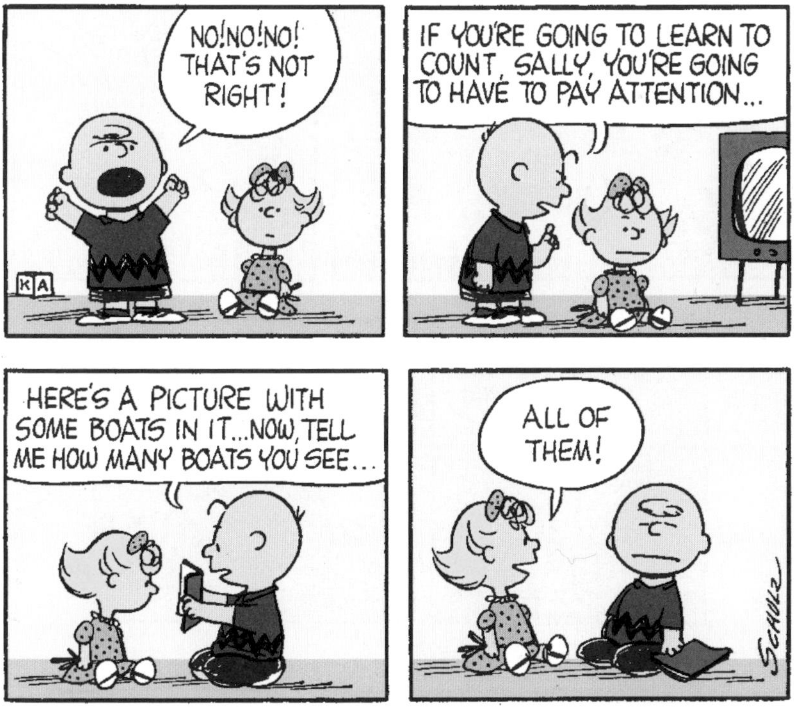
NO!NO!NO! THAT'S NOT RIGHT!
K A
IF YOU'RE GOING TO LEARN TO COUNT, SALLY, YOU'RE GOING TO HAVE TO PAY ATTENTION...
HERE'S A PICTURE WITH SOME BOATS IN IT...NOW, TELL ME HOW MANY BOATS YOU SEE...
ALL OF THEM!
SCHULZ

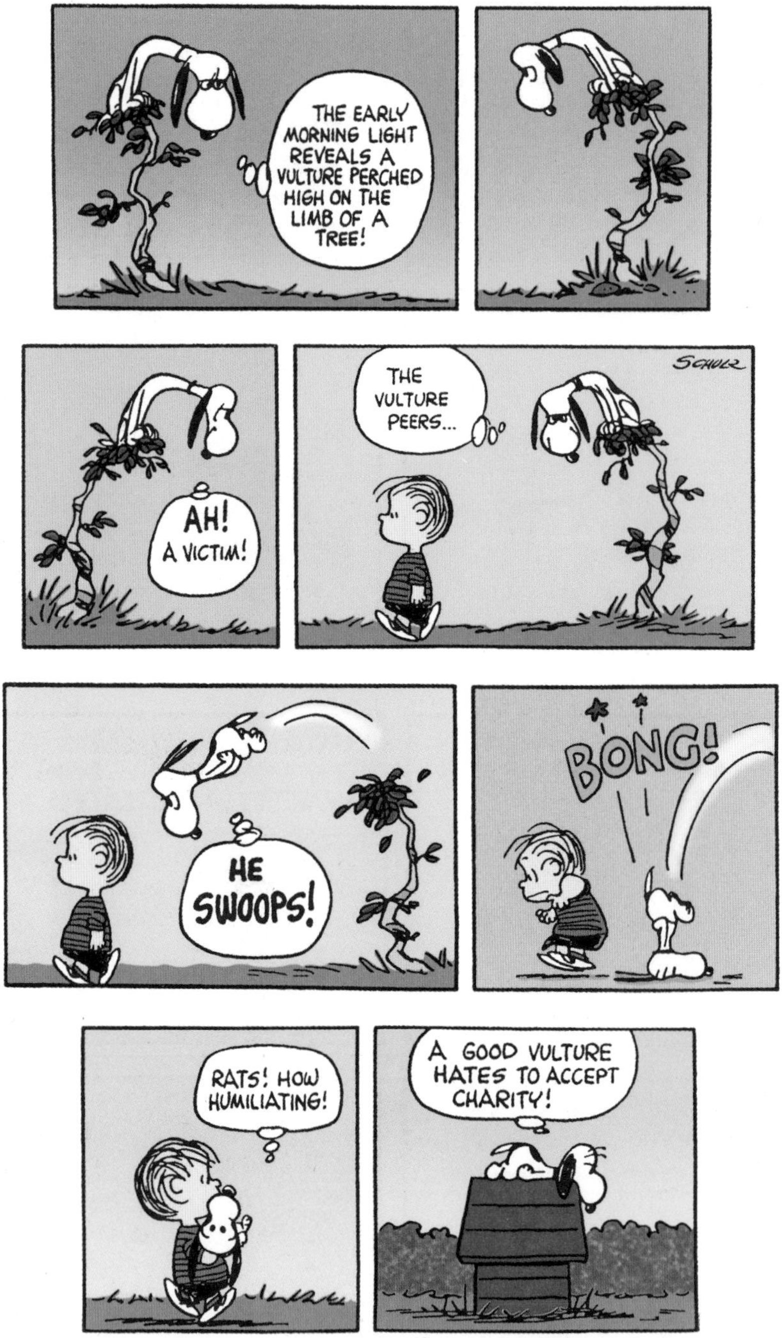
THE EARLY MORNING LIGHT REVEALS A VULTURE PERCHED HIGH ON THE LIMB OF A TREE!
SCHULZ
AH! A VICTIM!
THE VULTURE PEERS...
HE SWOOPS!
BONG!
RATS! HOW HUMILIATING!
A GOOD VULTURE HATES TO ACCEPT CHARITY!

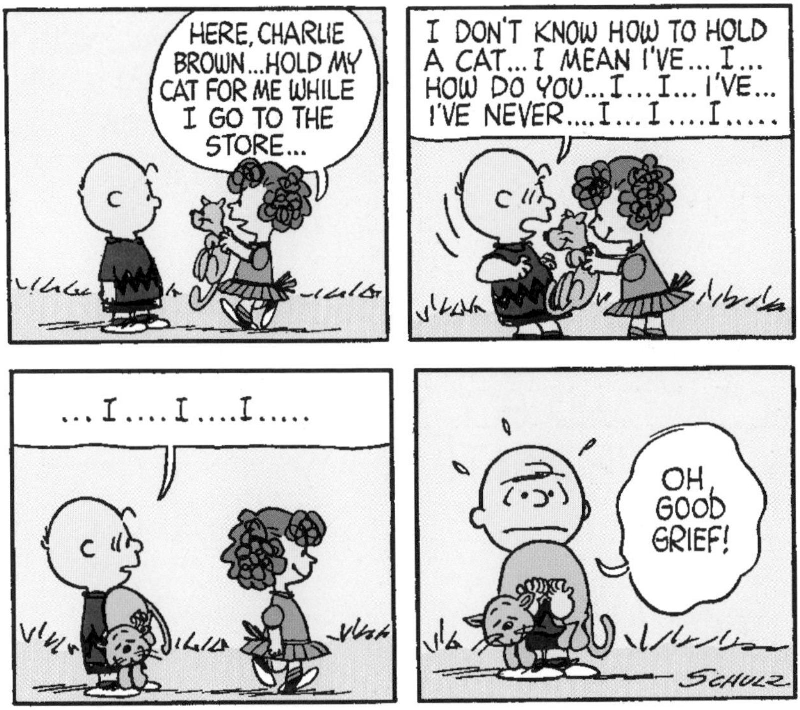
HERE, CHARLIE BROWN...HOLD MY CAT FOR ME WHILE I GO TO THE STORE...
I DON'T KNOW HOW TO HOLD A CAT...I MEAN I'VE...I...HOW DO YOU...I...I...I'VE...I'VE NEVER....I...I....I.....
...I....I....I.....
OH, GOOD GRIEF!
SCHULZ

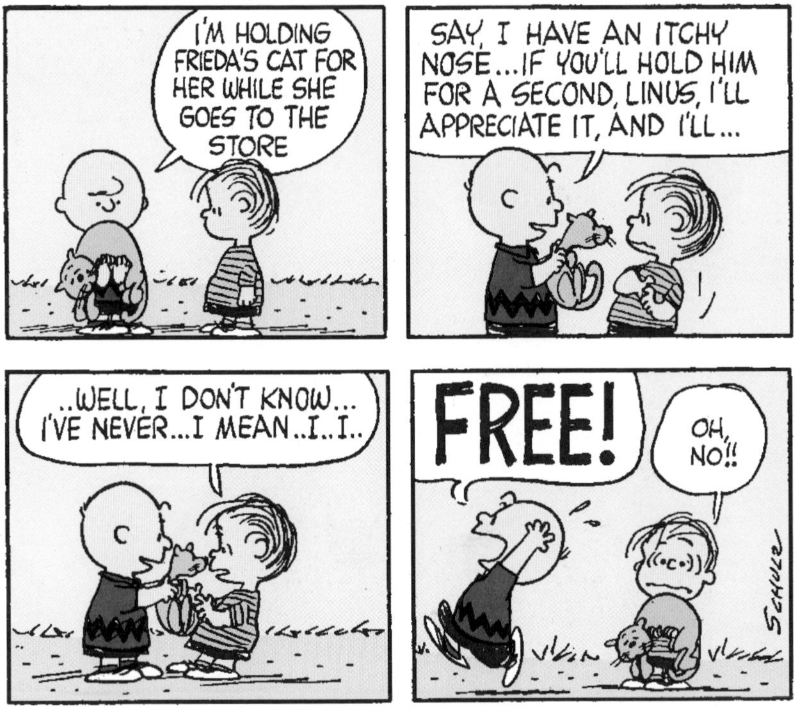
I'M HOLDING FRIEDA'S CAT FOR HER WHILE SHE GOES TO THE STORE
SAY, I HAVE AN ITCHY NOSE...IF YOU'LL HOLD HIM FOR A SECOND, LINUS, I'LL APPRECIATE IT, AND I'LL...
..WELL, I DON'T KNOW...I'VE NEVER...I MEAN..I..I..
FREE!
OH, NO!!
SCHULZ

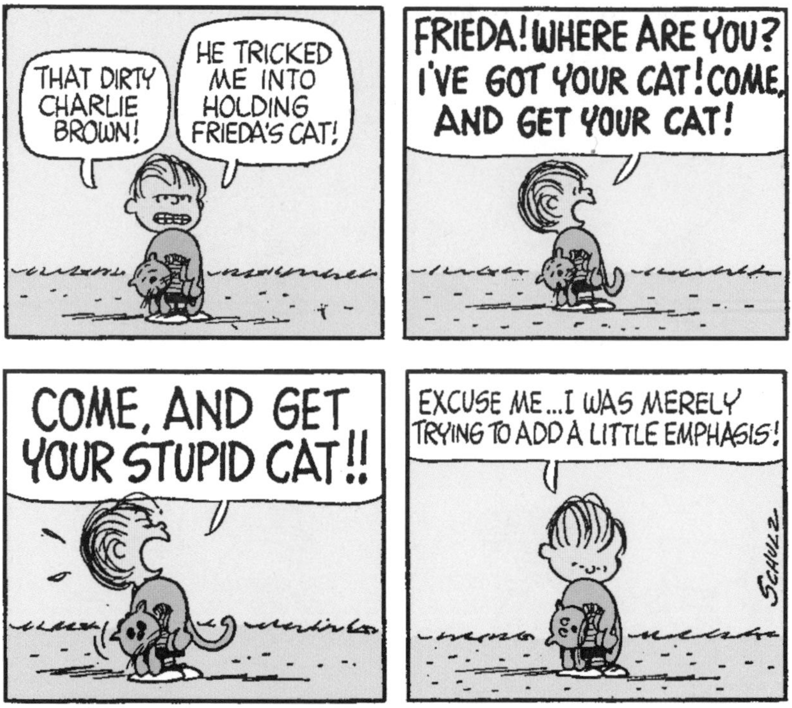
THAT DIRTY CHARLIE BROWN!
HE TRICKED ME INTO HOLDING FRIEDA'S CAT!
FRIEDA! WHERE ARE YOU? I'VE GOT YOUR CAT! COME, AND GET YOUR CAT!
COME, AND GET YOUR STUPID CAT!!
EXCUSE ME...I WAS MERELY TRYING TO ADD A LITTLE EMPHASIS!
SCHULZ

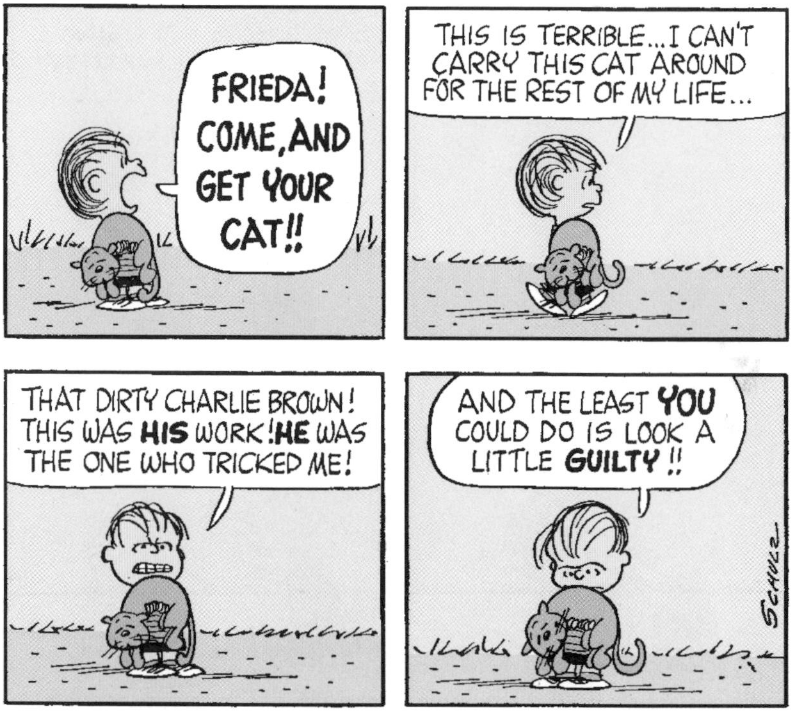
FRIEDA! COME, AND GET YOUR CAT!!
THIS IS TERRIBLE...I CAN'T CARRY THIS CAT AROUND FOR THE REST OF MY LIFE...
THAT DIRTY CHARLIE BROWN! THIS WAS HIS WORK! HE WAS THE ONE WHO TRICKED ME!
AND THE LEAST YOU COULD DO IS LOOK A LITTLE GUILTY!!
SCHULZ

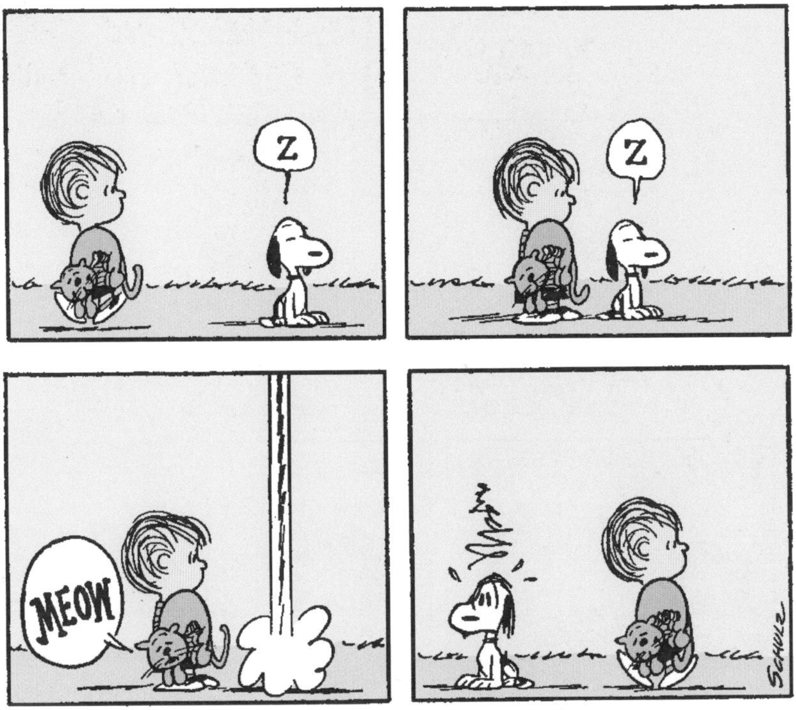
Z
Z
MEOW
SCHULZ

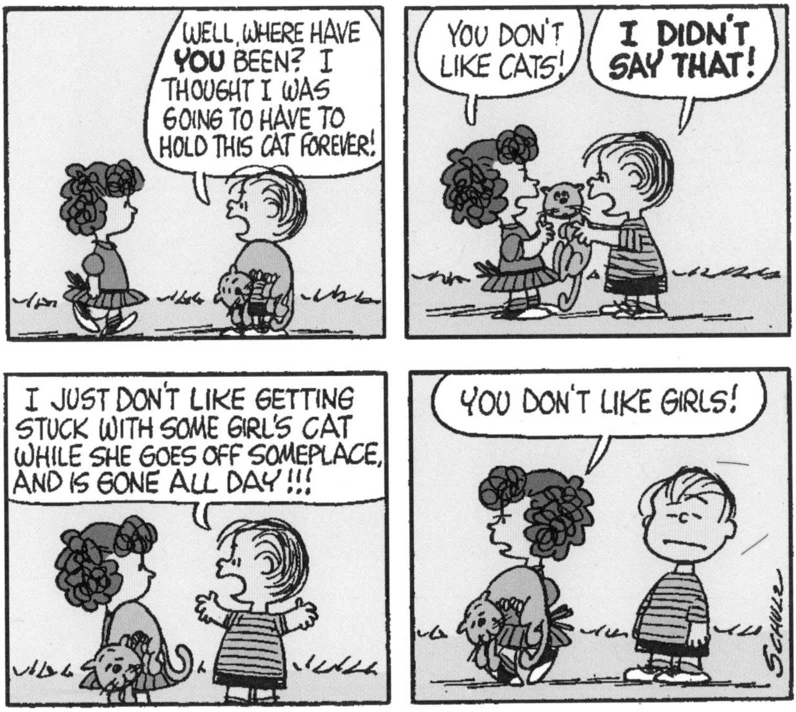
WELL, WHERE HAVE YOU BEEN? I THOUGHT I WAS GOING TO HAVE TO HOLD THIS CAT FOREVER!
YOU DON'T LIKE CATS!
I DIDN'T SAY THAT!
I JUST DON'T LIKE GETTING STUCK WITH SOME GIRL'S CAT WHILE SHE GOES OFF SOMEPLACE, AND IS GONE ALL DAY!!!
YOU DON'T LIKE GIRLS!
SCHULZ

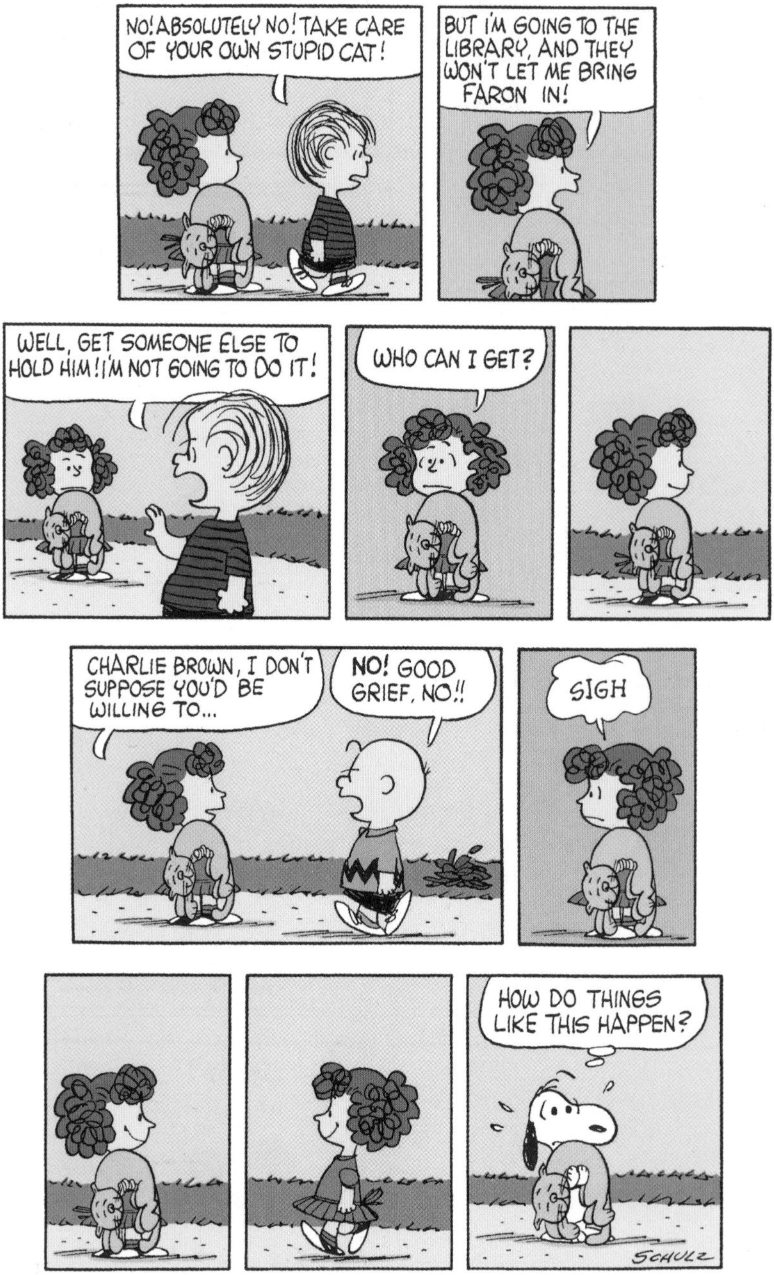
NO! ABSOLUTELY NO! TAKE CARE OF YOUR OWN STUPID CAT!
BUT I'M GOING TO THE LIBRARY, AND THEY WON'T LET ME BRING FARON IN!
WELL, GET SOMEONE ELSE TO HOLD HIM! I'M NOT GOING TO DO IT!
WHO CAN I GET?
CHARLIE BROWN, I DON'T SUPPOSE YOU'D BE WILLING TO...
NO! GOOD GRIEF, NO!!
SIGH
HOW DO THINGS LIKE THIS HAPPEN?
SCHULZ

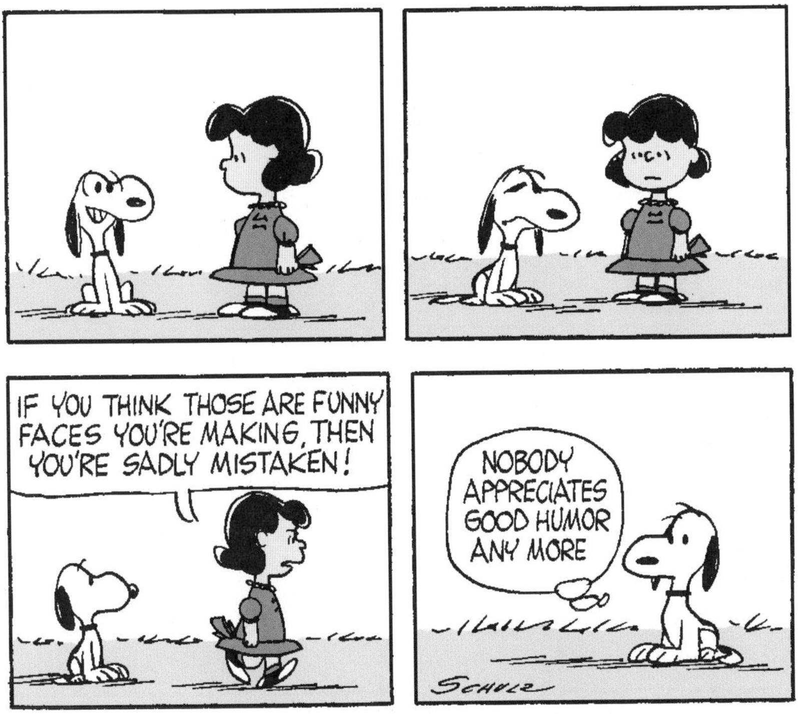
IF YOU THINK THOSE ARE FUNNY FACES YOU'RE MAKING, THEN YOU'RE SADLY MISTAKEN!
NOBODY APPRECIATES GOOD HUMOR ANY MORE
SCHULZ

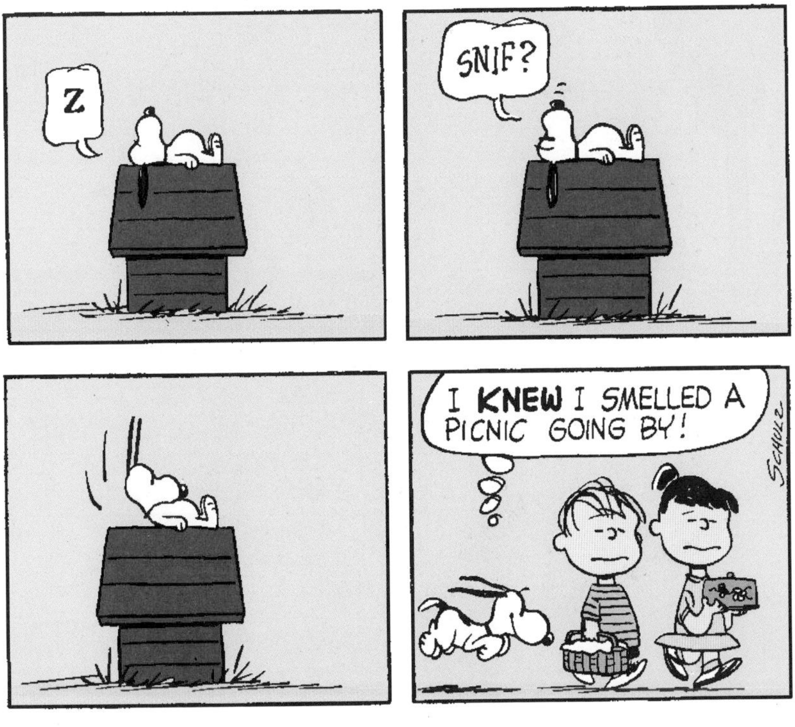
Z
SNIF?
I **KNEW** I SMELLED A PICNIC GOING BY!
SCHULZ

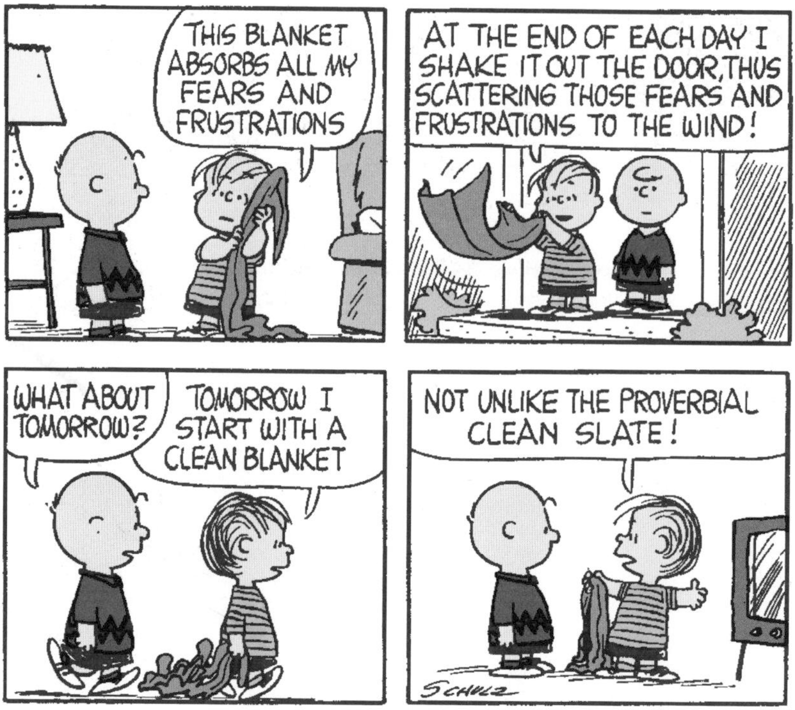
THIS BLANKET ABSORBS ALL MY FEARS AND FRUSTRATIONS
AT THE END OF EACH DAY I SHAKE IT OUT THE DOOR, THUS SCATTERING THOSE FEARS AND FRUSTRATIONS TO THE WIND!
WHAT ABOUT TOMORROW?
TOMORROW I START WITH A CLEAN BLANKET
NOT UNLIKE THE PROVERBIAL CLEAN SLATE!
SCHULZ

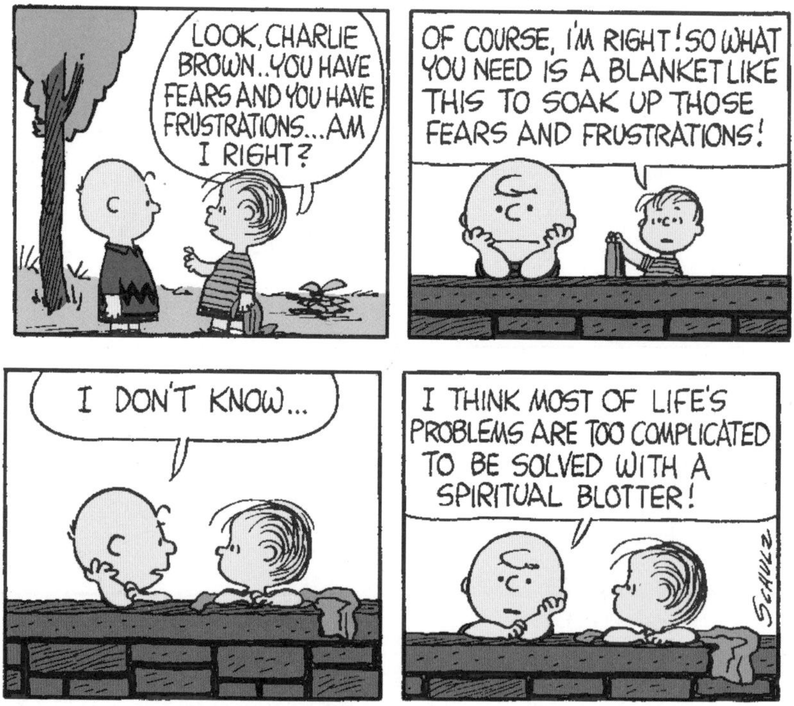
LOOK, CHARLIE BROWN..YOU HAVE FEARS AND YOU HAVE FRUSTRATIONS...AM I RIGHT?
OF COURSE, I'M RIGHT! SO WHAT YOU NEED IS A BLANKET LIKE THIS TO SOAK UP THOSE FEARS AND FRUSTRATIONS!
I DON'T KNOW...
I THINK MOST OF LIFE'S PROBLEMS ARE TOO COMPLICATED TO BE SOLVED WITH A SPIRITUAL BLOTTER!
SCHULZ

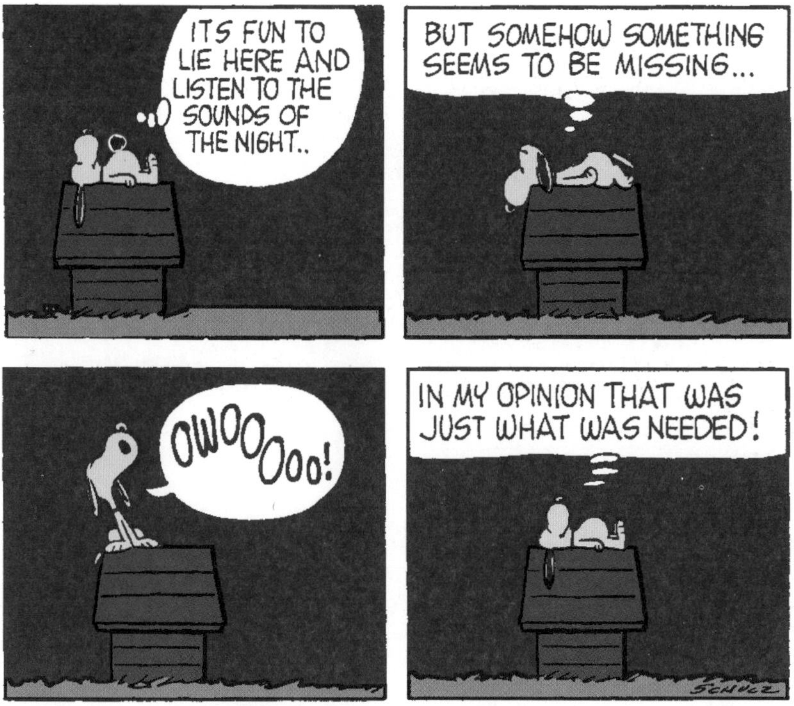
ITS FUN TO LIE HERE AND LISTEN TO THE SOUNDS OF THE NIGHT..
BUT SOMEHOW SOMETHING SEEMS TO BE MISSING...
OWOOOOoo!
IN MY OPINION THAT WAS JUST WHAT WAS NEEDED!
SCHULZ

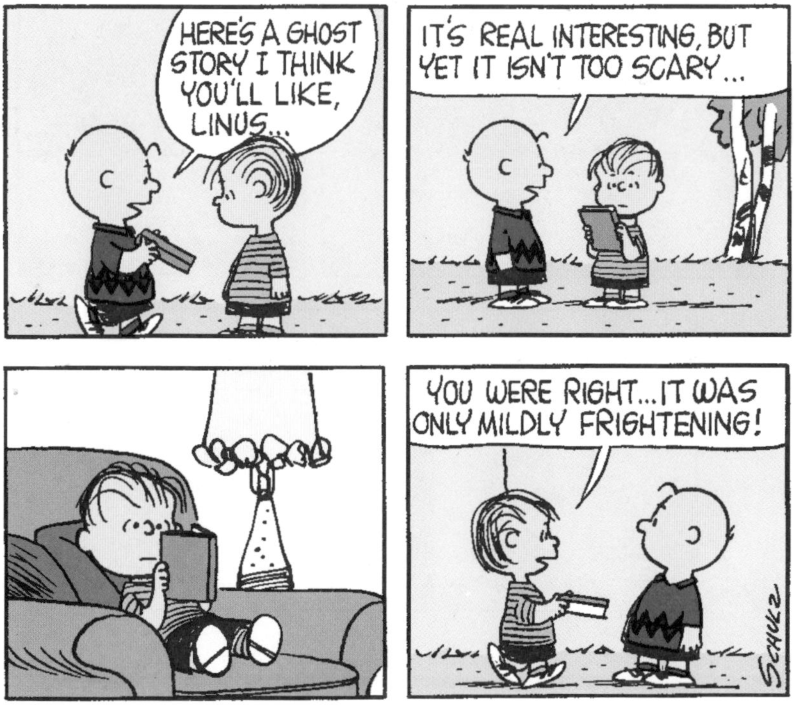
HERE'S A GHOST STORY I THINK YOU'LL LIKE, LINUS...
IT'S REAL INTERESTING, BUT YET IT ISN'T TOO SCARY...
YOU WERE RIGHT...IT WAS ONLY MILDLY FRIGHTENING!
SCHULZ

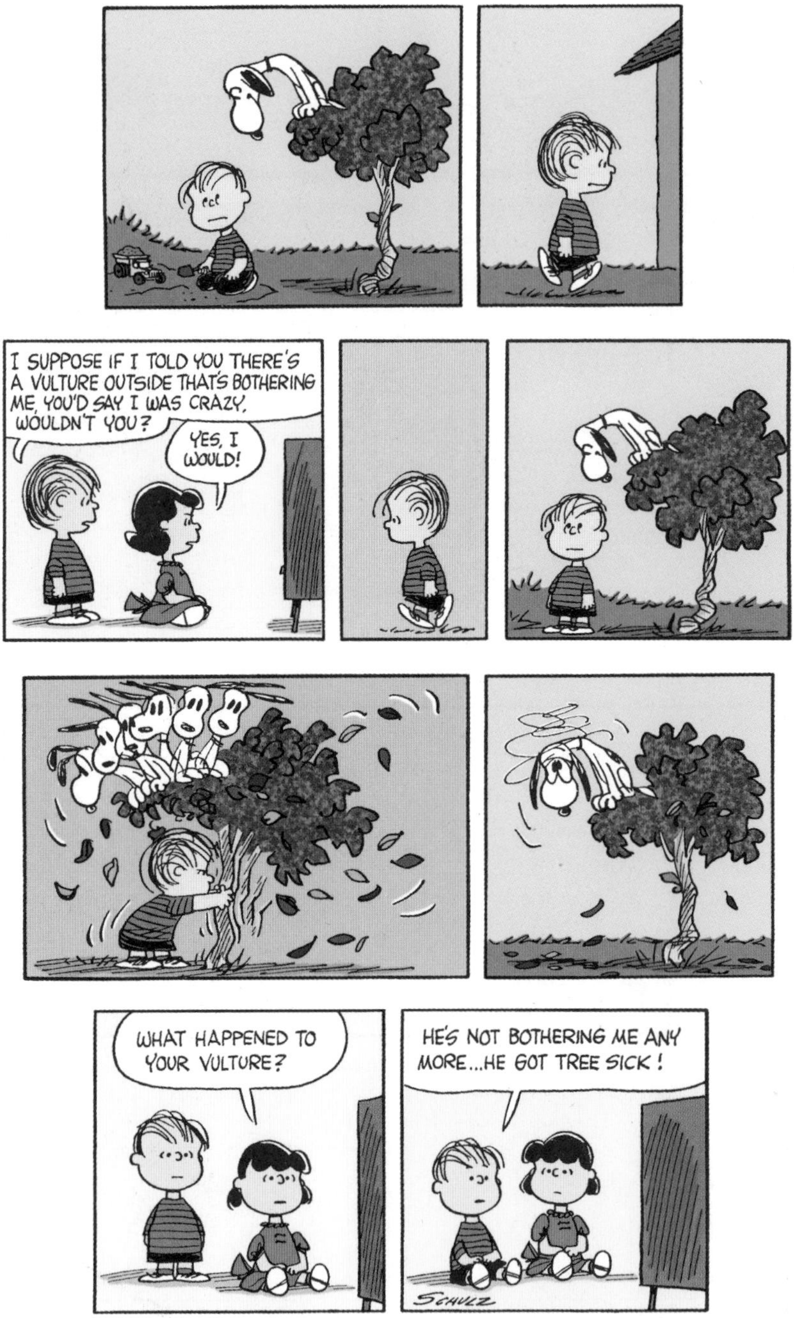
I SUPPOSE IF I TOLD YOU THERE'S A VULTURE OUTSIDE THAT'S BOTHERING ME, YOU'D SAY I WAS CRAZY, WOULDN'T YOU?
YES, I WOULD!
WHAT HAPPENED TO YOUR VULTURE?
HE'S NOT BOTHERING ME ANY MORE...HE GOT TREE SICK!
SCHULZ

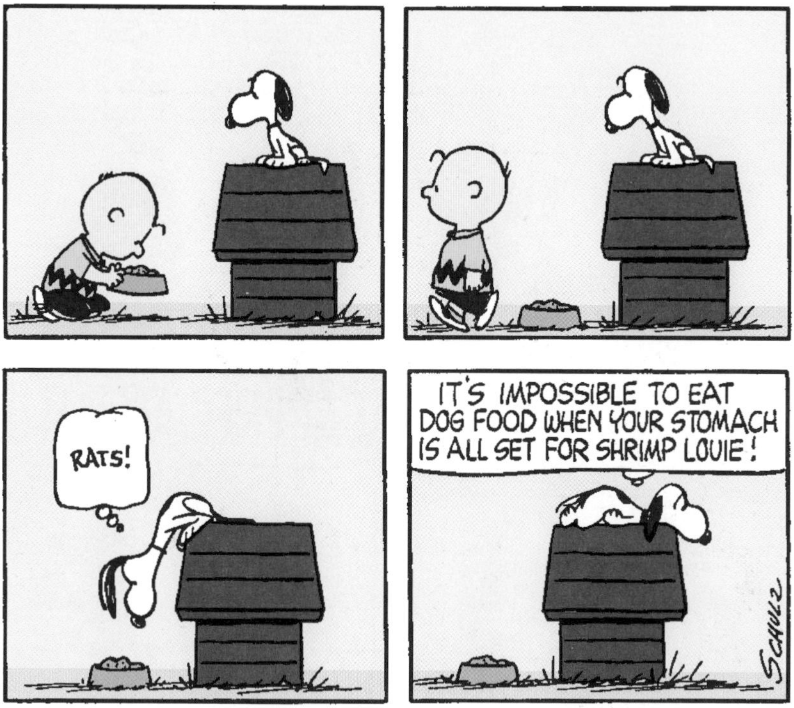
RATS!
IT'S IMPOSSIBLE TO EAT DOG FOOD WHEN YOUR STOMACH IS ALL SET FOR SHRIMP LOUIE!
SCHULZ

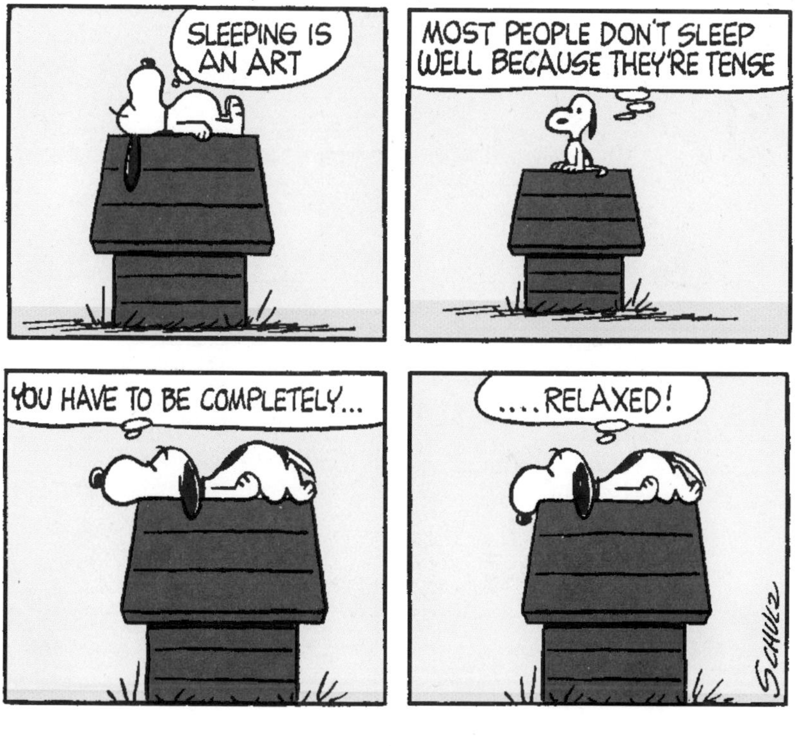
SLEEPING IS AN ART
MOST PEOPLE DON'T SLEEP WELL BECAUSE THEY'RE TENSE
YOU HAVE TO BE COMPLETELY...
....RELAXED!
SCHULZ

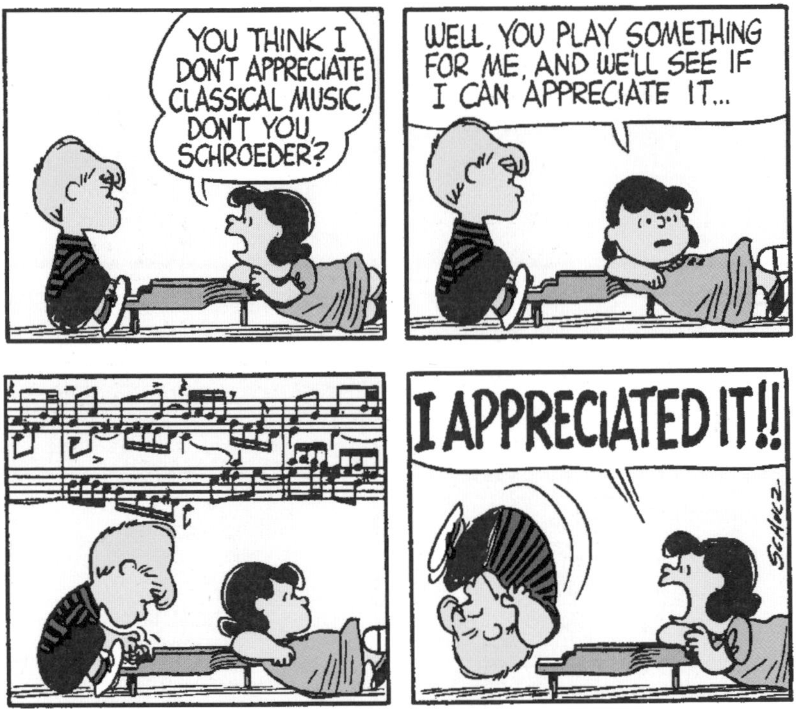
YOU THINK I DON'T APPRECIATE CLASSICAL MUSIC, DON'T YOU, SCHROEDER?
WELL, YOU PLAY SOMETHING FOR ME, AND WE'LL SEE IF I CAN APPRECIATE IT...
I APPRECIATED IT!!
SCHULZ

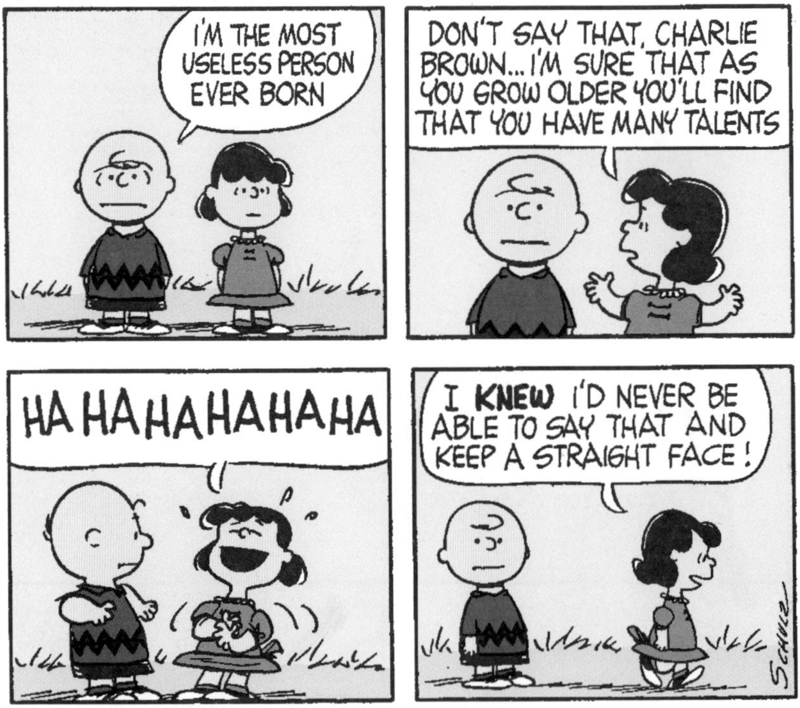
I'M THE MOST USELESS PERSON EVER BORN
DON'T SAY THAT, CHARLIE BROWN... I'M SURE THAT AS YOU GROW OLDER YOU'LL FIND THAT YOU HAVE MANY TALENTS
HA HA HA HA HA HA HA HA
I KNEW I'D NEVER BE ABLE TO SAY THAT AND KEEP A STRAIGHT FACE!
SCHULZ

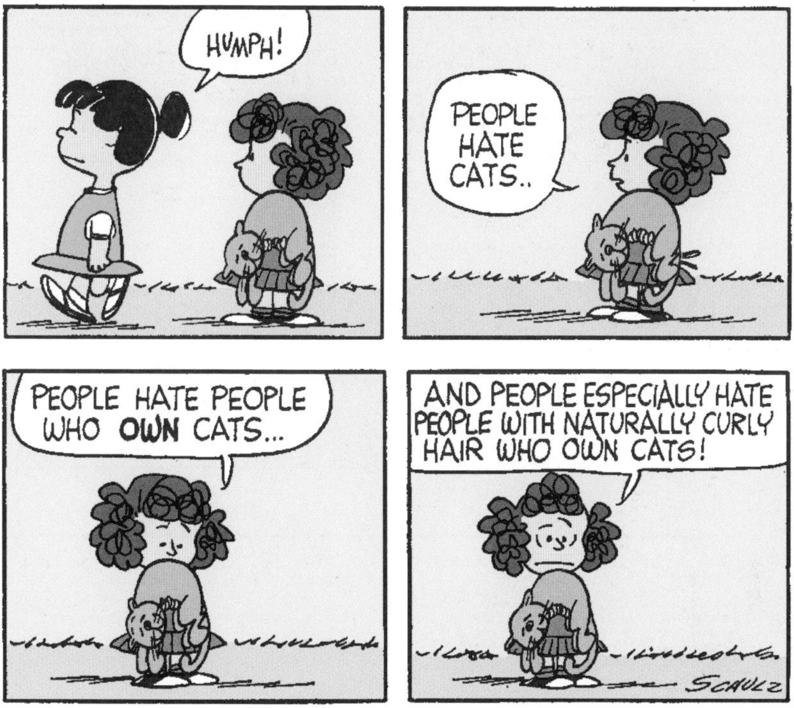
HUMPH!
PEOPLE HATE CATS..
PEOPLE HATE PEOPLE WHO **OWN** CATS...
AND PEOPLE ESPECIALLY HATE PEOPLE WITH NATURALLY CURLY HAIR WHO OWN CATS!
SCHULZ

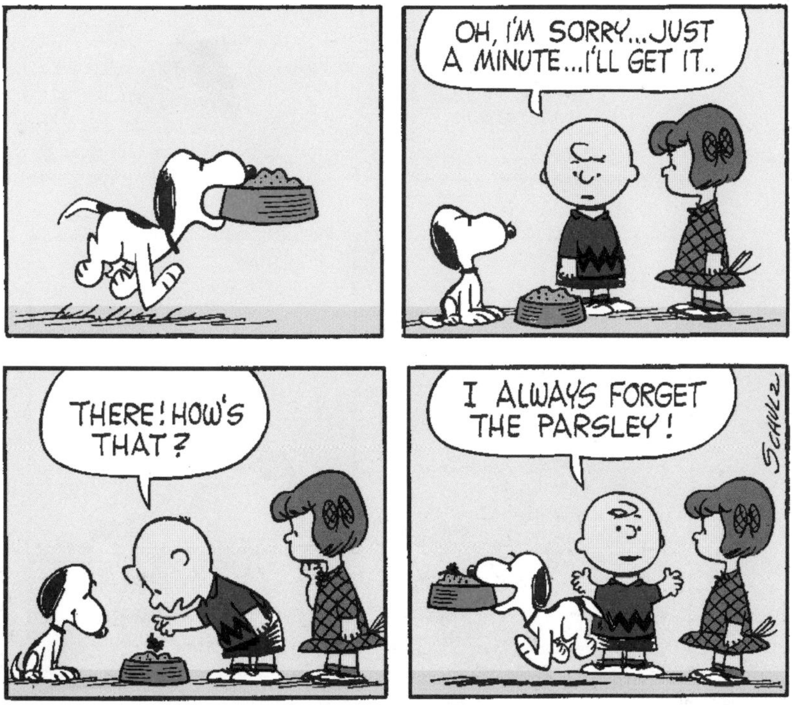
OH, I'M SORRY...JUST A MINUTE...I'LL GET IT..
THERE! HOW'S THAT?
I ALWAYS FORGET THE PARSLEY!
SCHULZ

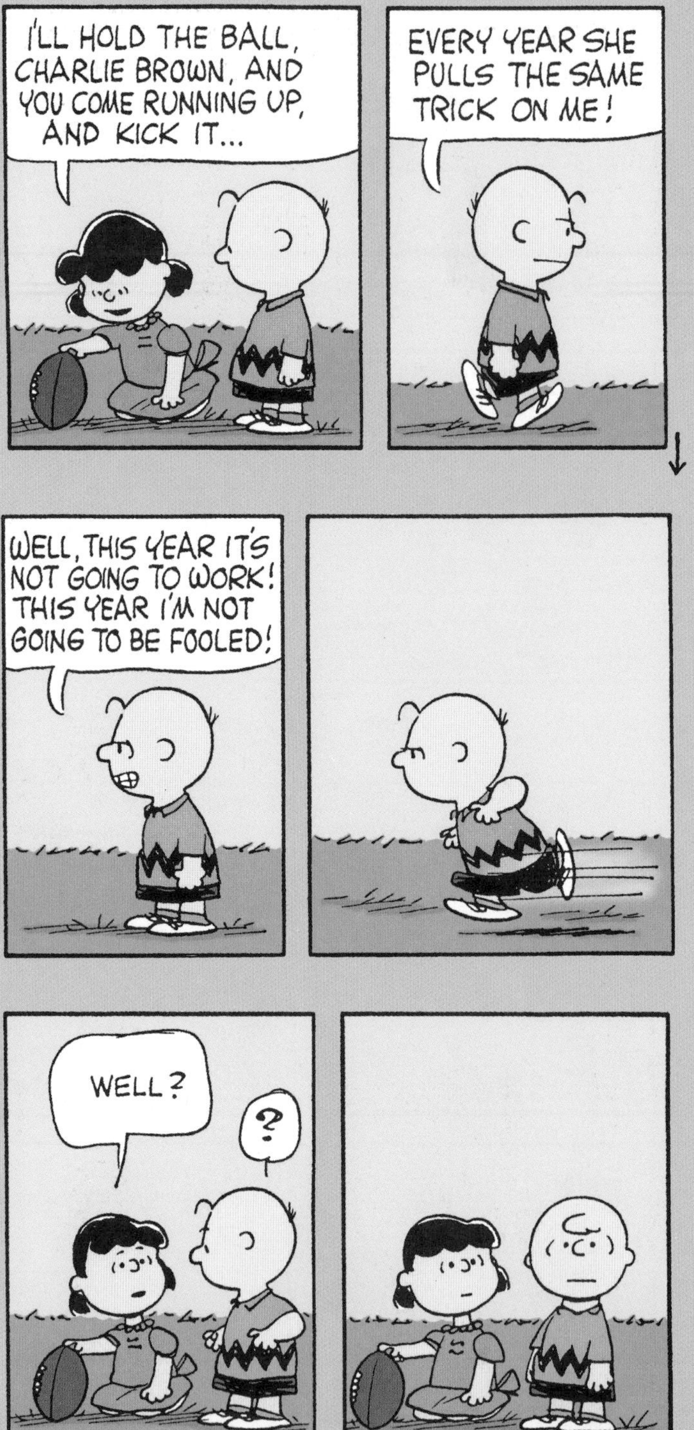
I'LL HOLD THE BALL, CHARLIE BROWN, AND YOU COME RUNNING UP, AND KICK IT...
EVERY YEAR SHE PULLS THE SAME TRICK ON ME!
WELL, THIS YEAR IT'S NOT GOING TO WORK! THIS YEAR I'M NOT GOING TO BE FOOLED!
WELL?
?

YOU THOUGHT I WAS GOING TO PULL THE BALL AWAY, DIDN'T YOU? WHY, CHARLIE BROWN, I'M ASHAMED OF YOU! I'M ALSO INSULTED!
DON'T YOU TRUST ANYONE ANY MORE? HAS YOUR MIND BECOME SO DARKENED WITH MISTRUST THAT YOU'VE LOST YOUR ABILITY TO BELIEVE IN PEOPLE?
AUGH!
WUMP!
ISN'T IT BETTER THIS WAY, CHARLIE BROWN? ISN'T IT BETTER TO TRUST PEOPLE?
SCHULZ

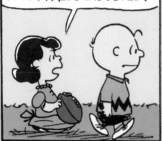

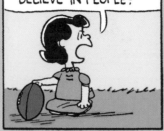

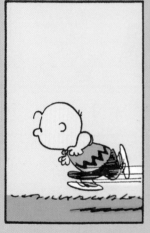

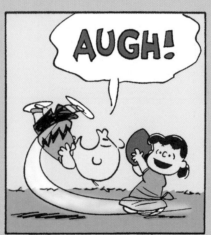

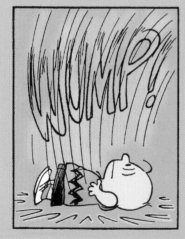

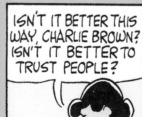

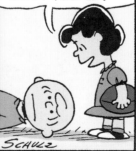

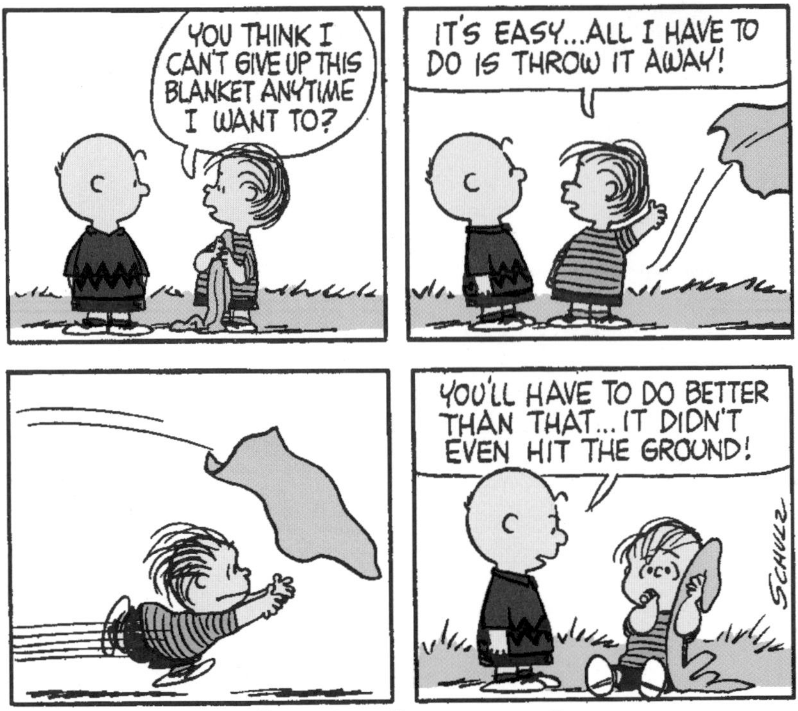
YOU THINK I CAN'T GIVE UP THIS BLANKET ANYTIME I WANT TO?
IT'S EASY...ALL I HAVE TO DO IS THROW IT AWAY!
YOU'LL HAVE TO DO BETTER THAN THAT... IT DIDN'T EVEN HIT THE GROUND!
SCHULZ

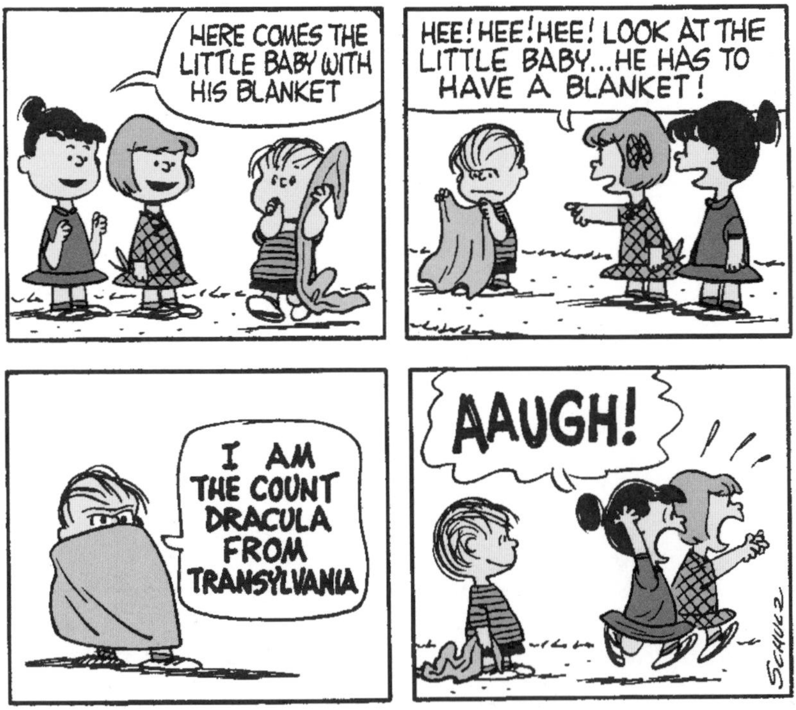
HERE COMES THE LITTLE BABY WITH HIS BLANKET
HEE! HEE! HEE! LOOK AT THE LITTLE BABY...HE HAS TO HAVE A BLANKET!
I AM THE COUNT DRACULA FROM TRANSYLVANIA
AAUGH!
SCHULZ

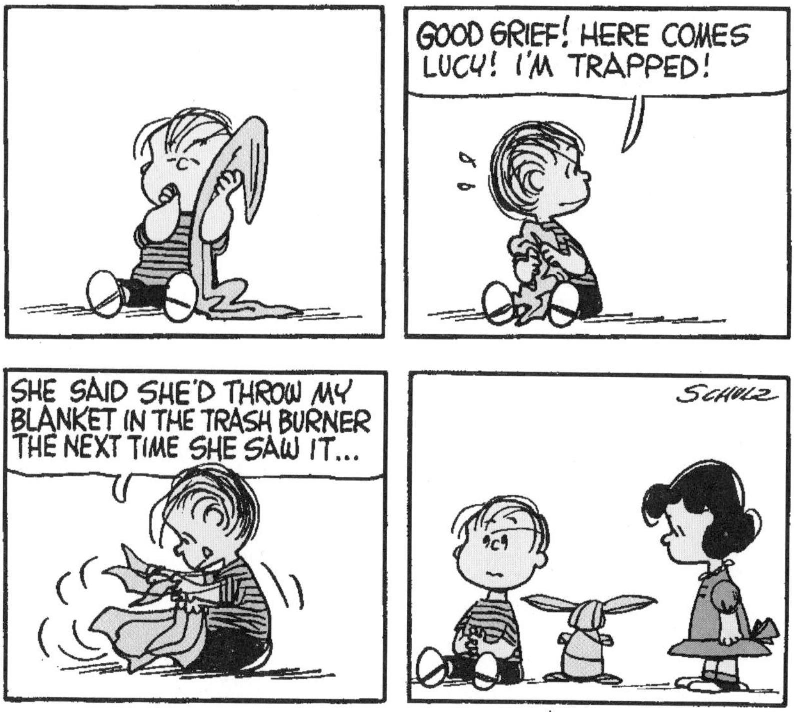
GOOD GRIEF! HERE COMES LUCY! I'M TRAPPED!
SHE SAID SHE'D THROW MY BLANKET IN THE TRASH BURNER THE NEXT TIME SHE SAW IT...
SCHULZ

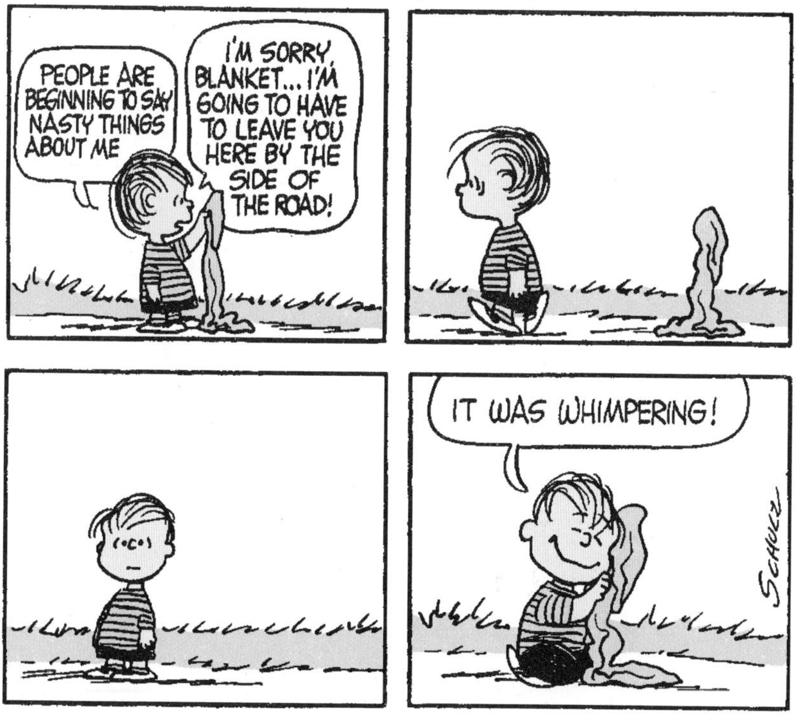
PEOPLE ARE BEGINNING TO SAY NASTY THINGS ABOUT ME
I'M SORRY, BLANKET... I'M GOING TO HAVE TO LEAVE YOU HERE BY THE SIDE OF THE ROAD!
IT WAS WHIMPERING!
SCHULZ

ALL RIGHT, WHERE IS IT?!

SOMEBODY HAS MY BLANKET, AND WHEN I FIND HIM, I'LL FIX HIM GOOD! I'M MAD! I'M REALLY MAD!!

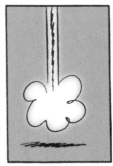

I'LL FIND HIM, TOO! I'LL FIND WHOEVER TOOK MY BLANKET, AND WHEN I'M THROUGH WITH HIM, HE'LL BE PLENTY SORRY!!

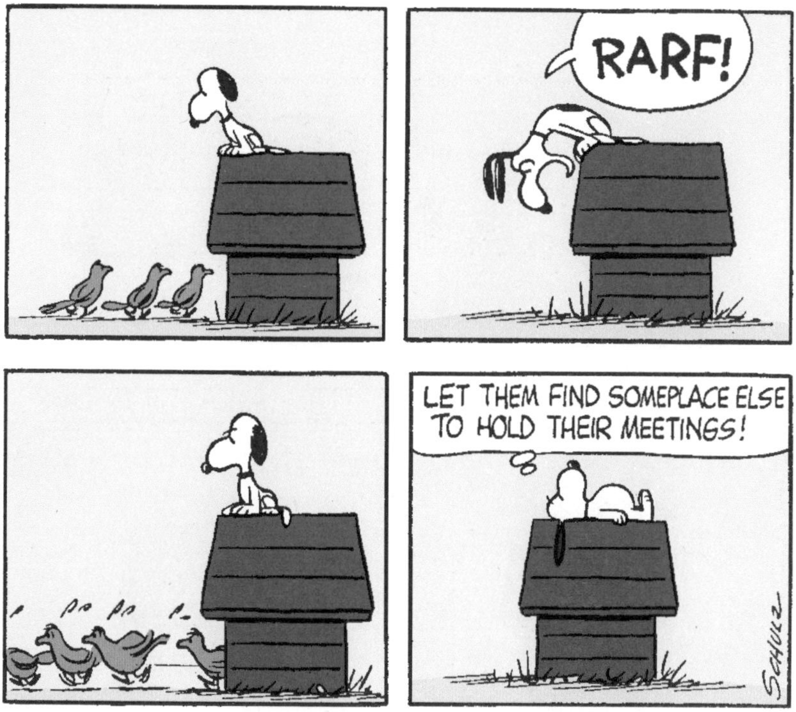
RARF!
LET THEM FIND SOMEPLACE ELSE TO HOLD THEIR MEETINGS!
SCHULZ

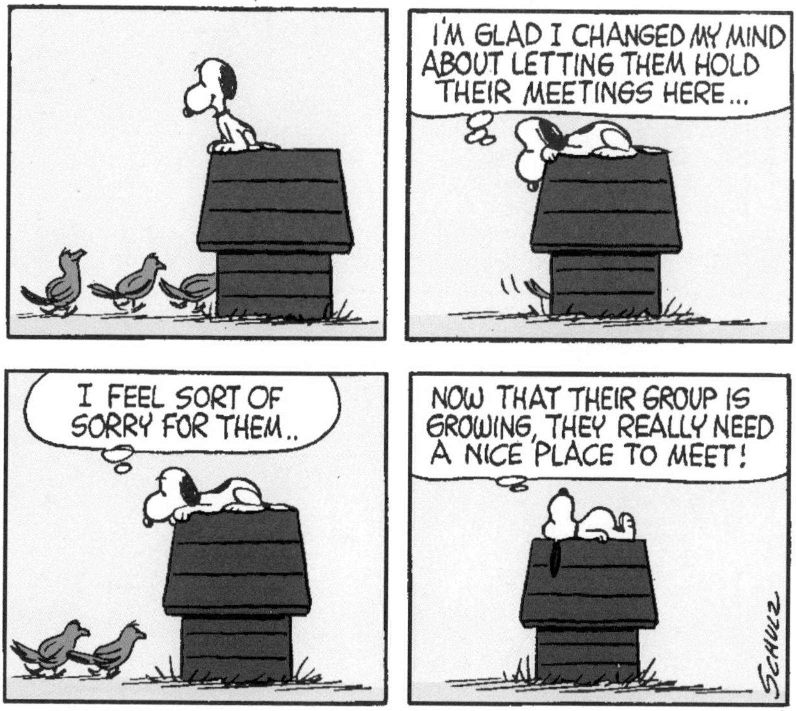
I'M GLAD I CHANGED MY MIND ABOUT LETTING THEM HOLD THEIR MEETINGS HERE...
I FEEL SORT OF SORRY FOR THEM..
NOW THAT THEIR GROUP IS GROWING, THEY REALLY NEED A NICE PLACE TO MEET!
SCHULZ

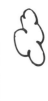

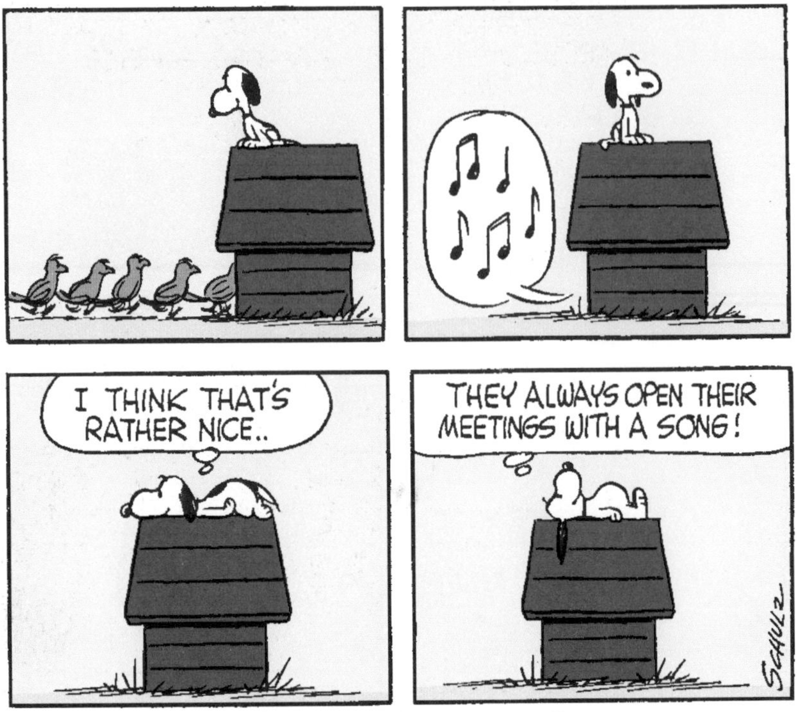
I THINK THAT'S RATHER NICE..
THEY ALWAYS OPEN THEIR MEETINGS WITH A SONG!
SCHULZ

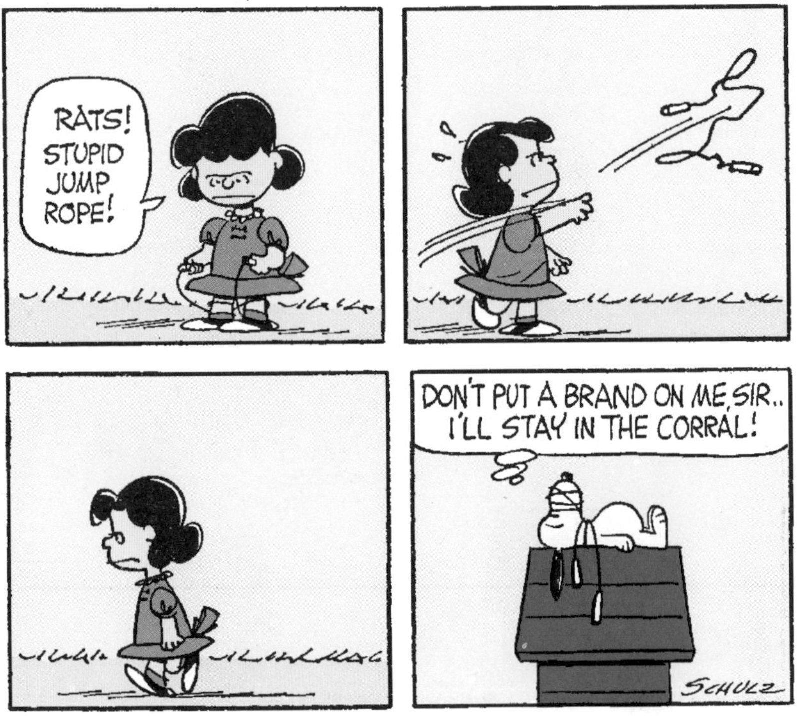
RATS! STUPID JUMP ROPE!
DON'T PUT A BRAND ON ME, SIR.. I'LL STAY IN THE CORRAL!
SCHULZ

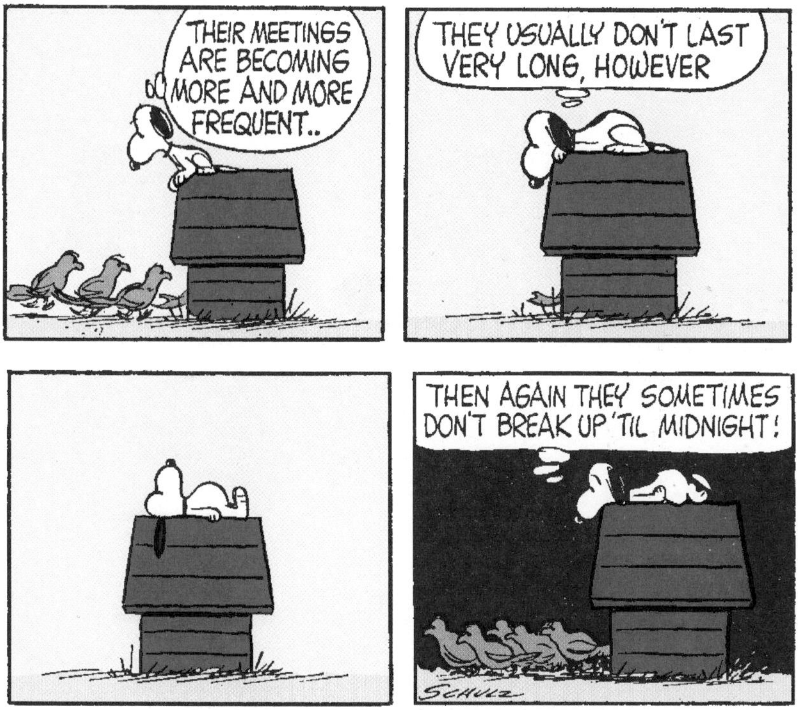
THEIR MEETINGS ARE BECOMING MORE AND MORE FREQUENT..
THEY USUALLY DON'T LAST VERY LONG, HOWEVER
THEN AGAIN THEY SOMETIMES DON'T BREAK UP 'TIL MIDNIGHT!
SCHULZ

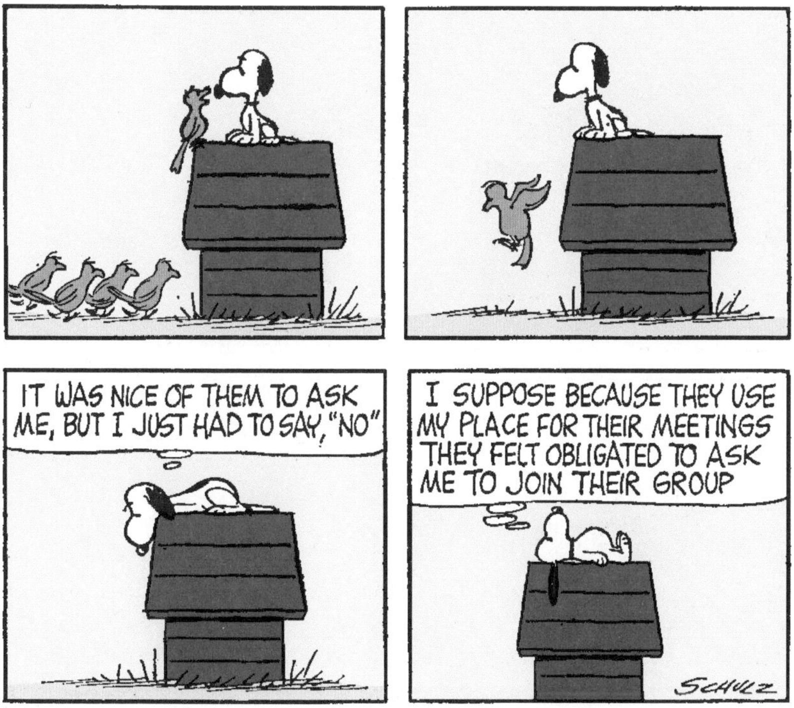
IT WAS NICE OF THEM TO ASK ME, BUT I JUST HAD TO SAY, "NO"
I SUPPOSE BECAUSE THEY USE MY PLACE FOR THEIR MEETINGS THEY FELT OBLIGATED TO ASK ME TO JOIN THEIR GROUP
SCHULZ

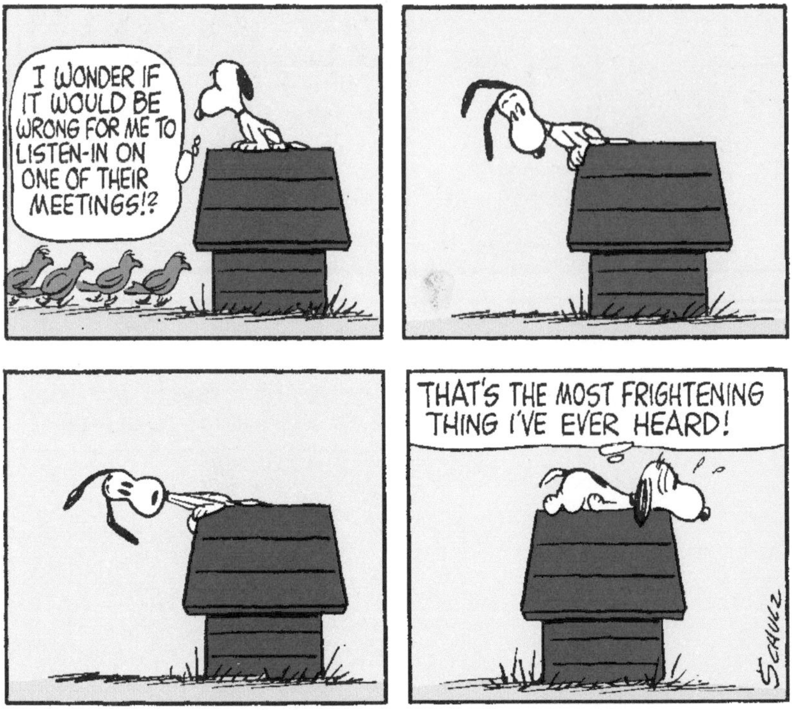
I WONDER IF IT WOULD BE WRONG FOR ME TO LISTEN-IN ON ONE OF THEIR MEETINGS!?
THAT'S THE MOST FRIGHTENING THING I'VE EVER HEARD!
SCHULZ

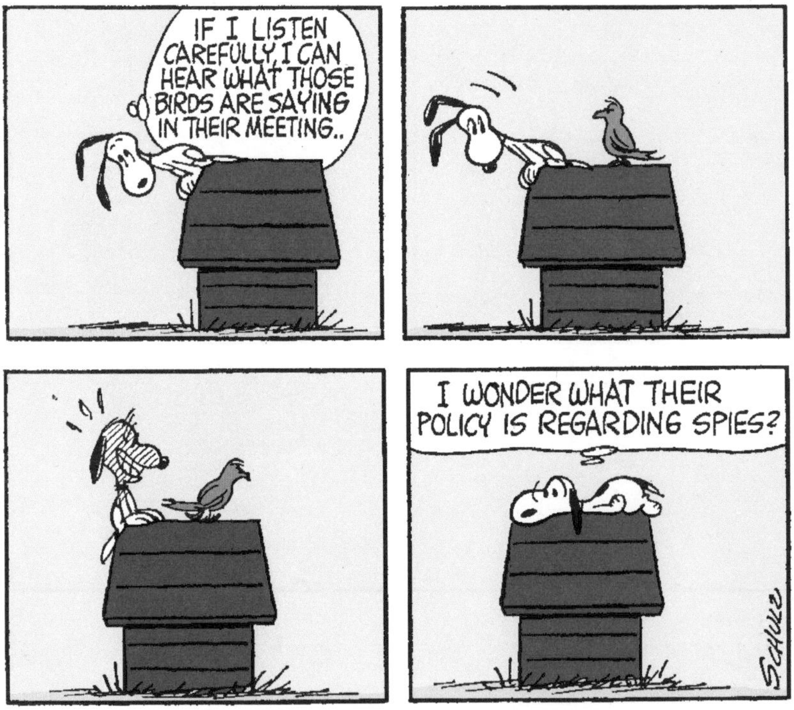
IF I LISTEN CAREFULLY, I CAN HEAR WHAT THOSE BIRDS ARE SAYING IN THEIR MEETING..
I WONDER WHAT THEIR POLICY IS REGARDING SPIES?
SCHULZ

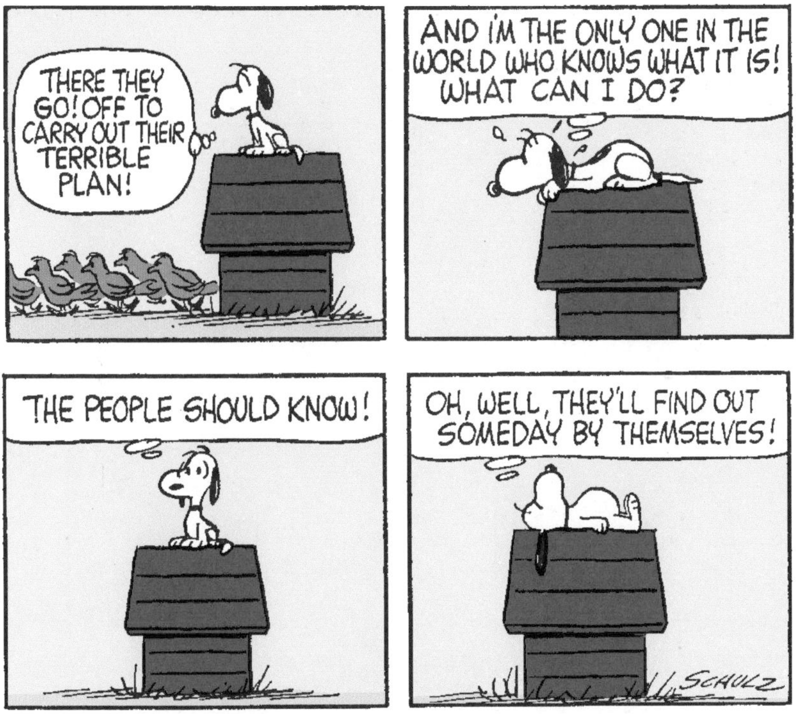
THERE THEY GO! OFF TO CARRY OUT THEIR TERRIBLE PLAN!
AND I'M THE ONLY ONE IN THE WORLD WHO KNOWS WHAT IT IS! WHAT CAN I DO?
THE PEOPLE SHOULD KNOW!
OH, WELL, THEY'LL FIND OUT SOMEDAY BY THEMSELVES!
SCHULZ

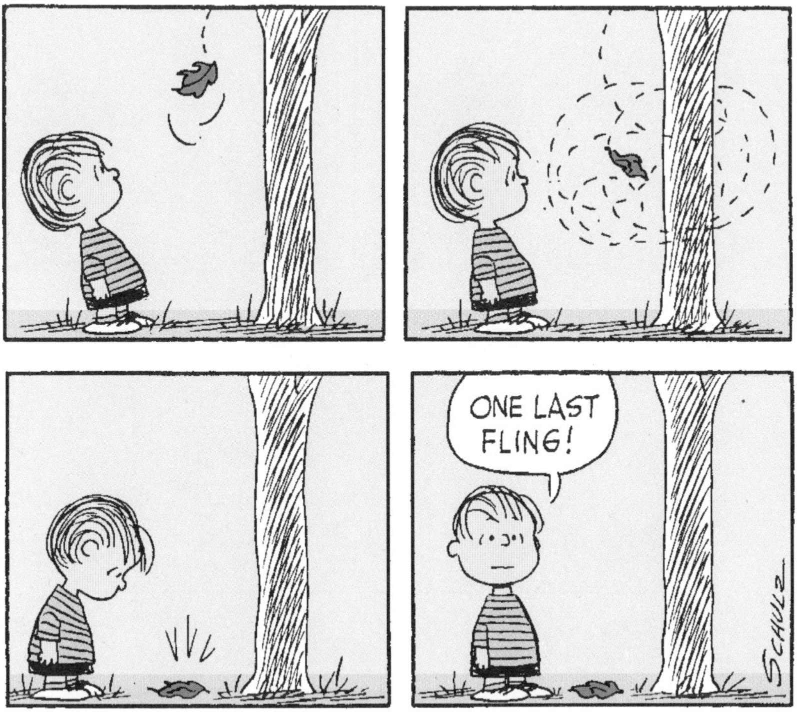
ONE LAST FLING!
SCHULZ

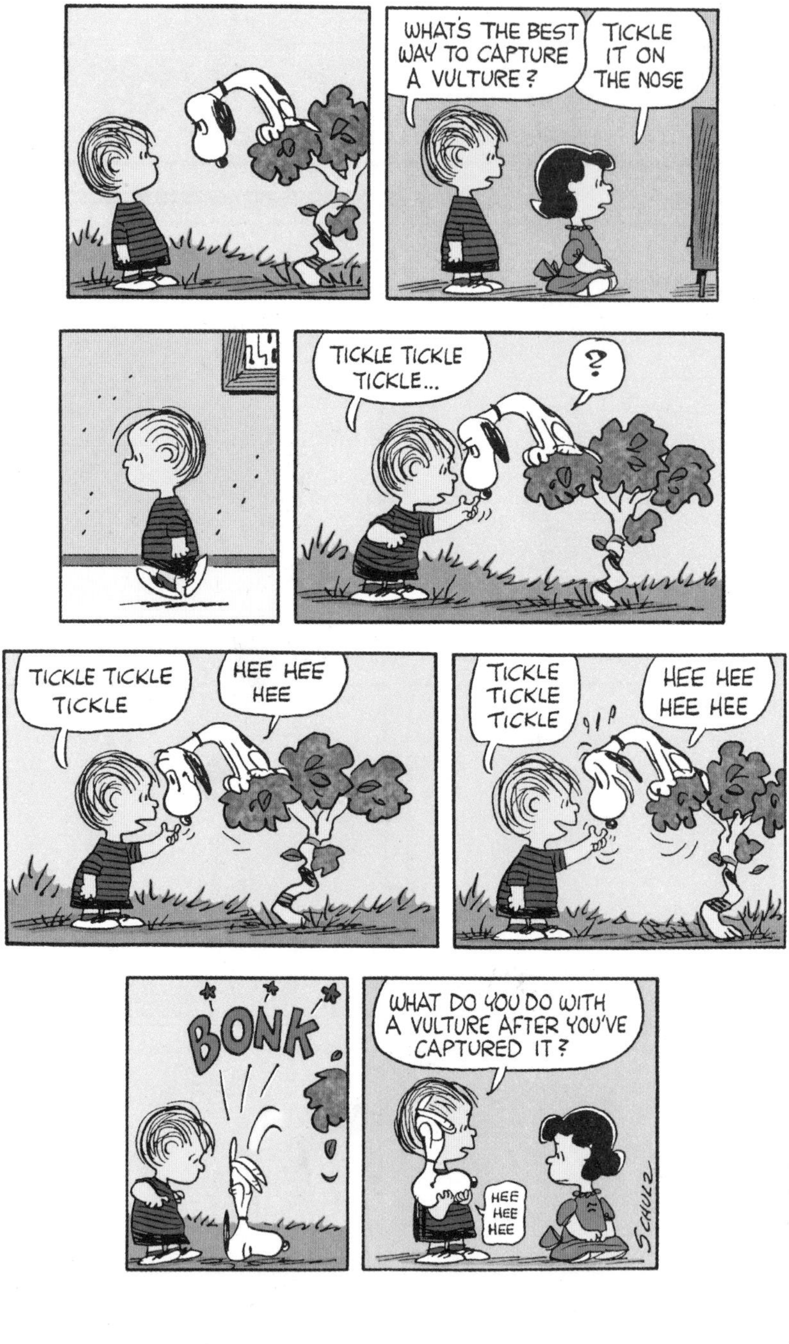
WHAT'S THE BEST WAY TO CAPTURE A VULTURE ?
TICKLE IT ON THE NOSE
TICKLE TICKLE TICKLE...
?
TICKLE TICKLE TICKLE
HEE HEE HEE
TICKLE TICKLE TICKLE
HEE HEE HEE HEE
BONK
WHAT DO YOU DO WITH A VULTURE AFTER YOU'VE CAPTURED IT ?
HEE HEE HEE
SCHULZ

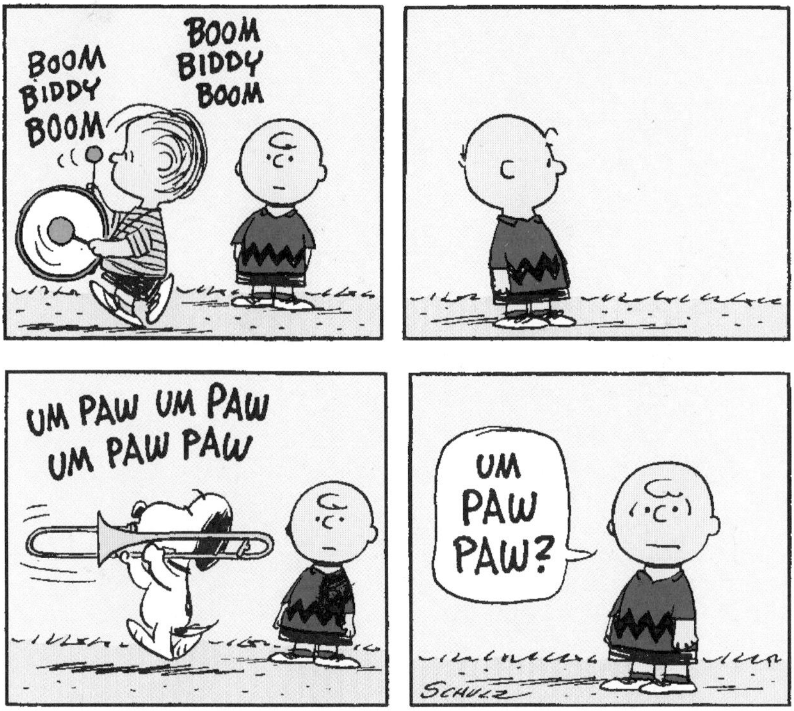
BOOM BIDDY BOOM
BOOM BIDDY BOOM
UM PAW UM PAW UM PAW PAW
UM PAW PAW?
SCHULZ

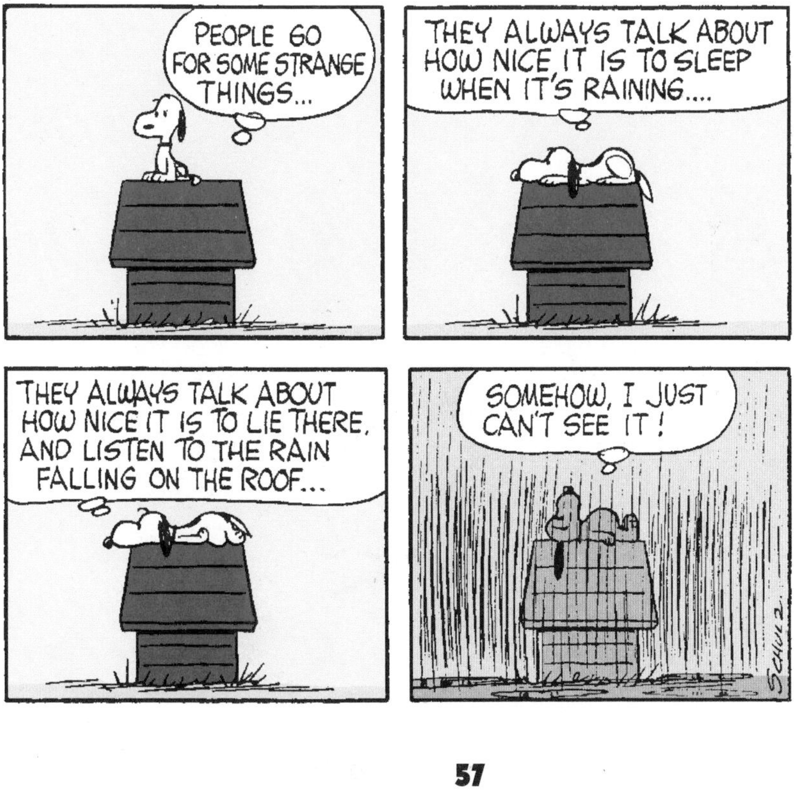
PEOPLE GO FOR SOME STRANGE THINGS...
THEY ALWAYS TALK ABOUT HOW NICE IT IS TO SLEEP WHEN IT'S RAINING....
THEY ALWAYS TALK ABOUT HOW NICE IT IS TO LIE THERE, AND LISTEN TO THE RAIN FALLING ON THE ROOF...
SOMEHOW, I JUST CAN'T SEE IT!
SCHULZ

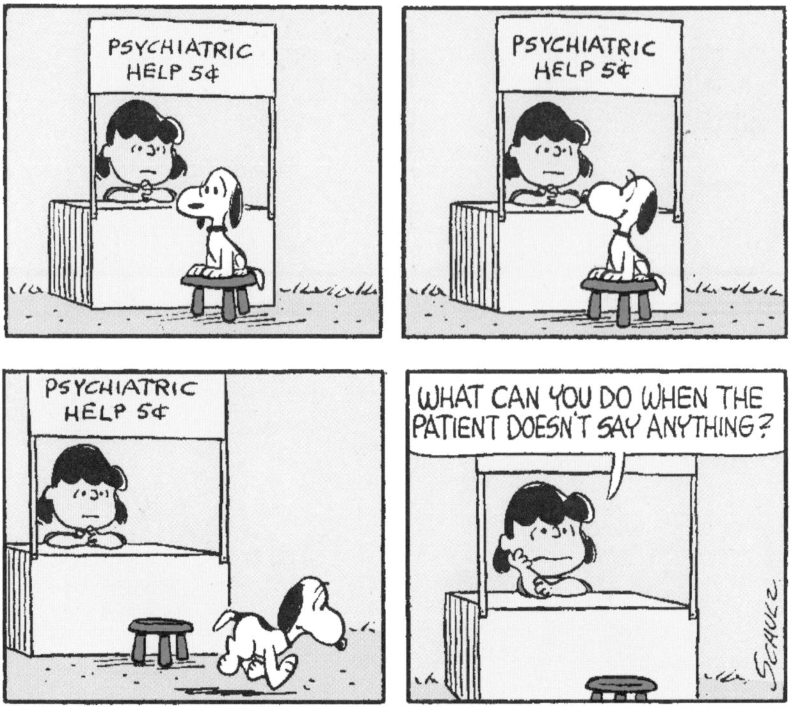
PSYCHIATRIC HELP 5¢
PSYCHIATRIC HELP 5¢
PSYCHIATRIC HELP 5¢
WHAT CAN YOU DO WHEN THE PATIENT DOESN'T SAY ANYTHING?
SCHULZ

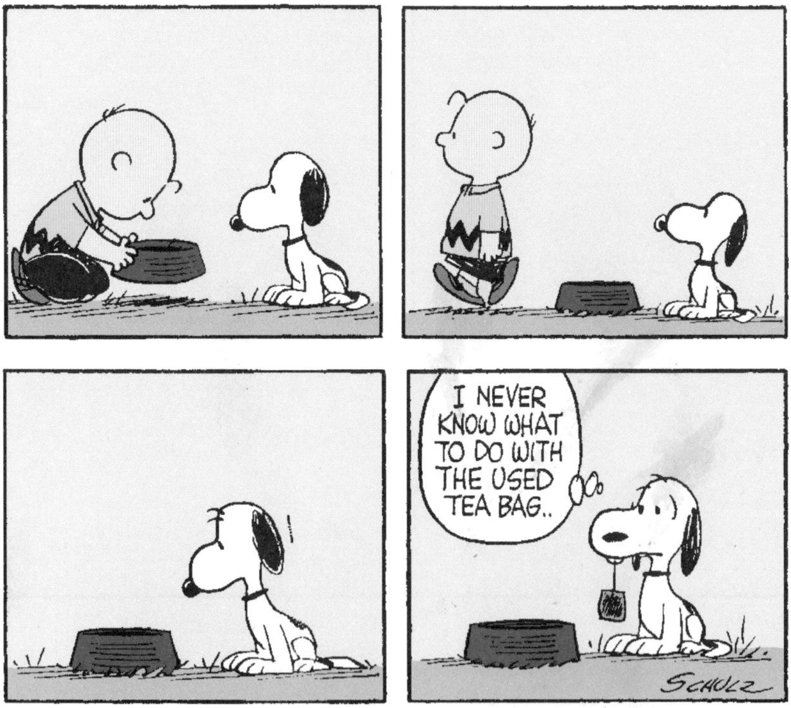
I NEVER KNOW WHAT TO DO WITH THE USED TEA BAG..
SCHULZ

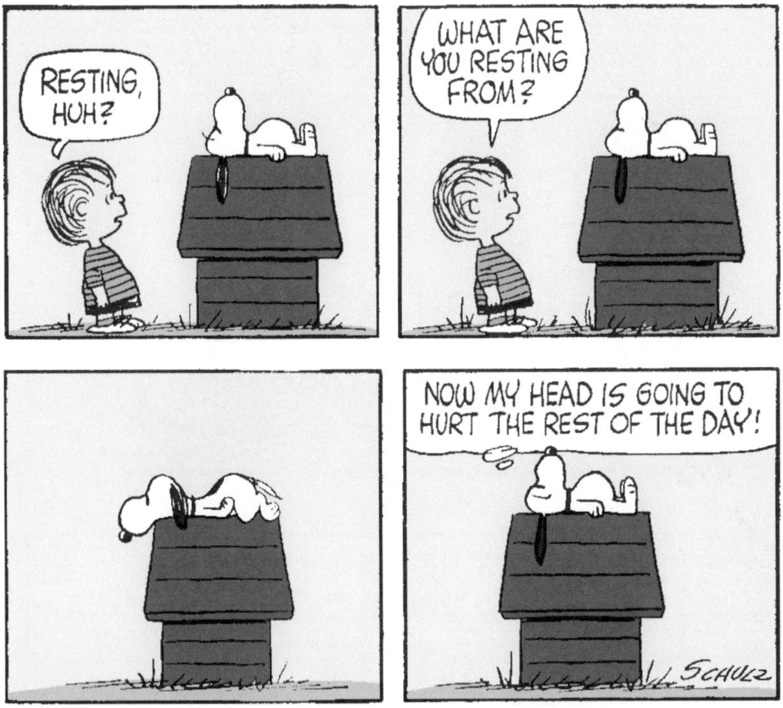
RESTING, HUH?
WHAT ARE YOU RESTING FROM?
NOW MY HEAD IS GOING TO HURT THE REST OF THE DAY!
SCHULZ

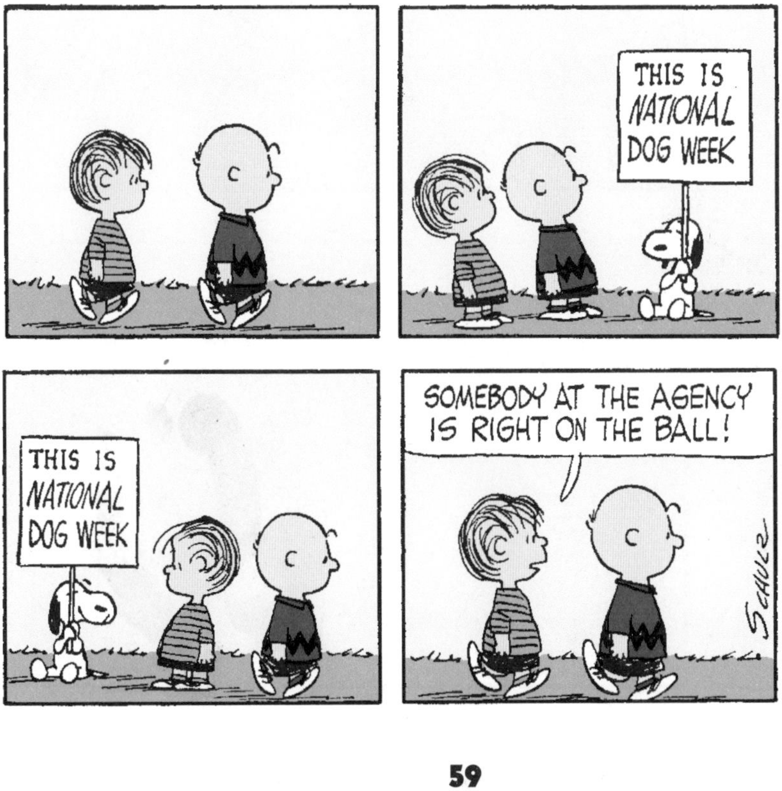
THIS IS NATIONAL DOG WEEK
THIS IS NATIONAL DOG WEEK
SOMEBODY AT THE AGENCY IS RIGHT ON THE BALL!
SCHULZ

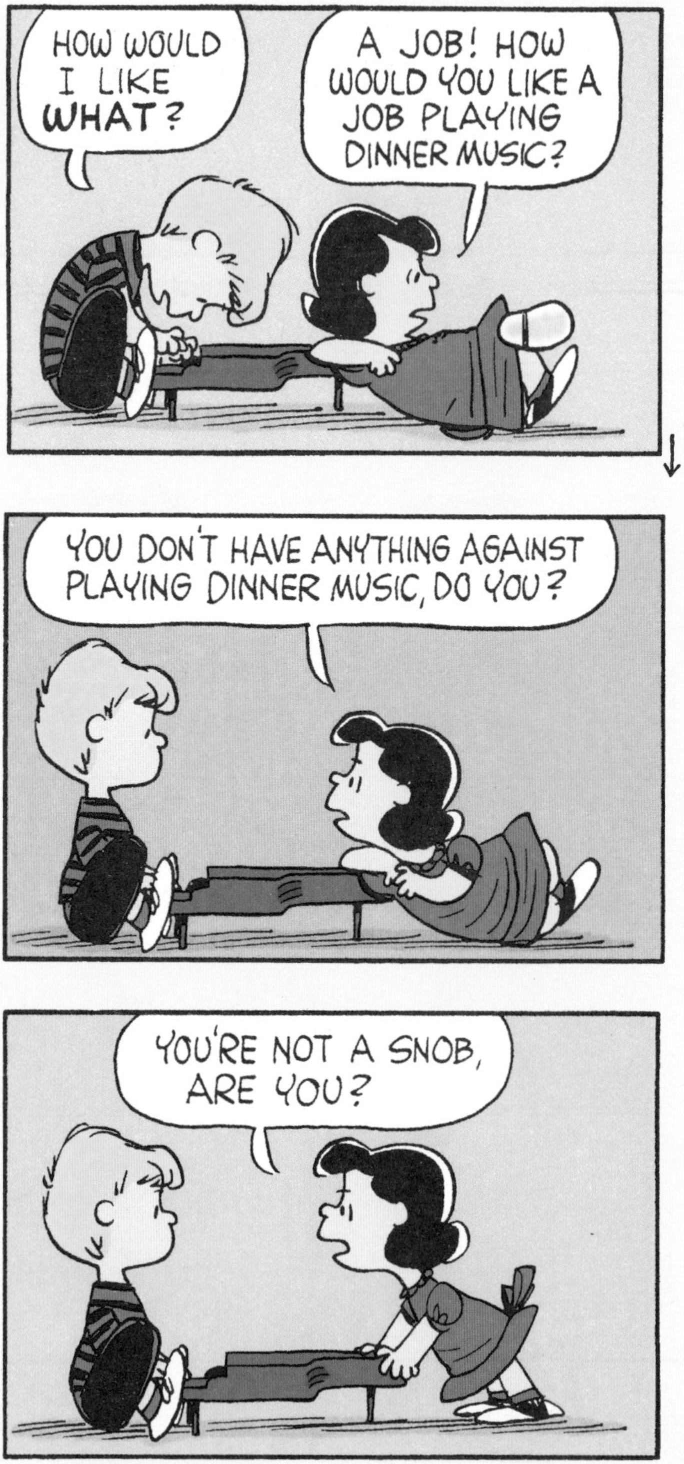
HOW WOULD I LIKE WHAT?
A JOB! HOW WOULD YOU LIKE A JOB PLAYING DINNER MUSIC?
YOU DON'T HAVE ANYTHING AGAINST PLAYING DINNER MUSIC, DO YOU?
YOU'RE NOT A SNOB, ARE YOU?

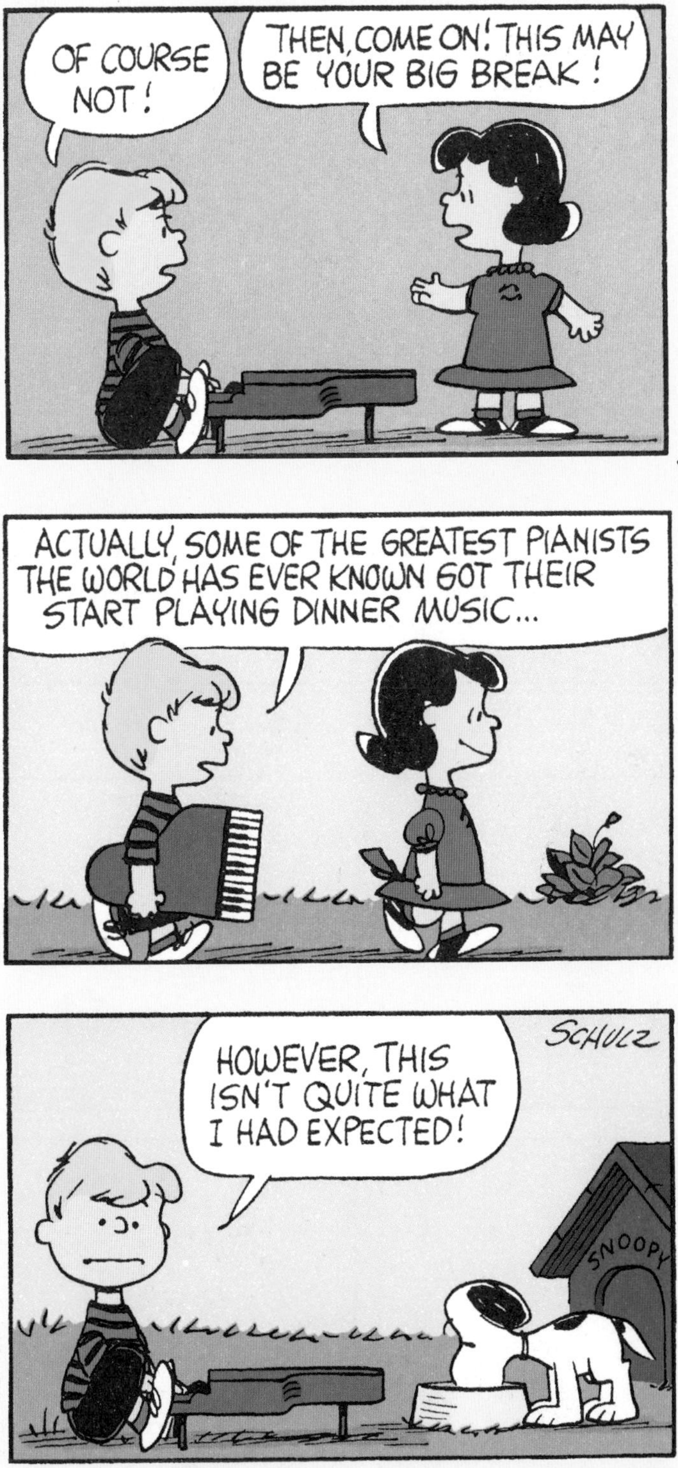
OF COURSE NOT!
THEN, COME ON! THIS MAY BE YOUR BIG BREAK!
ACTUALLY, SOME OF THE GREATEST PIANISTS THE WORLD HAS EVER KNOWN GOT THEIR START PLAYING DINNER MUSIC...
SCHULZ
HOWEVER, THIS ISN'T QUITE WHAT I HAD EXPECTED!
SNOOPY

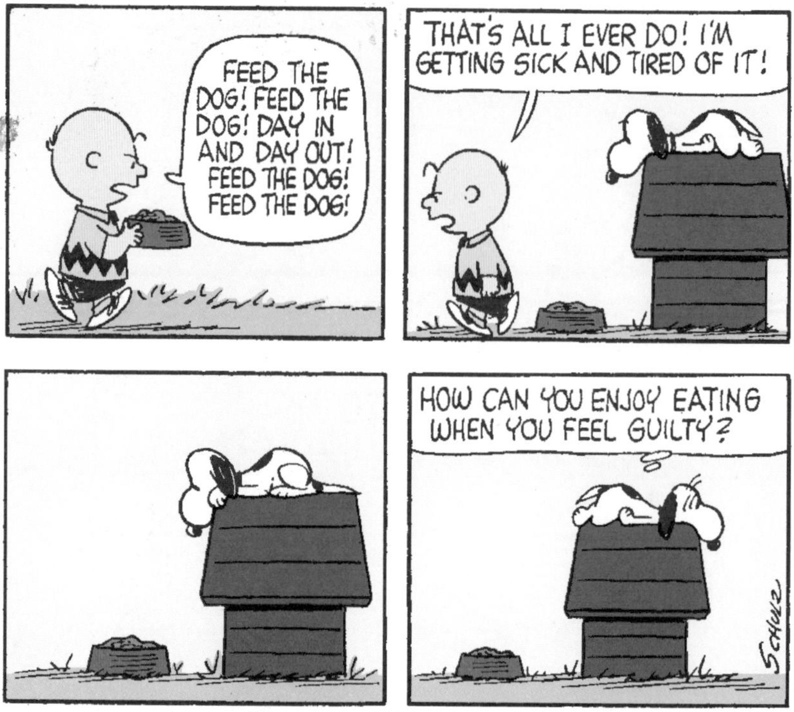
FEED THE DOG! FEED THE DOG! DAY IN AND DAY OUT! FEED THE DOG! FEED THE DOG!
THAT'S ALL I EVER DO! I'M GETTING SICK AND TIRED OF IT!
HOW CAN YOU ENJOY EATING WHEN YOU FEEL GUILTY?
SCHULZ

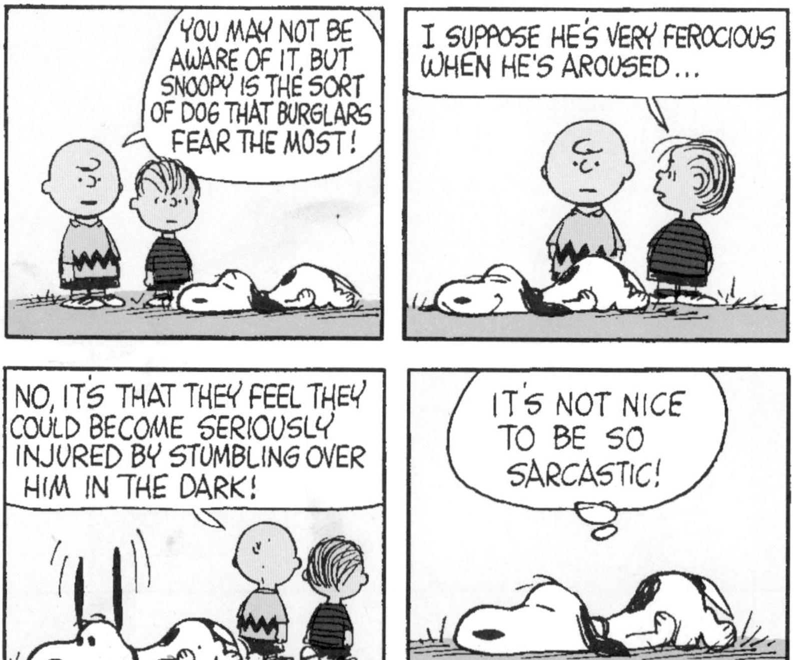
YOU MAY NOT BE AWARE OF IT, BUT SNOOPY IS THE SORT OF DOG THAT BURGLARS FEAR THE MOST!
I SUPPOSE HE'S VERY FEROCIOUS WHEN HE'S AROUSED...
NO, IT'S THAT THEY FEEL THEY COULD BECOME SERIOUSLY INJURED BY STUMBLING OVER HIM IN THE DARK!
IT'S NOT NICE TO BE SO SARCASTIC!
SCHULZ

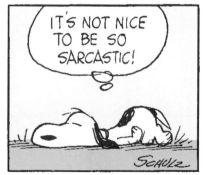

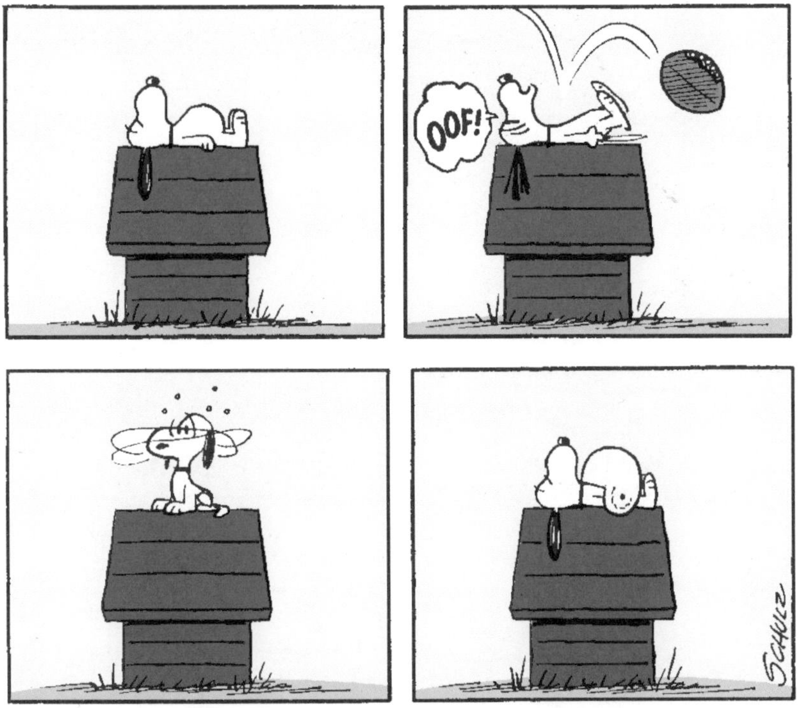
OOF!
SCHULZ

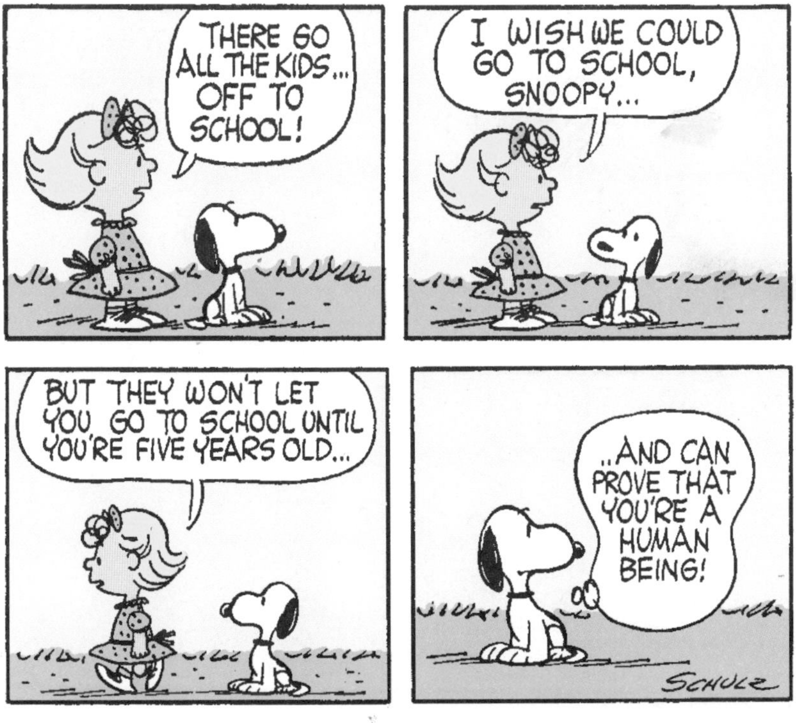
THERE GO ALL THE KIDS... OFF TO SCHOOL!
I WISH WE COULD GO TO SCHOOL, SNOOPY...
BUT THEY WON'T LET YOU GO TO SCHOOL UNTIL YOU'RE FIVE YEARS OLD...
..AND CAN PROVE THAT YOU'RE A HUMAN BEING!
SCHULZ

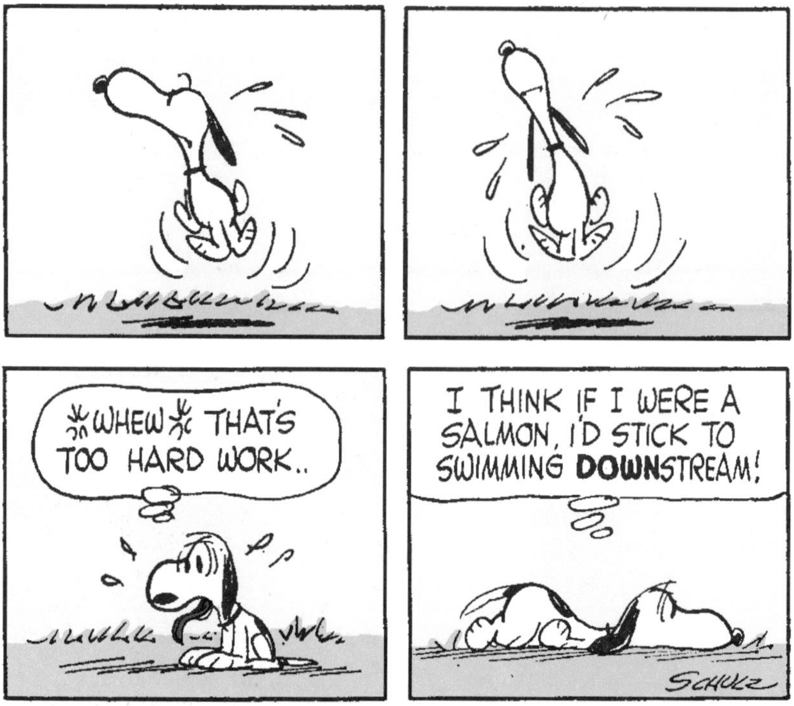
WHEW THAT'S TOO HARD WORK..
I THINK IF I WERE A SALMON, I'D STICK TO SWIMMING **DOWN**STREAM!
SCHULZ

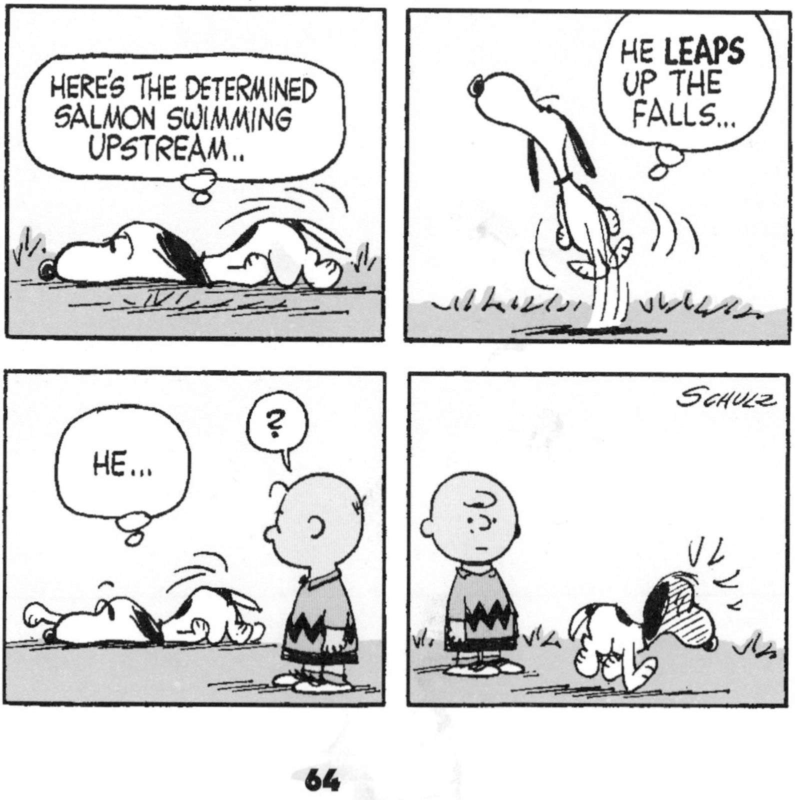
HERE'S THE DETERMINED SALMON SWIMMING UPSTREAM..
HE **LEAPS** UP THE FALLS...
HE...
?
SCHULZ

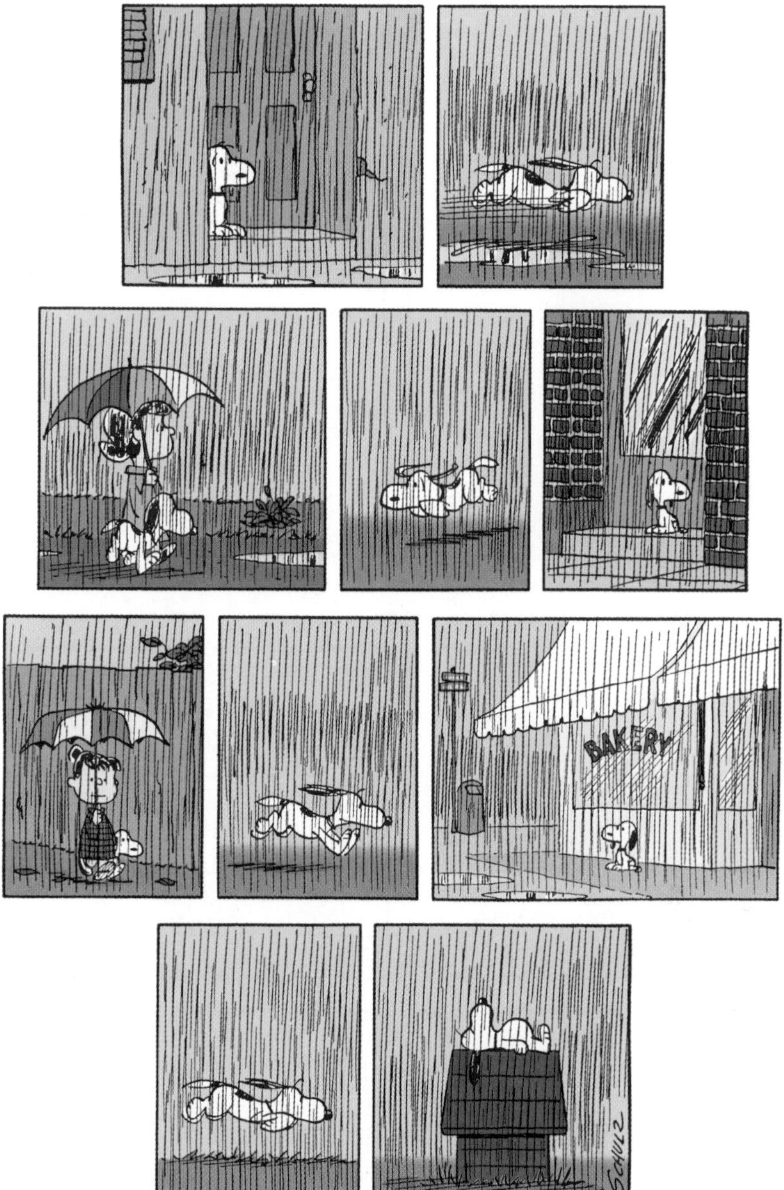
BAKERY
SCHULZ

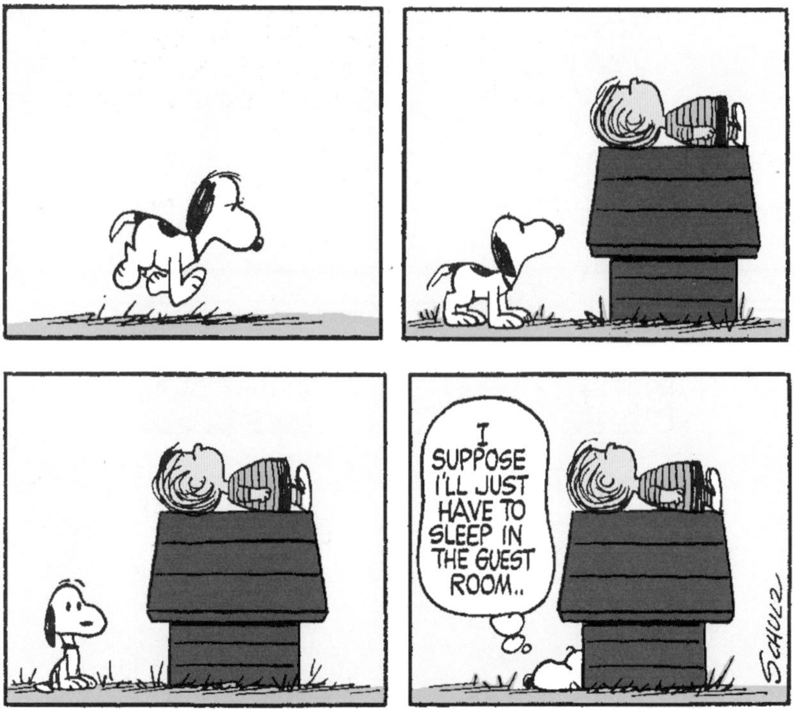
I SUPPOSE I'LL JUST HAVE TO SLEEP IN THE GUEST ROOM..

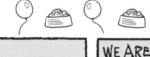

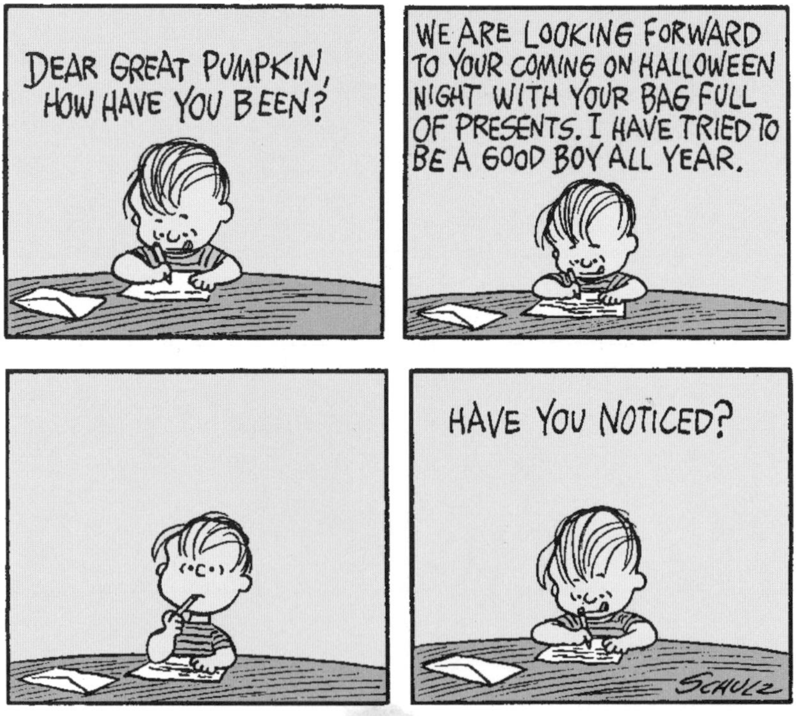
DEAR GREAT PUMPKIN, HOW HAVE YOU BEEN?
WE ARE LOOKING FORWARD TO YOUR COMING ON HALLOWEEN NIGHT WITH YOUR BAG FULL OF PRESENTS. I HAVE TRIED TO BE A GOOD BOY ALL YEAR.
HAVE YOU NOTICED?

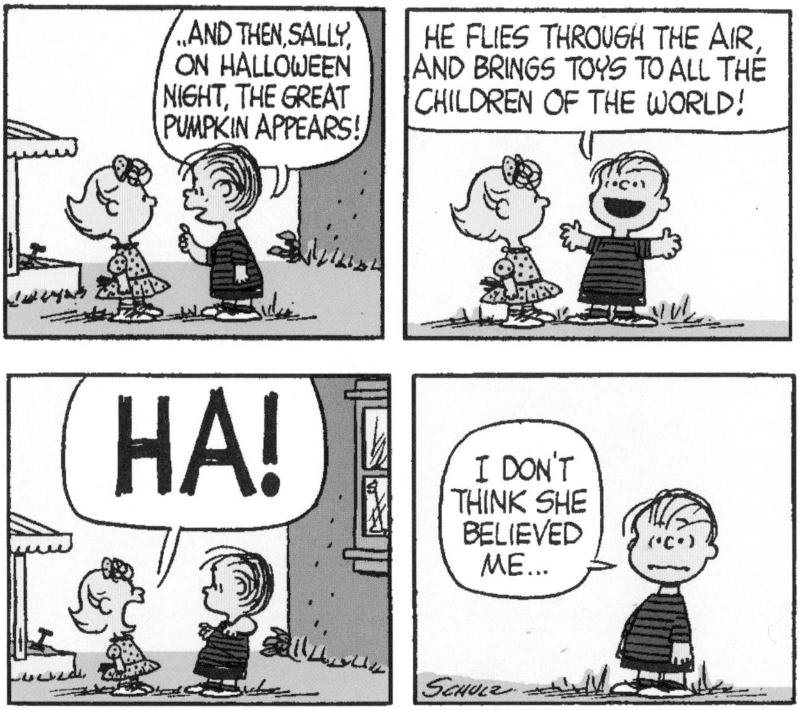
..AND THEN, SALLY, ON HALLOWEEN NIGHT, THE GREAT PUMPKIN APPEARS!
HE FLIES THROUGH THE AIR, AND BRINGS TOYS TO ALL THE CHILDREN OF THE WORLD!
HA!
I DON'T THINK SHE BELIEVED ME...
SCHULZ

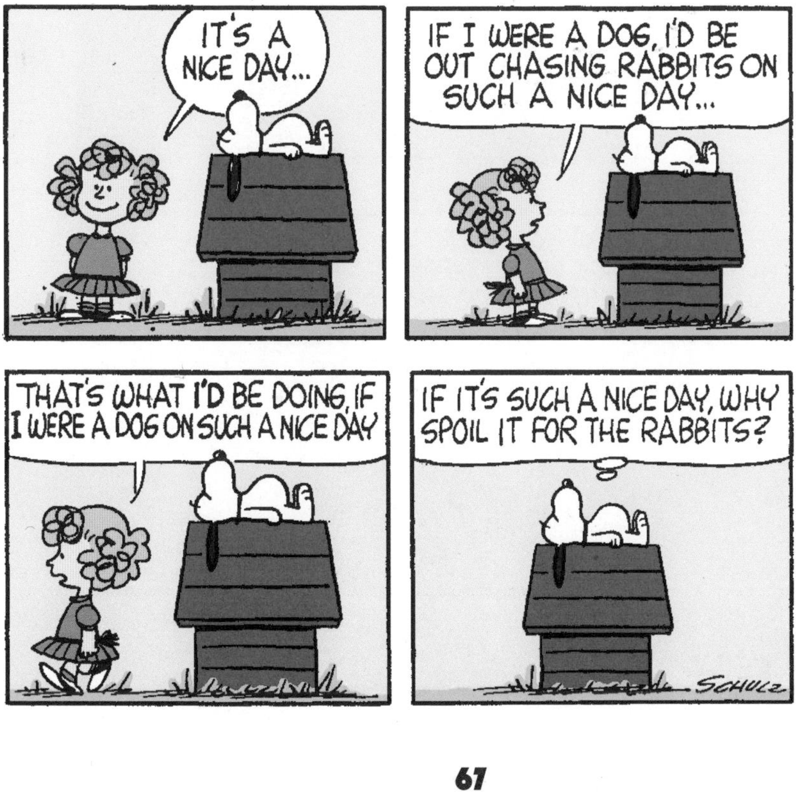
IT'S A NICE DAY...
IF I WERE A DOG, I'D BE OUT CHASING RABBITS ON SUCH A NICE DAY...
THAT'S WHAT I'D BE DOING, IF I WERE A DOG ON SUCH A NICE DAY
IF IT'S SUCH A NICE DAY, WHY SPOIL IT FOR THE RABBITS?
SCHULZ

ON HALLOWEEN NIGHT IN 1959 THE GREAT PUMPKIN APPEARED IN THE PUMPKIN PATCH OF BOOTS RUTMAN OF CONNECTICUT..
IF YOU DON'T BELIEVE ME, LOOK IN THE RECORD!
IN 1960 THE GREAT PUMPKIN APPEARED IN THE PUMPKIN PATCH OF R.W. DANIELS OF TEXAS...
AGAIN I SAY, IF YOU DON'T BELIEVE ME, LOOK IN THE RECORD!
NOW, SOMEWHERE IN THIS WORLD THE GREAT PUMPKIN HAS TO APPEAR **THIS** HALLOWEEN NIGHT!
WHY NOT **HERE**?!

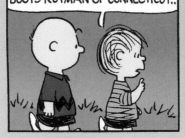

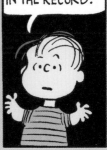

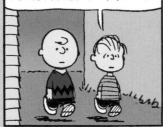

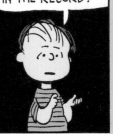

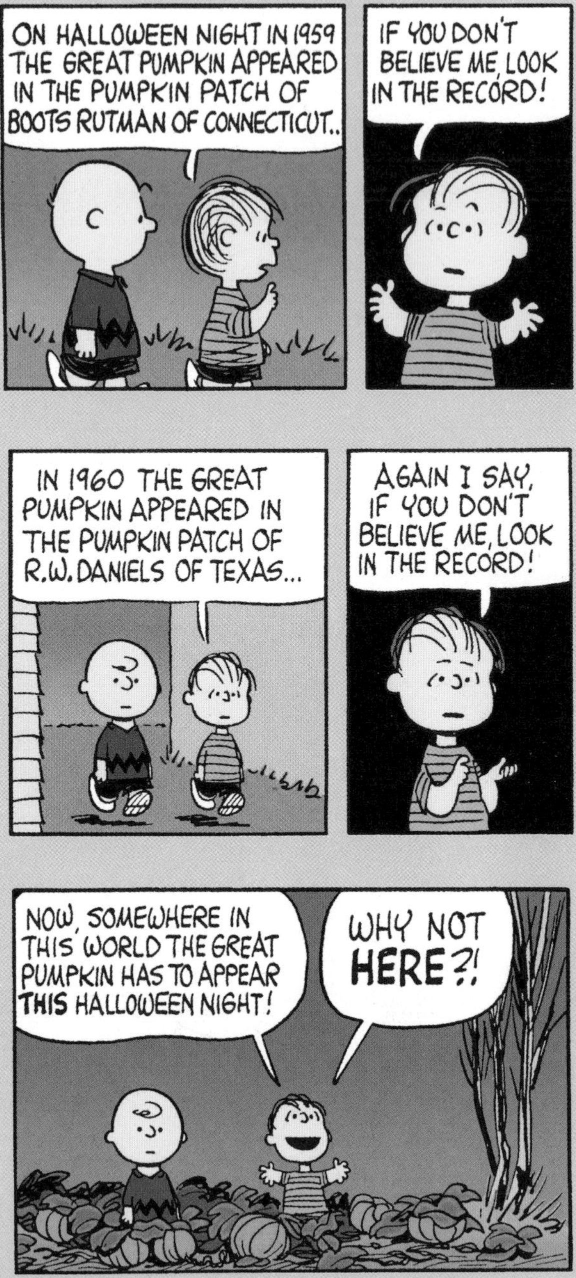

MAYBE THIS PUMPKIN PATCH ISN'T BIG ENOUGH?
SIZE HAS NOTHING TO DO WITH IT! IT'S SINCERITY THAT COUNTS! ASK BOOTS RUTMAN! ASK R.W. DANIELS!
MAYBE IT'S NEATNESS, TOO...MAYBE HE APPEARS IN THE PUMPKIN PATCH THAT HAS THE LEAST WEEDS
NO, NO, NO, NO, NO, NO, NO! IT'S SINCERITY THAT COUNTS! THE GREAT PUMPKIN WILL APPEAR IN WHICHEVER PUMPKIN PATCH HE DECIDES IS THE MOST SINCERE!!
I'D HATE TO HAVE TO MAKE SUCH A DECISION!
SCHULZ

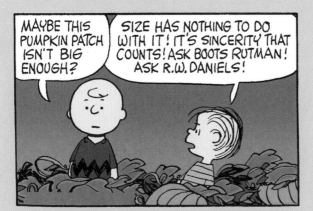

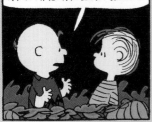

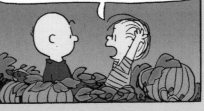

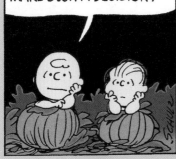

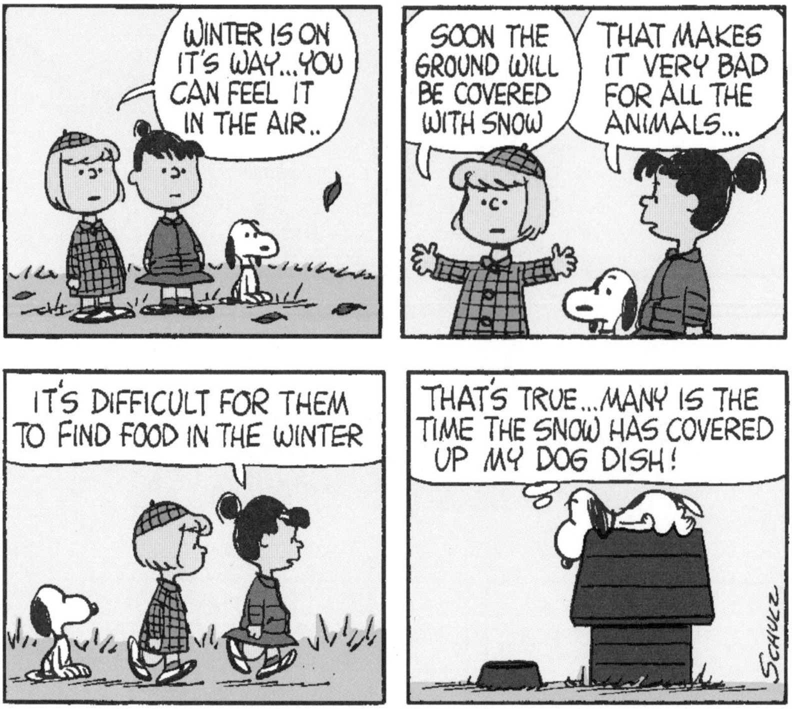
WINTER IS ON IT'S WAY...YOU CAN FEEL IT IN THE AIR..
SOON THE GROUND WILL BE COVERED WITH SNOW
THAT MAKES IT VERY BAD FOR ALL THE ANIMALS...
IT'S DIFFICULT FOR THEM TO FIND FOOD IN THE WINTER
THAT'S TRUE...MANY IS THE TIME THE SNOW HAS COVERED UP MY DOG DISH!
SCHULZ

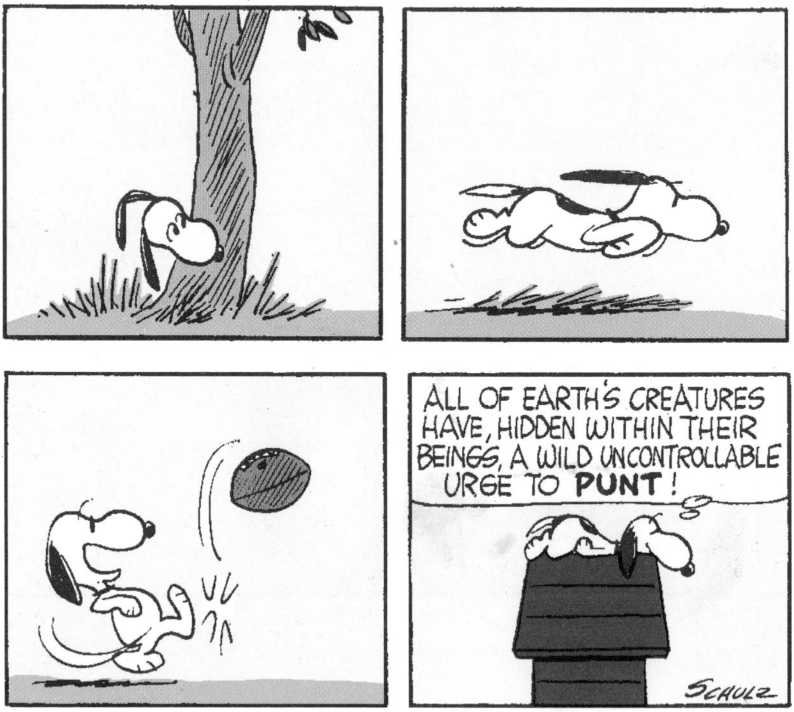
ALL OF EARTH'S CREATURES HAVE, HIDDEN WITHIN THEIR BEINGS, A WILD UNCONTROLLABLE URGE TO **PUNT**!
SCHULZ

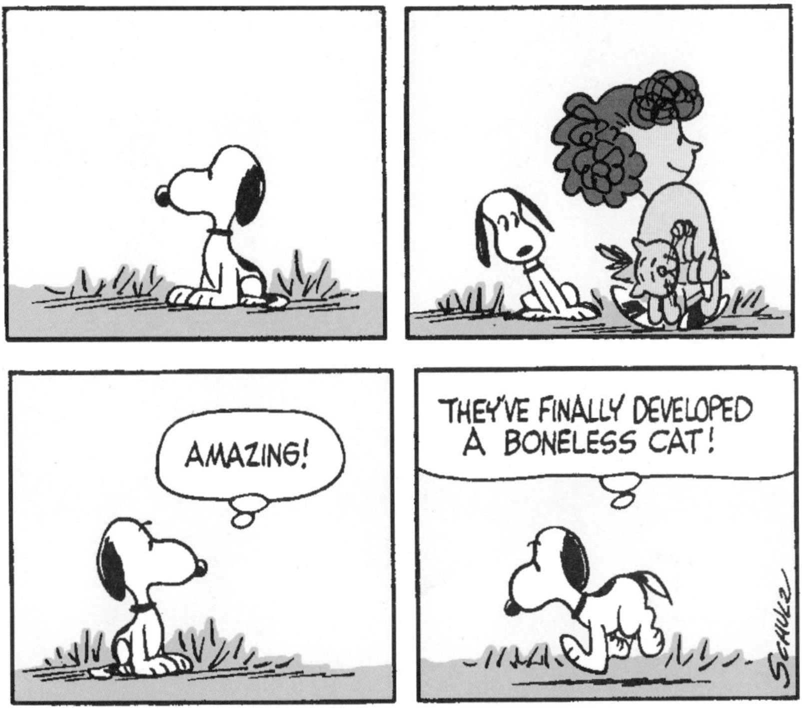
AMAZING!
THEY'VE FINALLY DEVELOPED A BONELESS CAT!
SCHULZ

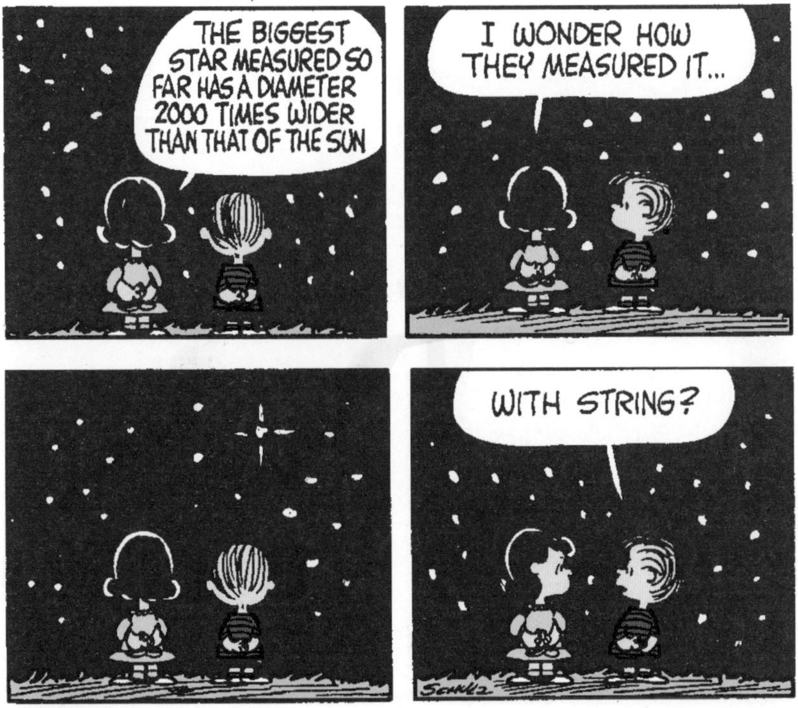
THE BIGGEST STAR MEASURED SO FAR HAS A DIAMETER 2000 TIMES WIDER THAN THAT OF THE SUN
I WONDER HOW THEY MEASURED IT...
WITH STRING?
SCHULZ

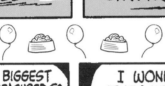

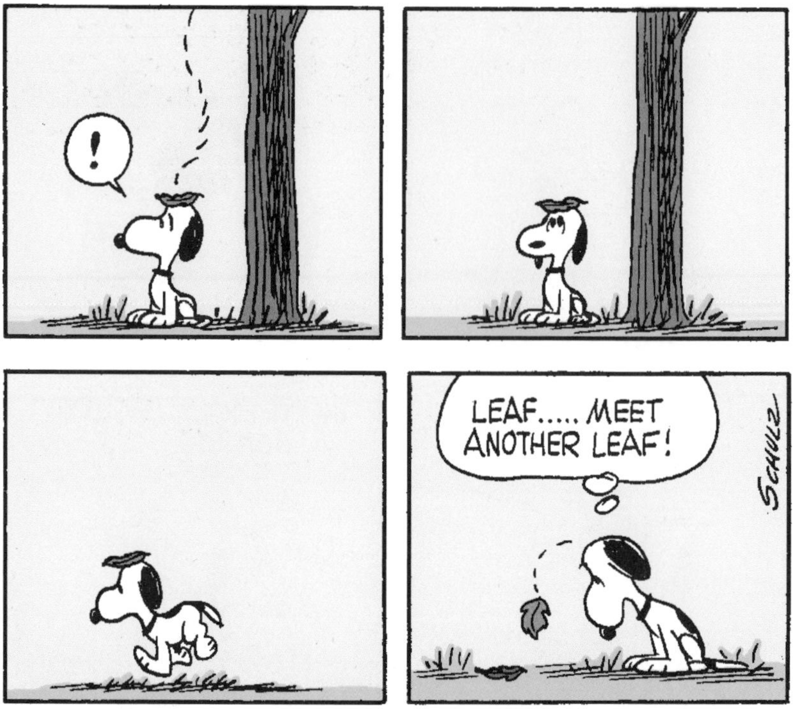
!
LEAF..... MEET ANOTHER LEAF!
SCHULZ

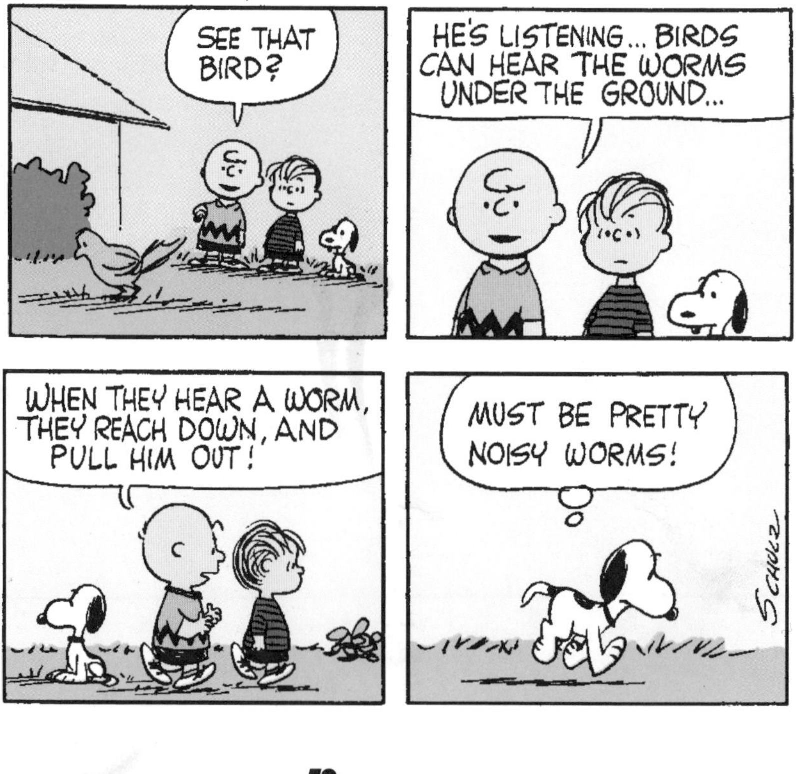
SEE THAT BIRD?
HE'S LISTENING... BIRDS CAN HEAR THE WORMS UNDER THE GROUND...
WHEN THEY HEAR A WORM, THEY REACH DOWN, AND PULL HIM OUT!
MUST BE PRETTY NOISY WORMS!
SCHULZ

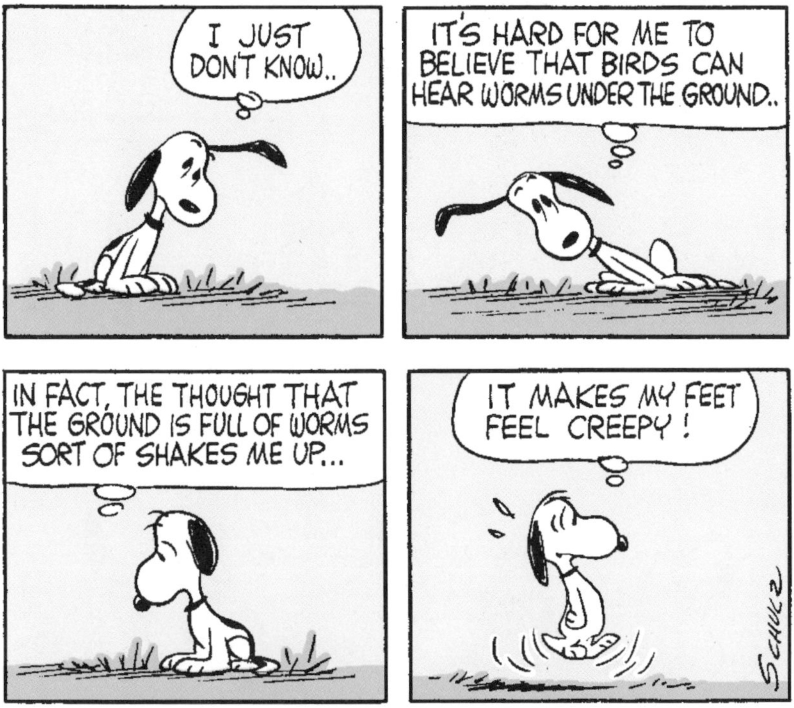
I JUST DON'T KNOW..
IT'S HARD FOR ME TO BELIEVE THAT BIRDS CAN HEAR WORMS UNDER THE GROUND..
IN FACT, THE THOUGHT THAT THE GROUND IS FULL OF WORMS SORT OF SHAKES ME UP...
IT MAKES MY FEET FEEL CREEPY!
SCHULZ

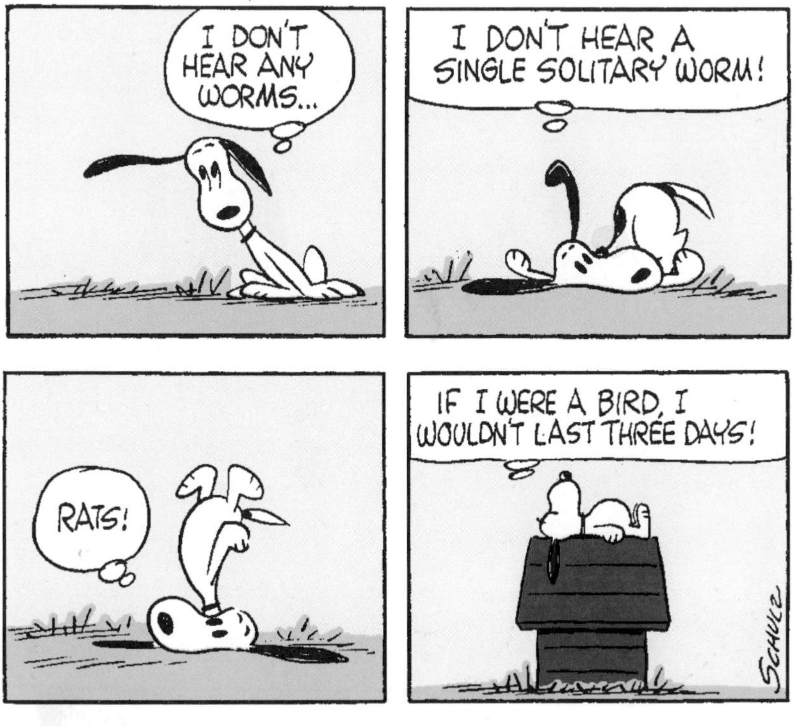
I DON'T HEAR ANY WORMS...
I DON'T HEAR A SINGLE SOLITARY WORM!
RATS!
IF I WERE A BIRD, I WOULDN'T LAST THREE DAYS!
SCHULZ

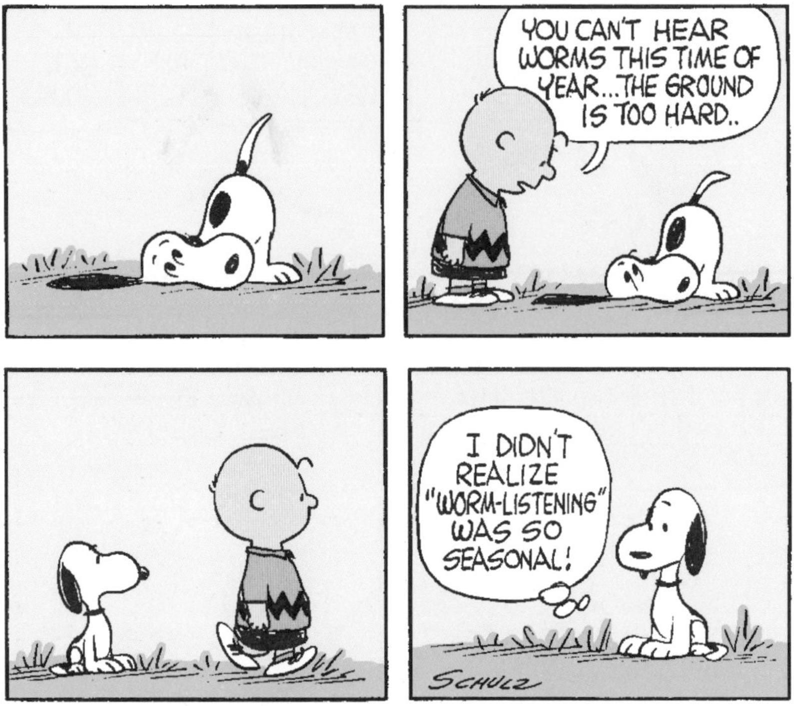
YOU CAN'T HEAR WORMS THIS TIME OF YEAR...THE GROUND IS TOO HARD..
I DIDN'T REALIZE "WORM-LISTENING" WAS SO SEASONAL!
SCHULZ

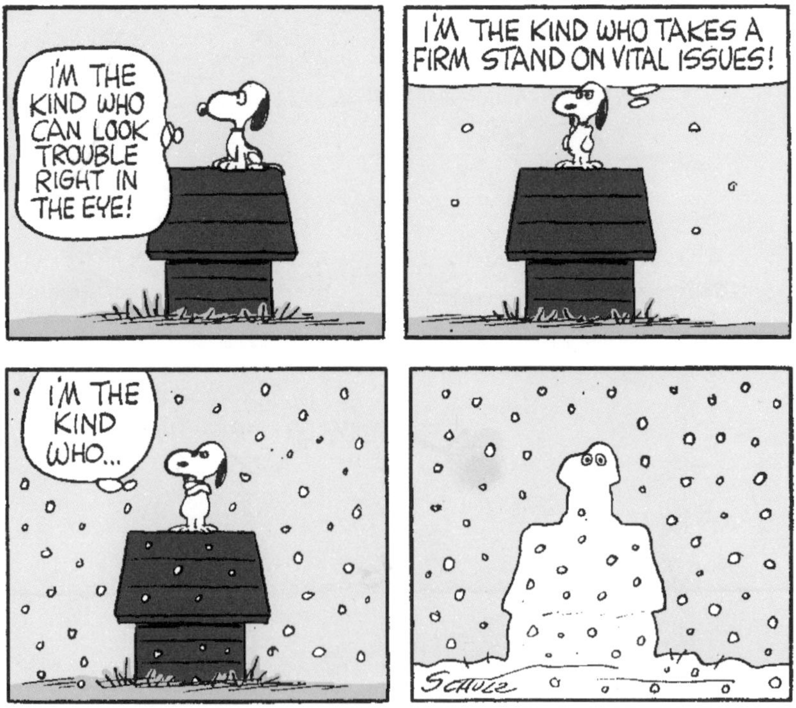
I'M THE KIND WHO CAN LOOK TROUBLE RIGHT IN THE EYE!
I'M THE KIND WHO TAKES A FIRM STAND ON VITAL ISSUES!
I'M THE KIND WHO...
SCHULZ

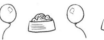

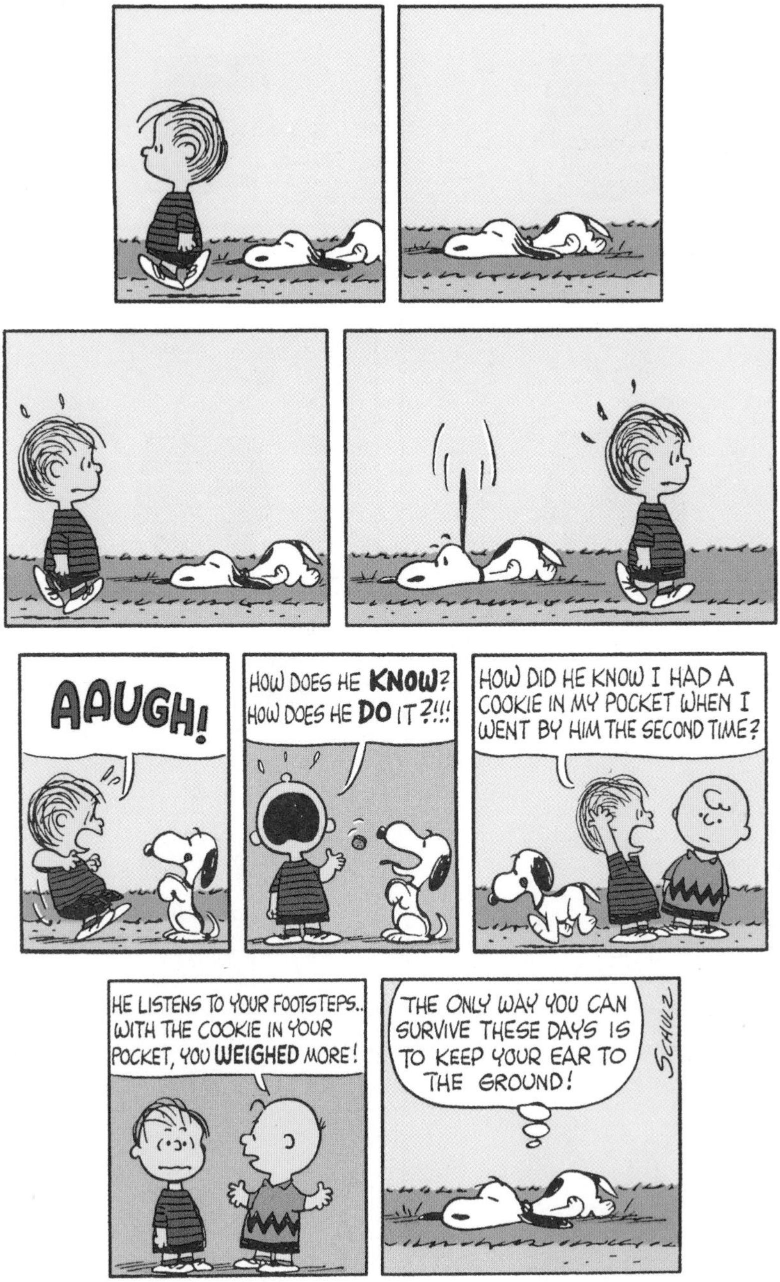
AAUGH!
HOW DOES HE KNOW? HOW DOES HE DO IT?!!!
HOW DID HE KNOW I HAD A COOKIE IN MY POCKET WHEN I WENT BY HIM THE SECOND TIME?
HE LISTENS TO YOUR FOOTSTEPS.. WITH THE COOKIE IN YOUR POCKET, YOU WEIGHED MORE!
THE ONLY WAY YOU CAN SURVIVE THESE DAYS IS TO KEEP YOUR EAR TO THE GROUND!
SCHULZ

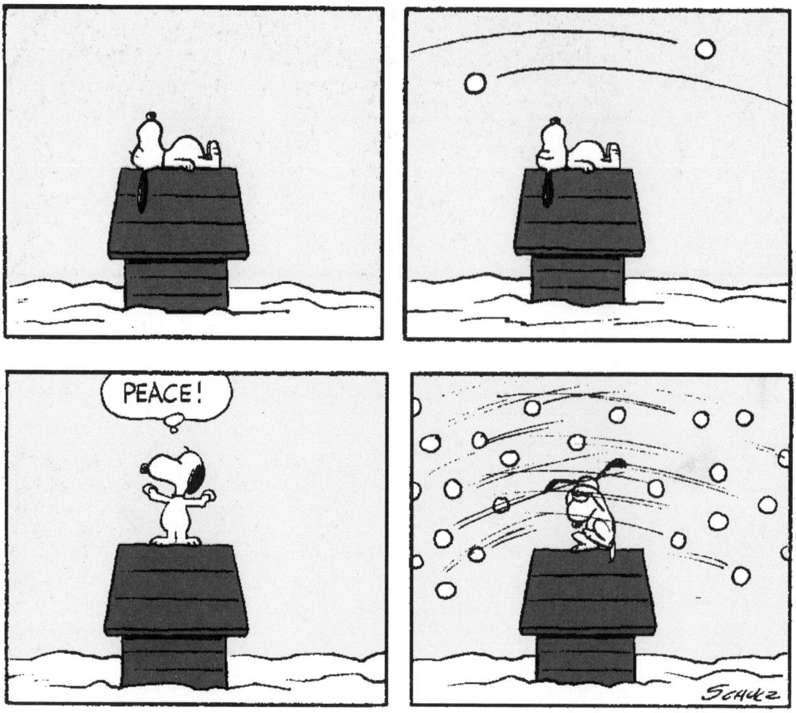
PEACE!
SCHULZ

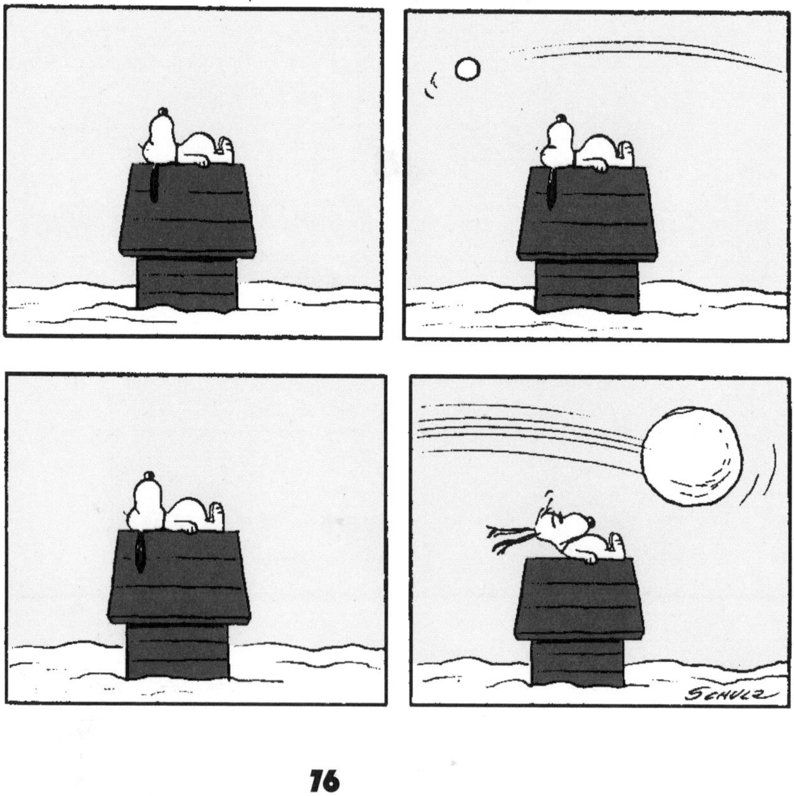
SCHULZ

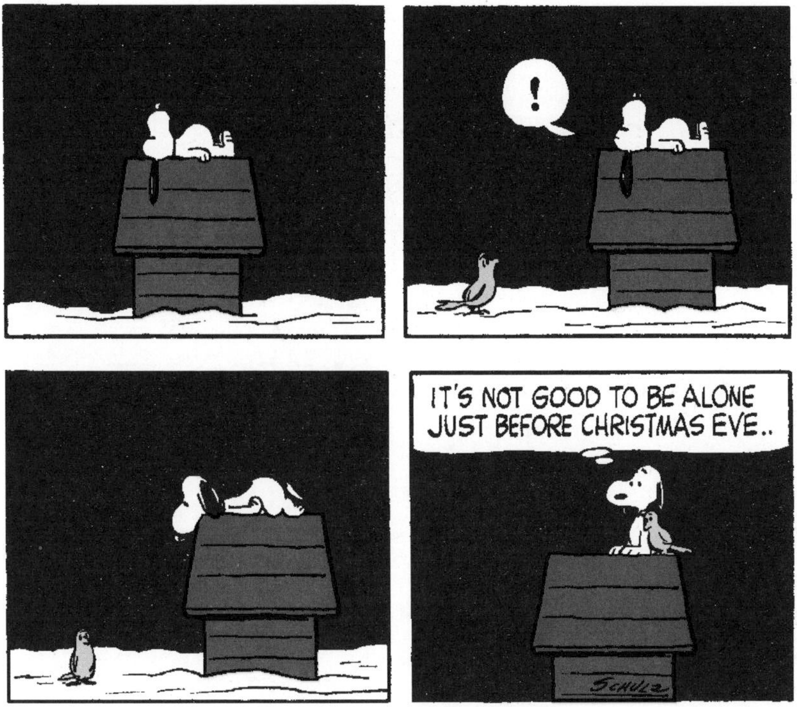
!
IT'S NOT GOOD TO BE ALONE JUST BEFORE CHRISTMAS EVE..
SCHULZ

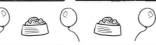

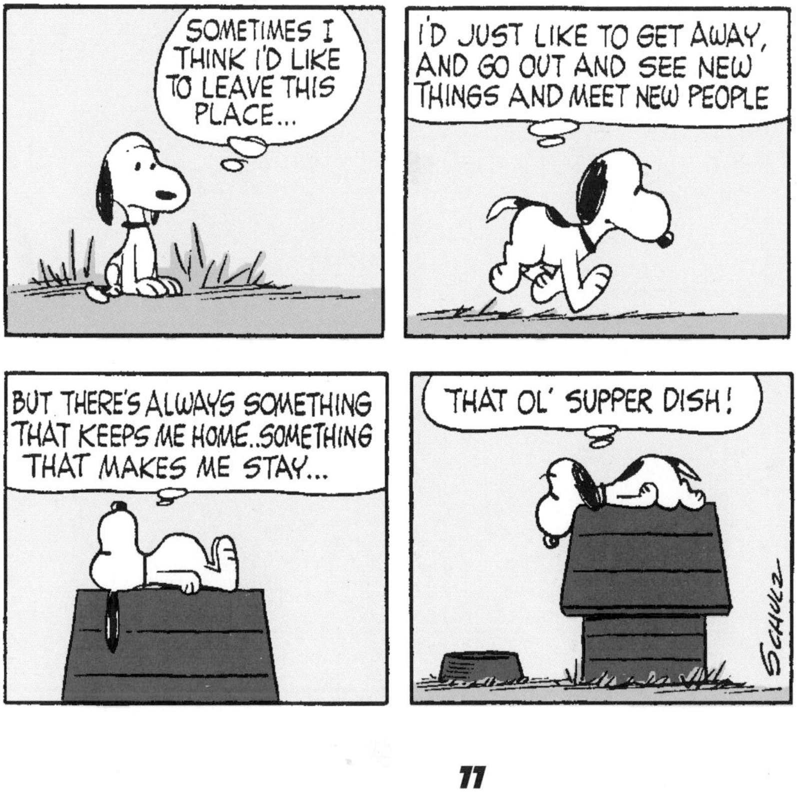
SOMETIMES I THINK I'D LIKE TO LEAVE THIS PLACE...
I'D JUST LIKE TO GET AWAY, AND GO OUT AND SEE NEW THINGS AND MEET NEW PEOPLE
BUT THERE'S ALWAYS SOMETHING THAT KEEPS ME HOME..SOMETHING THAT MAKES ME STAY...
THAT OL' SUPPER DISH!
SCHULZ

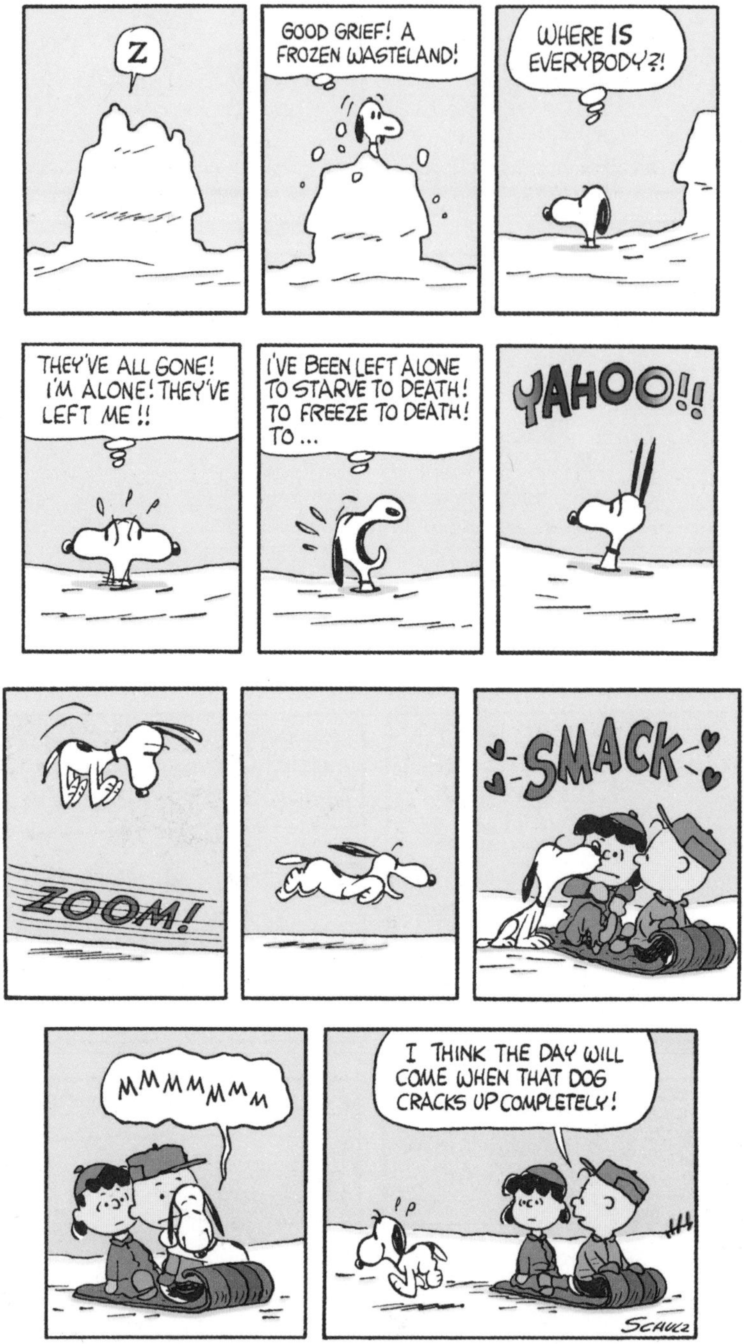
Z
GOOD GRIEF! A FROZEN WASTELAND!
WHERE IS EVERYBODY?!
THEY'VE ALL GONE! I'M ALONE! THEY'VE LEFT ME!!
I'VE BEEN LEFT ALONE TO STARVE TO DEATH! TO FREEZE TO DEATH! TO...
YAHOO!!
ZOOM!
SMACK
MMMMMMMM
I THINK THE DAY WILL COME WHEN THAT DOG CRACKS UP COMPLETELY!
SCHULZ

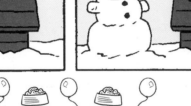

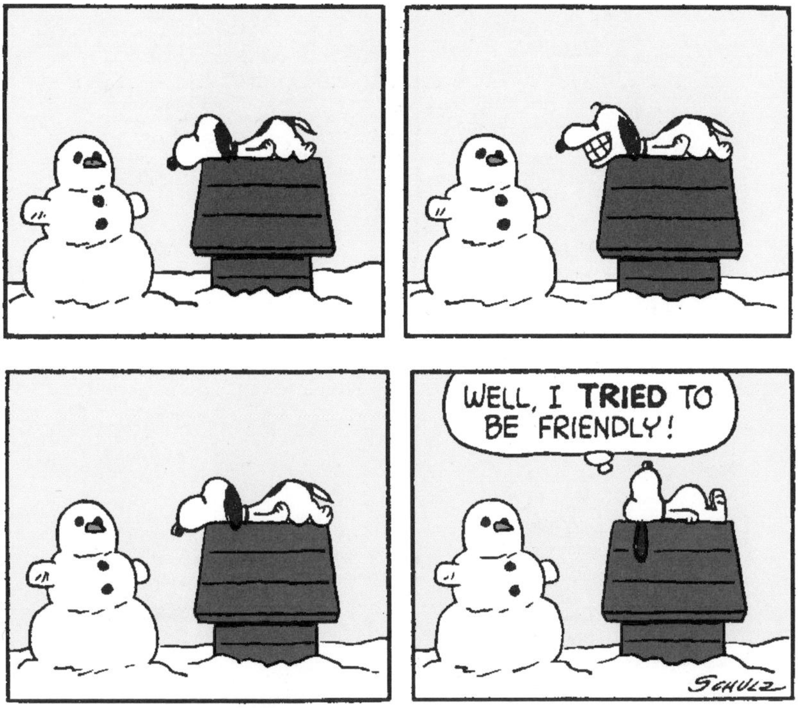
WELL, I **TRIED** TO BE FRIENDLY!
SCHULZ

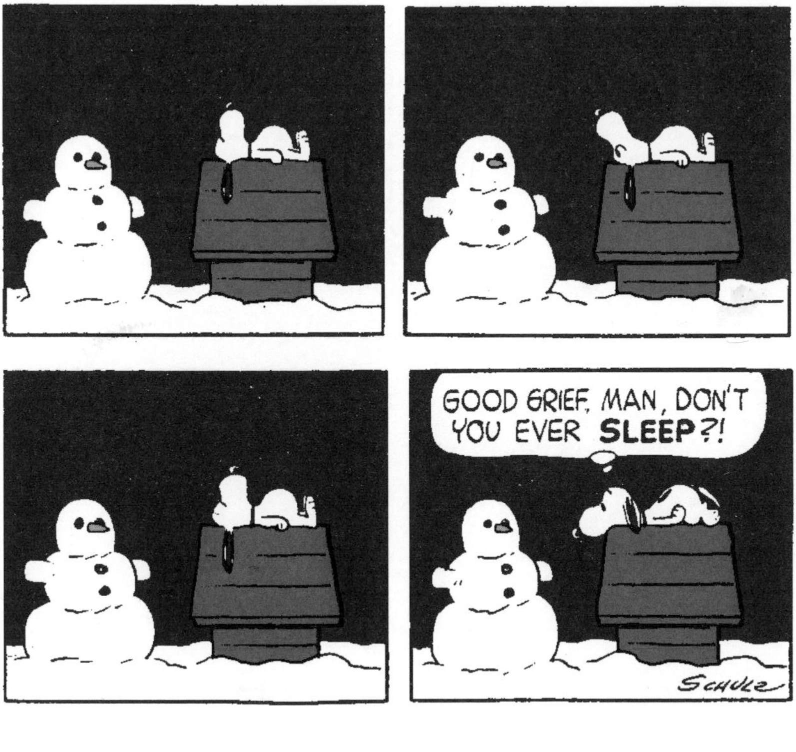
GOOD GRIEF, MAN, DON'T YOU EVER **SLEEP**?!
SCHULZ

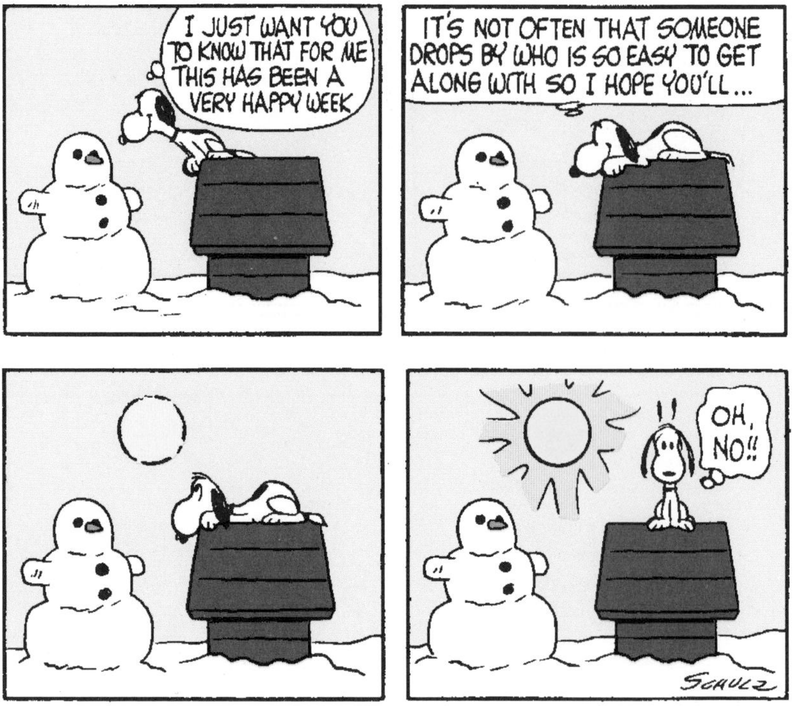
I JUST WANT YOU TO KNOW THAT FOR ME THIS HAS BEEN A VERY HAPPY WEEK
IT'S NOT OFTEN THAT SOMEONE DROPS BY WHO IS SO EASY TO GET ALONG WITH SO I HOPE YOU'LL...
OH, NO!!
SCHULZ

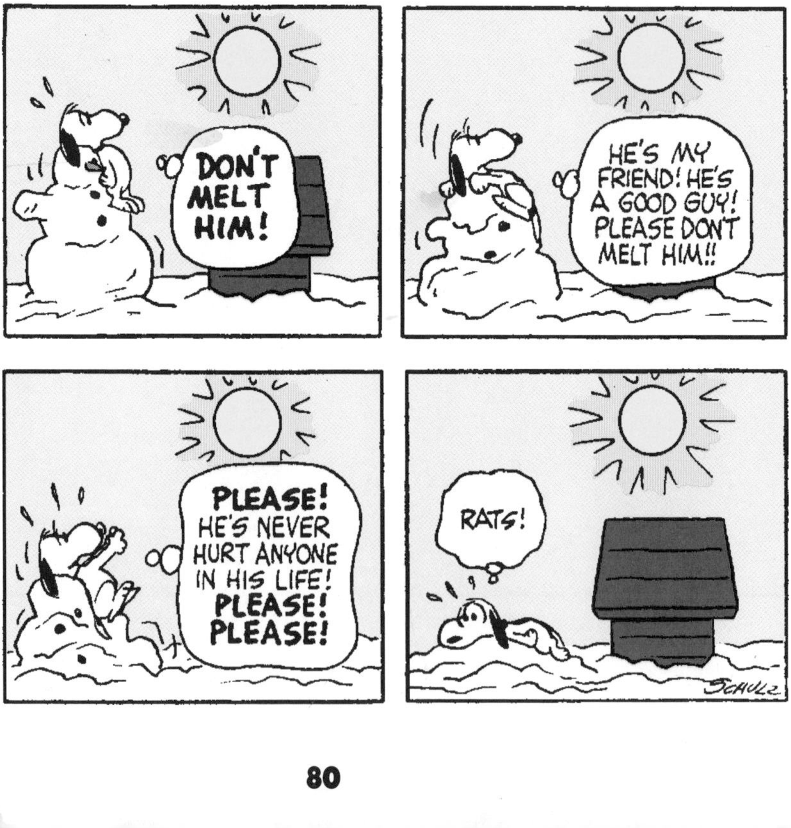
DON'T MELT HIM!
HE'S MY FRIEND! HE'S A GOOD GUY! PLEASE DON'T MELT HIM!!
PLEASE! HE'S NEVER HURT ANYONE IN HIS LIFE! PLEASE! PLEASE!
RATS!
SCHULZ

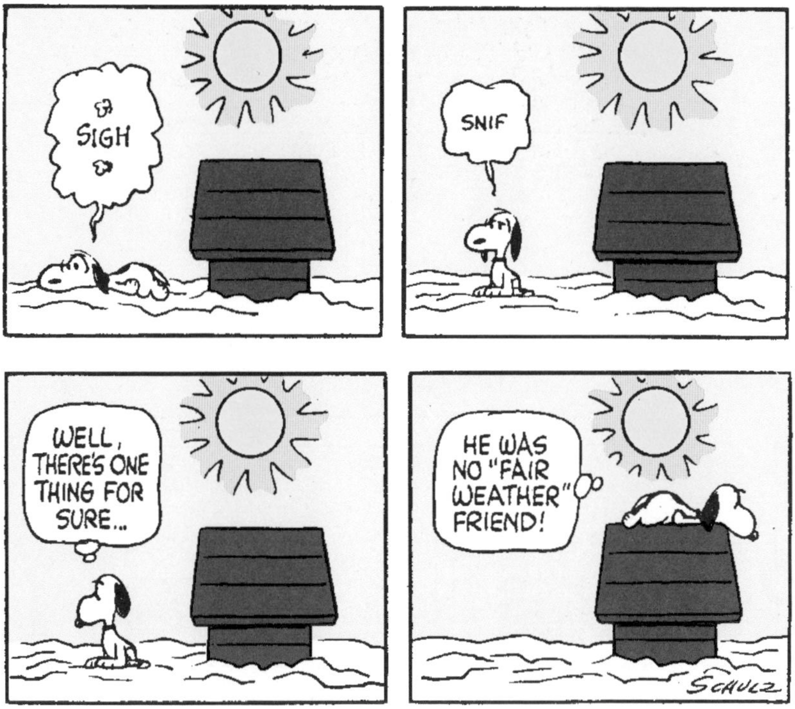
SIGH
SNIF
WELL, THERE'S ONE THING FOR SURE...
HE WAS NO "FAIR WEATHER" FRIEND!

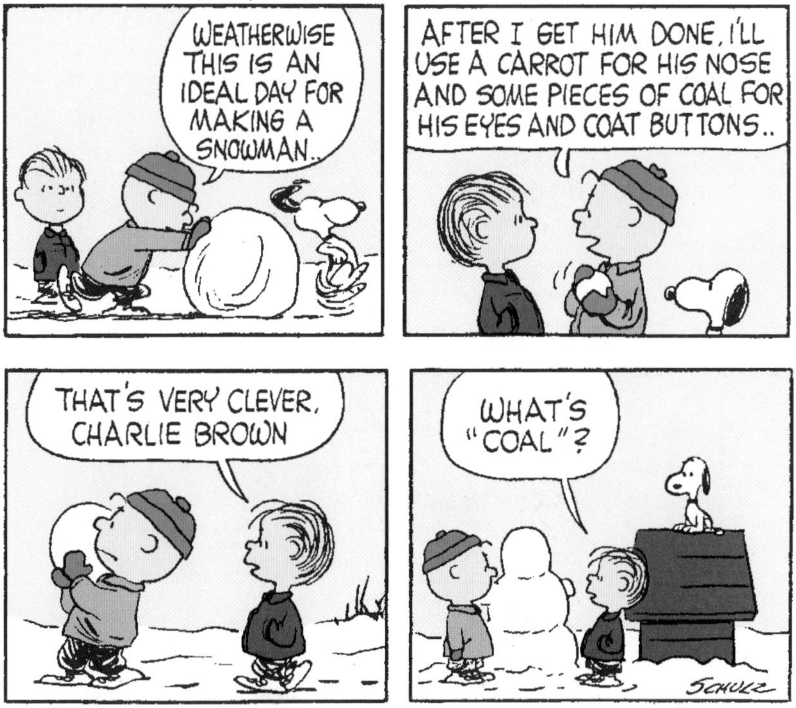
WEATHERWISE THIS IS AN IDEAL DAY FOR MAKING A SNOWMAN..
AFTER I GET HIM DONE, I'LL USE A CARROT FOR HIS NOSE AND SOME PIECES OF COAL FOR HIS EYES AND COAT BUTTONS..
THAT'S VERY CLEVER, CHARLIE BROWN
WHAT'S "COAL"?

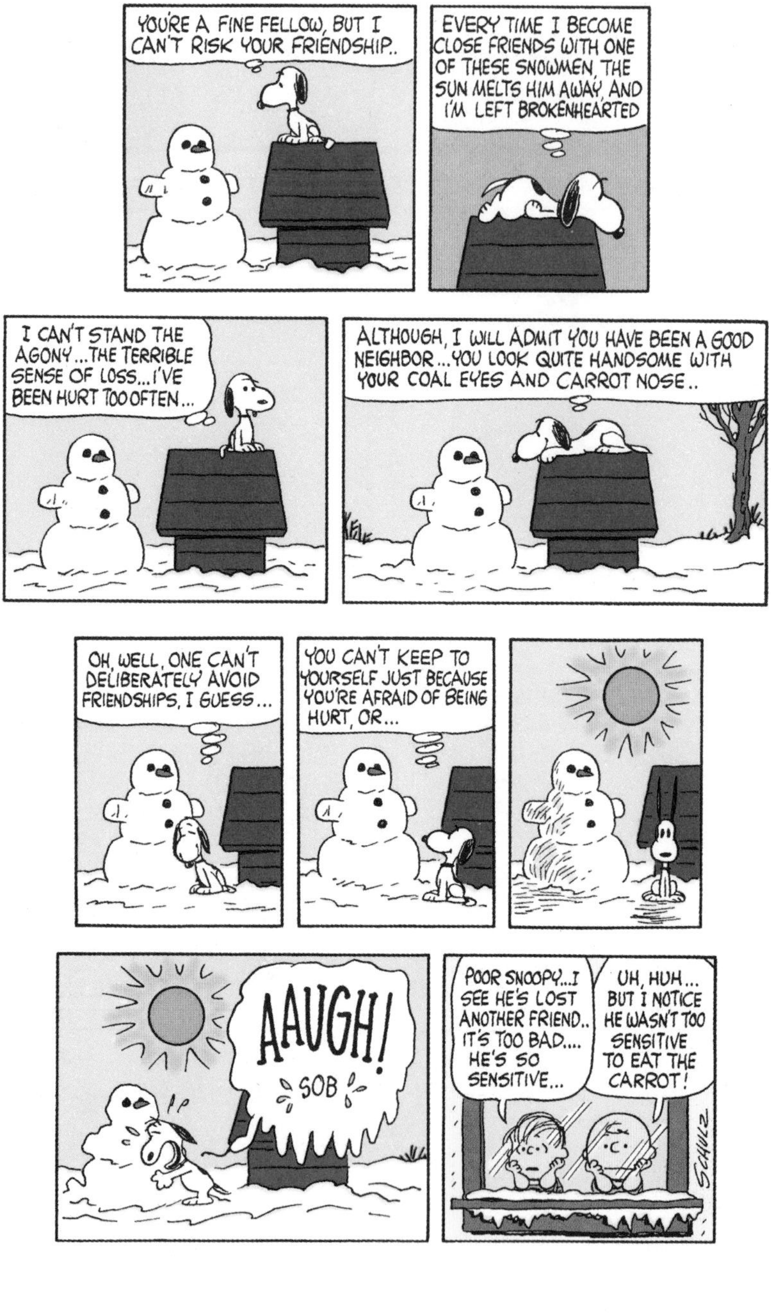

YOU'RE A FINE FELLOW, BUT I CAN'T RISK YOUR FRIENDSHIP..
EVERY TIME I BECOME CLOSE FRIENDS WITH ONE OF THESE SNOWMEN, THE SUN MELTS HIM AWAY, AND I'M LEFT BROKENHEARTED
I CAN'T STAND THE AGONY...THE TERRIBLE SENSE OF LOSS...I'VE BEEN HURT TOO OFTEN...
ALTHOUGH, I WILL ADMIT YOU HAVE BEEN A GOOD NEIGHBOR...YOU LOOK QUITE HANDSOME WITH YOUR COAL EYES AND CARROT NOSE..
OH, WELL, ONE CAN'T DELIBERATELY AVOID FRIENDSHIPS, I GUESS...
YOU CAN'T KEEP TO YOURSELF JUST BECAUSE YOU'RE AFRAID OF BEING HURT, OR...
AAUGH!
SOB
POOR SNOOPY...I SEE HE'S LOST ANOTHER FRIEND.. IT'S TOO BAD.... HE'S SO SENSITIVE...
UH, HUH... BUT I NOTICE HE WASN'T TOO SENSITIVE TO EAT THE CARROT!
SCHULZ

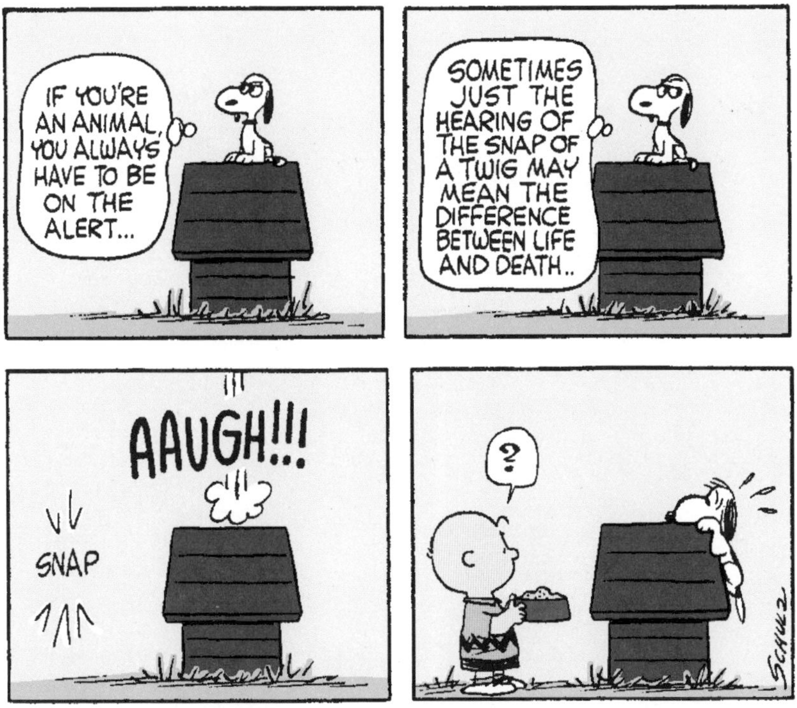
IF YOU'RE AN ANIMAL, YOU ALWAYS HAVE TO BE ON THE ALERT...
SOMETIMES JUST THE HEARING OF THE SNAP OF A TWIG MAY MEAN THE DIFFERENCE BETWEEN LIFE AND DEATH..
AAUGH!!!
SNAP
?
SCHULZ

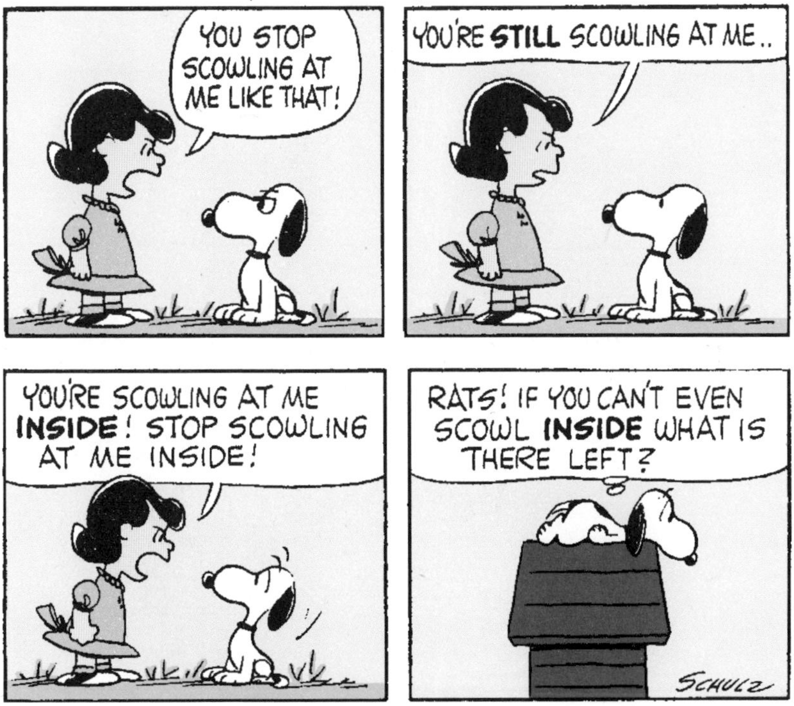
YOU STOP SCOWLING AT ME LIKE THAT!
YOU'RE **STILL** SCOWLING AT ME..
YOU'RE SCOWLING AT ME **INSIDE**! STOP SCOWLING AT ME INSIDE!
RATS! IF YOU CAN'T EVEN SCOWL **INSIDE** WHAT IS THERE LEFT?
SCHULZ

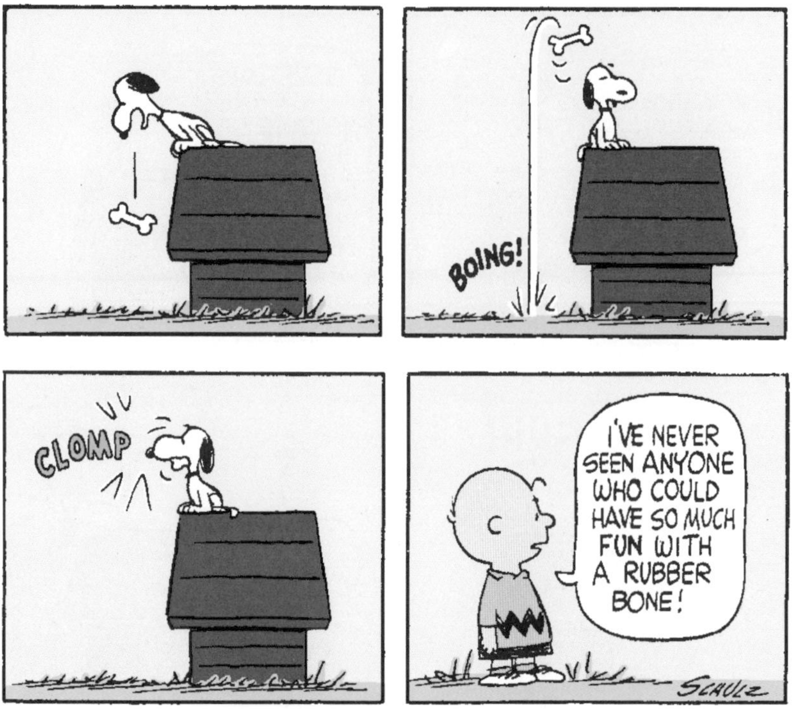
BOING!
CLOMP
I'VE NEVER SEEN ANYONE WHO COULD HAVE SO MUCH FUN WITH A RUBBER BONE!
SCHULZ

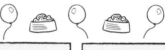

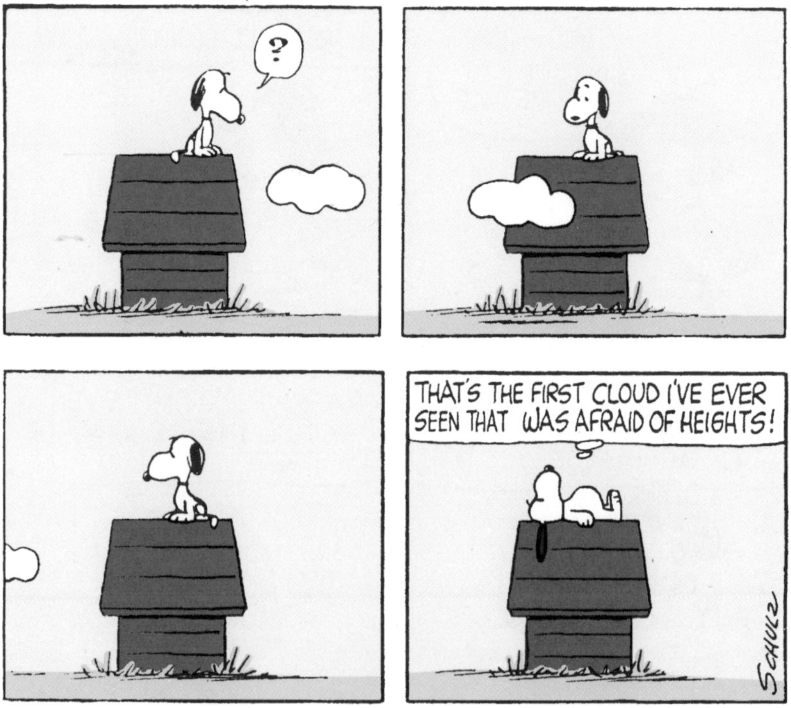
?
THAT'S THE FIRST CLOUD I'VE EVER SEEN THAT WAS AFRAID OF HEIGHTS!
SCHULZ

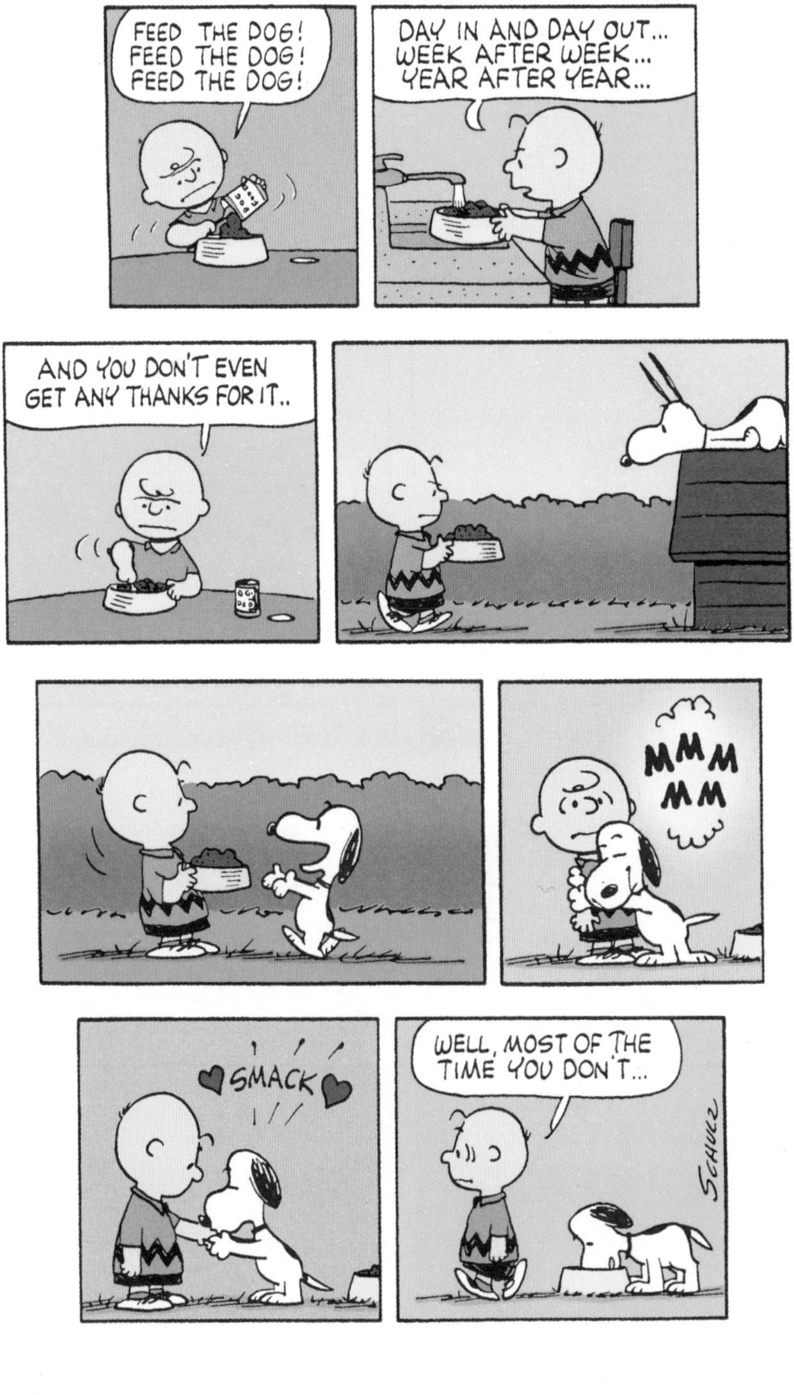
FEED THE DOG! FEED THE DOG! FEED THE DOG!
DAY IN AND DAY OUT... WEEK AFTER WEEK... YEAR AFTER YEAR...
AND YOU DON'T EVEN GET ANY THANKS FOR IT..
MMM MM
SMACK
WELL, MOST OF THE TIME YOU DON'T...
SCHULZ

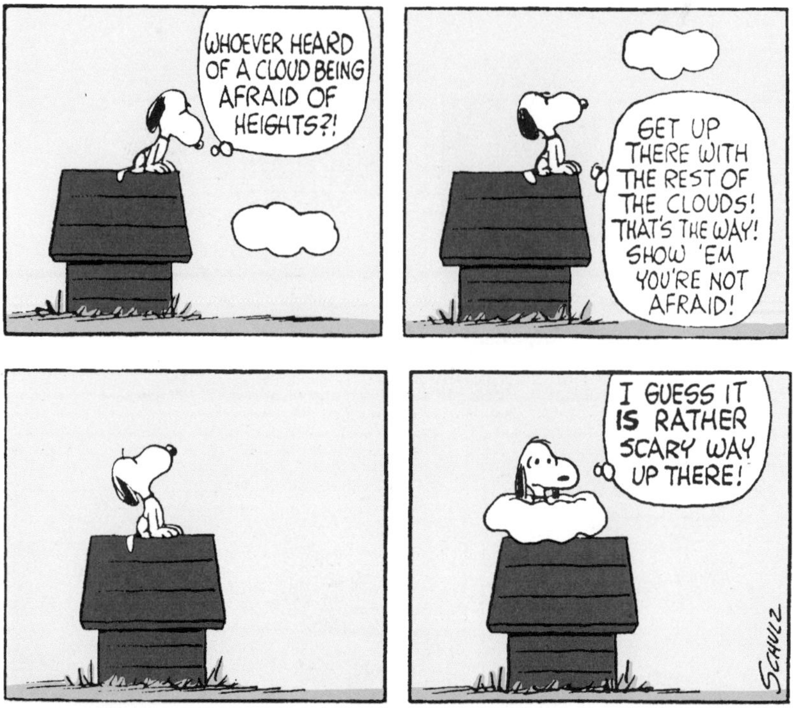
WHOEVER HEARD OF A CLOUD BEING AFRAID OF HEIGHTS?!
GET UP THERE WITH THE REST OF THE CLOUDS! THAT'S THE WAY! SHOW 'EM YOU'RE NOT AFRAID!
I GUESS IT **IS** RATHER SCARY WAY UP THERE!

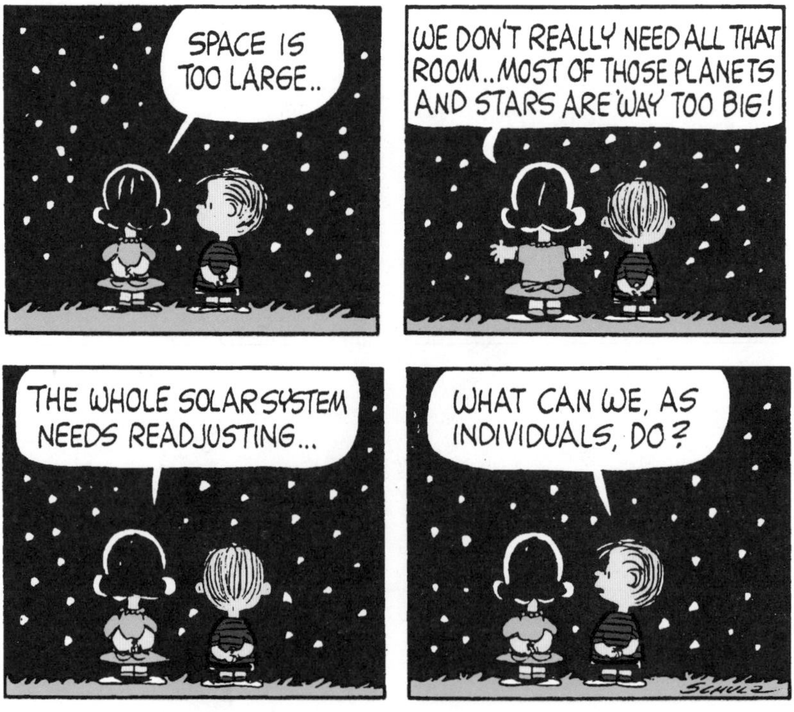
SPACE IS TOO LARGE..
WE DON'T REALLY NEED ALL THAT ROOM..MOST OF THOSE PLANETS AND STARS ARE 'WAY TOO BIG!
THE WHOLE SOLAR SYSTEM NEEDS READJUSTING...
WHAT CAN WE, AS INDIVIDUALS, DO?

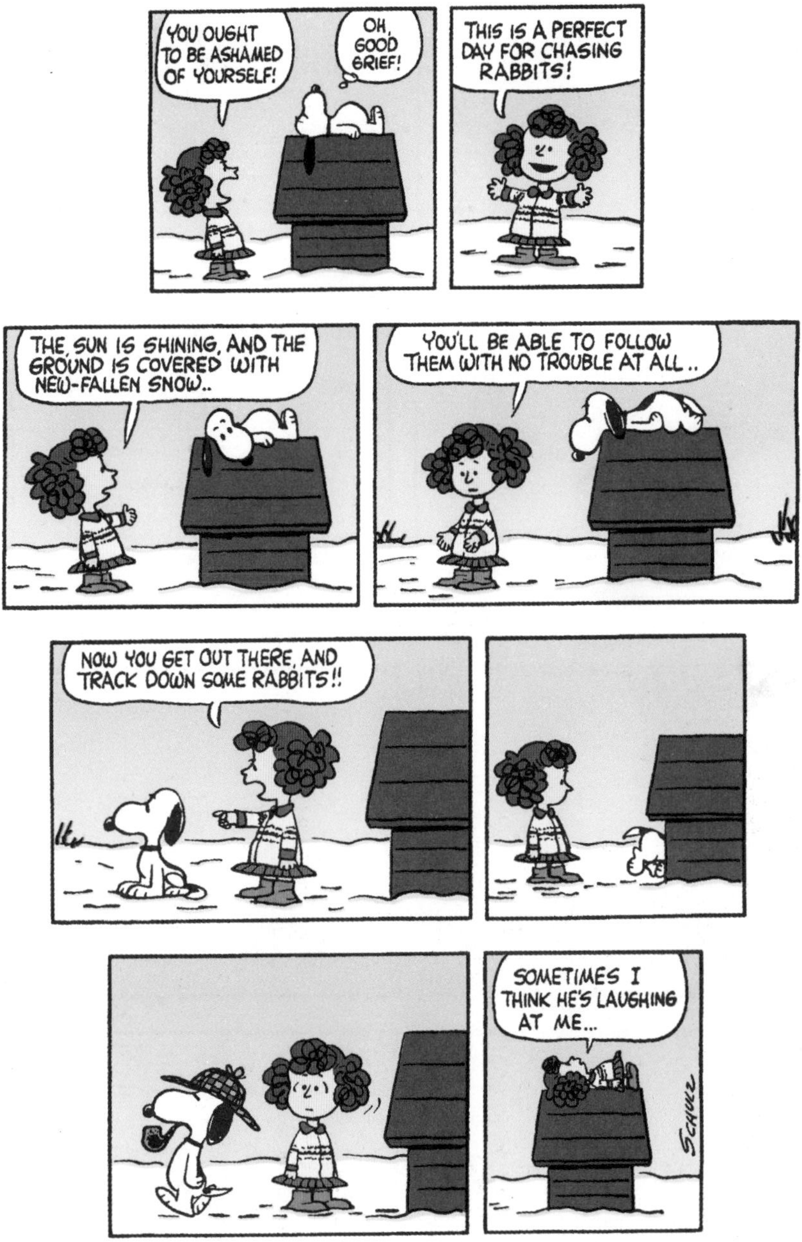
YOU OUGHT TO BE ASHAMED OF YOURSELF!
OH, GOOD GRIEF!
THIS IS A PERFECT DAY FOR CHASING RABBITS!
THE SUN IS SHINING, AND THE GROUND IS COVERED WITH NEW-FALLEN SNOW..
YOU'LL BE ABLE TO FOLLOW THEM WITH NO TROUBLE AT ALL..
NOW YOU GET OUT THERE, AND TRACK DOWN SOME RABBITS!!
SOMETIMES I THINK HE'S LAUGHING AT ME...
SCHULZ

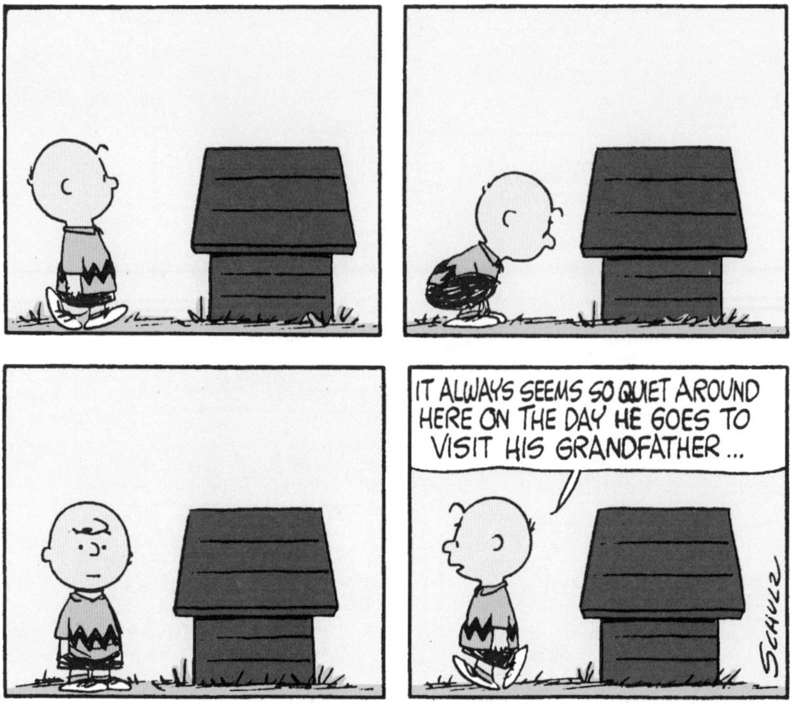
IT ALWAYS SEEMS SO QUIET AROUND HERE ON THE DAY HE GOES TO VISIT HIS GRANDFATHER ...
SCHULZ

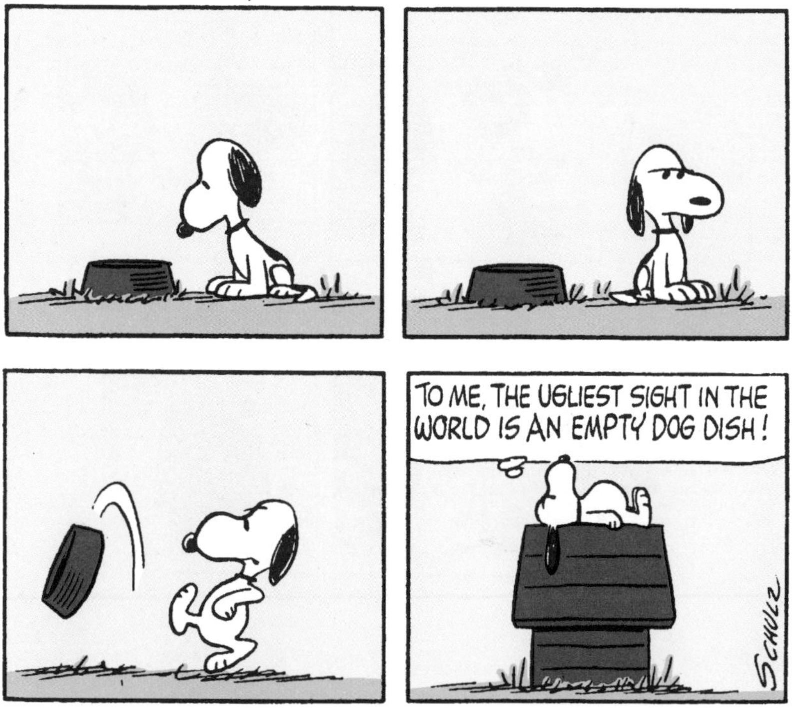
TO ME, THE UGLIEST SIGHT IN THE WORLD IS AN EMPTY DOG DISH!
SCHULZ

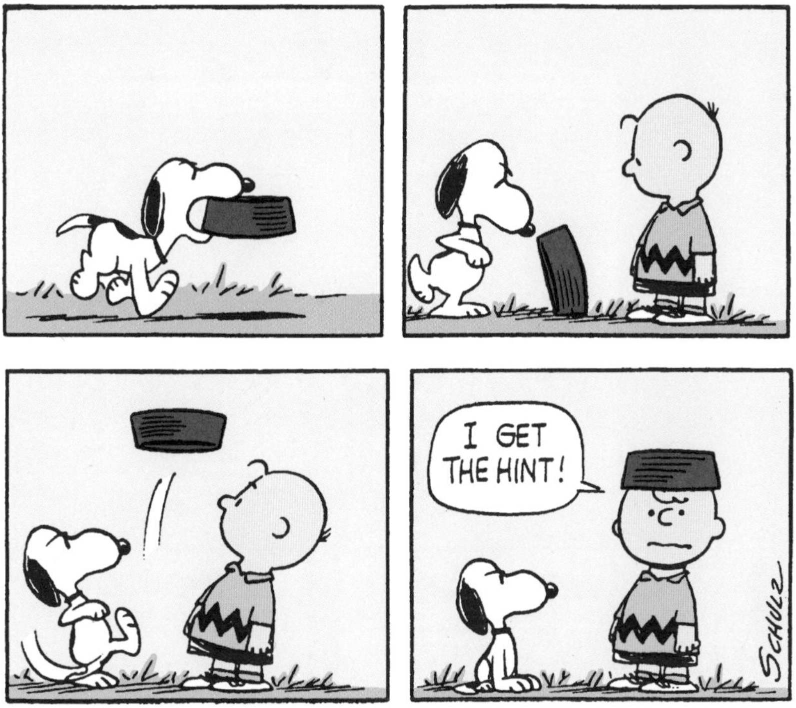
I GET THE HINT!
SCHULZ

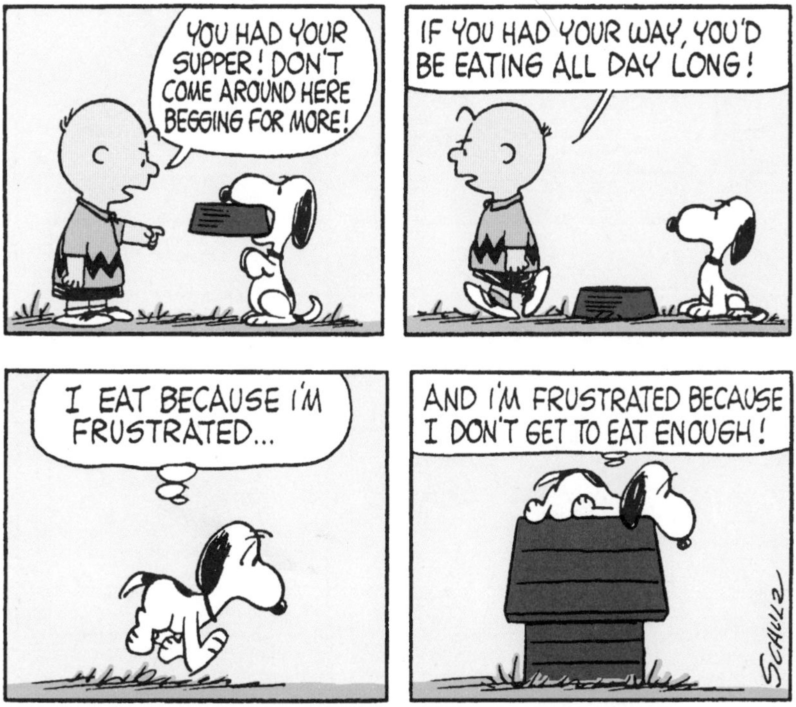
YOU HAD YOUR SUPPER! DON'T COME AROUND HERE BEGGING FOR MORE!
IF YOU HAD YOUR WAY, YOU'D BE EATING ALL DAY LONG!
I EAT BECAUSE I'M FRUSTRATED...
AND I'M FRUSTRATED BECAUSE I DON'T GET TO EAT ENOUGH!
SCHULZ

IT'S SNOWING! IT'S SNOWING!
IT'S BEAUTIFUL! IT'S BEAUTIFUL!
EVERYBODY DANCE!
IT'S SNOWING! IT'S SNOWING!
WHAT A SIGHT!
OH, IT'S BEAUTIFUL! IT'S BEAUTIFUL!

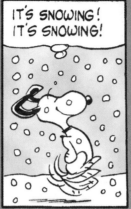

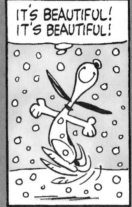

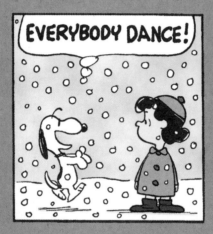

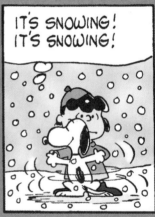

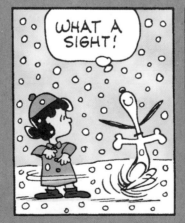

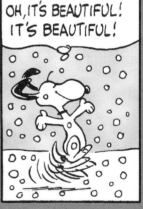

EVERYBODY DANCE
IT'S SNOWING! IT'S BEAUTIFUL! IT'S...
?
RATS!
I OVERDID IT!
SCHULZ

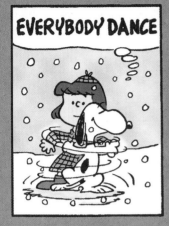

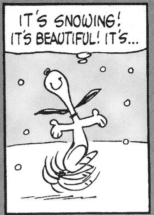

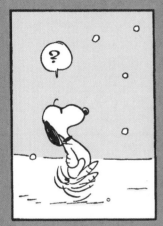

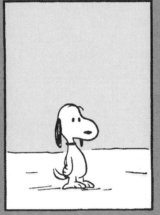

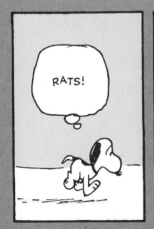

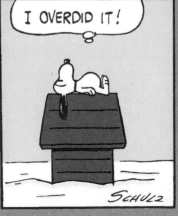

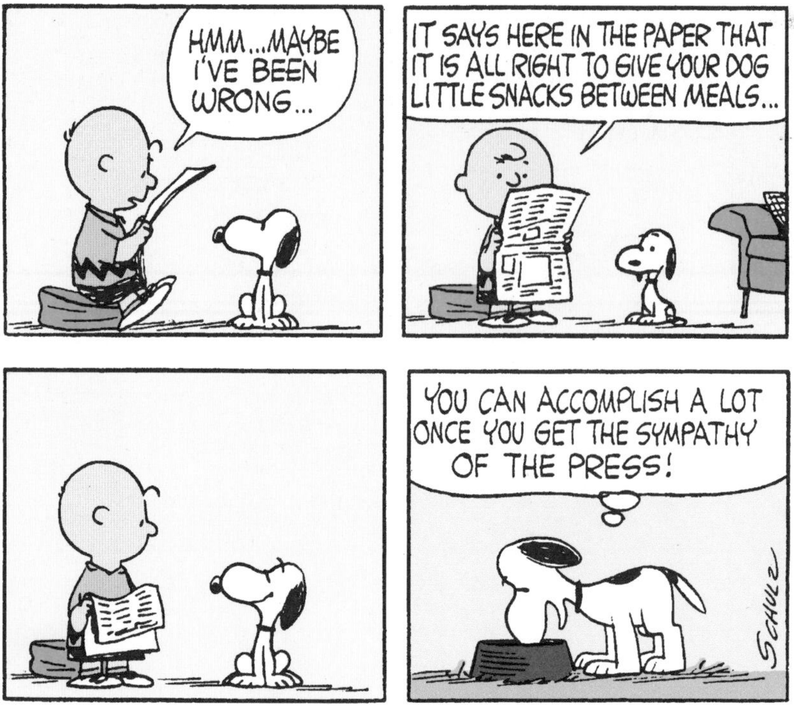
HMM...MAYBE I'VE BEEN WRONG...
IT SAYS HERE IN THE PAPER THAT IT IS ALL RIGHT TO GIVE YOUR DOG LITTLE SNACKS BETWEEN MEALS...
YOU CAN ACCOMPLISH A LOT ONCE YOU GET THE SYMPATHY OF THE PRESS!
SCHULZ

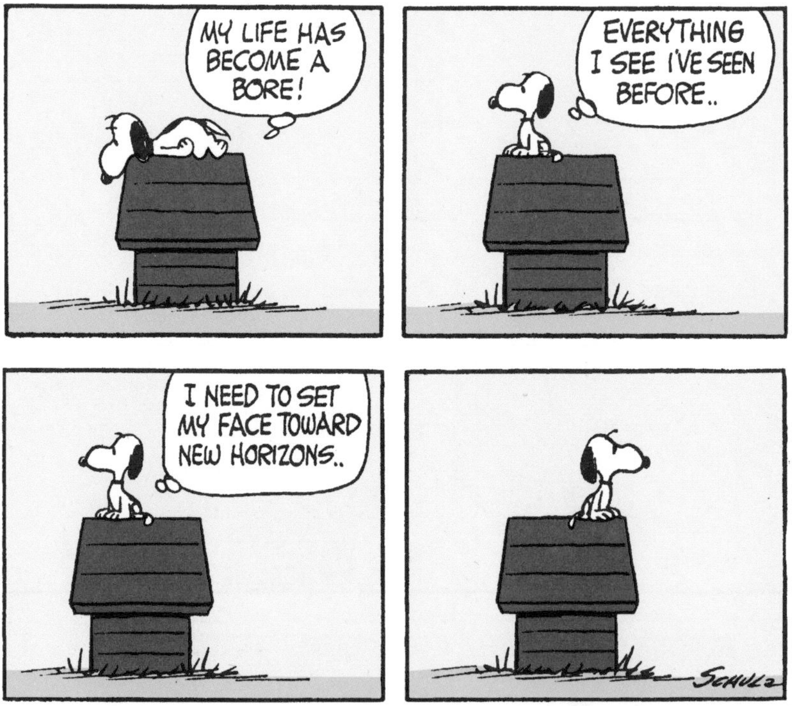
MY LIFE HAS BECOME A BORE!
EVERYTHING I SEE I'VE SEEN BEFORE..
I NEED TO SET MY FACE TOWARD NEW HORIZONS..
SCHULZ

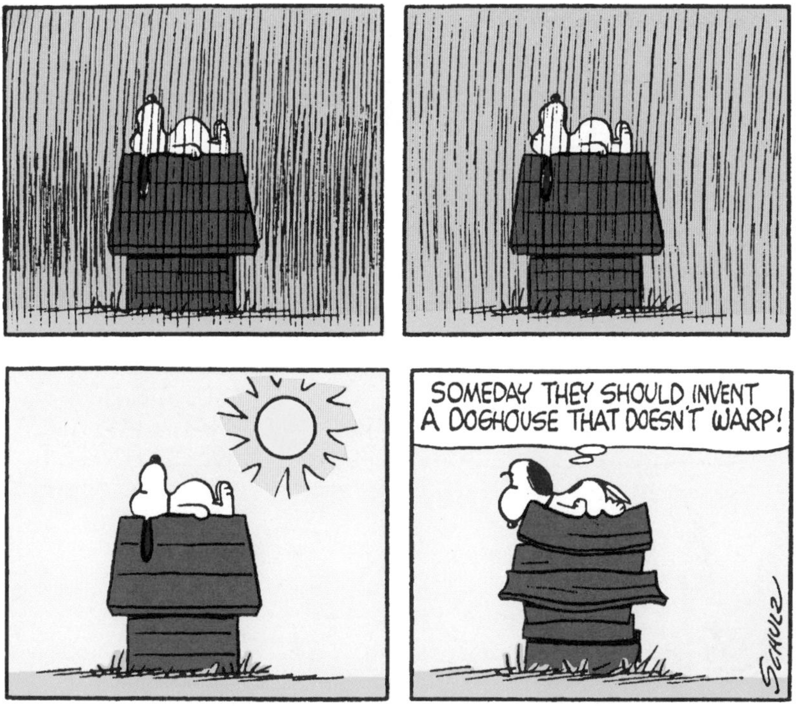
SOMEDAY THEY SHOULD INVENT A DOGHOUSE THAT DOESN'T WARP!
SCHULZ

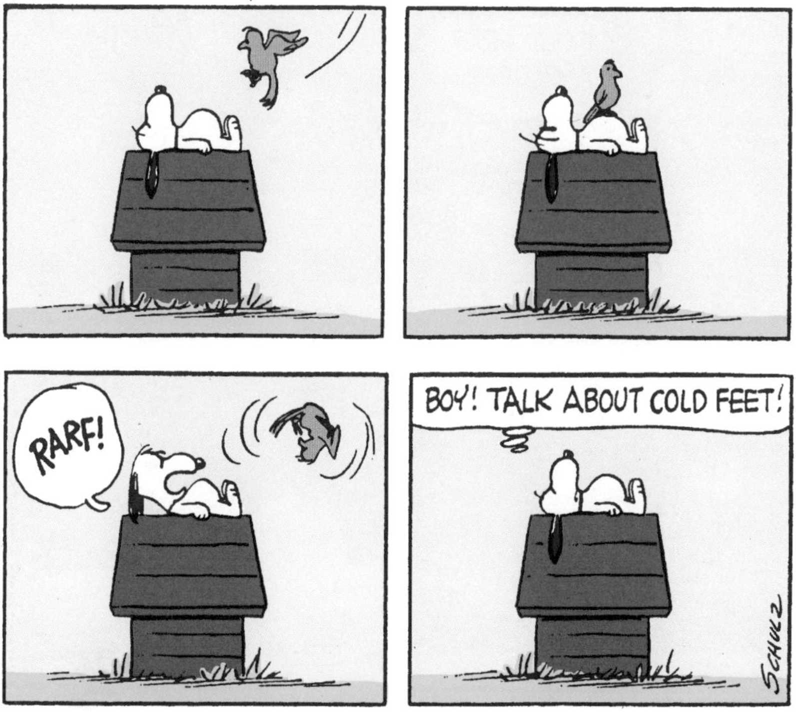
RARF!
BOY! TALK ABOUT COLD FEET!
SCHULZ

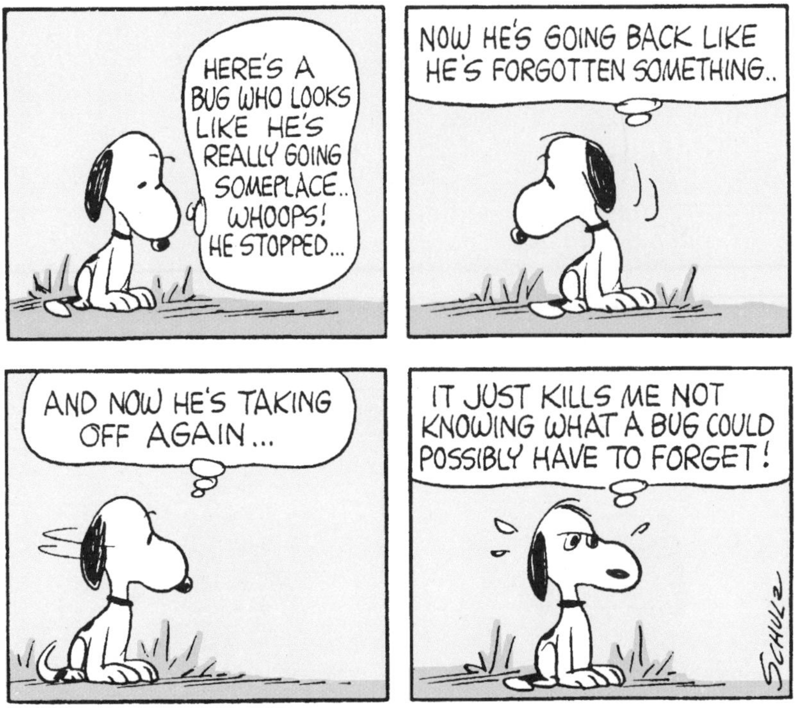
HERE'S A BUG WHO LOOKS LIKE HE'S REALLY GOING SOMEPLACE.. WHOOPS! HE STOPPED...
NOW HE'S GOING BACK LIKE HE'S FORGOTTEN SOMETHING..
AND NOW HE'S TAKING OFF AGAIN...
IT JUST KILLS ME NOT KNOWING WHAT A BUG COULD POSSIBLY HAVE TO FORGET!
SCHULZ

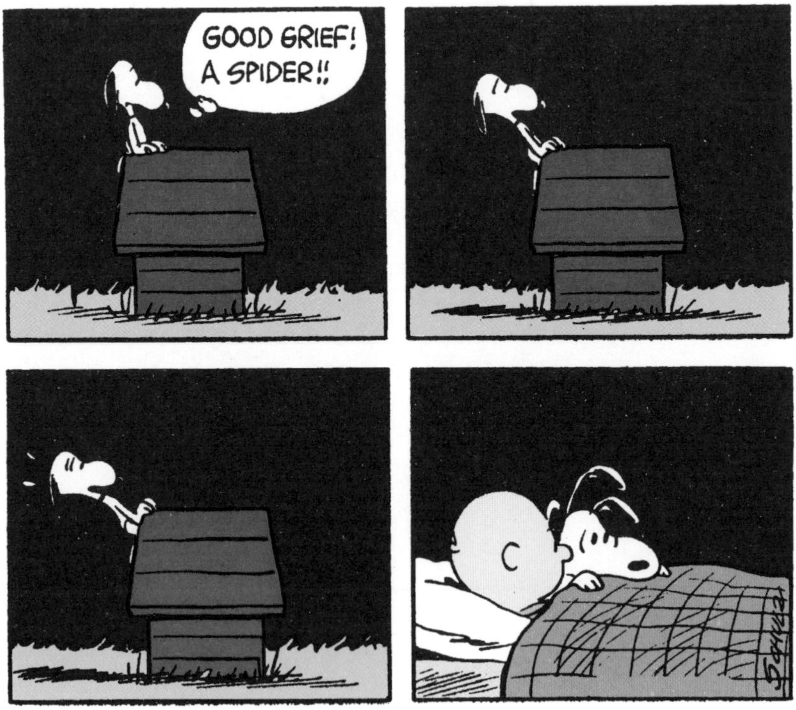
GOOD GRIEF! A SPIDER!!
SCHULZ

NOW I'M TOO TIRED TO EAT!
SCHULZ

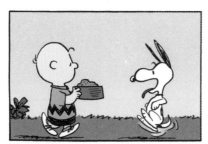

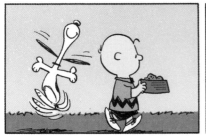

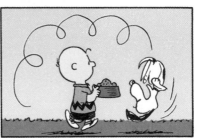

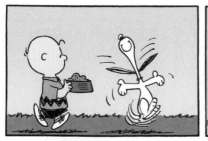

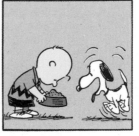

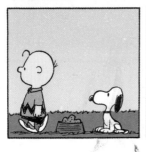

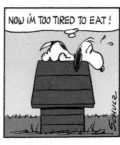

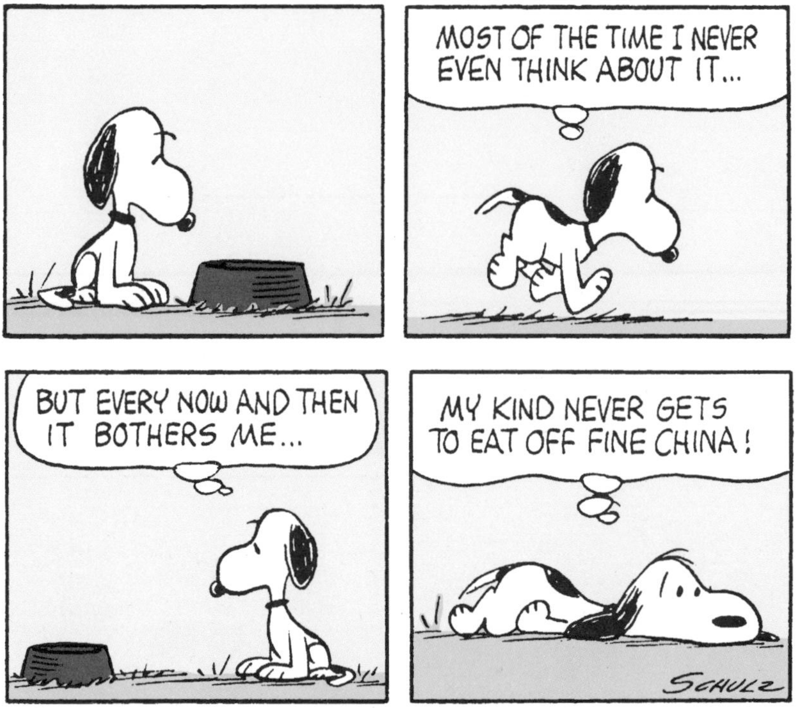
MOST OF THE TIME I NEVER EVEN THINK ABOUT IT...
BUT EVERY NOW AND THEN IT BOTHERS ME...
MY KIND NEVER GETS TO EAT OFF FINE CHINA!
SCHULZ

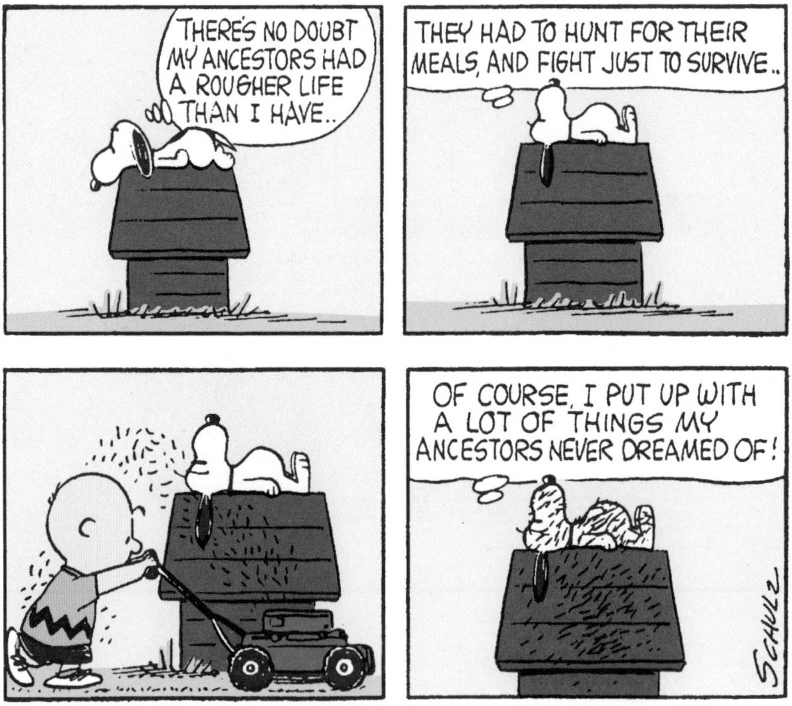
THERE'S NO DOUBT MY ANCESTORS HAD A ROUGHER LIFE THAN I HAVE..
THEY HAD TO HUNT FOR THEIR MEALS, AND FIGHT JUST TO SURVIVE..
OF COURSE, I PUT UP WITH A LOT OF THINGS MY ANCESTORS NEVER DREAMED OF!
SCHULZ

Z
Z
Z
Z
Z
SCHULZ
?

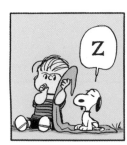

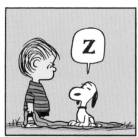

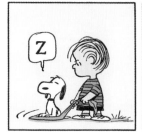

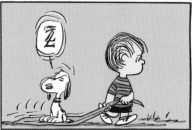

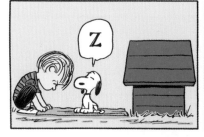

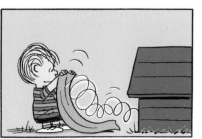

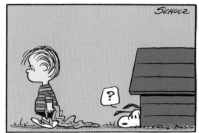

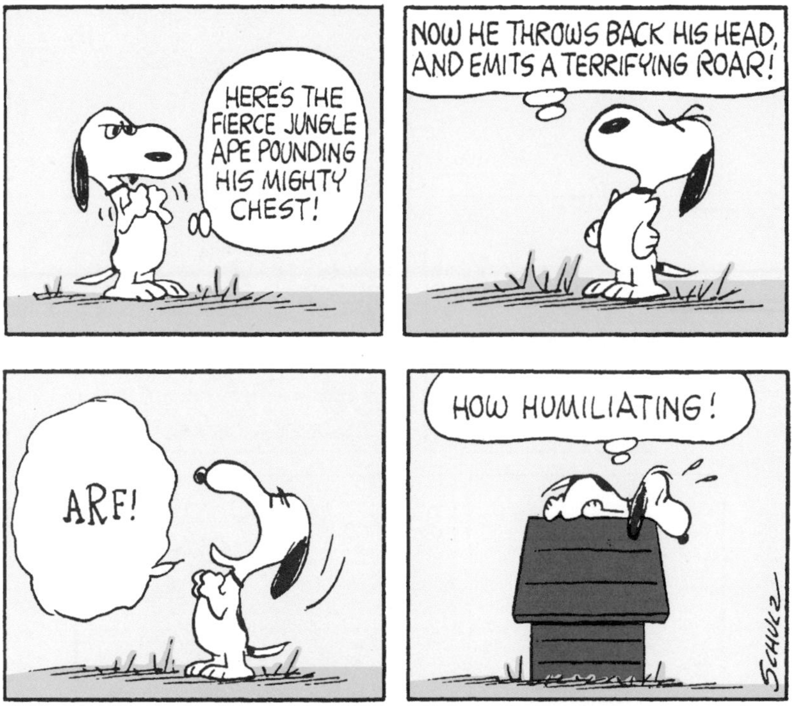
HERE'S THE FIERCE JUNGLE APE POUNDING HIS MIGHTY CHEST!
NOW HE THROWS BACK HIS HEAD, AND EMITS A TERRIFYING ROAR!
ARF!
HOW HUMILIATING!
SCHULZ

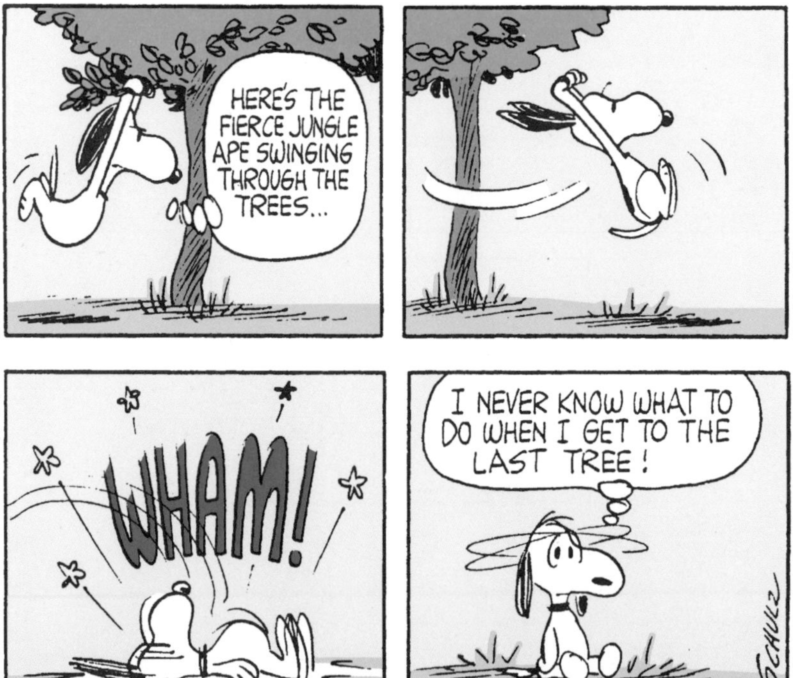
HERE'S THE FIERCE JUNGLE APE SWINGING THROUGH THE TREES...
WHAM!
I NEVER KNOW WHAT TO DO WHEN I GET TO THE LAST TREE!
SCHULZ

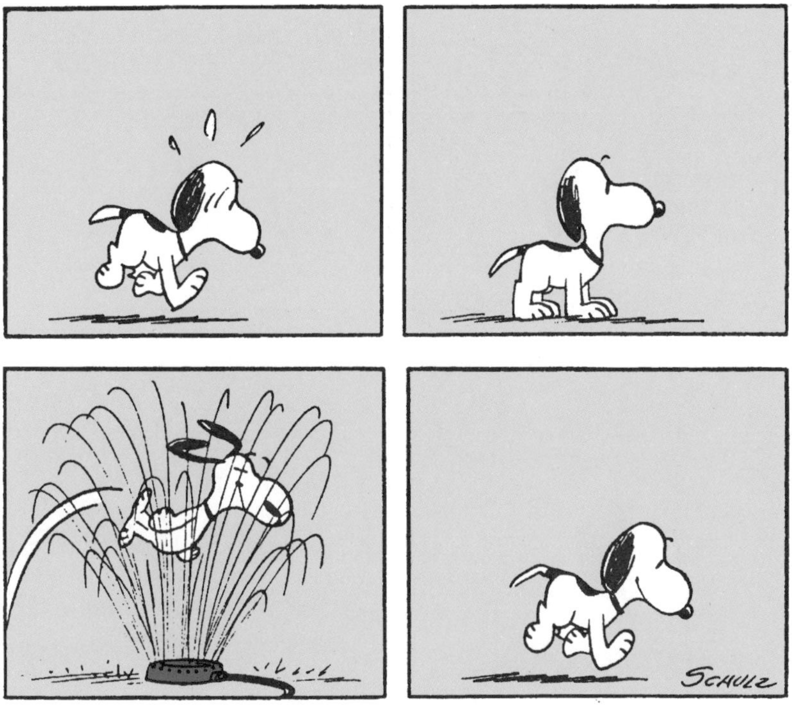
SCHULZ

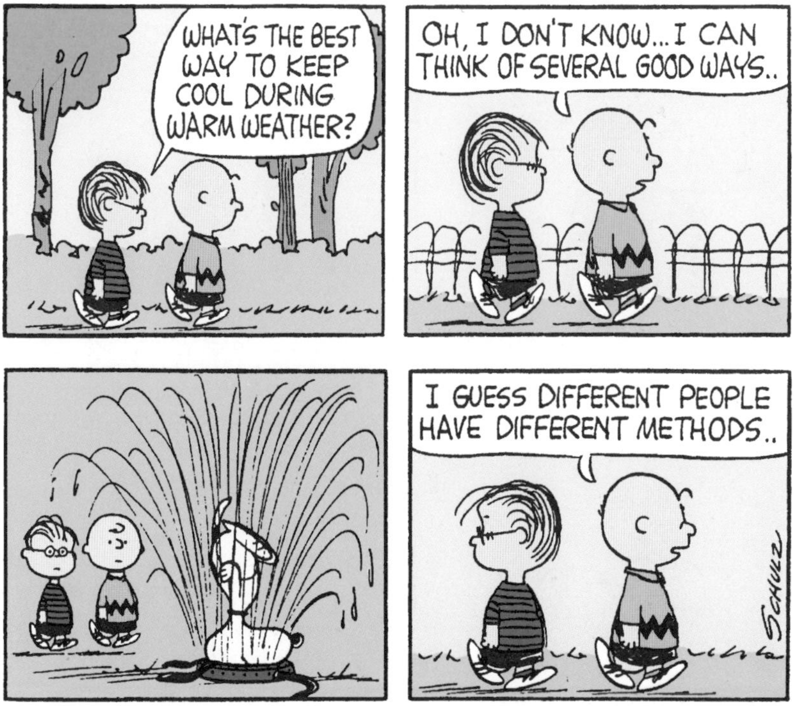
WHAT'S THE BEST WAY TO KEEP COOL DURING WARM WEATHER?
OH, I DON'T KNOW... I CAN THINK OF SEVERAL GOOD WAYS..
I GUESS DIFFERENT PEOPLE HAVE DIFFERENT METHODS..
SCHULZ

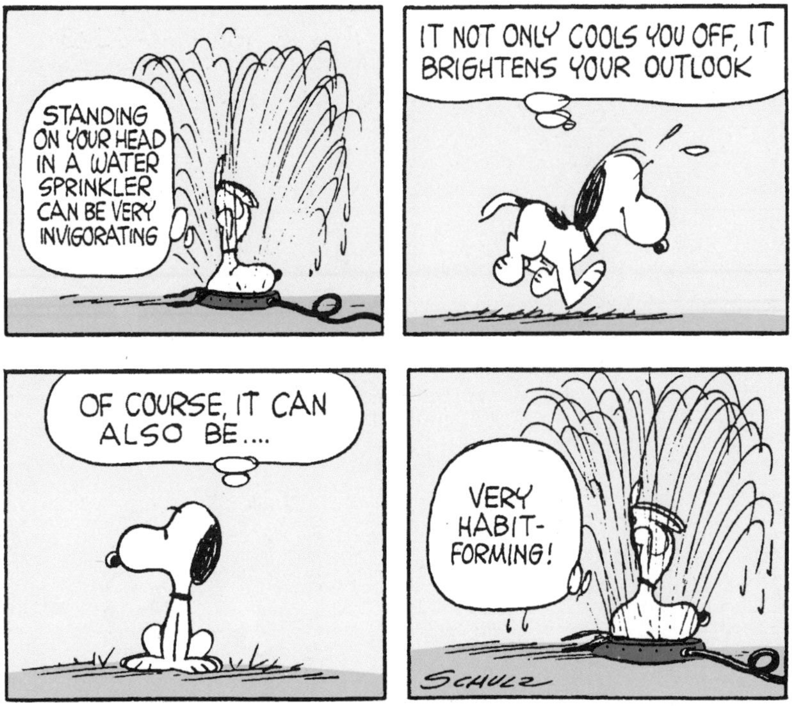
STANDING ON YOUR HEAD IN A WATER SPRINKLER CAN BE VERY INVIGORATING
IT NOT ONLY COOLS YOU OFF, IT BRIGHTENS YOUR OUTLOOK
OF COURSE, IT CAN ALSO BE....
VERY HABIT-FORMING!
SCHULZ

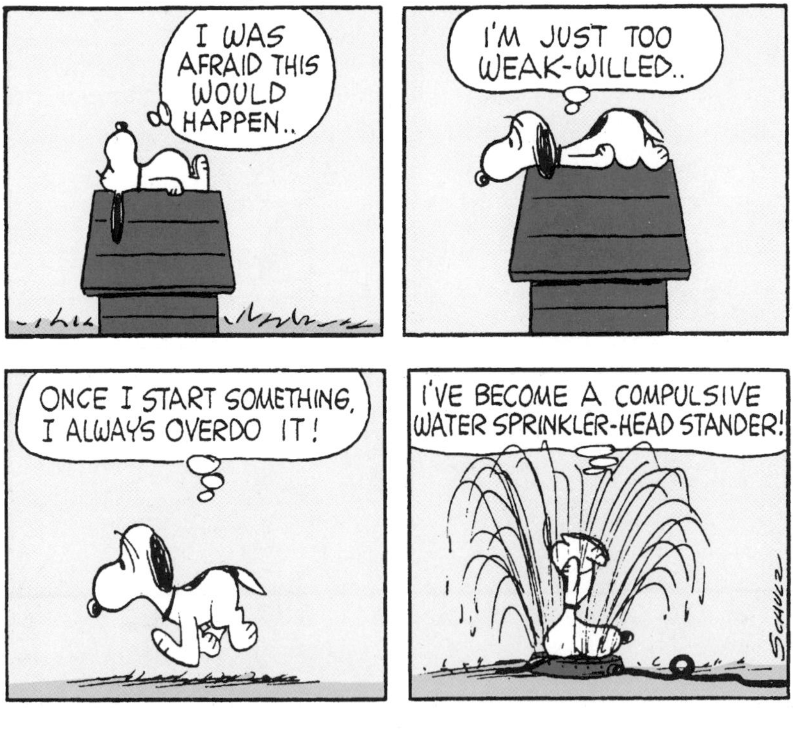
I WAS AFRAID THIS WOULD HAPPEN..
I'M JUST TOO WEAK-WILLED..
ONCE I START SOMETHING, I ALWAYS OVERDO IT!
I'VE BECOME A COMPULSIVE WATER SPRINKLER-HEAD STANDER!
SCHULZ

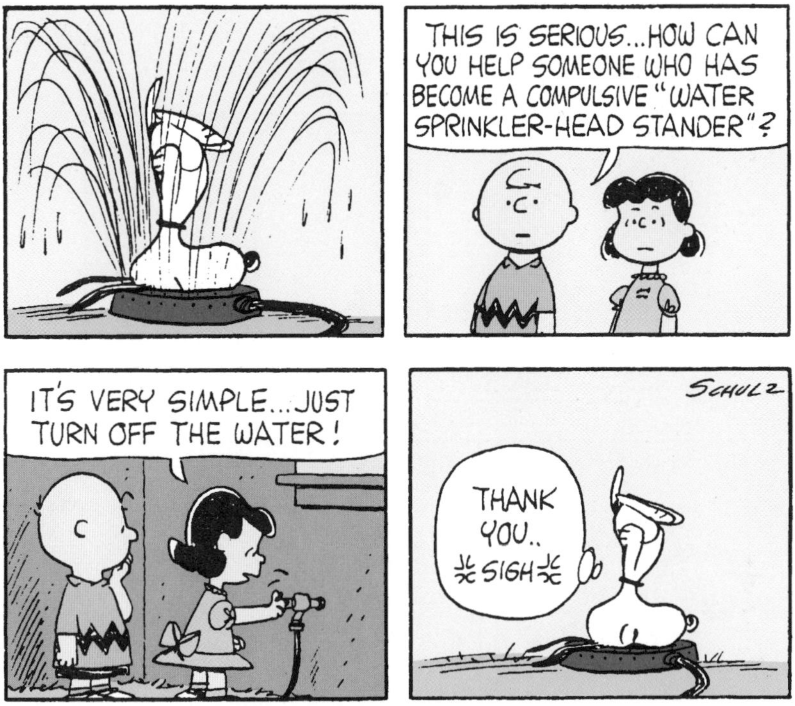
THIS IS SERIOUS...HOW CAN YOU HELP SOMEONE WHO HAS BECOME A COMPULSIVE "WATER SPRINKLER-HEAD STANDER"?
IT'S VERY SIMPLE...JUST TURN OFF THE WATER!
SCHULZ
THANK YOU..
SIGH

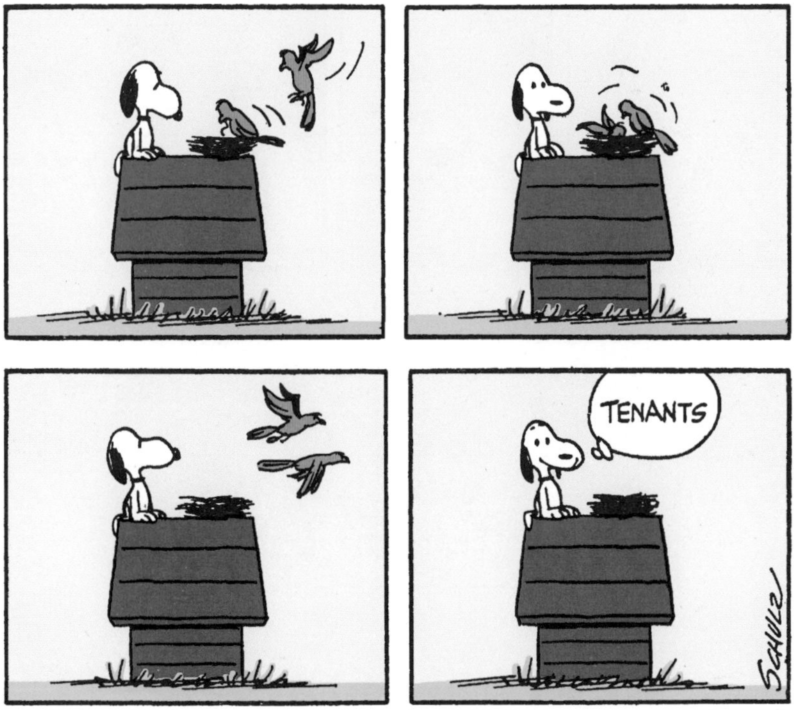
TENANTS
SCHULZ

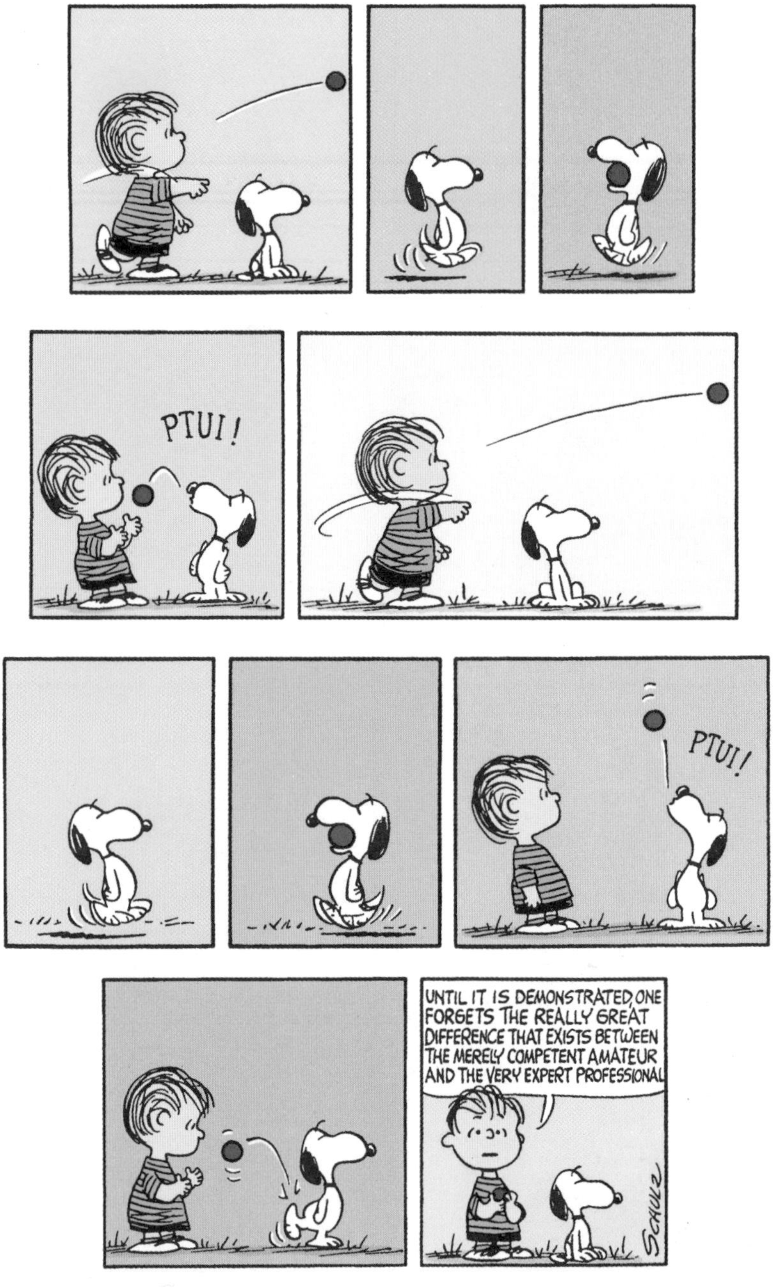
PTUI!
PTUI!
UNTIL IT IS DEMONSTRATED, ONE FORGETS THE REALLY GREAT DIFFERENCE THAT EXISTS BETWEEN THE MERELY COMPETENT AMATEUR AND THE VERY EXPERT PROFESSIONAL
SCHULZ

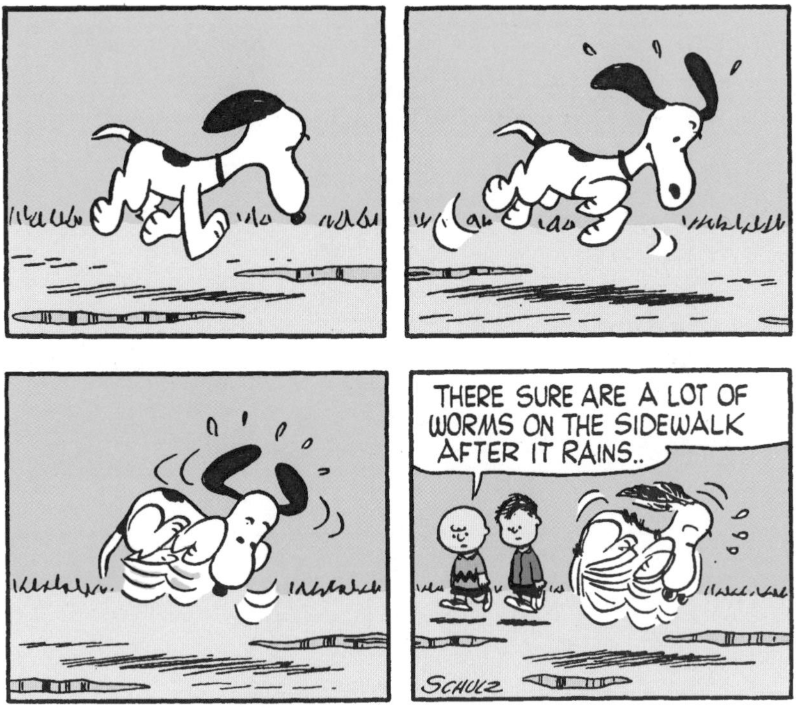
THERE SURE ARE A LOT OF WORMS ON THE SIDEWALK AFTER IT RAINS..
SCHULZ

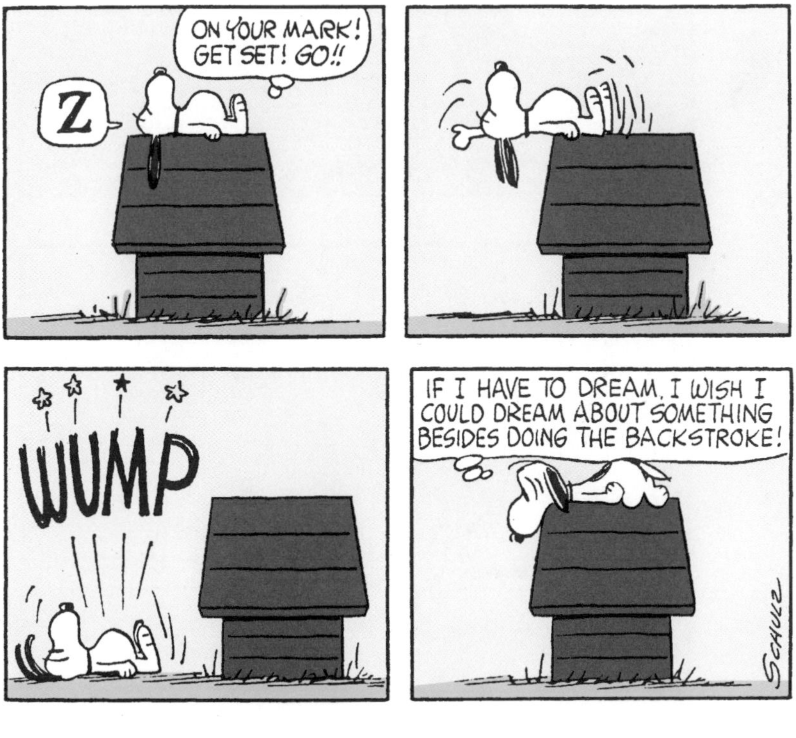
Z
ON YOUR MARK! GET SET! GO!!
WUMP
IF I HAVE TO DREAM, I WISH I COULD DREAM ABOUT SOMETHING BESIDES DOING THE BACKSTROKE!
SCHULZ

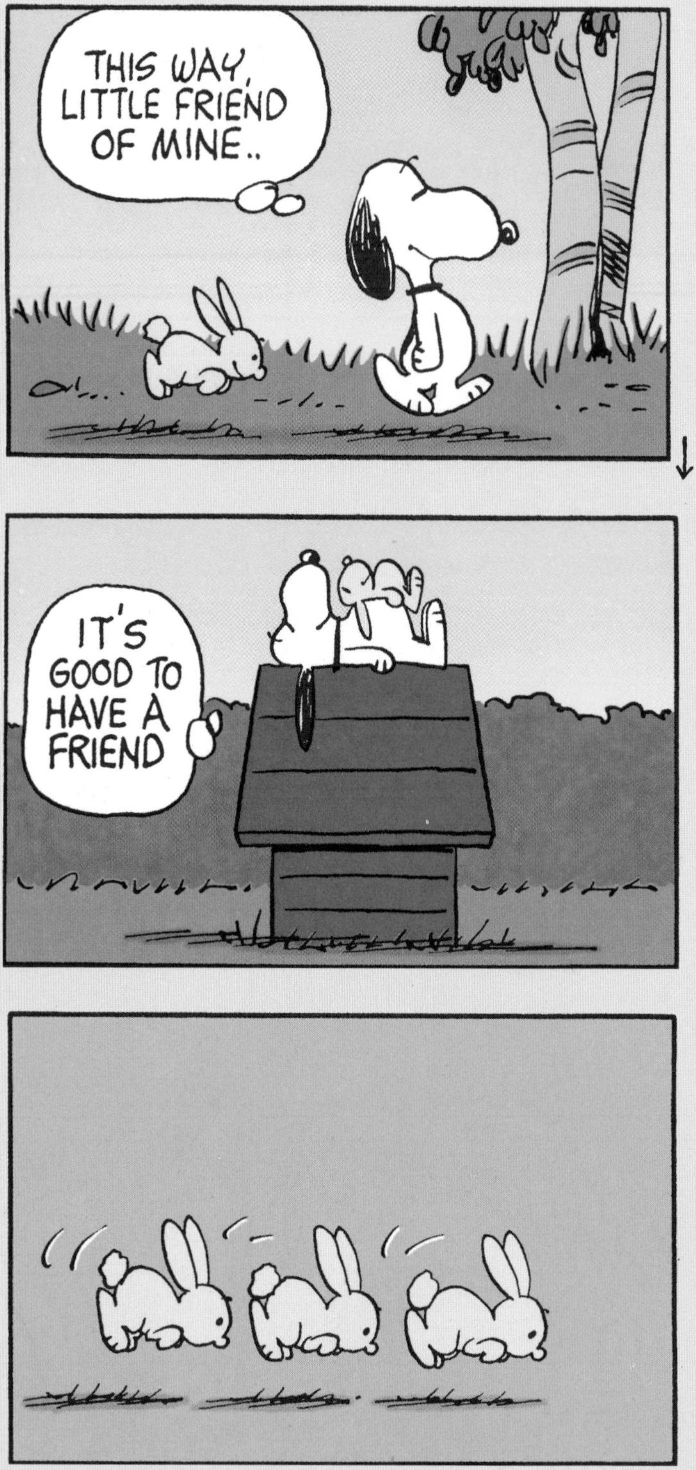
THIS WAY, LITTLE FRIEND OF MINE..
IT'S GOOD TO HAVE A FRIEND

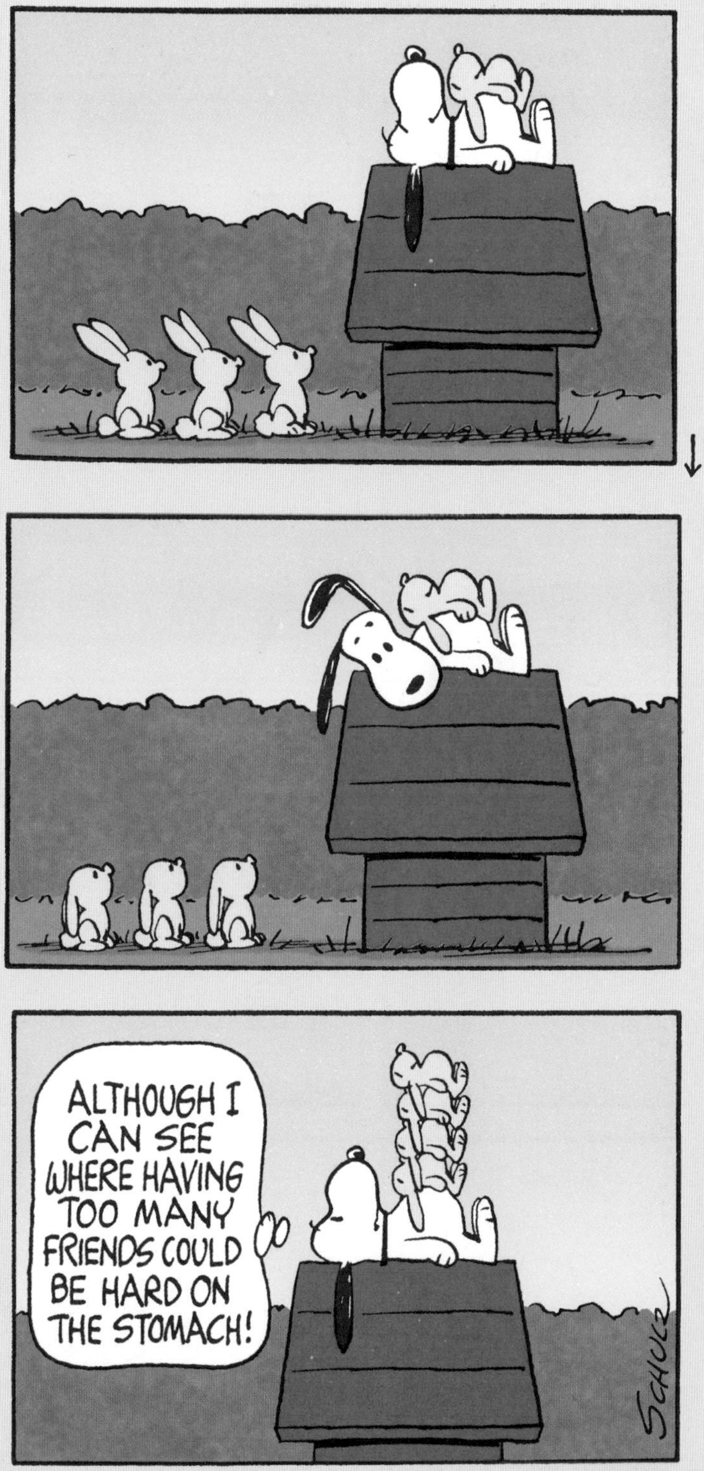
ALTHOUGH I CAN SEE WHERE HAVING TOO MANY FRIENDS COULD BE HARD ON THE STOMACH!
SCHULZ

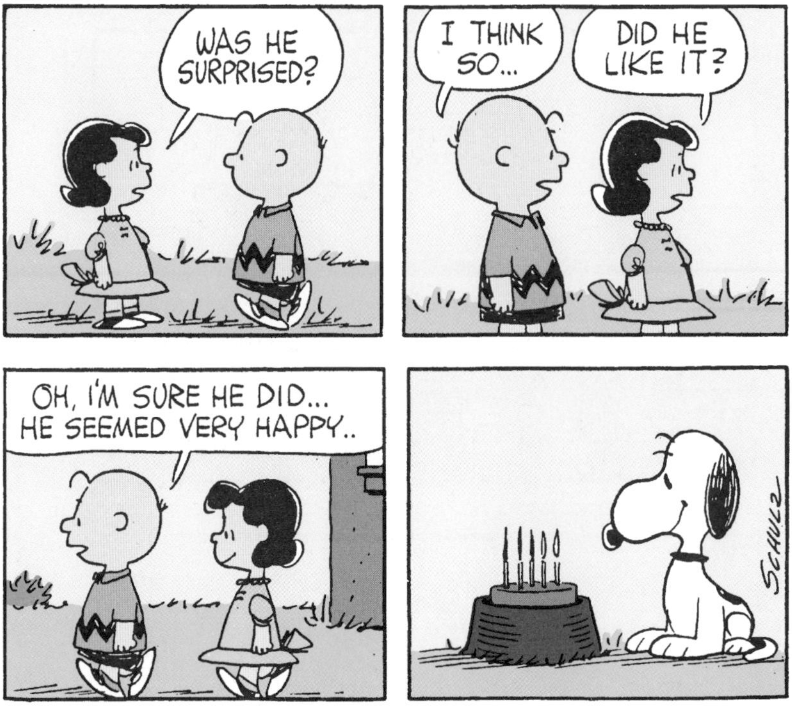
WAS HE SURPRISED?
I THINK SO...
DID HE LIKE IT?
OH, I'M SURE HE DID... HE SEEMED VERY HAPPY..
SCHULZ

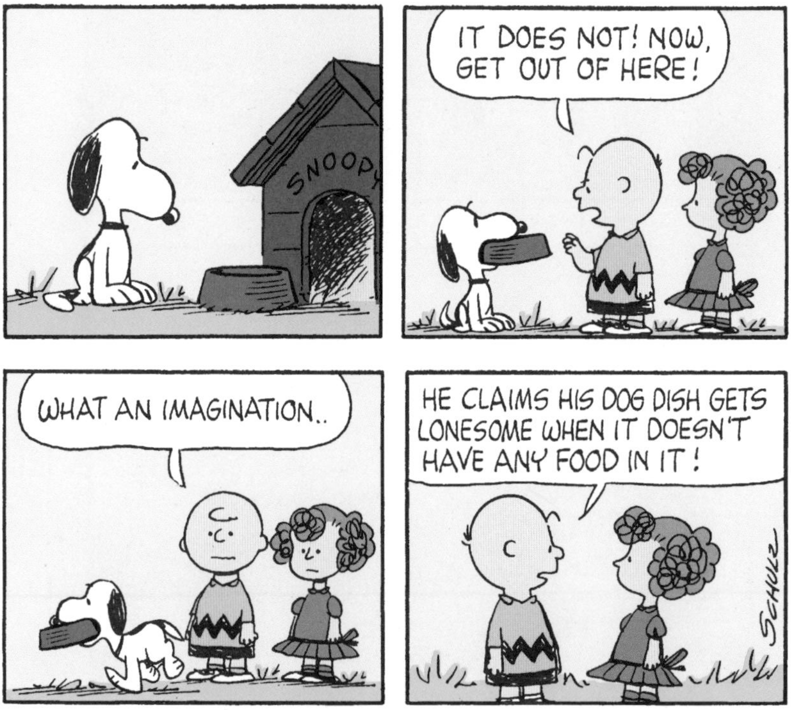
SNOOPY
IT DOES NOT! NOW, GET OUT OF HERE!
WHAT AN IMAGINATION..
HE CLAIMS HIS DOG DISH GETS LONESOME WHEN IT DOESN'T HAVE ANY FOOD IN IT!
SCHULZ

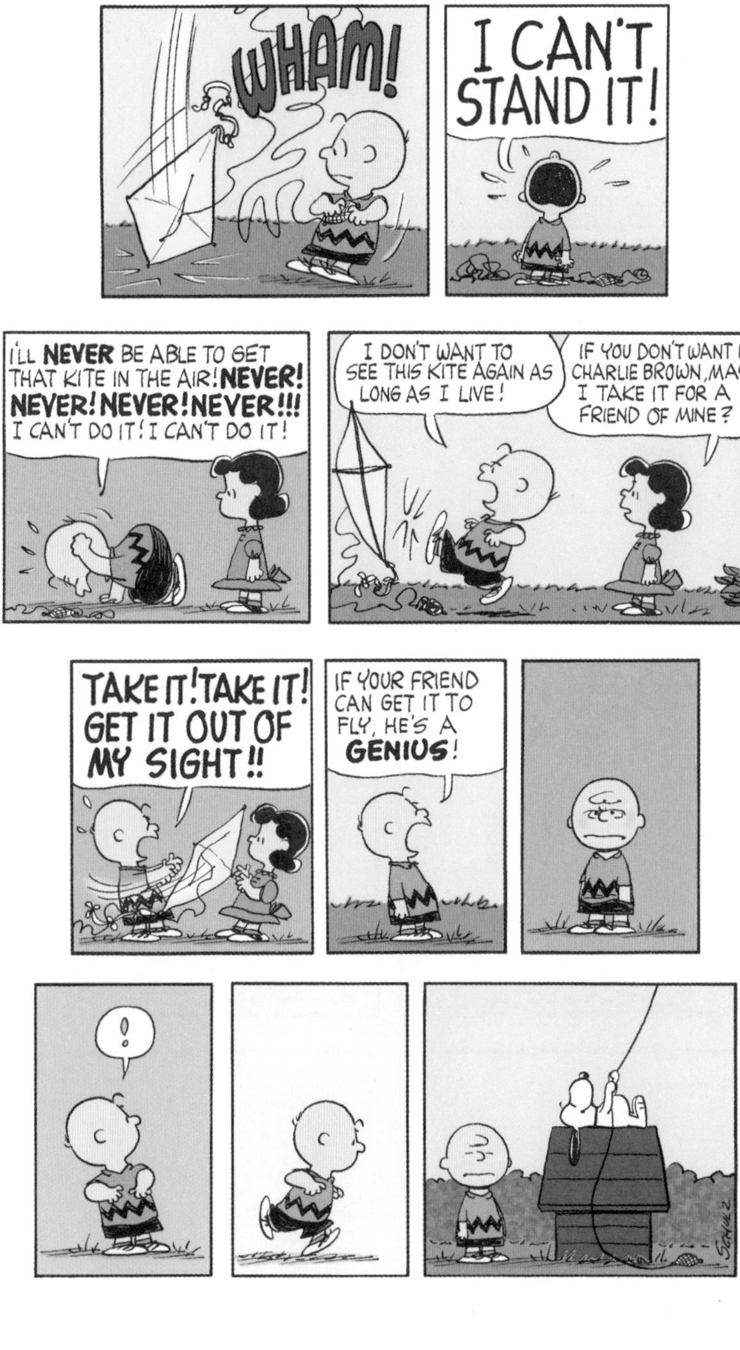

WHAM!
I CAN'T STAND IT!
I'LL NEVER BE ABLE TO GET THAT KITE IN THE AIR! NEVER! NEVER! NEVER! NEVER!!! I CAN'T DO IT! I CAN'T DO IT!
I DON'T WANT TO SEE THIS KITE AGAIN AS LONG AS I LIVE!
IF YOU DON'T WANT IT, CHARLIE BROWN, MAY I TAKE IT FOR A FRIEND OF MINE?
TAKE IT! TAKE IT! GET IT OUT OF MY SIGHT!!
IF YOUR FRIEND CAN GET IT TO FLY, HE'S A GENIUS!
!
SCHULZ

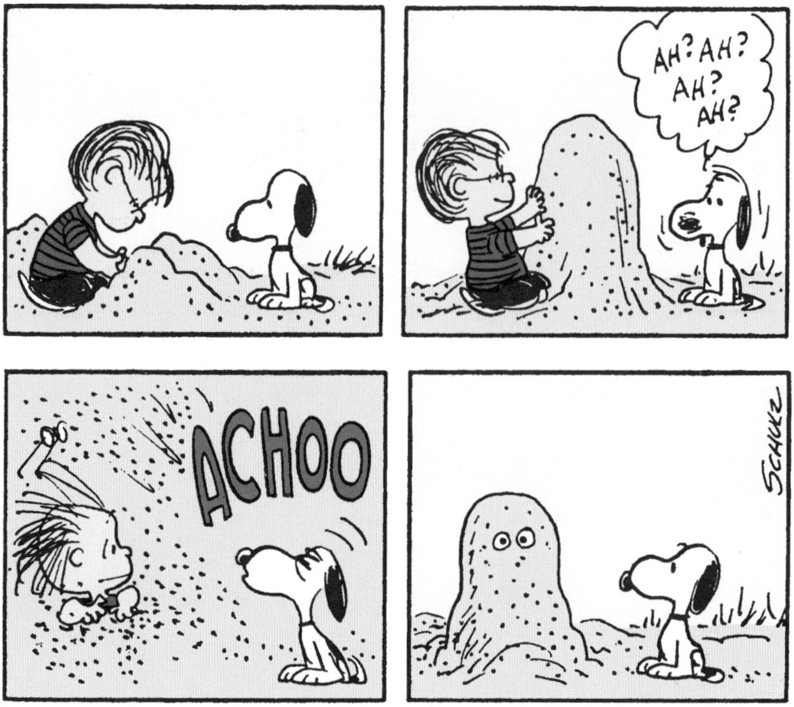
AH? AH?
AH?
AH?
ACHOO
SCHULZ

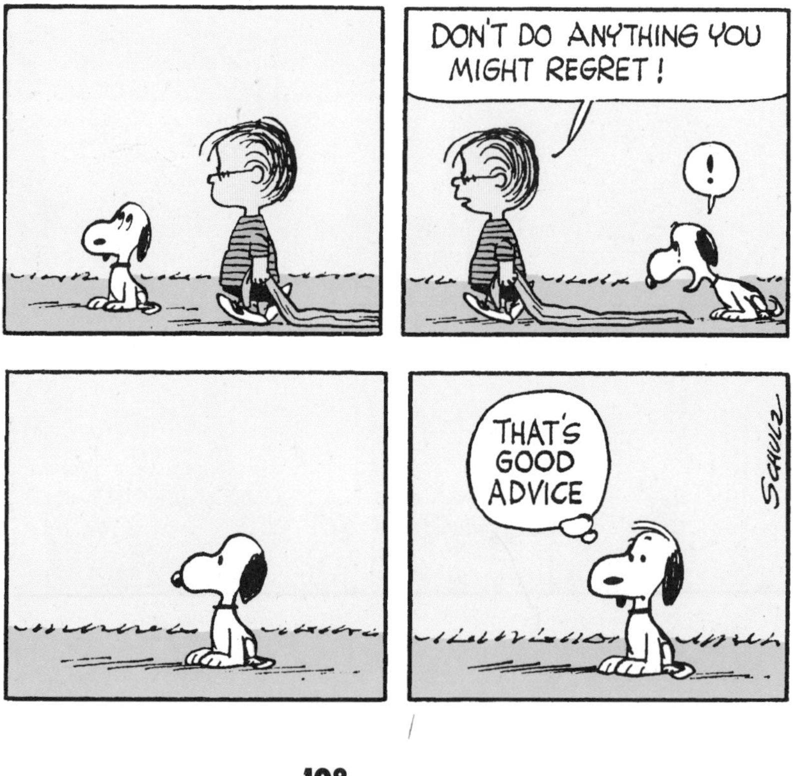
DON'T DO ANYTHING YOU MIGHT REGRET!
!
THAT'S GOOD ADVICE
SCHULZ

WISE GUY!

IT'S A STORM AT SEA!

THE FIERCE GALE LASHES THE RAIN INTO THE FACE OF THE CAPTAIN AS HE STANDS ON DECK!

DON'T YOU LOVE THE FEEL OF A SOFT, GENTLE SUMMER SHOWER?

SIGH

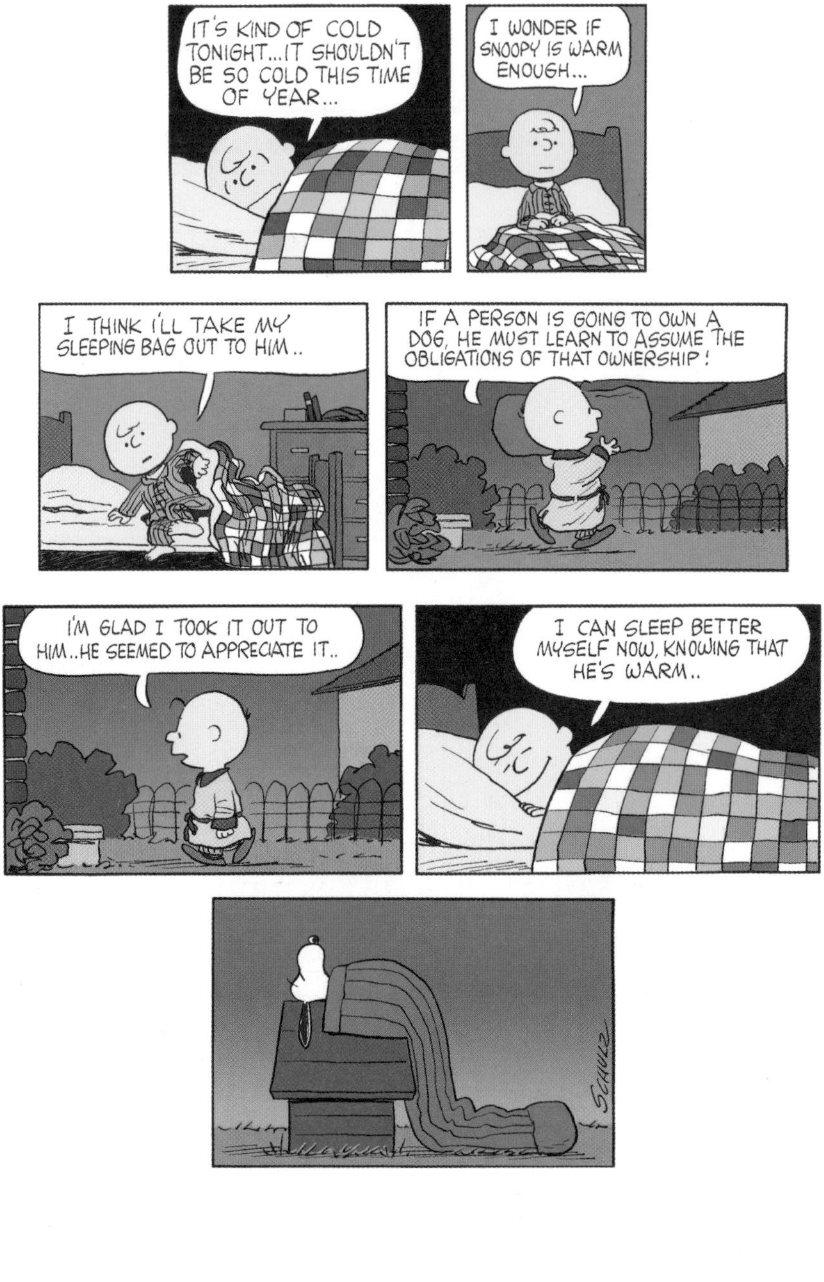
IT'S KIND OF COLD TONIGHT...IT SHOULDN'T BE SO COLD THIS TIME OF YEAR...
I WONDER IF SNOOPY IS WARM ENOUGH...
I THINK I'LL TAKE MY SLEEPING BAG OUT TO HIM..
IF A PERSON IS GOING TO OWN A DOG, HE MUST LEARN TO ASSUME THE OBLIGATIONS OF THAT OWNERSHIP!
I'M GLAD I TOOK IT OUT TO HIM..HE SEEMED TO APPRECIATE IT..
I CAN SLEEP BETTER MYSELF NOW, KNOWING THAT HE'S WARM..
SCHULZ

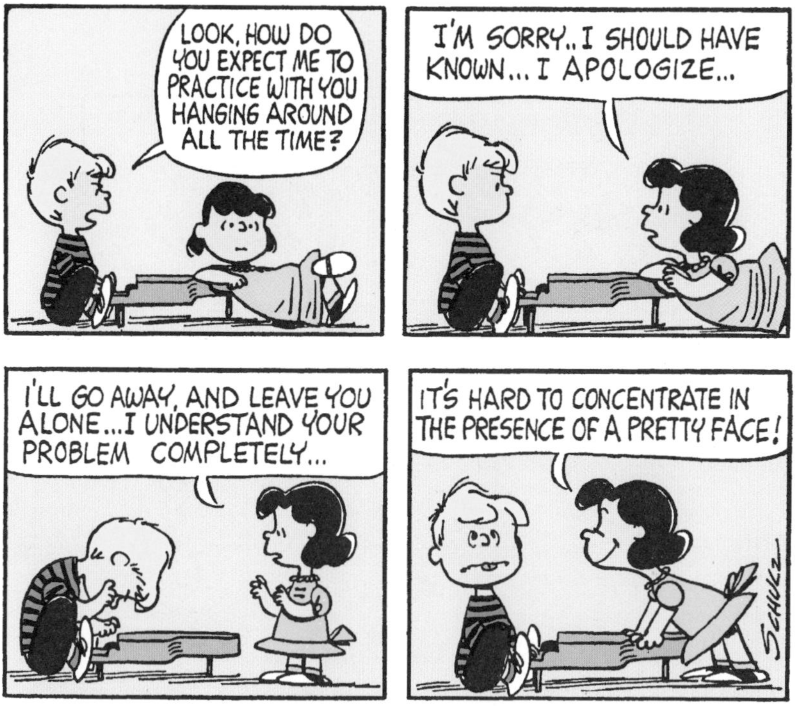
LOOK, HOW DO YOU EXPECT ME TO PRACTICE WITH YOU HANGING AROUND ALL THE TIME?
I'M SORRY.. I SHOULD HAVE KNOWN... I APOLOGIZE...
I'LL GO AWAY, AND LEAVE YOU ALONE...I UNDERSTAND YOUR PROBLEM COMPLETELY...
IT'S HARD TO CONCENTRATE IN THE PRESENCE OF A PRETTY FACE!
SCHULZ

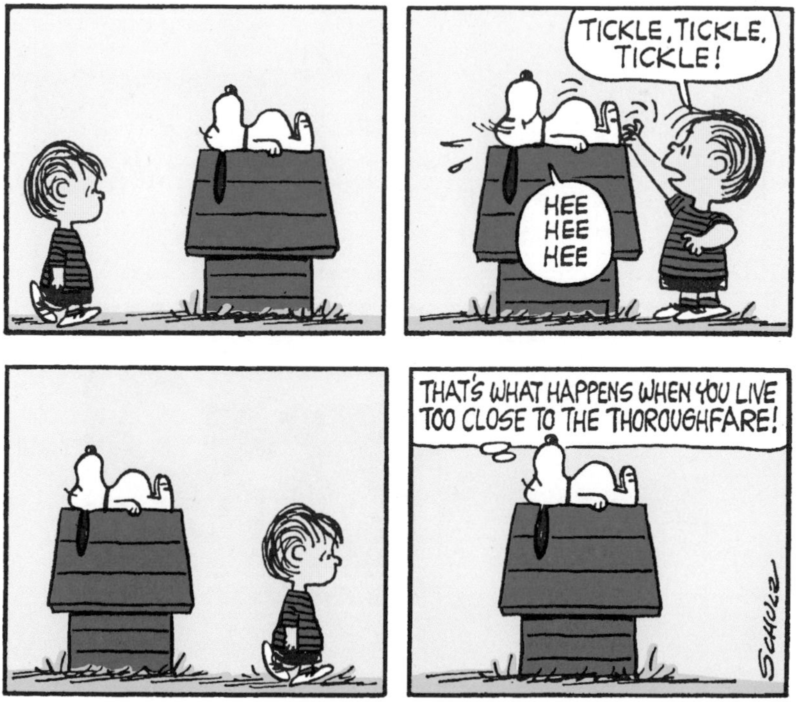
TICKLE, TICKLE, TICKLE!
HEE HEE HEE
THAT'S WHAT HAPPENS WHEN YOU LIVE TOO CLOSE TO THE THOROUGHFARE!
SCHULZ

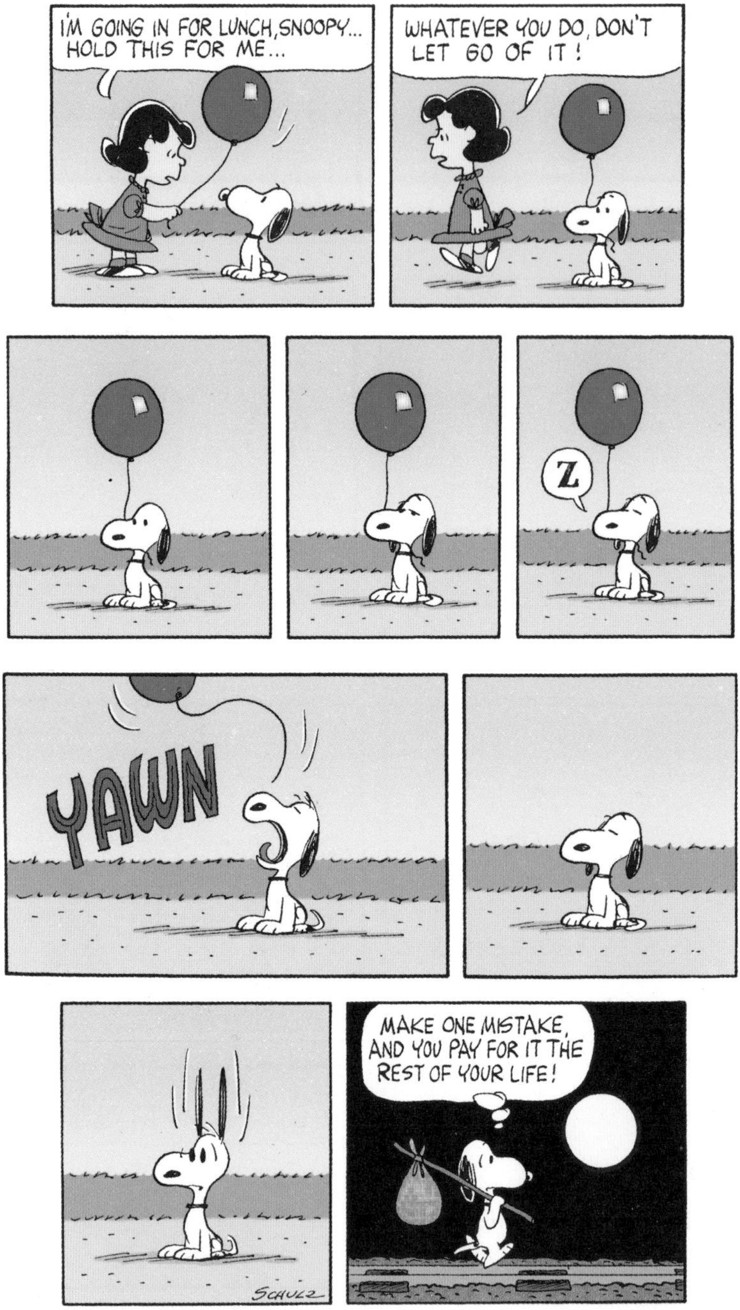
I'M GOING IN FOR LUNCH, SNOOPY... HOLD THIS FOR ME...
WHATEVER YOU DO, DON'T LET GO OF IT!
Z
YAWN
MAKE ONE MISTAKE, AND YOU PAY FOR IT THE REST OF YOUR LIFE!
SCHULZ

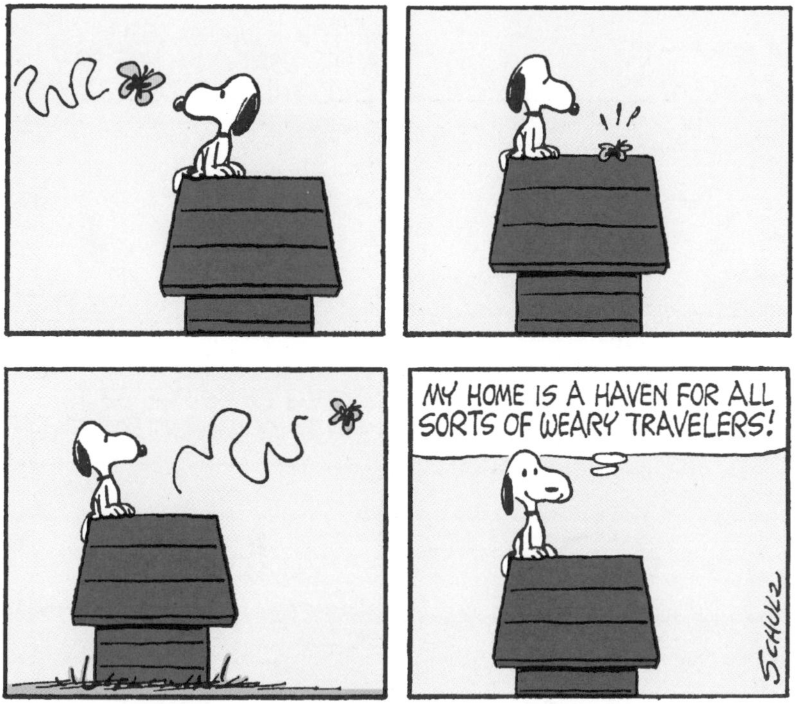
MY HOME IS A HAVEN FOR ALL SORTS OF WEARY TRAVELERS!
SCHULZ

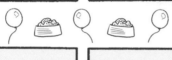

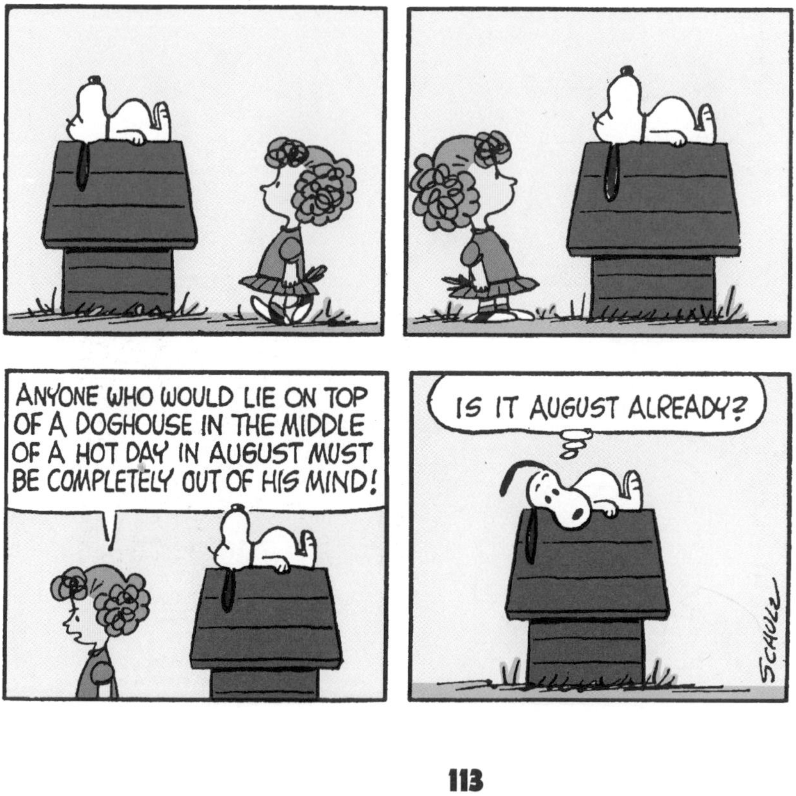
ANYONE WHO WOULD LIE ON TOP OF A DOGHOUSE IN THE MIDDLE OF A HOT DAY IN AUGUST MUST BE COMPLETELY OUT OF HIS MIND!
IS IT AUGUST ALREADY?
SCHULZ

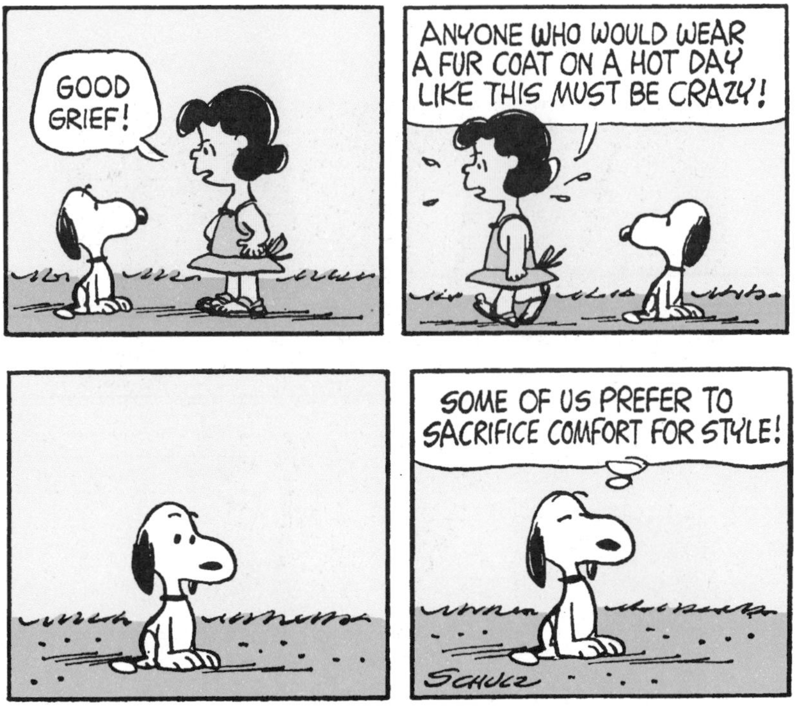
GOOD GRIEF!
ANYONE WHO WOULD WEAR A FUR COAT ON A HOT DAY LIKE THIS MUST BE CRAZY!
SOME OF US PREFER TO SACRIFICE COMFORT FOR STYLE!
SCHULZ

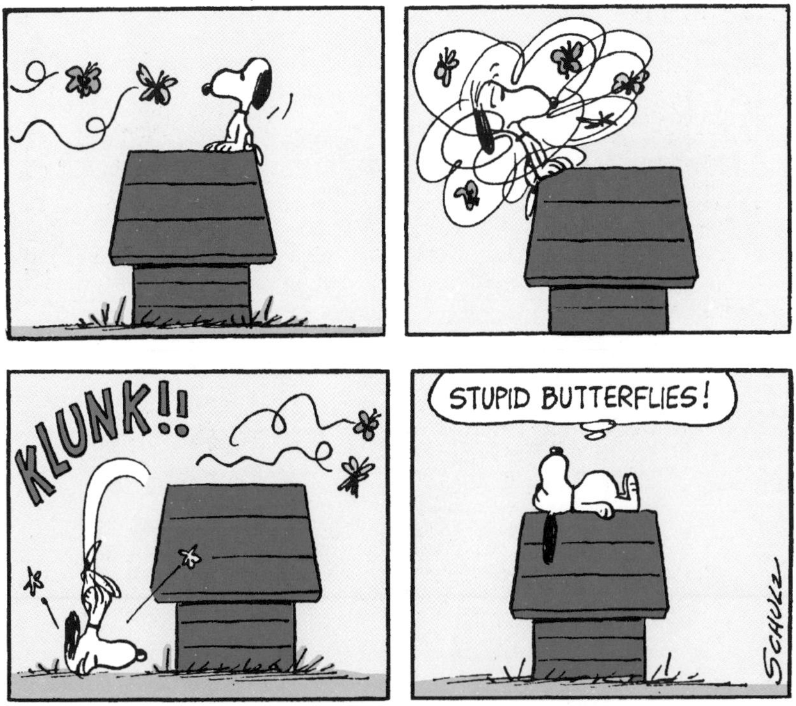
KLUNK!!
STUPID BUTTERFLIES!
SCHULZ

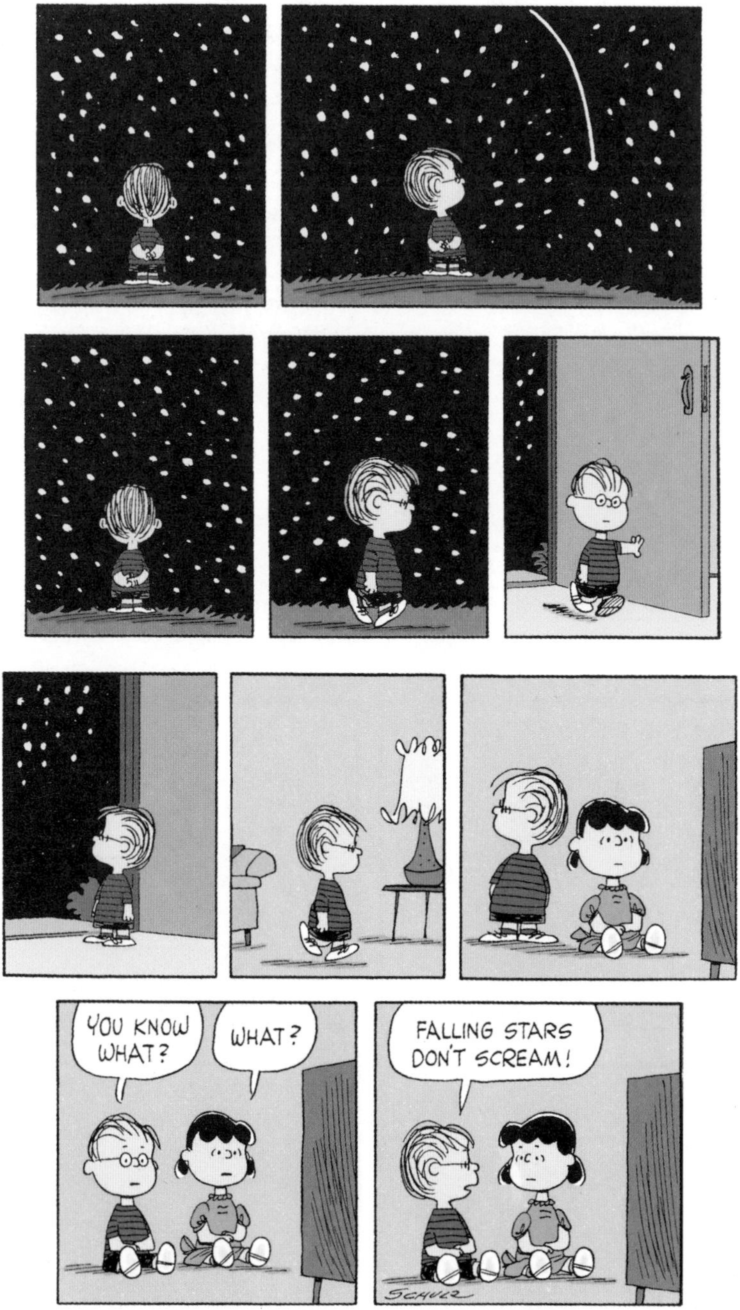
YOU KNOW WHAT?
WHAT?
FALLING STARS DON'T SCREAM!
SCHULZ

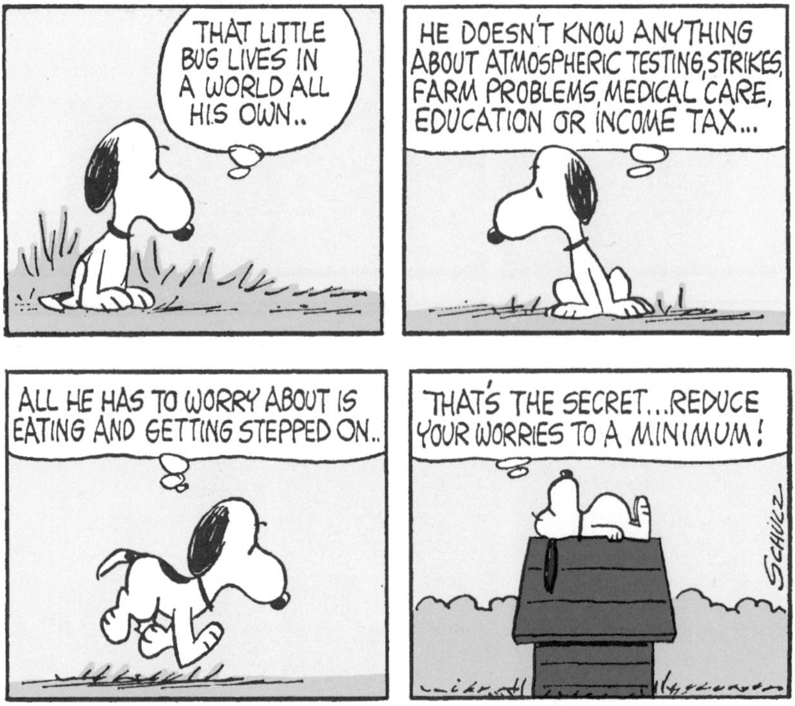
THAT LITTLE BUG LIVES IN A WORLD ALL HIS OWN..
HE DOESN'T KNOW ANYTHING ABOUT ATMOSPHERIC TESTING, STRIKES, FARM PROBLEMS, MEDICAL CARE, EDUCATION OR INCOME TAX...
ALL HE HAS TO WORRY ABOUT IS EATING AND GETTING STEPPED ON..
THAT'S THE SECRET...REDUCE YOUR WORRIES TO A MINIMUM!
SCHULZ

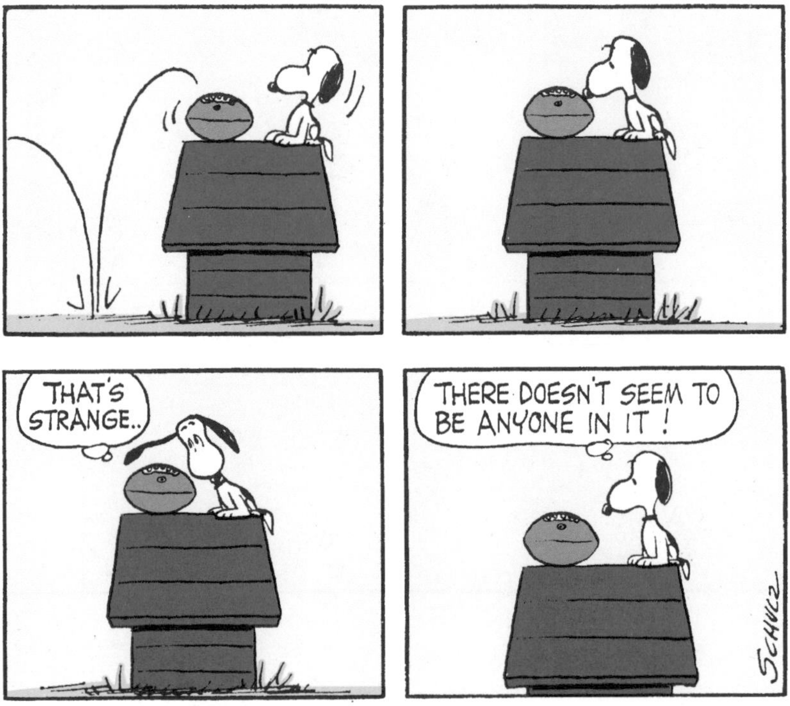
THAT'S STRANGE..
THERE DOESN'T SEEM TO BE ANYONE IN IT!
SCHULZ

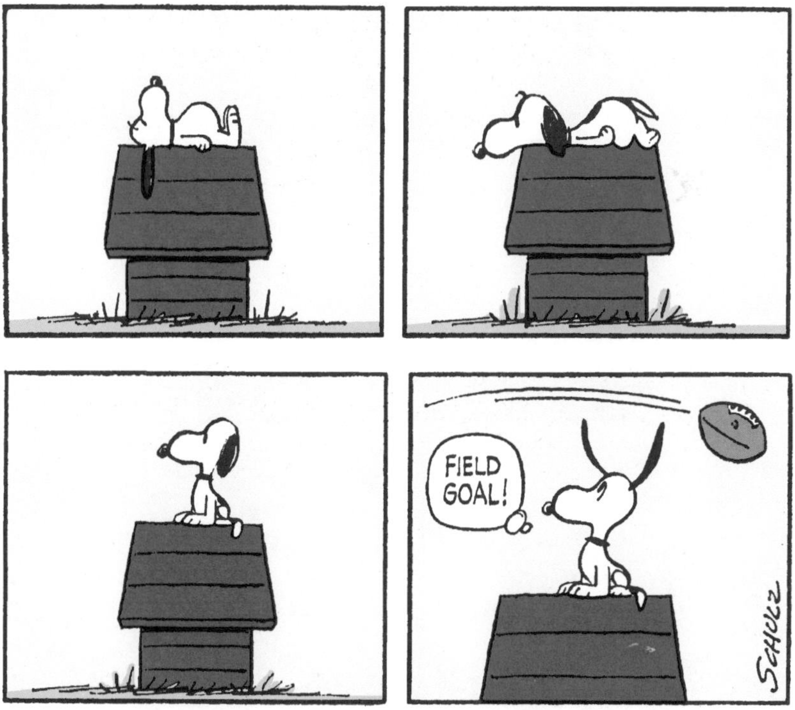
FIELD GOAL!
SCHULZ

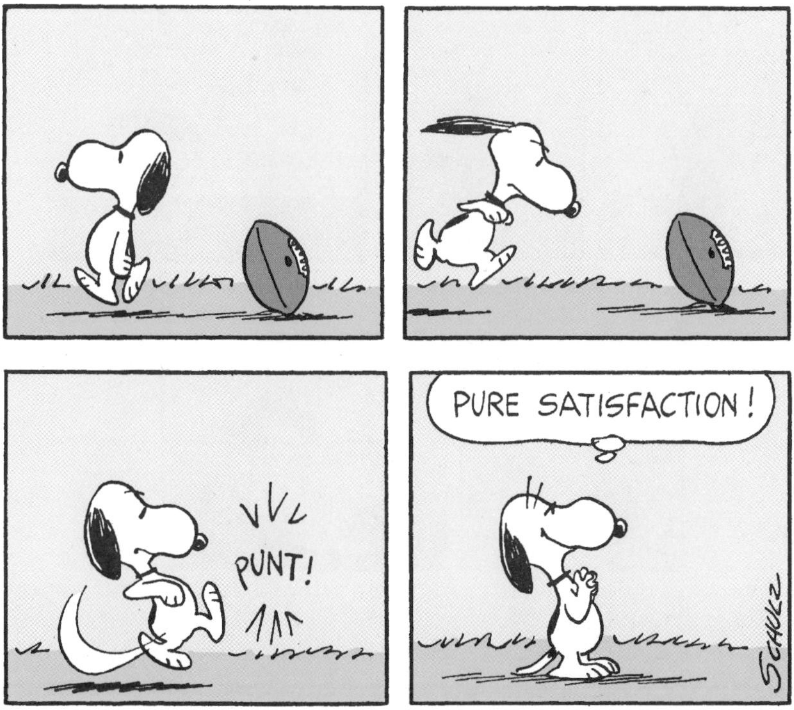
PUNT!
PURE SATISFACTION!
SCHULZ

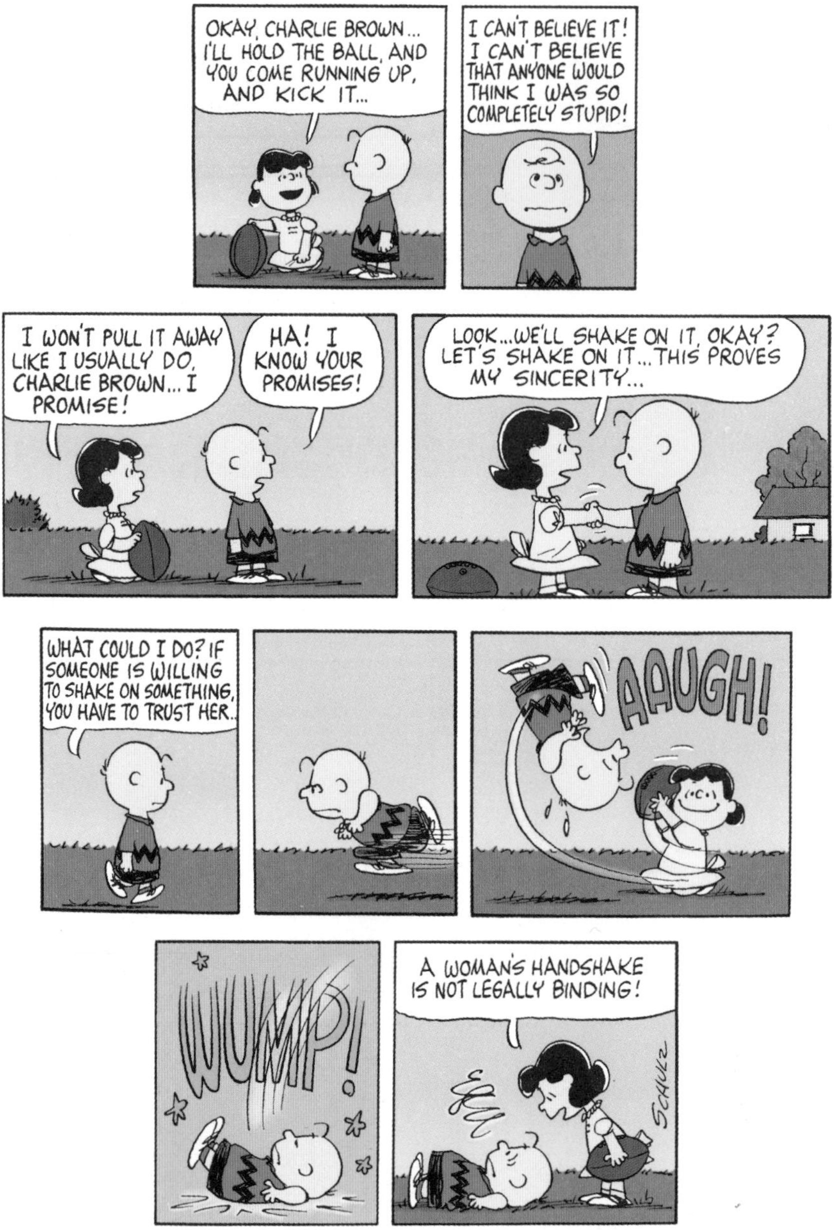
OKAY, CHARLIE BROWN... I'LL HOLD THE BALL, AND YOU COME RUNNING UP, AND KICK IT...
I CAN'T BELIEVE IT! I CAN'T BELIEVE THAT ANYONE WOULD THINK I WAS SO COMPLETELY STUPID!
I WON'T PULL IT AWAY LIKE I USUALLY DO, CHARLIE BROWN... I PROMISE!
HA! I KNOW YOUR PROMISES!
LOOK...WE'LL SHAKE ON IT, OKAY? LET'S SHAKE ON IT...THIS PROVES MY SINCERITY...
WHAT COULD I DO? IF SOMEONE IS WILLING TO SHAKE ON SOMETHING, YOU HAVE TO TRUST HER..
AAUGH!
WUMP!
A WOMAN'S HANDSHAKE IS NOT LEGALLY BINDING!
SCHULZ

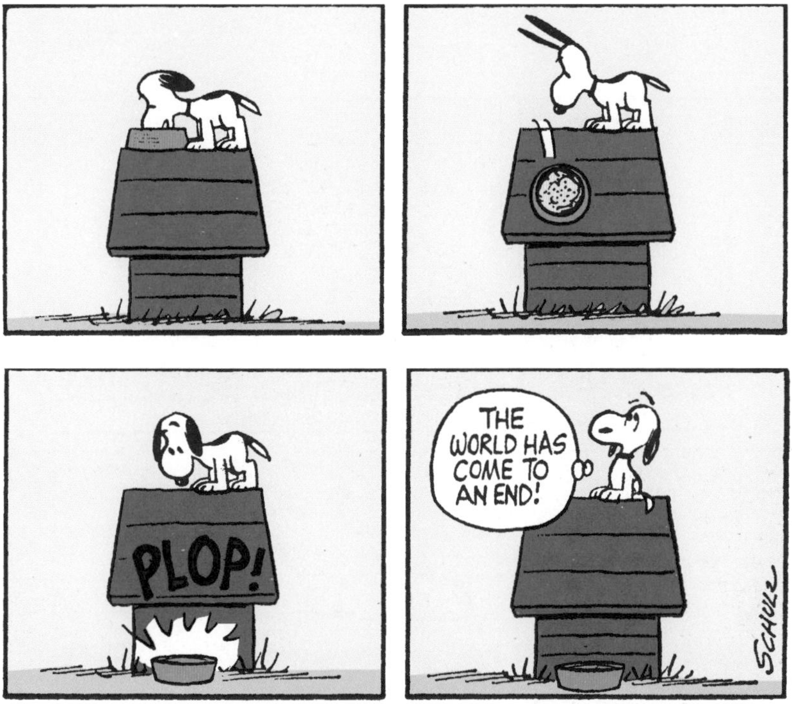
PLOP!
THE WORLD HAS COME TO AN END!
SCHULZ

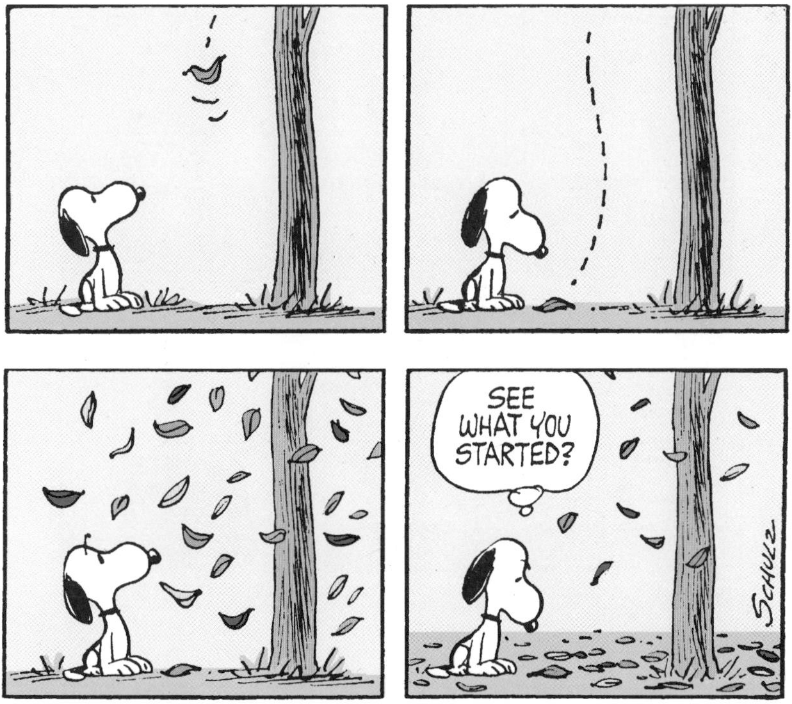
SEE WHAT YOU STARTED?
SCHULZ

STUPID LEAVES!
SCHULZ

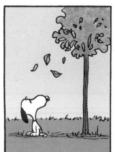

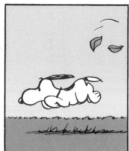

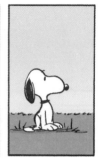

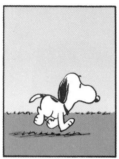

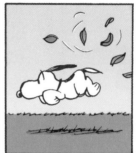

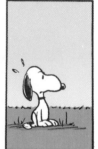

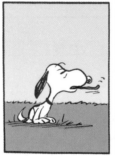

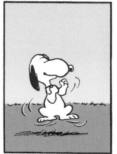

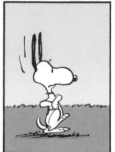

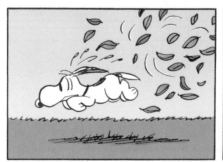

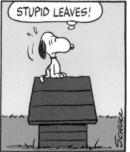

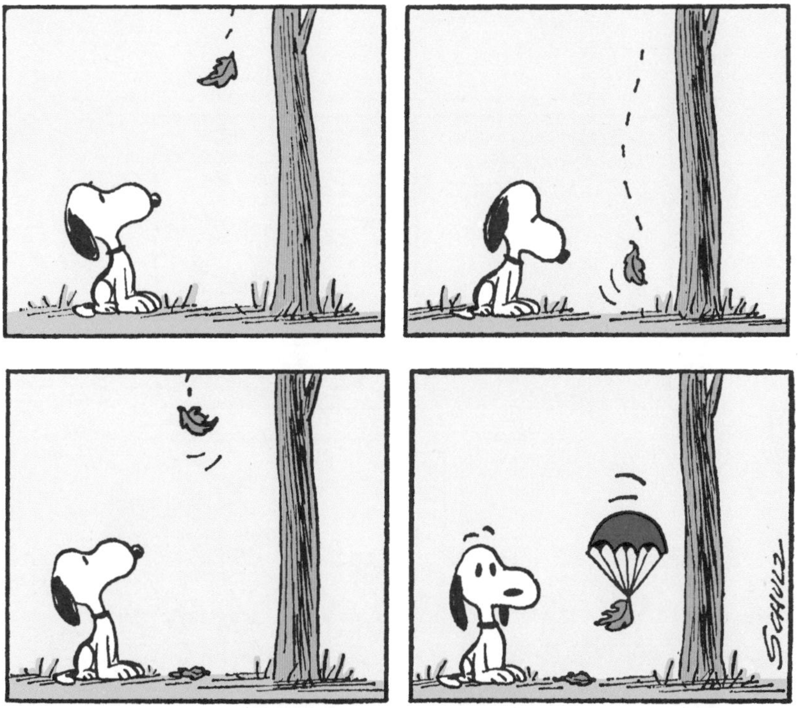
SCHULZ

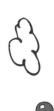

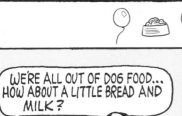

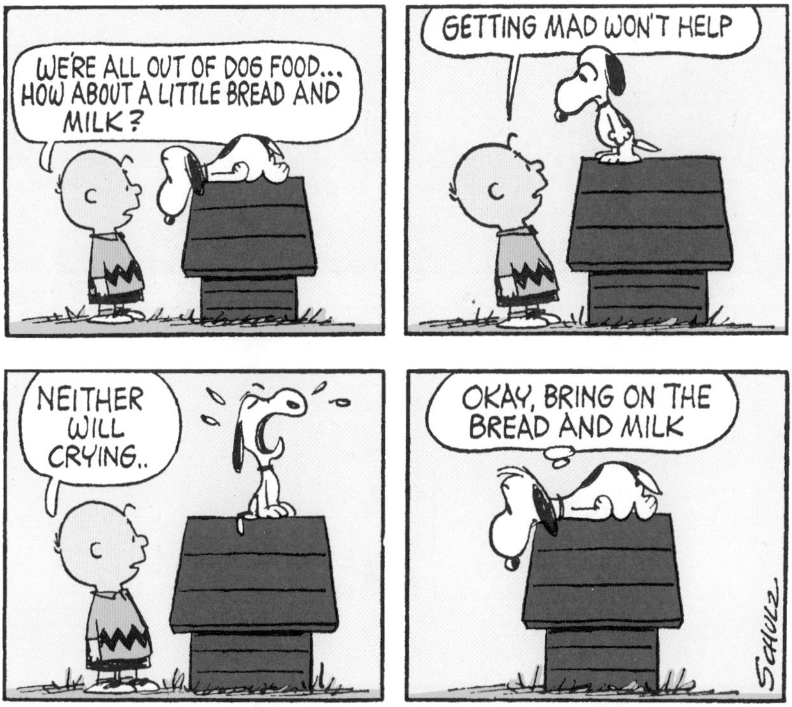
WE'RE ALL OUT OF DOG FOOD... HOW ABOUT A LITTLE BREAD AND MILK?
GETTING MAD WON'T HELP
NEITHER WILL CRYING..
OKAY, BRING ON THE BREAD AND MILK
SCHULZ

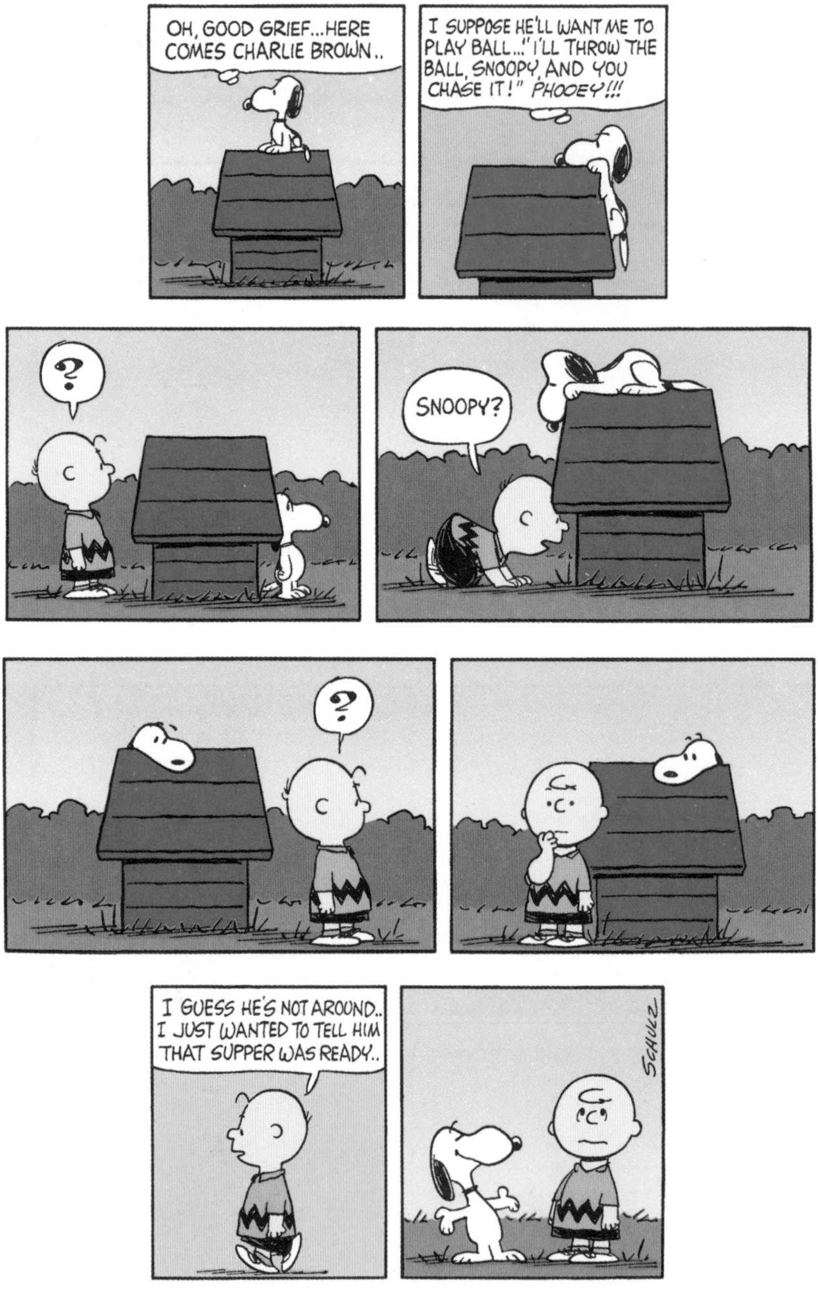
OH, GOOD GRIEF...HERE COMES CHARLIE BROWN..
I SUPPOSE HE'LL WANT ME TO PLAY BALL..."I'LL THROW THE BALL, SNOOPY, AND YOU CHASE IT!" PHOOEY!!!
?
SNOOPY?
?
I GUESS HE'S NOT AROUND.. I JUST WANTED TO TELL HIM THAT SUPPER WAS READY..
SCHULZ

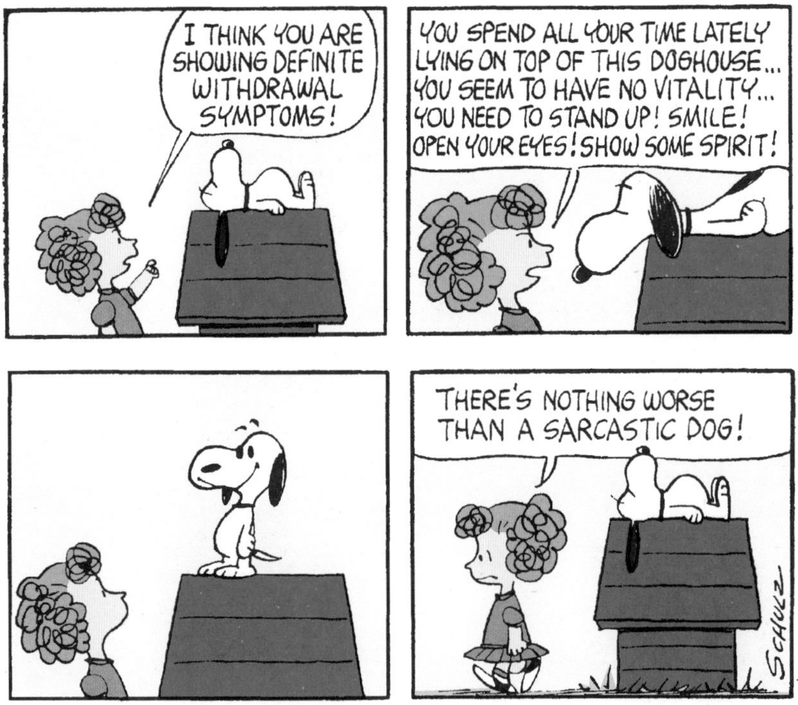
I THINK YOU ARE SHOWING DEFINITE WITHDRAWAL SYMPTOMS!
YOU SPEND ALL YOUR TIME LATELY LYING ON TOP OF THIS DOGHOUSE... YOU SEEM TO HAVE NO VITALITY... YOU NEED TO STAND UP! SMILE! OPEN YOUR EYES! SHOW SOME SPIRIT!
THERE'S NOTHING WORSE THAN A SARCASTIC DOG!
SCHULZ

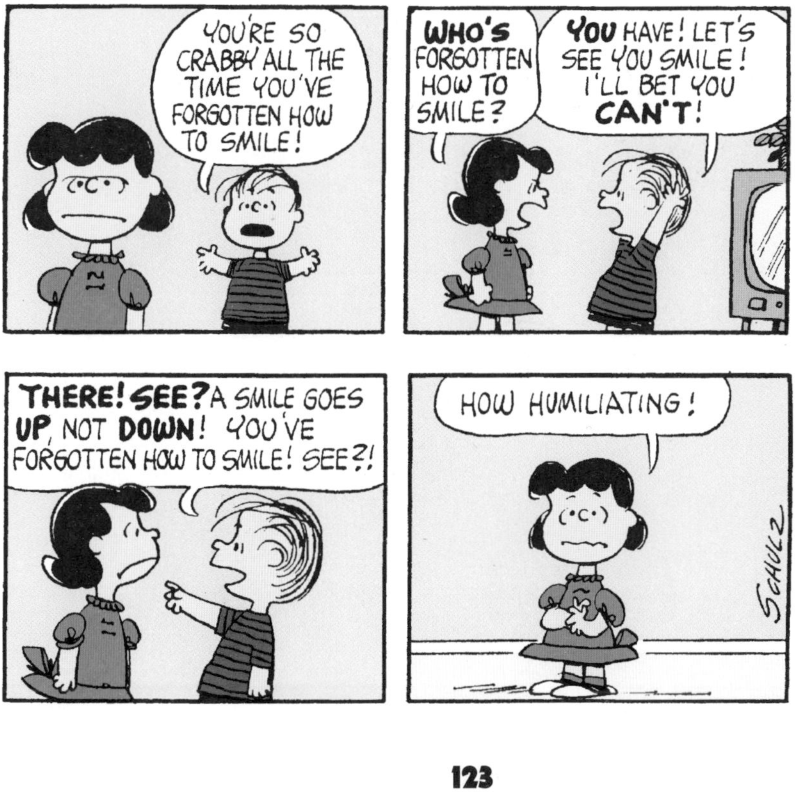
YOU'RE SO CRABBY ALL THE TIME YOU'VE FORGOTTEN HOW TO SMILE!
WHO'S FORGOTTEN HOW TO SMILE?
YOU HAVE! LET'S SEE YOU SMILE! I'LL BET YOU CAN'T!
THERE! SEE? A SMILE GOES UP, NOT DOWN! YOU'VE FORGOTTEN HOW TO SMILE! SEE?!
HOW HUMILIATING!
SCHULZ

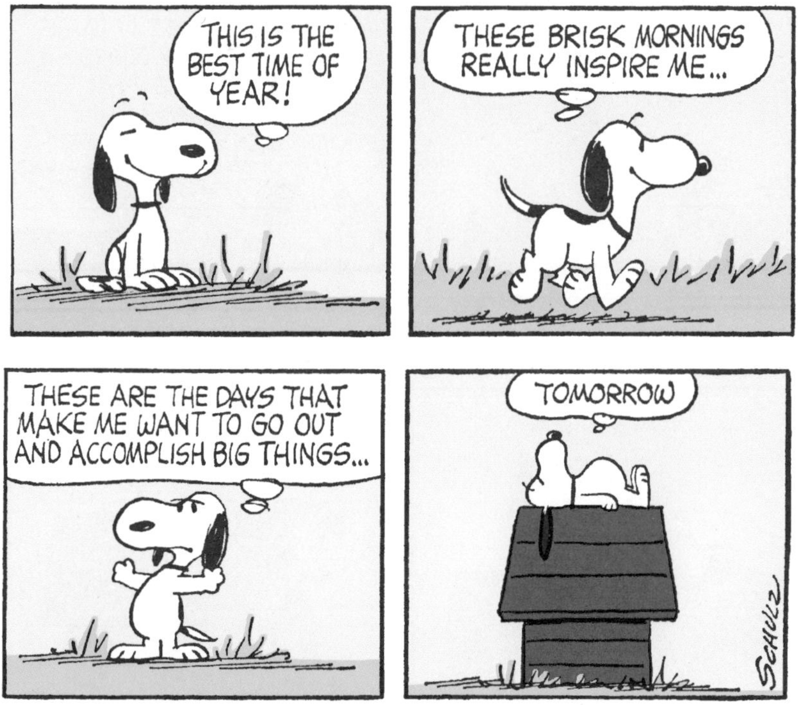
THIS IS THE BEST TIME OF YEAR!
THESE BRISK MORNINGS REALLY INSPIRE ME...
THESE ARE THE DAYS THAT MAKE ME WANT TO GO OUT AND ACCOMPLISH BIG THINGS...
TOMORROW
SCHULZ

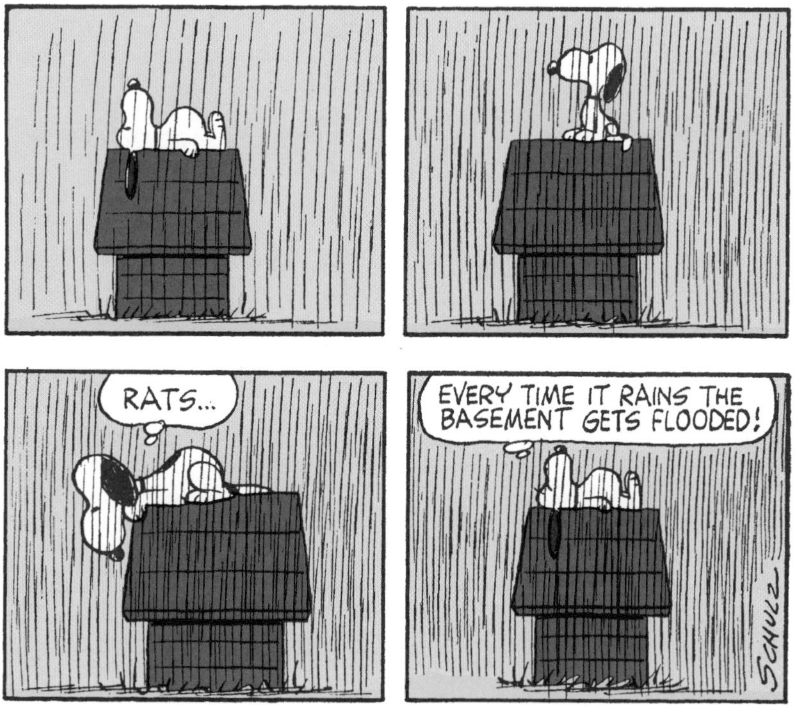
RATS...
EVERY TIME IT RAINS THE BASEMENT GETS FLOODED!
SCHULZ

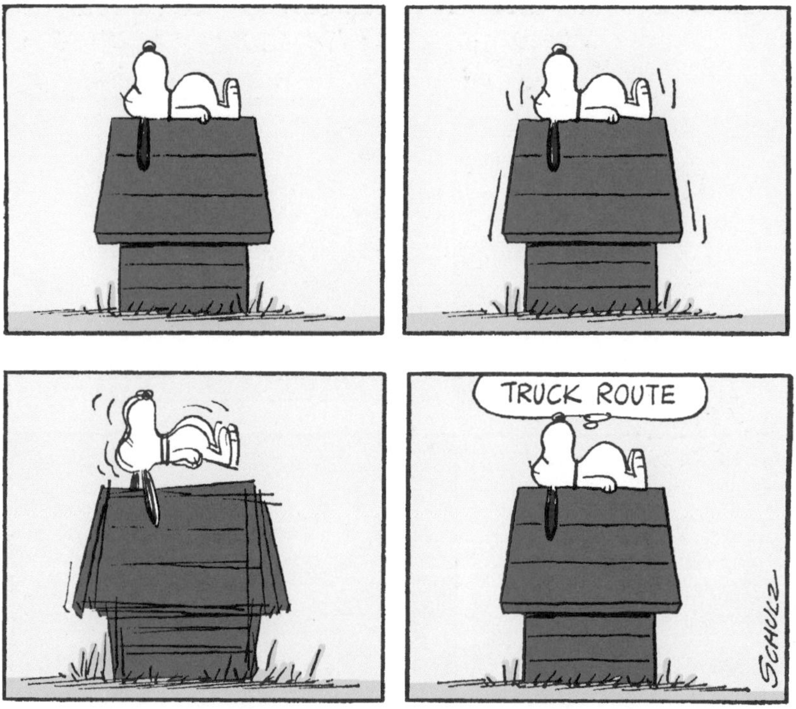
TRUCK ROUTE
SCHULZ

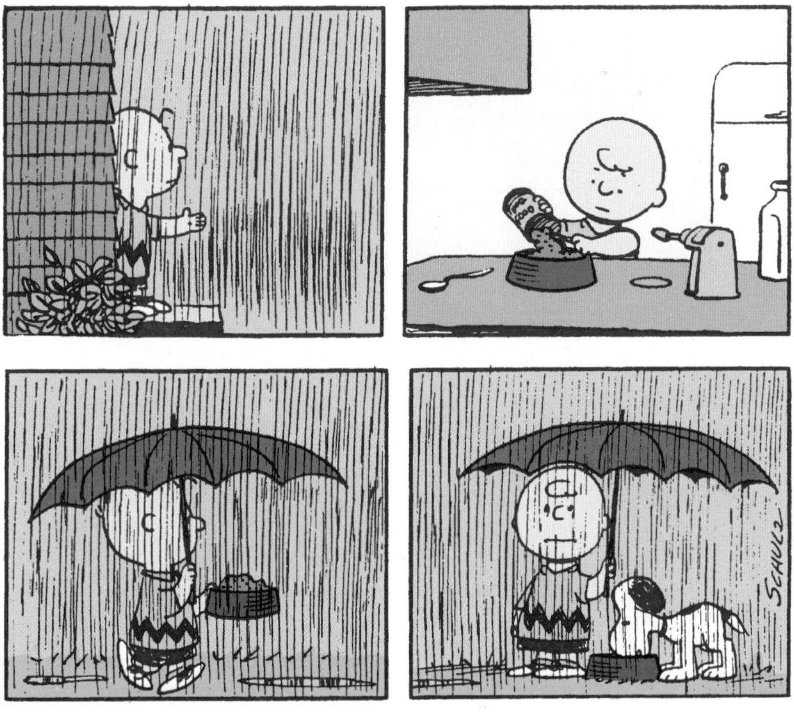
SCHULZ

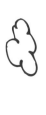

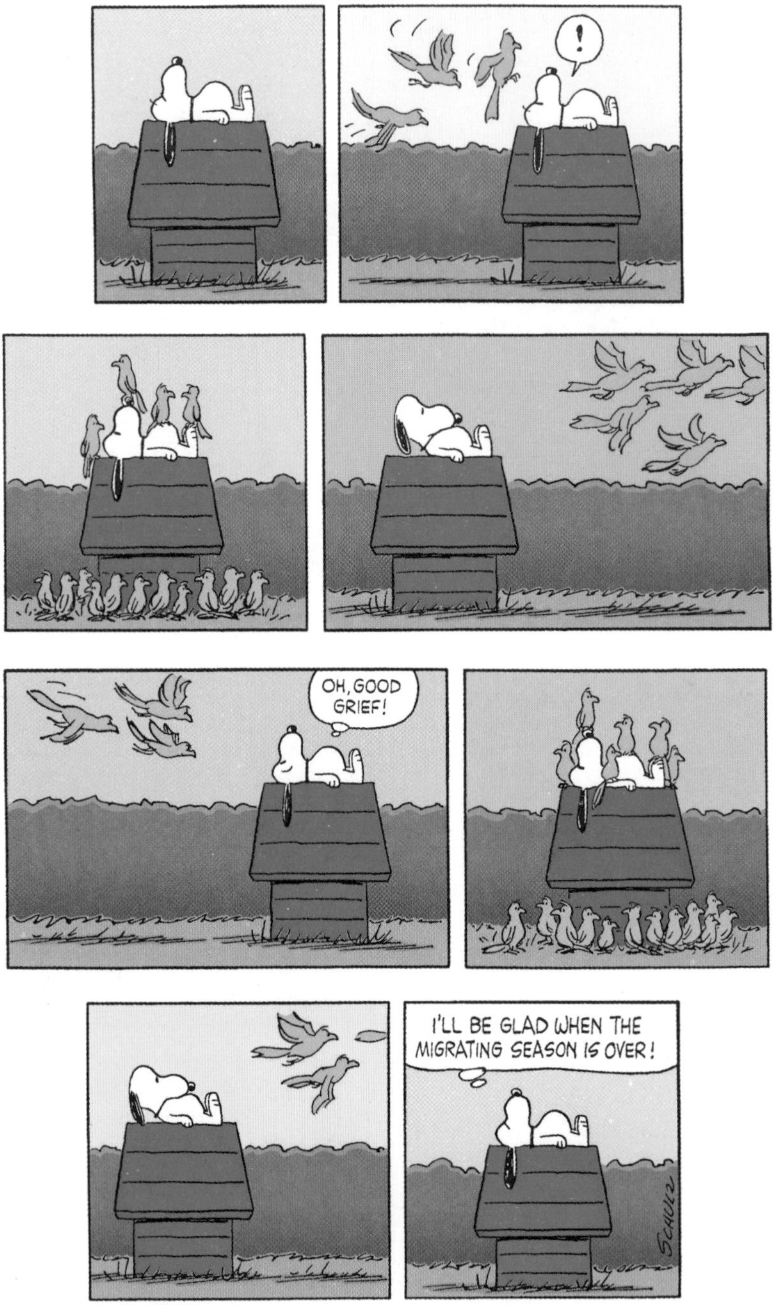
!
OH, GOOD GRIEF!
I'LL BE GLAD WHEN THE MIGRATING SEASON IS OVER!
SCHULZ

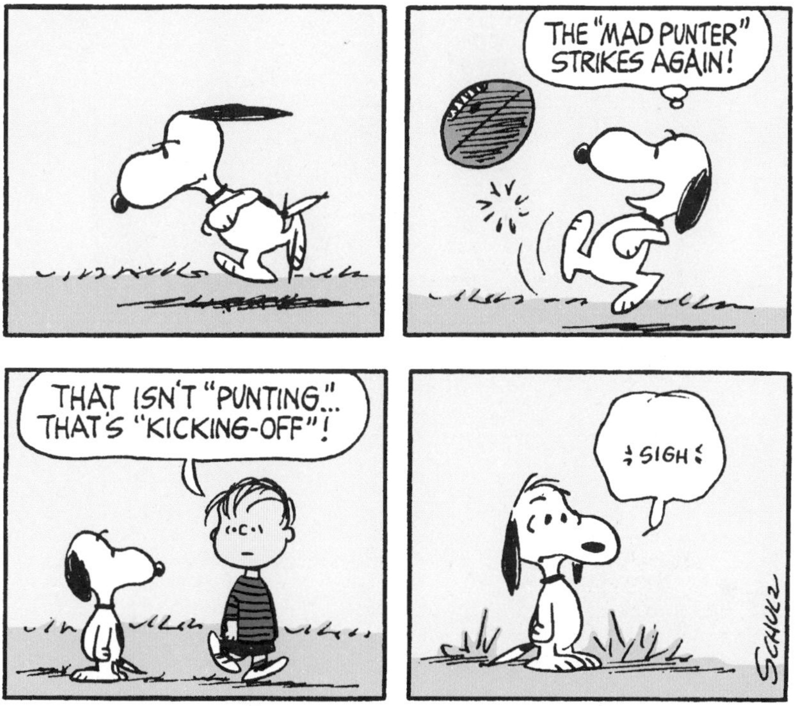
THE "MAD PUNTER" STRIKES AGAIN!
THAT ISN'T "PUNTING"... THAT'S "KICKING-OFF"!
SIGH

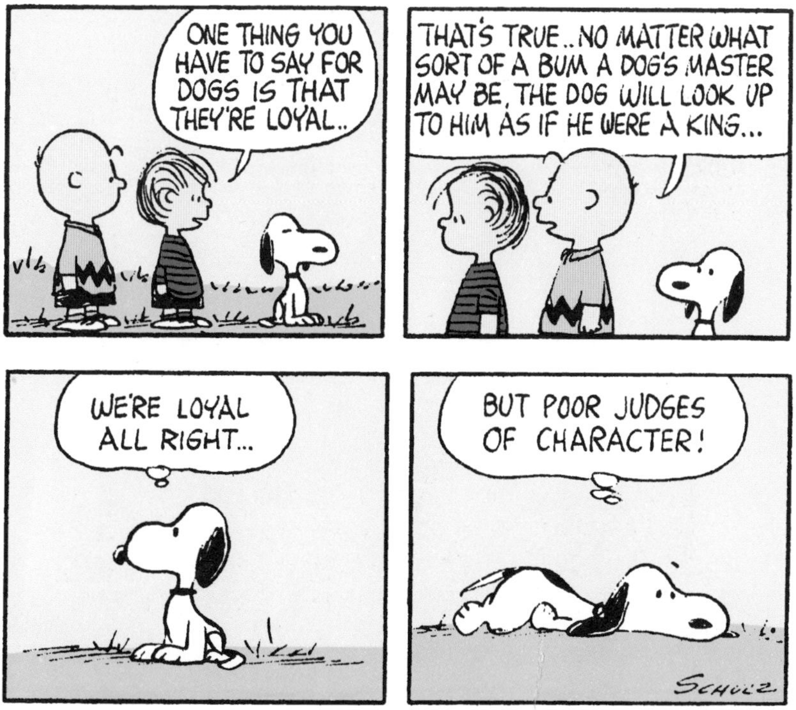
ONE THING YOU HAVE TO SAY FOR DOGS IS THAT THEY'RE LOYAL..
THAT'S TRUE..NO MATTER WHAT SORT OF A BUM A DOG'S MASTER MAY BE, THE DOG WILL LOOK UP TO HIM AS IF HE WERE A KING...
WE'RE LOYAL ALL RIGHT...
BUT POOR JUDGES OF CHARACTER!

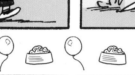

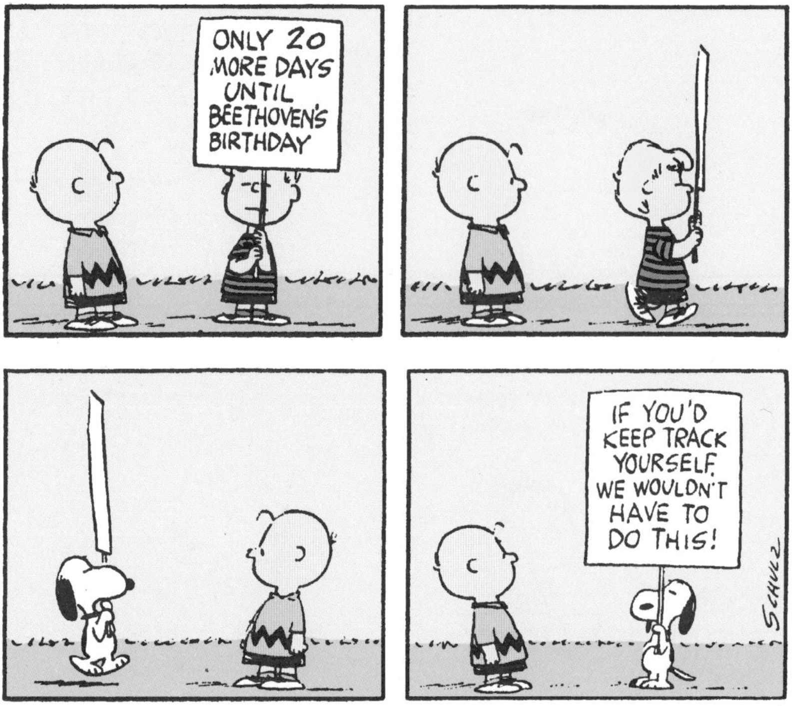
ONLY 20 MORE DAYS UNTIL BEETHOVEN'S BIRTHDAY
IF YOU'D KEEP TRACK YOURSELF, WE WOULDN'T HAVE TO DO THIS!
SCHULZ

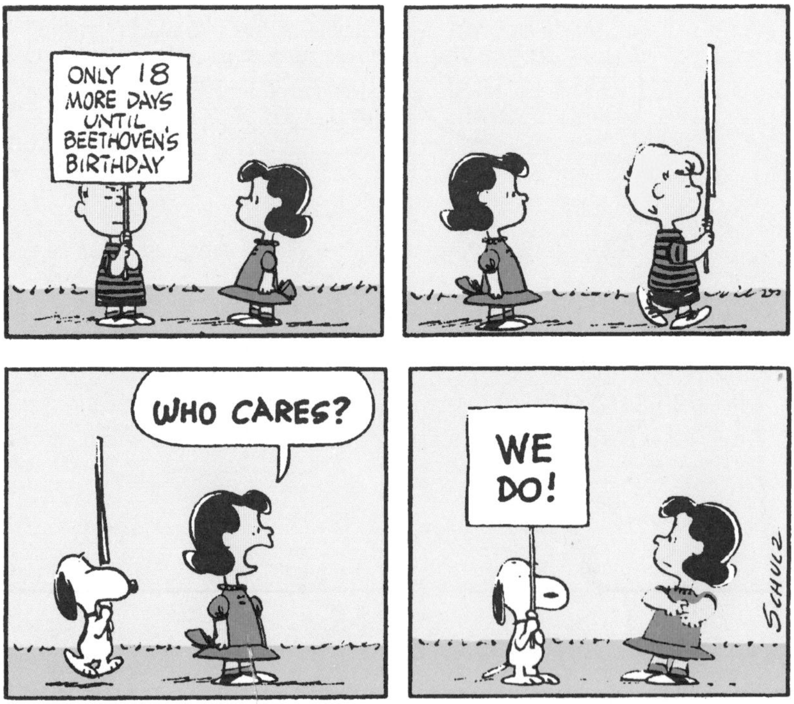
ONLY 18 MORE DAYS UNTIL BEETHOVEN'S BIRTHDAY
WHO CARES?
WE DO!
SCHULZ

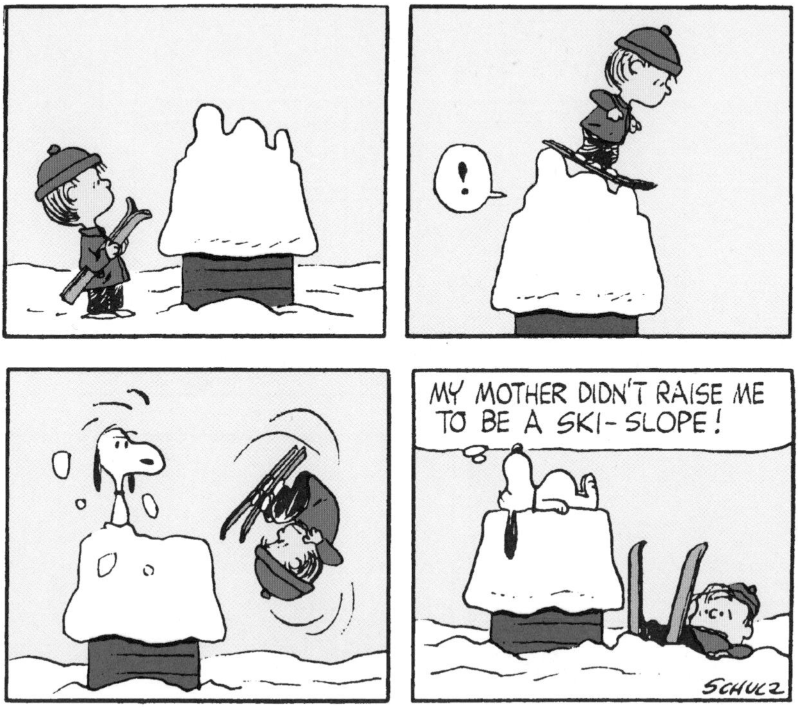
!
MY MOTHER DIDN'T RAISE ME TO BE A SKI-SLOPE!
SCHULZ

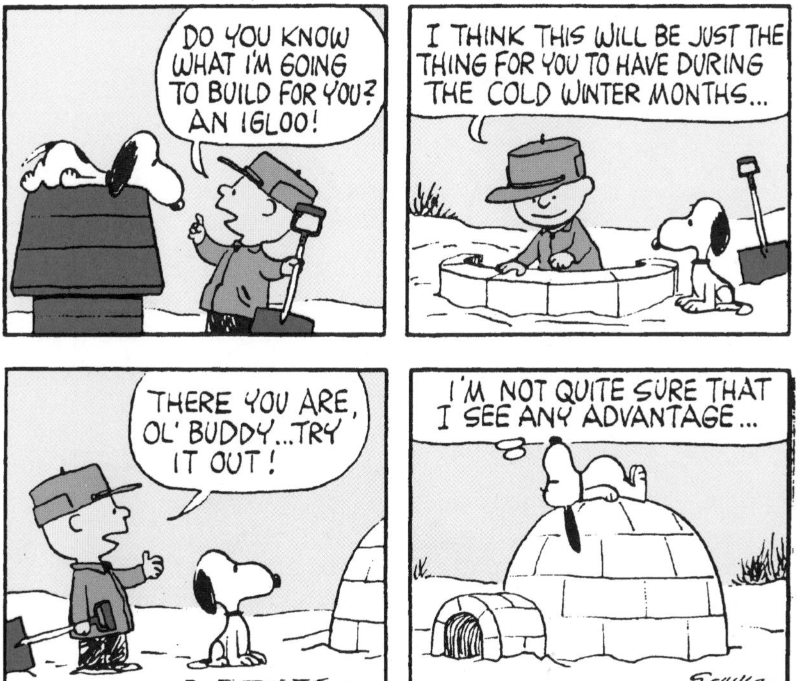
DO YOU KNOW WHAT I'M GOING TO BUILD FOR YOU? AN IGLOO!
I THINK THIS WILL BE JUST THE THING FOR YOU TO HAVE DURING THE COLD WINTER MONTHS...
THERE YOU ARE, OL' BUDDY...TRY IT OUT!
I'M NOT QUITE SURE THAT I SEE ANY ADVANTAGE...
SCHULZ

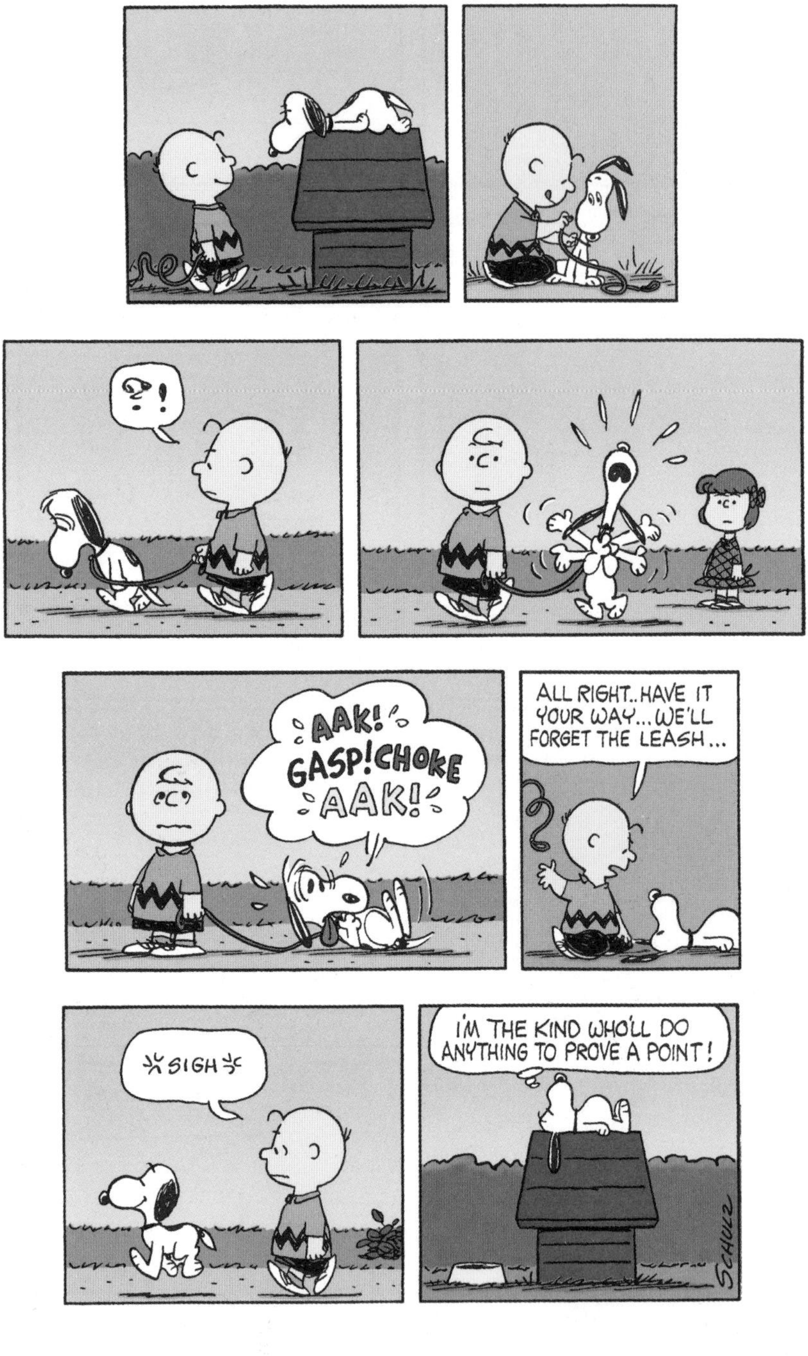
?!
AAK! GASP! CHOKE AAK!
ALL RIGHT..HAVE IT YOUR WAY...WE'LL FORGET THE LEASH...
SIGH
I'M THE KIND WHO'LL DO ANYTHING TO PROVE A POINT!
SCHULZ

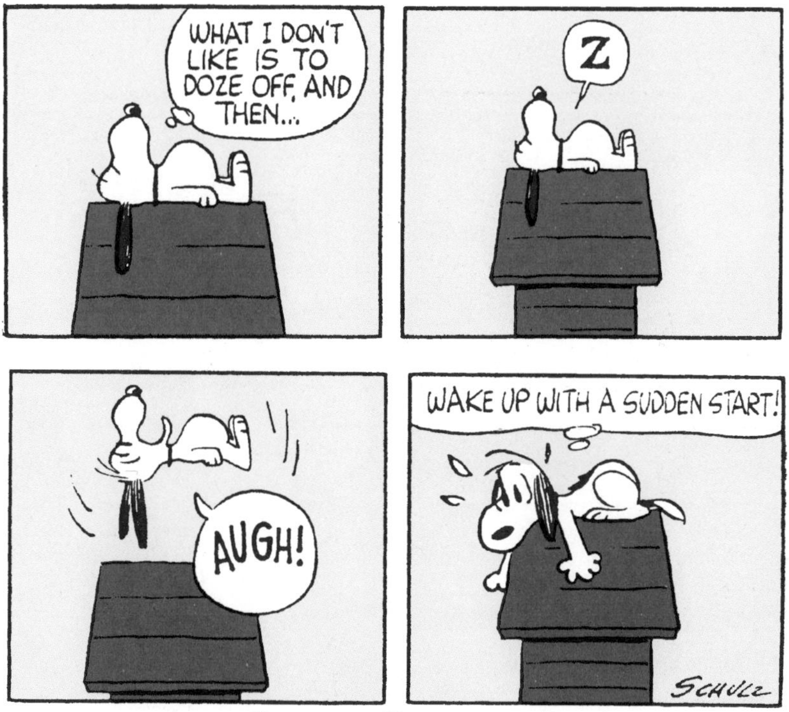
WHAT I DON'T LIKE IS TO DOZE OFF, AND THEN...
Z
AUGH!
WAKE UP WITH A SUDDEN START!
SCHULZ

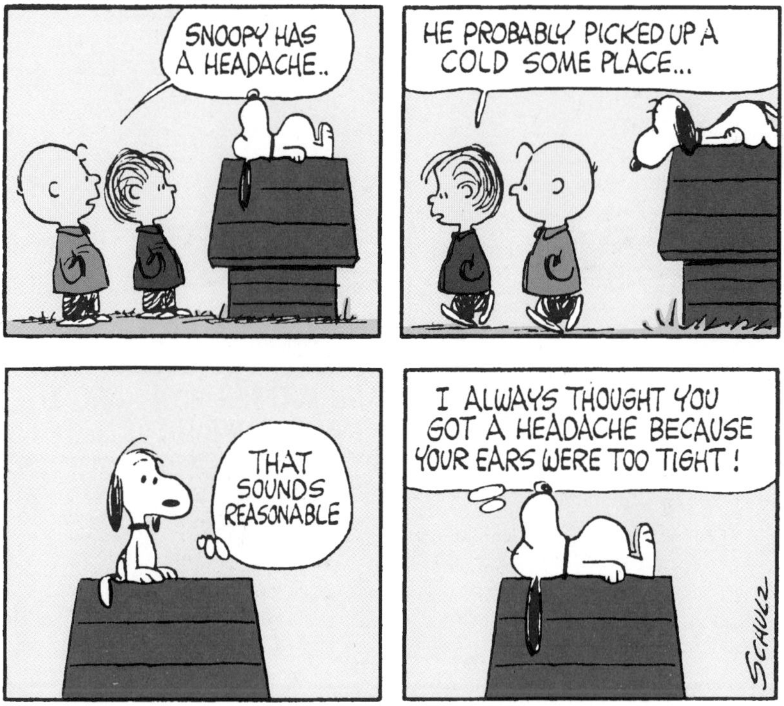
SNOOPY HAS A HEADACHE..
HE PROBABLY PICKED UP A COLD SOME PLACE...
THAT SOUNDS REASONABLE
I ALWAYS THOUGHT YOU GOT A HEADACHE BECAUSE YOUR EARS WERE TOO TIGHT!
SCHULZ

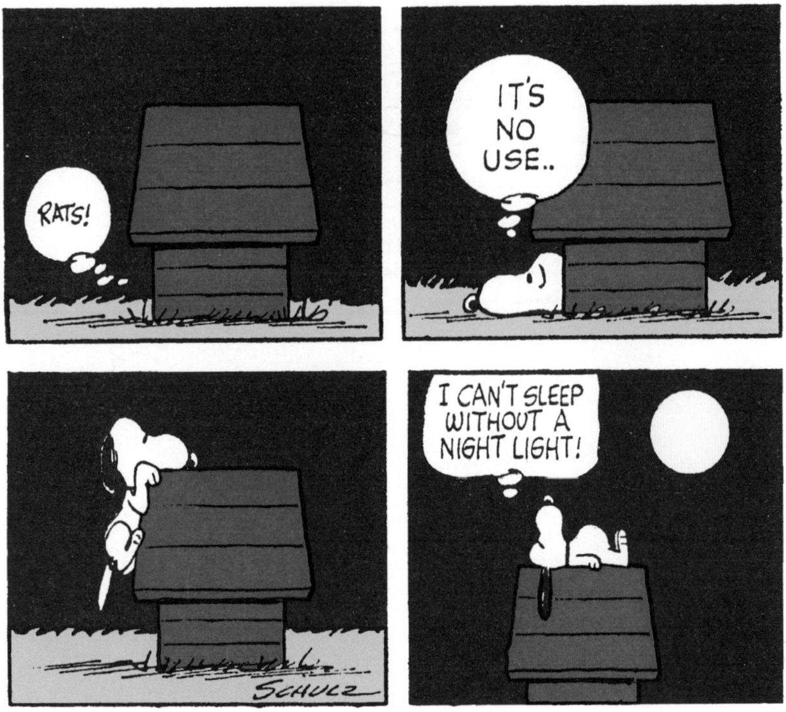
RATS!
IT'S NO USE..
I CAN'T SLEEP WITHOUT A NIGHT LIGHT!
SCHULZ

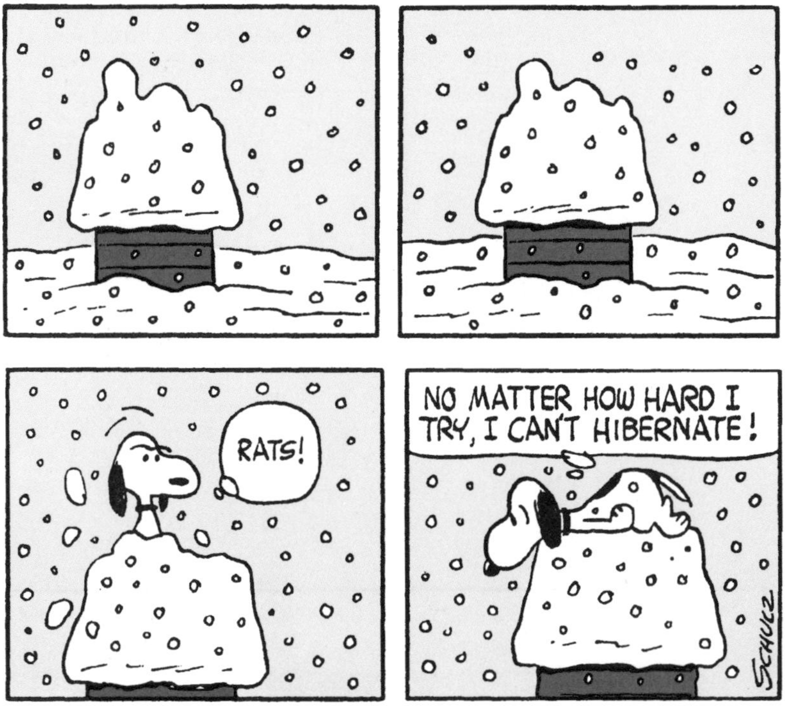
RATS!
NO MATTER HOW HARD I TRY, I CAN'T HIBERNATE!
SCHULZ

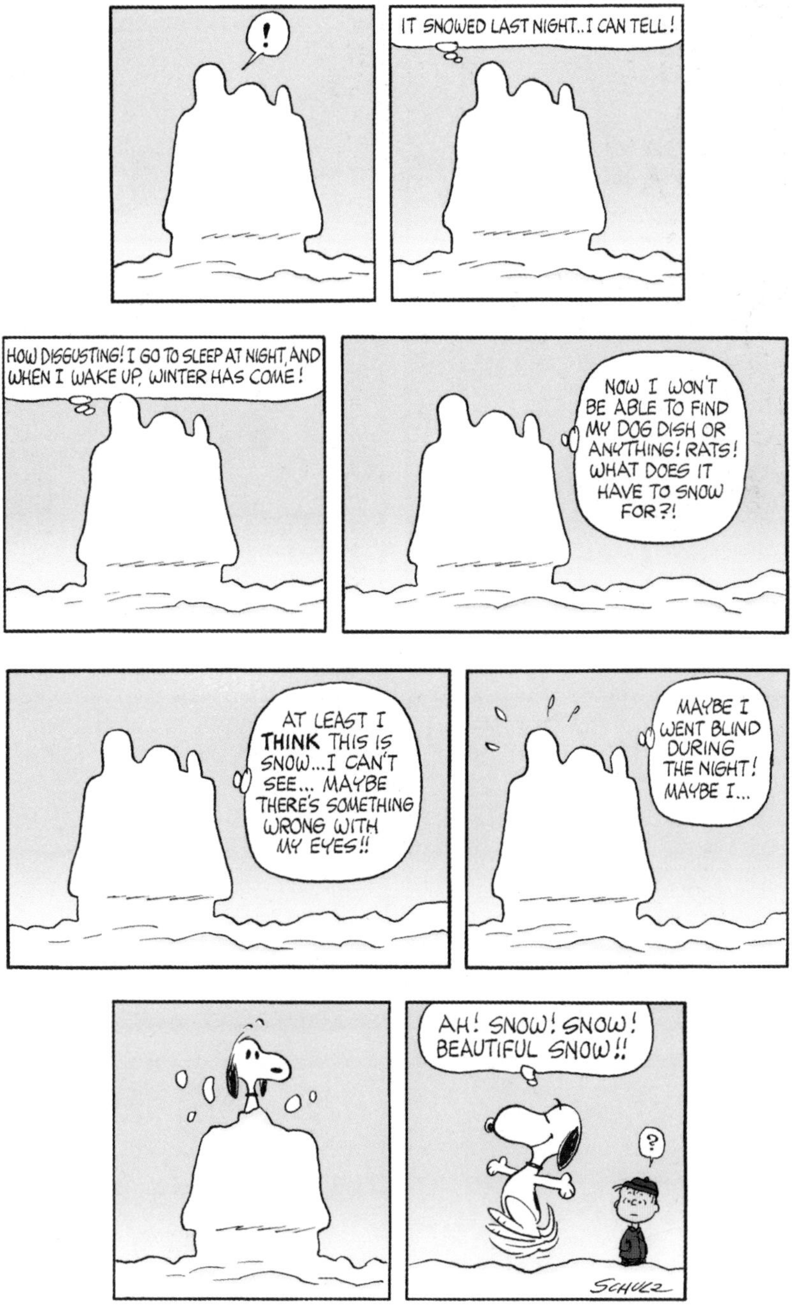
!
IT SNOWED LAST NIGHT..I CAN TELL!
HOW DISGUSTING! I GO TO SLEEP AT NIGHT, AND WHEN I WAKE UP, WINTER HAS COME!
NOW I WON'T BE ABLE TO FIND MY DOG DISH OR ANYTHING! RATS! WHAT DOES IT HAVE TO SNOW FOR?!
AT LEAST I **THINK** THIS IS SNOW...I CAN'T SEE... MAYBE THERE'S SOMETHING WRONG WITH MY EYES!!
MAYBE I WENT BLIND DURING THE NIGHT! MAYBE I...
AH! SNOW! SNOW! BEAUTIFUL SNOW!!
?
SCHULZ

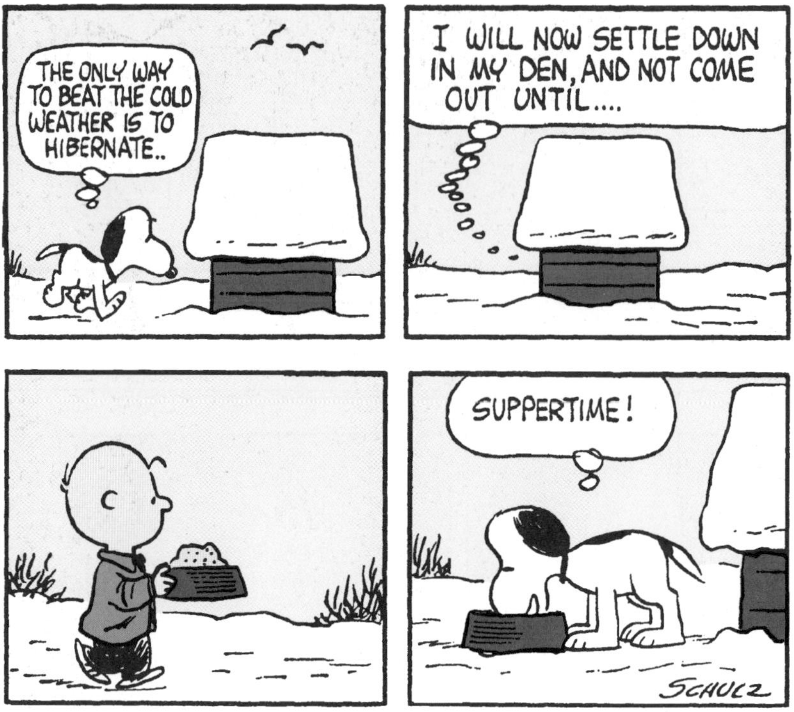
THE ONLY WAY TO BEAT THE COLD WEATHER IS TO HIBERNATE..
I WILL NOW SETTLE DOWN IN MY DEN, AND NOT COME OUT UNTIL....
SUPPERTIME!
SCHULZ

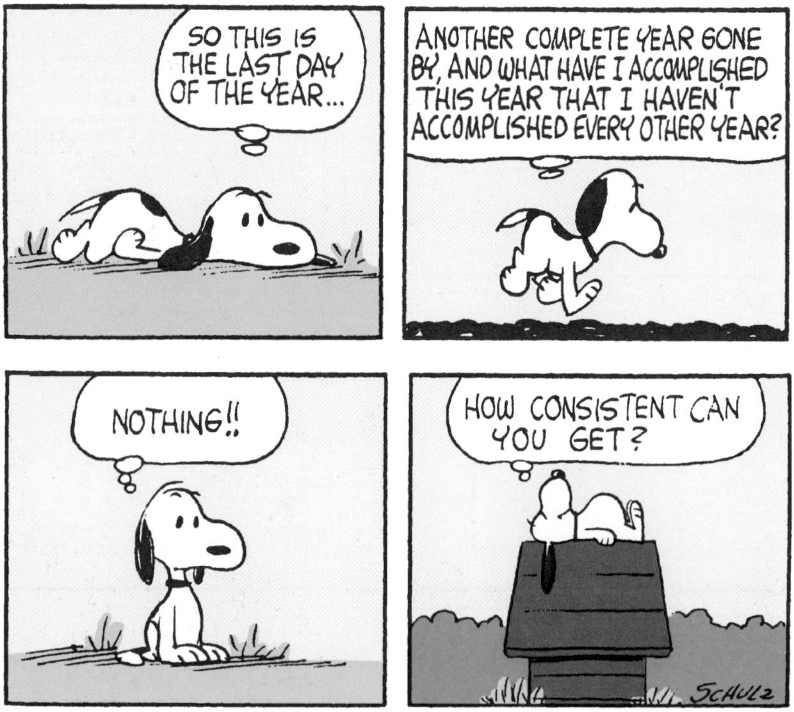
SO THIS IS THE LAST DAY OF THE YEAR...
ANOTHER COMPLETE YEAR GONE BY, AND WHAT HAVE I ACCOMPLISHED THIS YEAR THAT I HAVEN'T ACCOMPLISHED EVERY OTHER YEAR?
NOTHING!!
HOW CONSISTENT CAN YOU GET?
SCHULZ

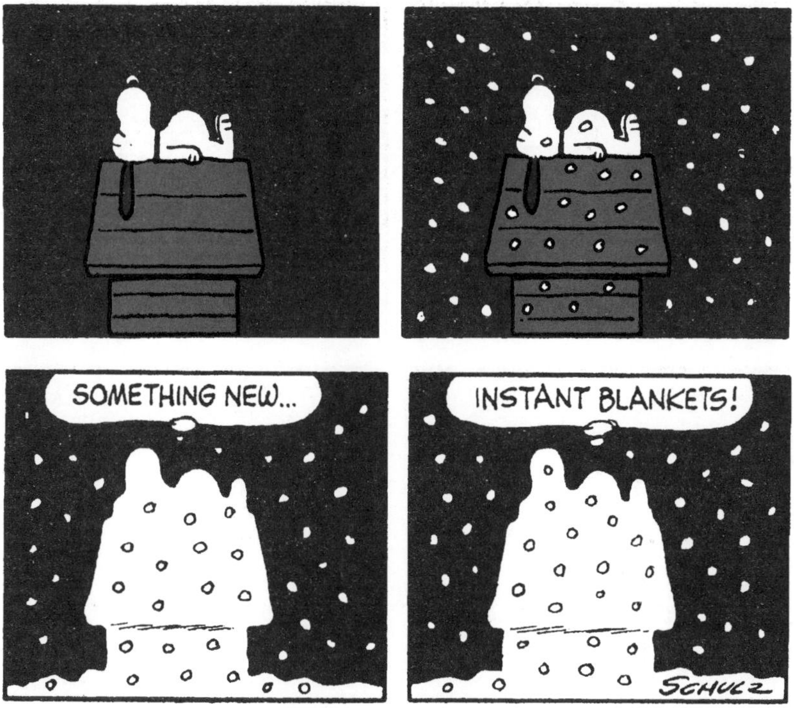
SOMETHING NEW...
INSTANT BLANKETS!
SCHULZ

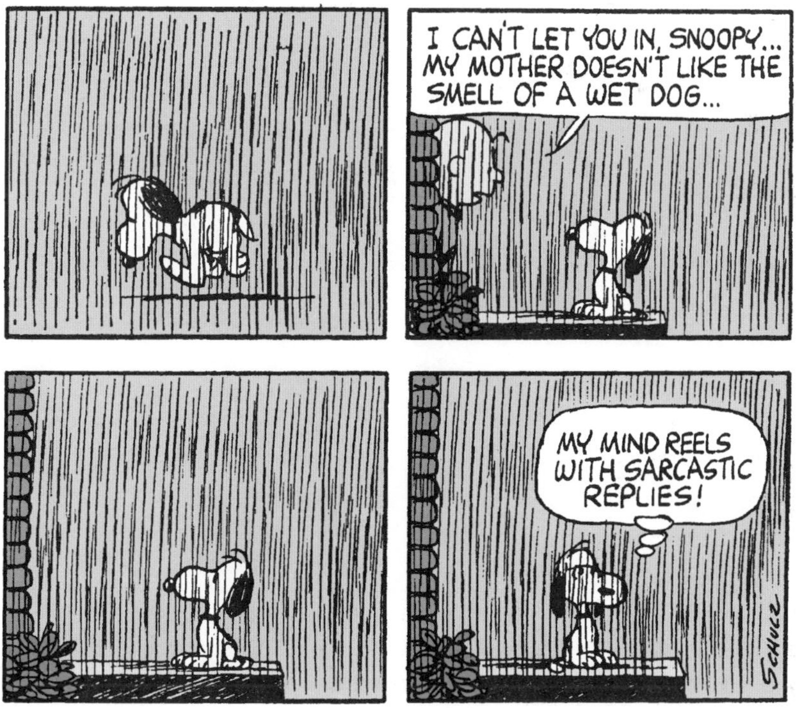
I CAN'T LET YOU IN, SNOOPY... MY MOTHER DOESN'T LIKE THE SMELL OF A WET DOG...
MY MIND REELS WITH SARCASTIC REPLIES!
SCHULZ

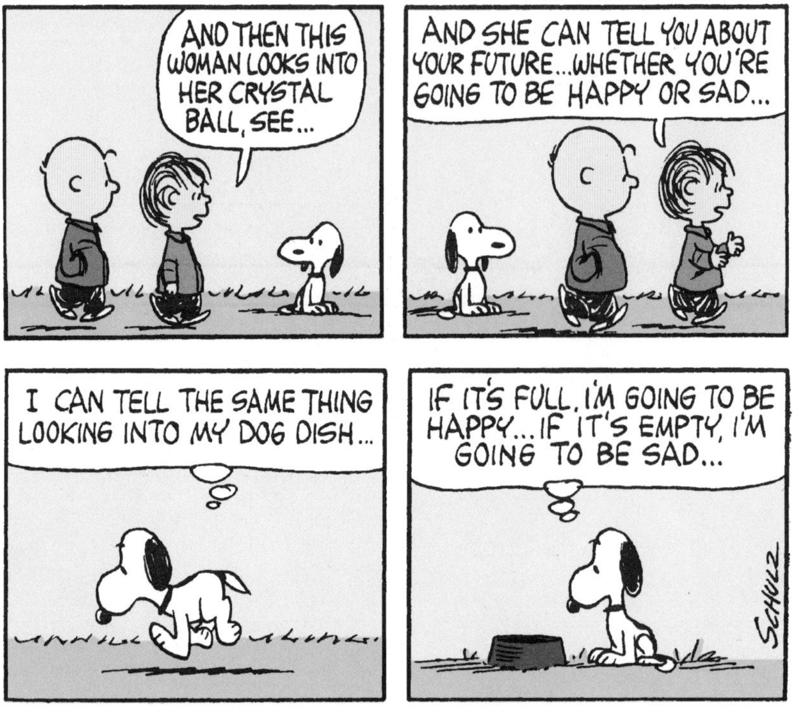
AND THEN THIS WOMAN LOOKS INTO HER CRYSTAL BALL, SEE...
AND SHE CAN TELL YOU ABOUT YOUR FUTURE...WHETHER YOU'RE GOING TO BE HAPPY OR SAD...
I CAN TELL THE SAME THING LOOKING INTO MY DOG DISH...
IF IT'S FULL, I'M GOING TO BE HAPPY...IF IT'S EMPTY, I'M GOING TO BE SAD...
SCHULZ

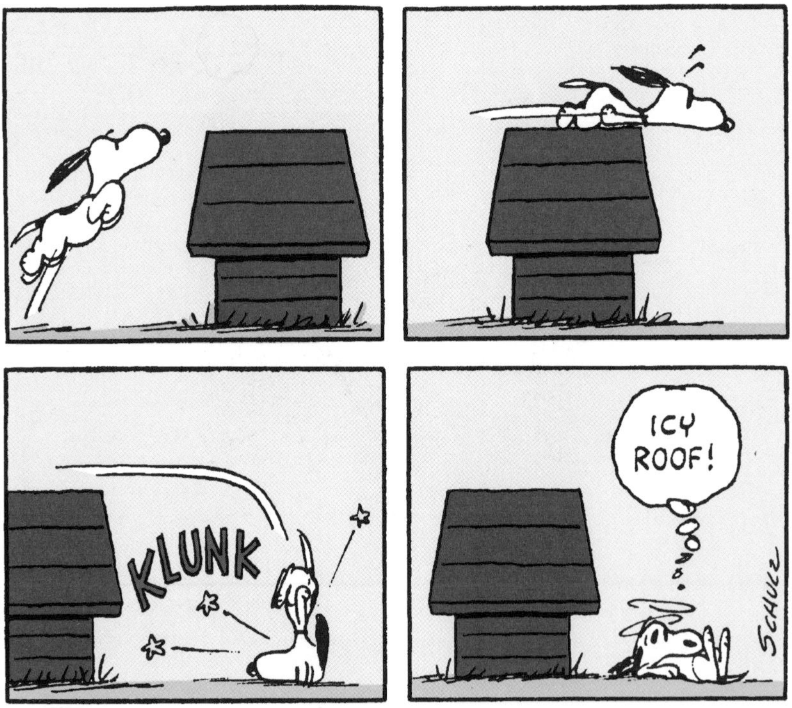
KLUNK
ICY ROOF!
SCHULZ

GOOD GRIEF! MY FEET ARE LIKE ICE!
I'M GOING TO HAVE TO DO SOMETHING TO HELP SNOOPY
HIS FEET GET AWFULLY COLD AT NIGHT..
HOW ABOUT A BLANKET?
BLANKETS HAVE A WAY OF SLIPPING OFF..
HOW ABOUT SOCKS? MAYBE HE COULD WEAR SOME WOOL SOCKS...OR MAYBE EVEN BOOTS...HOW ABOUT SOME BOOTS?
BOOTS! I THINK YOU HAVE SOMETHING THERE...
SCHULZ

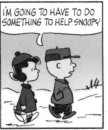

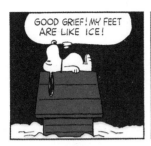

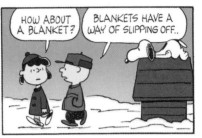

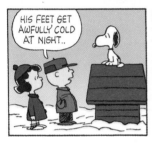

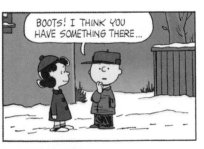

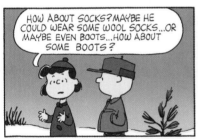

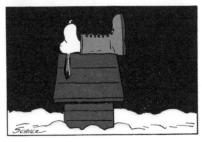

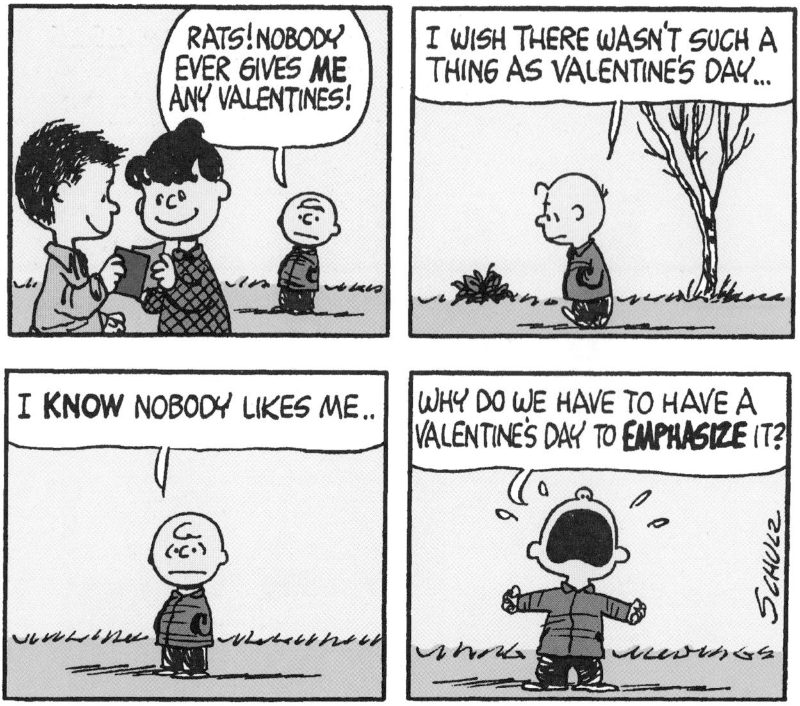
RATS! NOBODY EVER GIVES ME ANY VALENTINES!
I WISH THERE WASN'T SUCH A THING AS VALENTINE'S DAY...
I KNOW NOBODY LIKES ME..
WHY DO WE HAVE TO HAVE A VALENTINE'S DAY TO EMPHASIZE IT?
SCHULZ

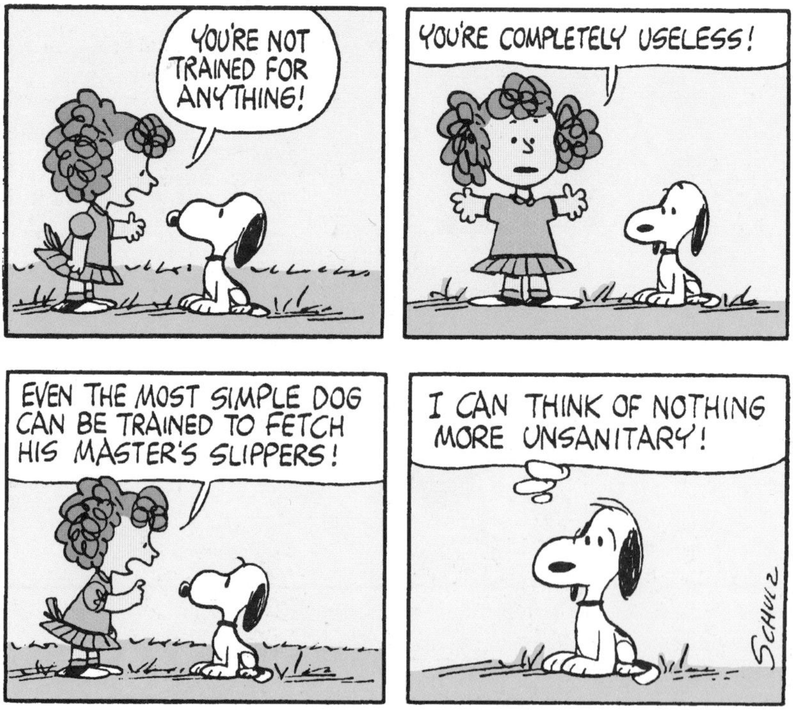
YOU'RE NOT TRAINED FOR ANYTHING!
YOU'RE COMPLETELY USELESS!
EVEN THE MOST SIMPLE DOG CAN BE TRAINED TO FETCH HIS MASTER'S SLIPPERS!
I CAN THINK OF NOTHING MORE UNSANITARY!
SCHULZ

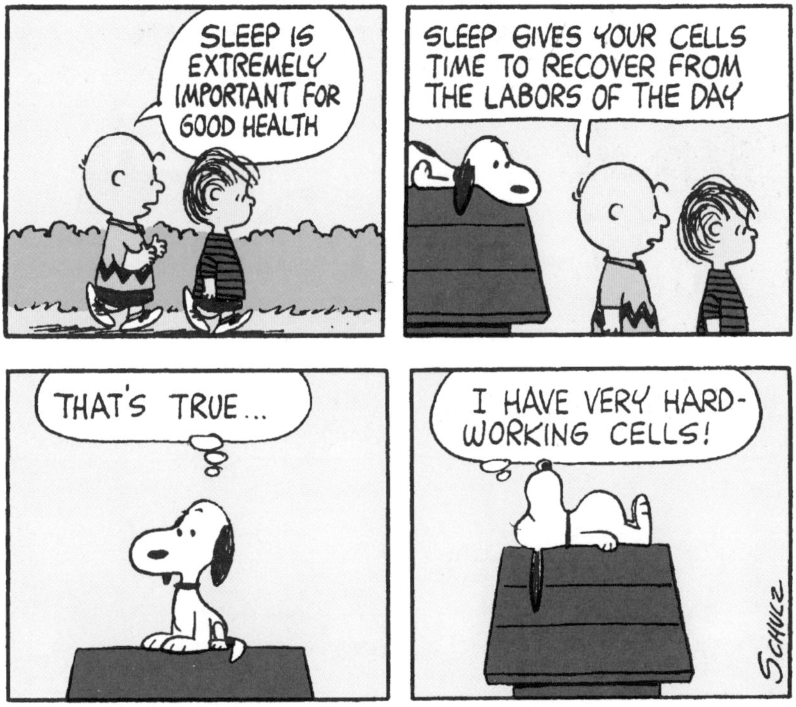
SLEEP IS EXTREMELY IMPORTANT FOR GOOD HEALTH
SLEEP GIVES YOUR CELLS TIME TO RECOVER FROM THE LABORS OF THE DAY
THAT'S TRUE...
I HAVE VERY HARD-WORKING CELLS!
SCHULZ

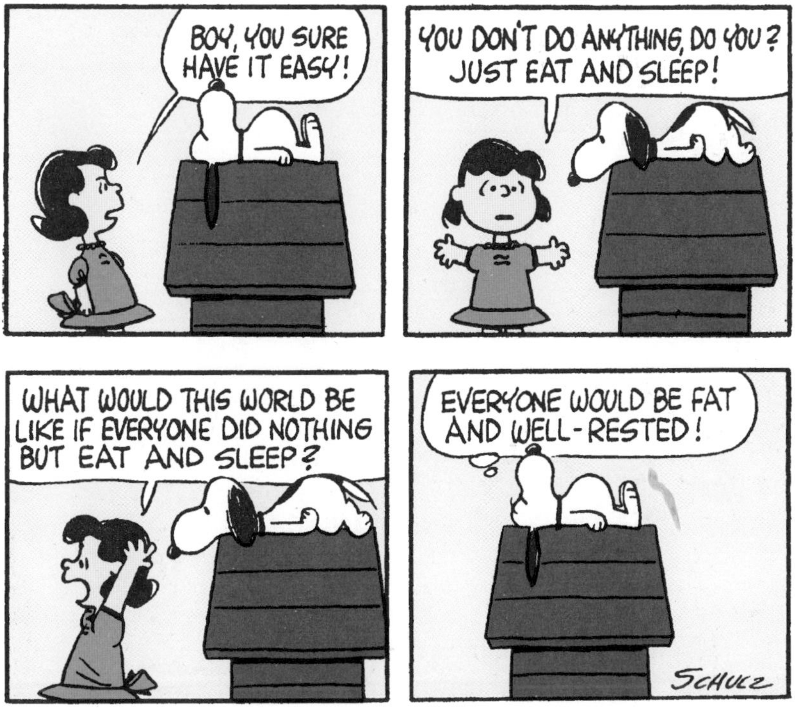
BOY, YOU SURE HAVE IT EASY!
YOU DON'T DO ANYTHING, DO YOU? JUST EAT AND SLEEP!
WHAT WOULD THIS WORLD BE LIKE IF EVERYONE DID NOTHING BUT EAT AND SLEEP?
EVERYONE WOULD BE FAT AND WELL-RESTED!
SCHULZ

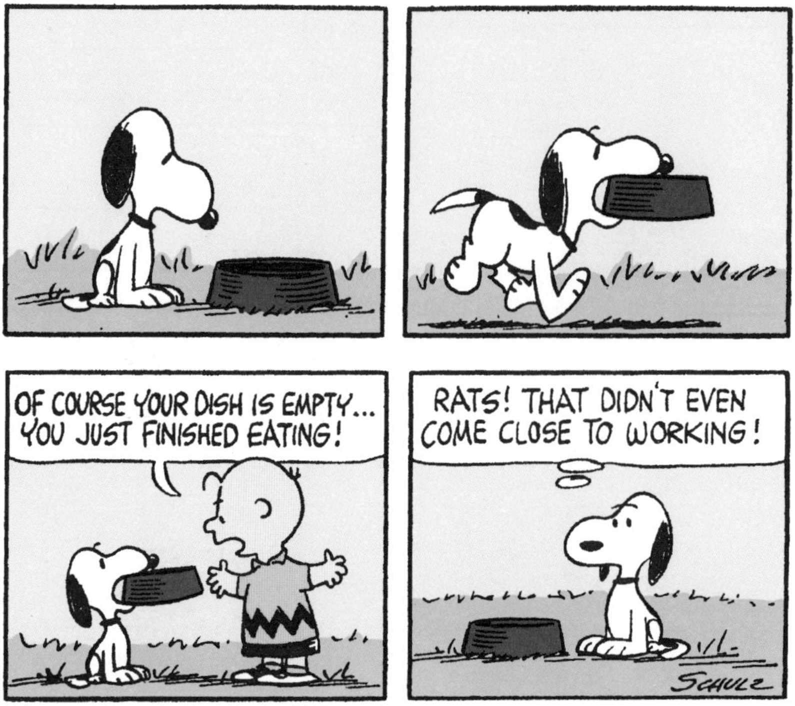
OF COURSE YOUR DISH IS EMPTY... YOU JUST FINISHED EATING!
RATS! THAT DIDN'T EVEN COME CLOSE TO WORKING!
SCHULZ

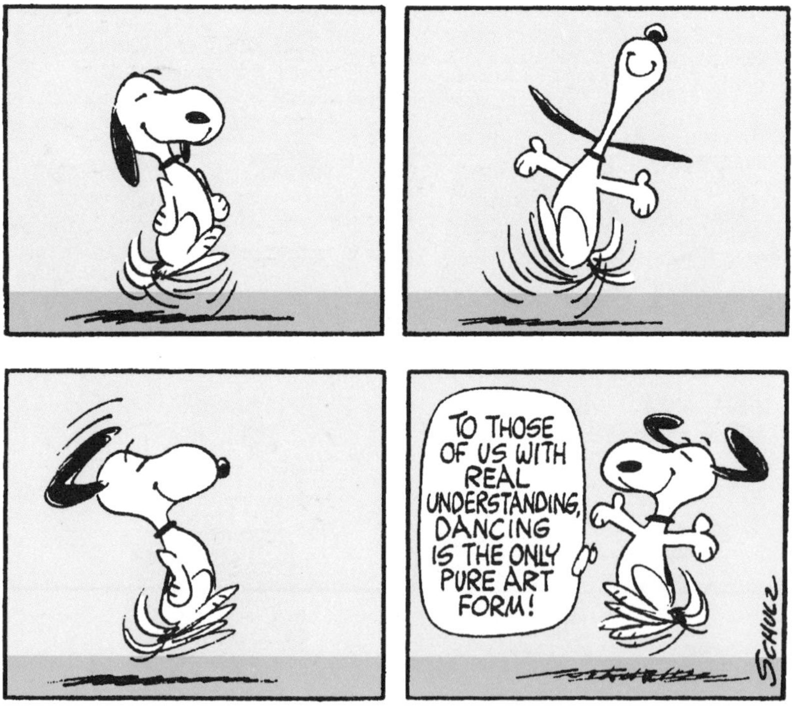
TO THOSE OF US WITH REAL UNDERSTANDING, DANCING IS THE ONLY PURE ART FORM!
SCHULZ

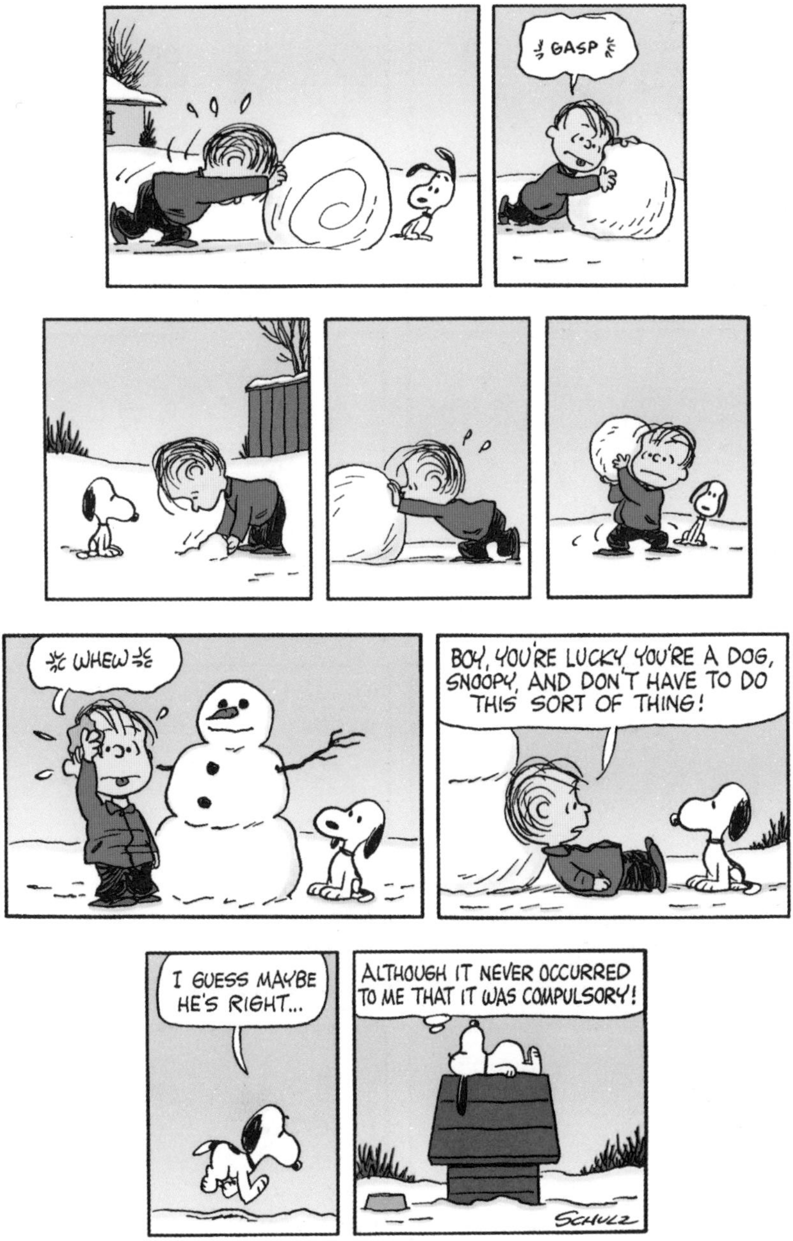
GASP
WHEW
BOY, YOU'RE LUCKY YOU'RE A DOG, SNOOPY, AND DON'T HAVE TO DO THIS SORT OF THING!
I GUESS MAYBE HE'S RIGHT...
ALTHOUGH IT NEVER OCCURRED TO ME THAT IT WAS COMPULSORY!
SCHULZ

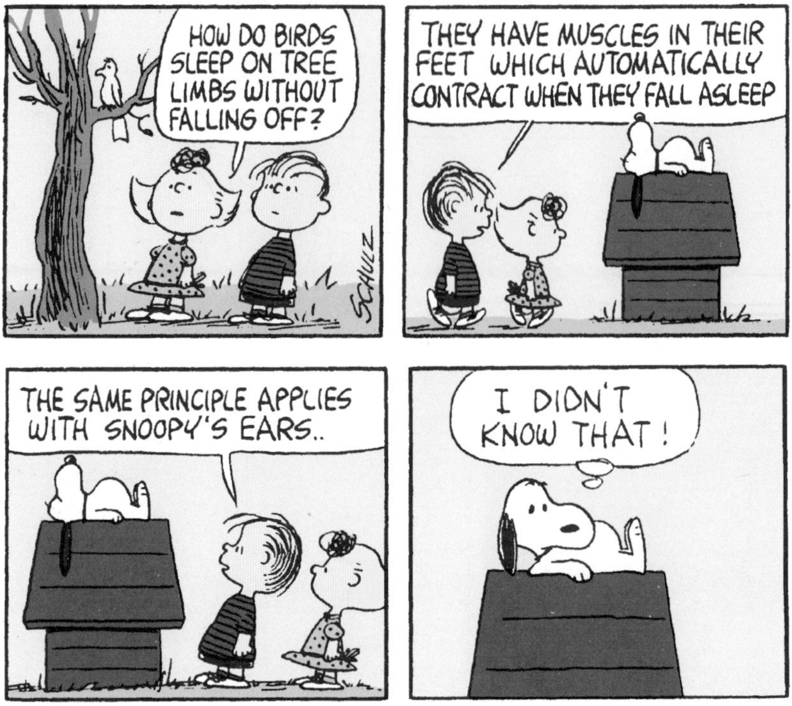
HOW DO BIRDS SLEEP ON TREE LIMBS WITHOUT FALLING OFF?
SCHULZ
THEY HAVE MUSCLES IN THEIR FEET WHICH AUTOMATICALLY CONTRACT WHEN THEY FALL ASLEEP
THE SAME PRINCIPLE APPLIES WITH SNOOPY'S EARS..
I DIDN'T KNOW THAT!

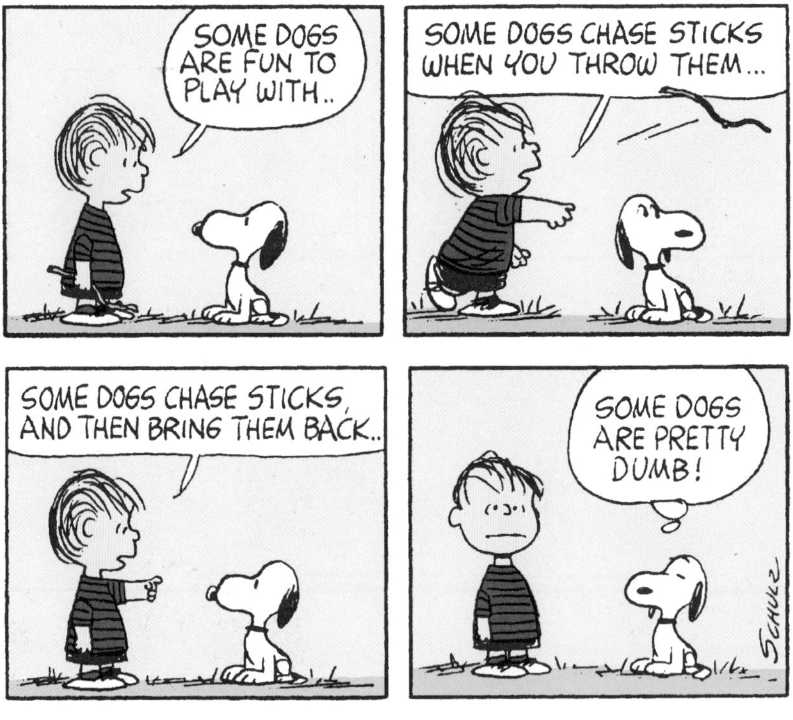
SOME DOGS ARE FUN TO PLAY WITH..
SOME DOGS CHASE STICKS WHEN YOU THROW THEM...
SOME DOGS CHASE STICKS, AND THEN BRING THEM BACK..
SOME DOGS ARE PRETTY DUMB!
SCHULZ

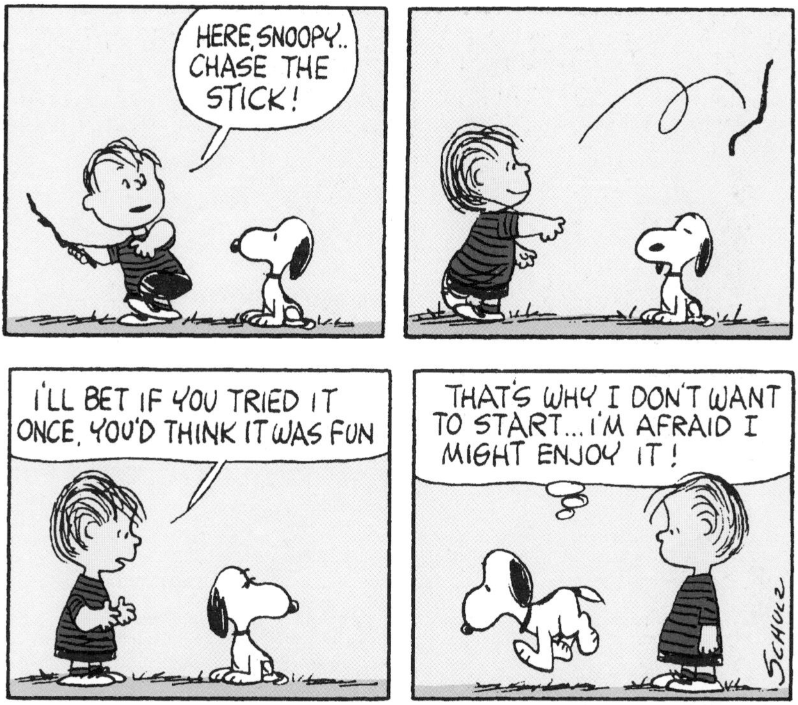
HERE, SNOOPY.. CHASE THE STICK!
I'LL BET IF YOU TRIED IT ONCE, YOU'D THINK IT WAS FUN
THAT'S WHY I DON'T WANT TO START... I'M AFRAID I MIGHT ENJOY IT!
SCHULZ

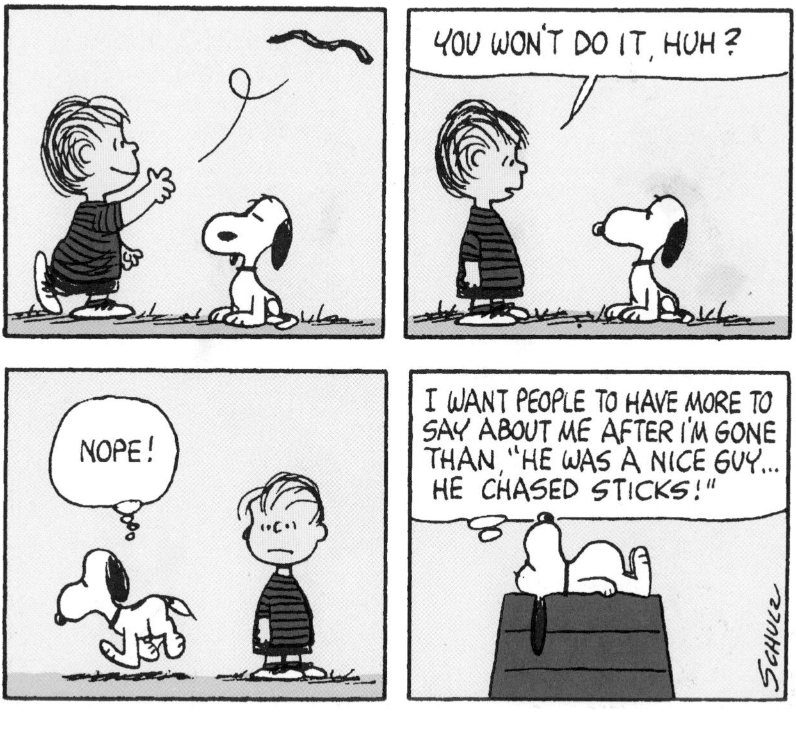
YOU WON'T DO IT, HUH?
NOPE!
I WANT PEOPLE TO HAVE MORE TO SAY ABOUT ME AFTER I'M GONE THAN, "HE WAS A NICE GUY... HE CHASED STICKS!"
SCHULZ

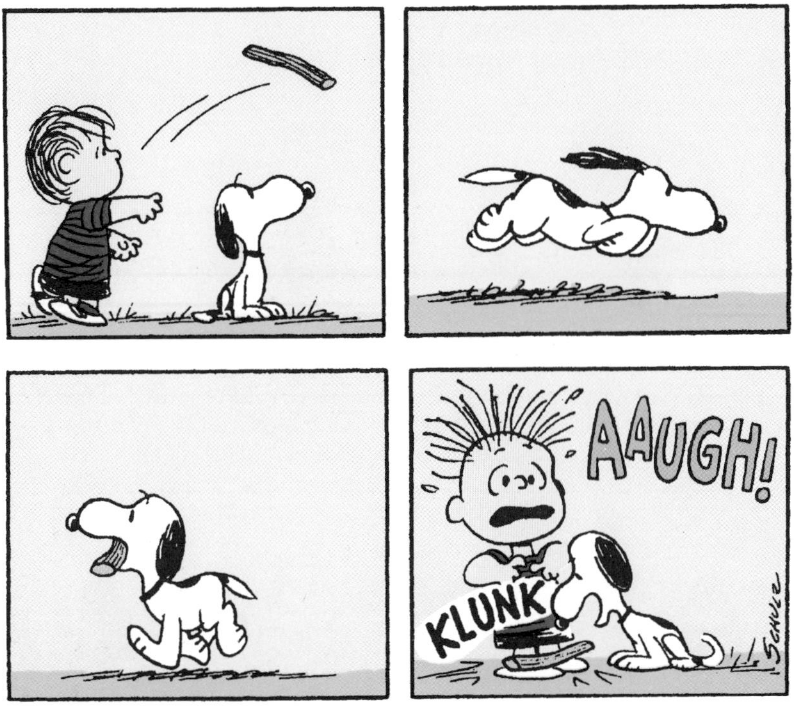

AAUGH!
KLUNK
SCHULZ

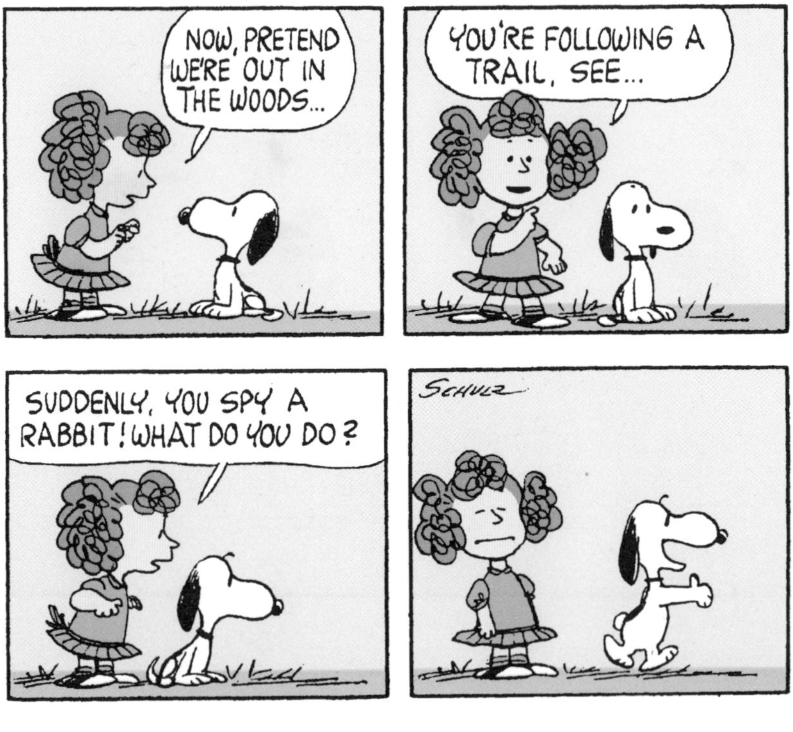

NOW, PRETEND WE'RE OUT IN THE WOODS...
YOU'RE FOLLOWING A TRAIL, SEE...
SUDDENLY, YOU SPY A RABBIT! WHAT DO YOU DO?
SCHULZ

I WORRY ABOUT SNOOPY.. HE STILL SEEMS TO GET COLD AT NIGHT...
I'VE TRIED JUST ABOUT EVERYTHING I CAN THINK OF TO HELP HIM...
I'VE GIVEN HIM BLANKETS, I'VE GIVEN HIM STRAW... I'VE DONE EVERYTHING I CAN THINK OF...
I HAVE AN IDEA...
WHY COULDN'T HE SLEEP INSIDE THE DOGHOUSE INSTEAD OF ON TOP?
I GUESS IT **WAS** SORT OF A RIDICULOUS SUGGESTION!
SCHULZ

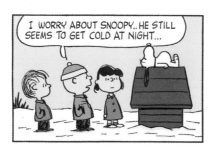

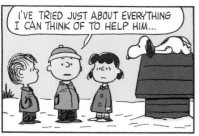

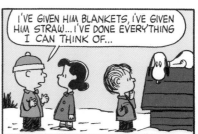

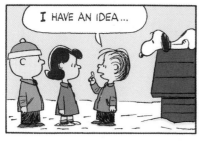

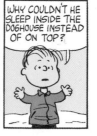

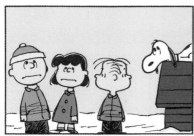

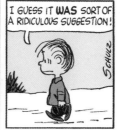

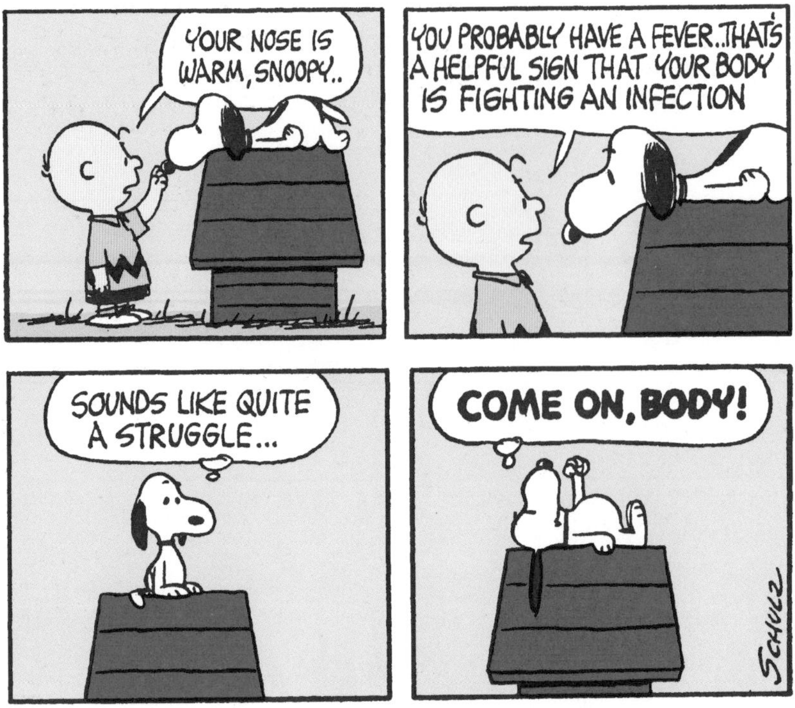
YOUR NOSE IS WARM, SNOOPY..
YOU PROBABLY HAVE A FEVER..THAT'S A HELPFUL SIGN THAT YOUR BODY IS FIGHTING AN INFECTION
SOUNDS LIKE QUITE A STRUGGLE...
COME ON, BODY!
SCHULZ

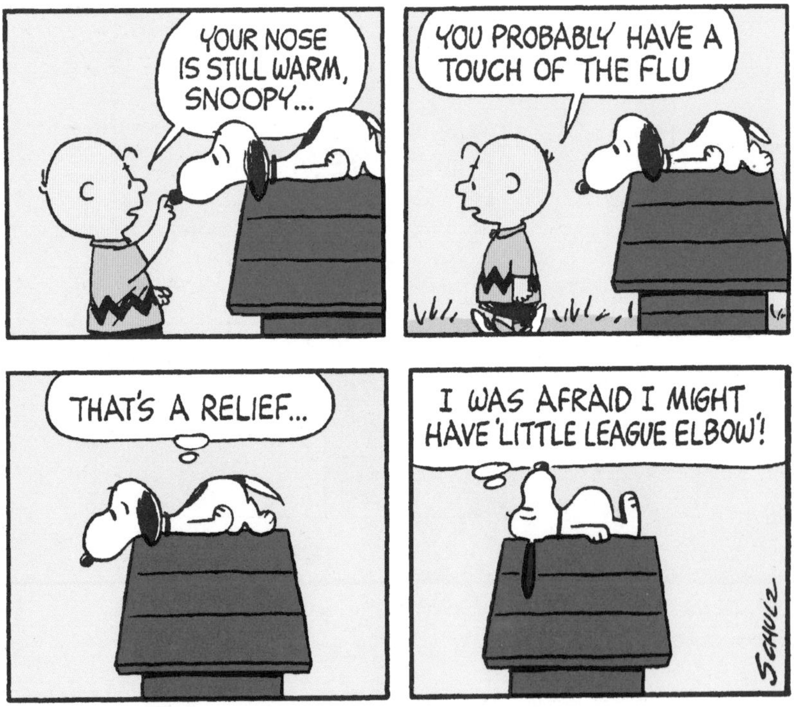
YOUR NOSE IS STILL WARM, SNOOPY...
YOU PROBABLY HAVE A TOUCH OF THE FLU
THAT'S A RELIEF...
I WAS AFRAID I MIGHT HAVE 'LITTLE LEAGUE ELBOW'!
SCHULZ

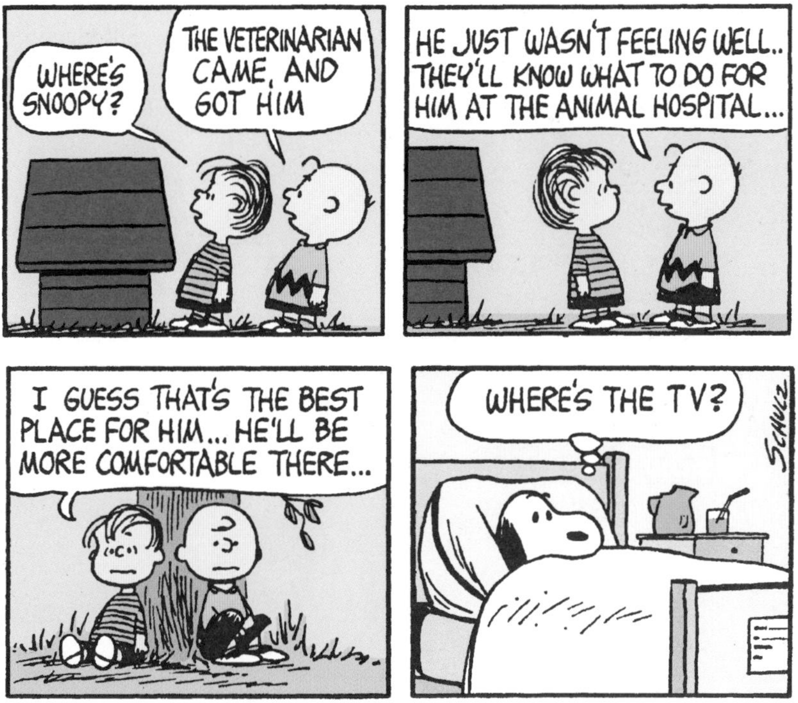
WHERE'S SNOOPY?
THE VETERINARIAN CAME, AND GOT HIM
HE JUST WASN'T FEELING WELL.. THEY'LL KNOW WHAT TO DO FOR HIM AT THE ANIMAL HOSPITAL...
I GUESS THAT'S THE BEST PLACE FOR HIM... HE'LL BE MORE COMFORTABLE THERE...
WHERE'S THE TV?
SCHULZ

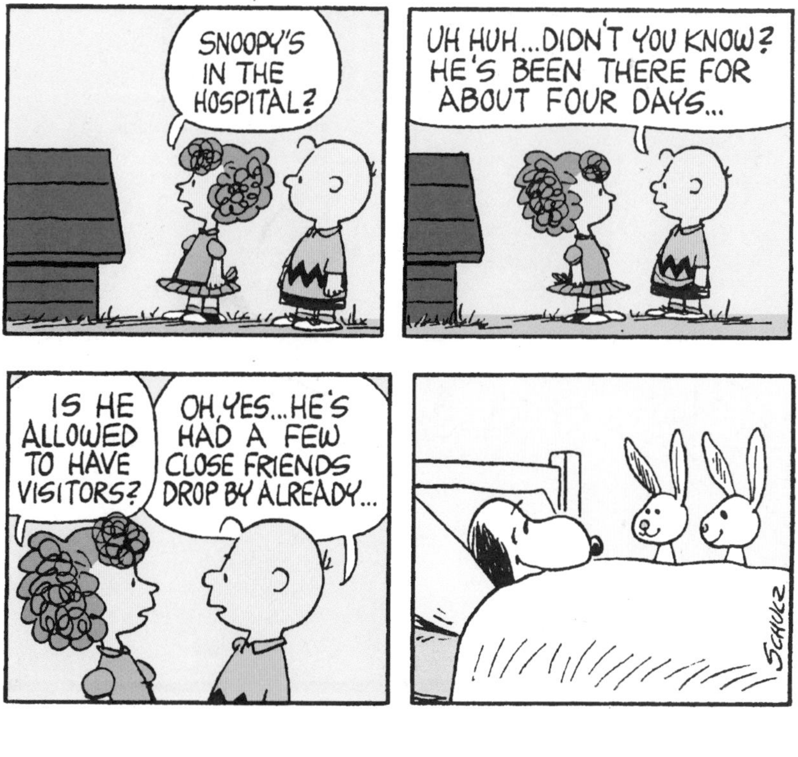
SNOOPY'S IN THE HOSPITAL?
UH HUH...DIDN'T YOU KNOW? HE'S BEEN THERE FOR ABOUT FOUR DAYS...
IS HE ALLOWED TO HAVE VISITORS?
OH, YES...HE'S HAD A FEW CLOSE FRIENDS DROP BY ALREADY...
SCHULZ

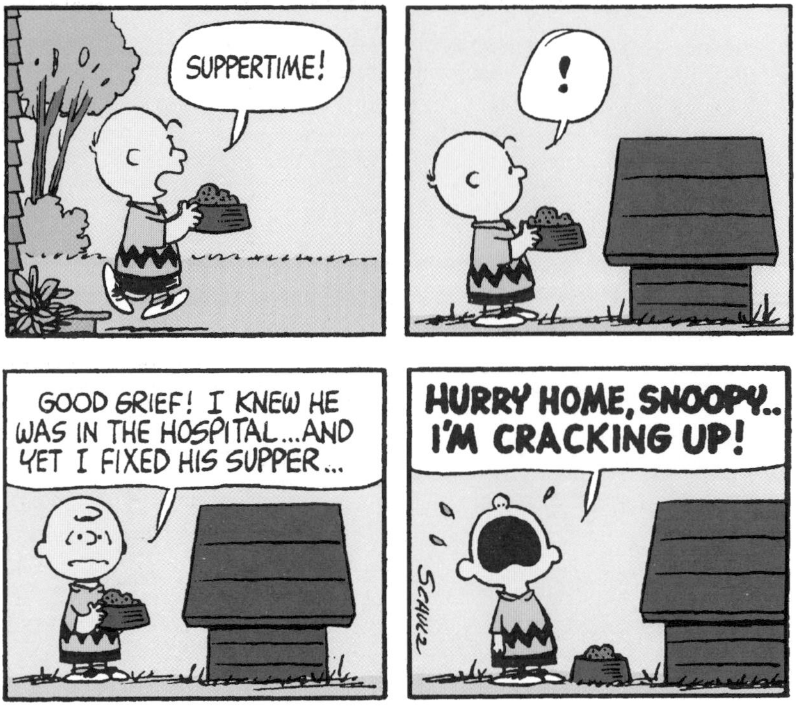
SUPPERTIME!
!
GOOD GRIEF! I KNEW HE WAS IN THE HOSPITAL...AND YET I FIXED HIS SUPPER...
HURRY HOME, SNOOPY.. I'M CRACKING UP!
SCHULZ

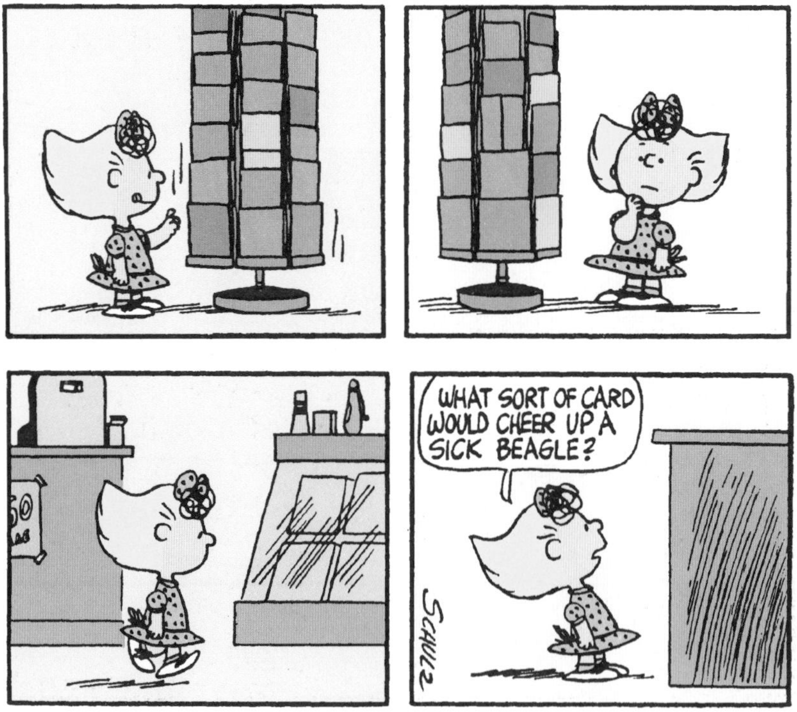
WHAT SORT OF CARD WOULD CHEER UP A SICK BEAGLE?
SCHULZ

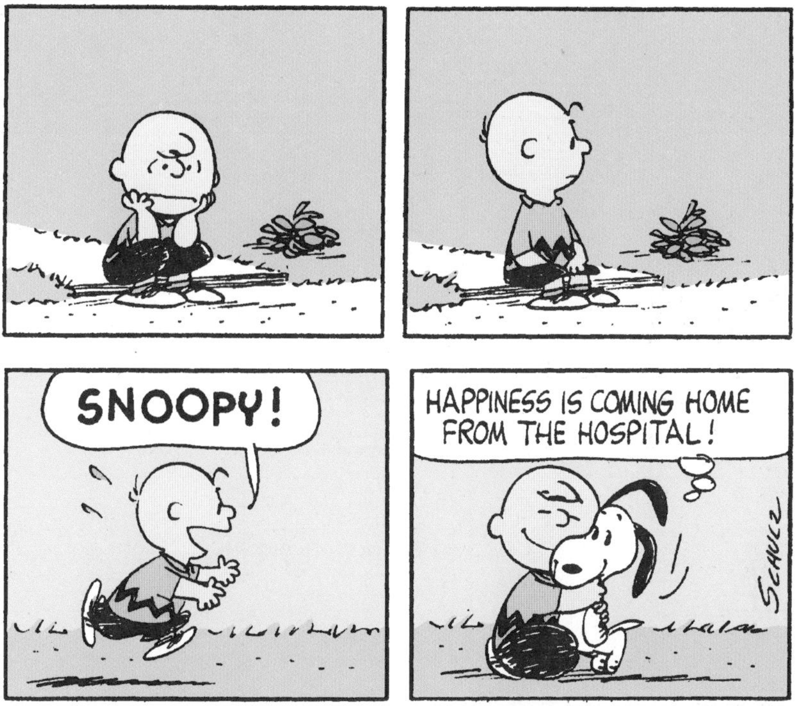
SNOOPY!
HAPPINESS IS COMING HOME FROM THE HOSPITAL!
SCHULZ

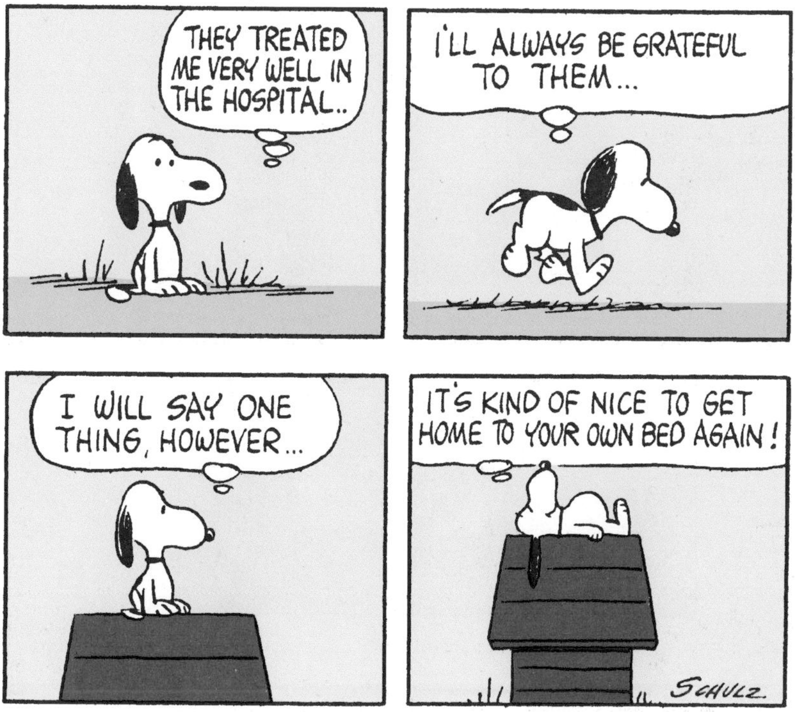
THEY TREATED ME VERY WELL IN THE HOSPITAL..
I'LL ALWAYS BE GRATEFUL TO THEM...
I WILL SAY ONE THING, HOWEVER...
IT'S KIND OF NICE TO GET HOME TO YOUR OWN BED AGAIN!
SCHULZ

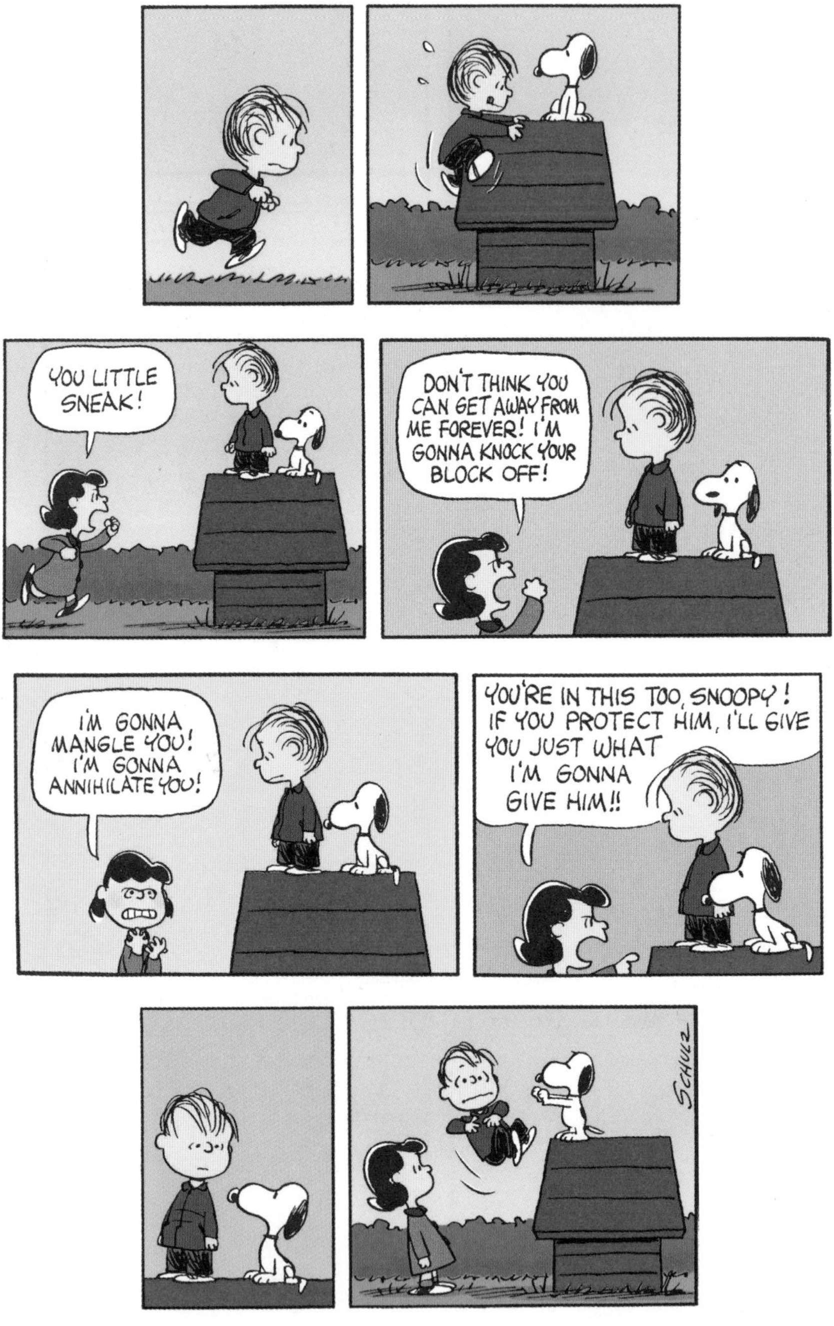
YOU LITTLE SNEAK!
DON'T THINK YOU CAN GET AWAY FROM ME FOREVER! I'M GONNA KNOCK YOUR BLOCK OFF!
I'M GONNA MANGLE YOU! I'M GONNA ANNIHILATE YOU!
YOU'RE IN THIS TOO, SNOOPY! IF YOU PROTECT HIM, I'LL GIVE YOU JUST WHAT I'M GONNA GIVE HIM!!
SCHULZ

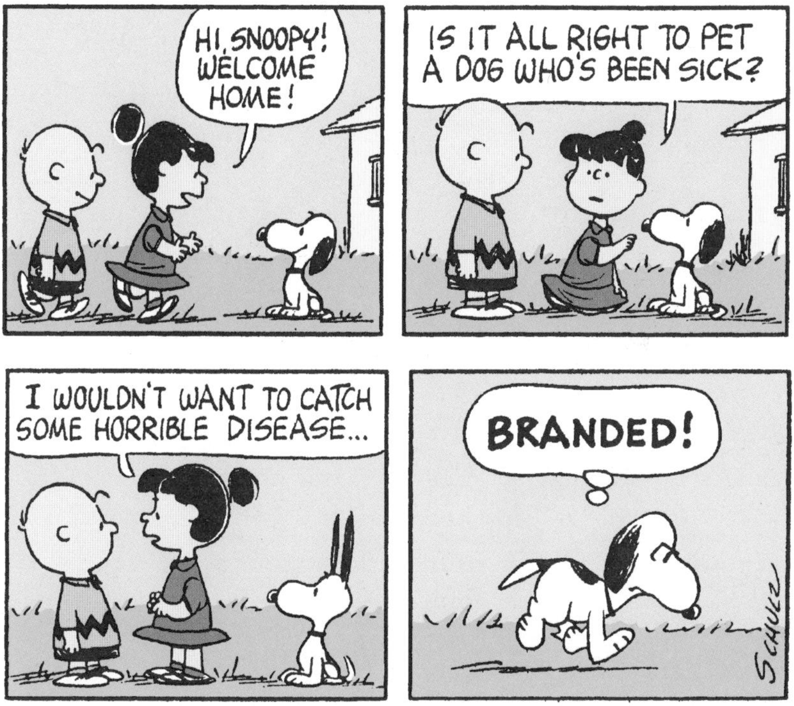
HI, SNOOPY! WELCOME HOME!
IS IT ALL RIGHT TO PET A DOG WHO'S BEEN SICK?
I WOULDN'T WANT TO CATCH SOME HORRIBLE DISEASE...
BRANDED!
SCHULZ

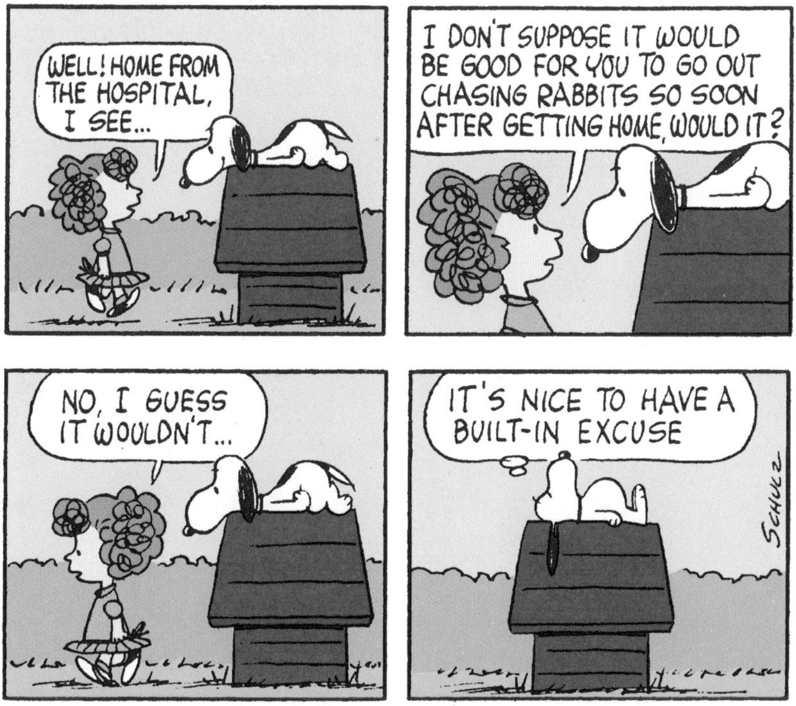
WELL! HOME FROM THE HOSPITAL, I SEE...
I DON'T SUPPOSE IT WOULD BE GOOD FOR YOU TO GO OUT CHASING RABBITS SO SOON AFTER GETTING HOME, WOULD IT?
NO, I GUESS IT WOULDN'T...
IT'S NICE TO HAVE A BUILT-IN EXCUSE
SCHULZ

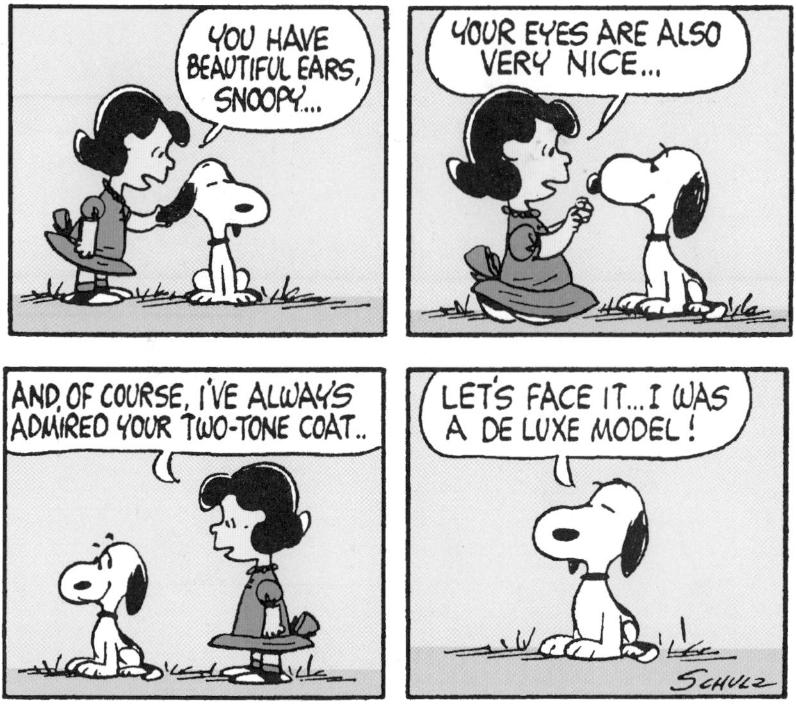
YOU HAVE BEAUTIFUL EARS, SNOOPY....
YOUR EYES ARE ALSO VERY NICE...
AND, OF COURSE, I'VE ALWAYS ADMIRED YOUR TWO-TONE COAT..
LET'S FACE IT... I WAS A DE LUXE MODEL!
SCHULZ

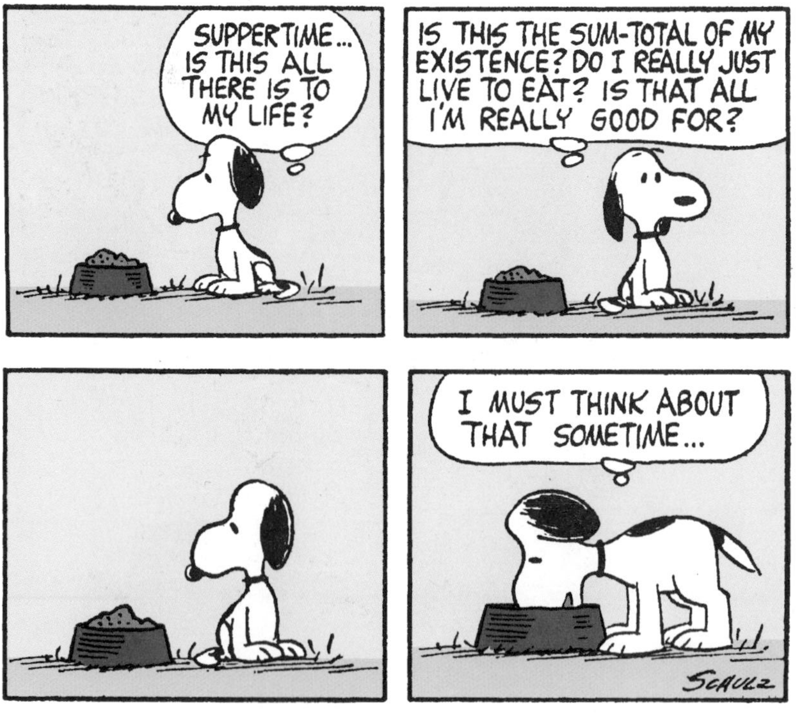
SUPPERTIME... IS THIS ALL THERE IS TO MY LIFE?
IS THIS THE SUM-TOTAL OF MY EXISTENCE? DO I REALLY JUST LIVE TO EAT? IS THAT ALL I'M REALLY GOOD FOR?
I MUST THINK ABOUT THAT SOMETIME...
SCHULZ

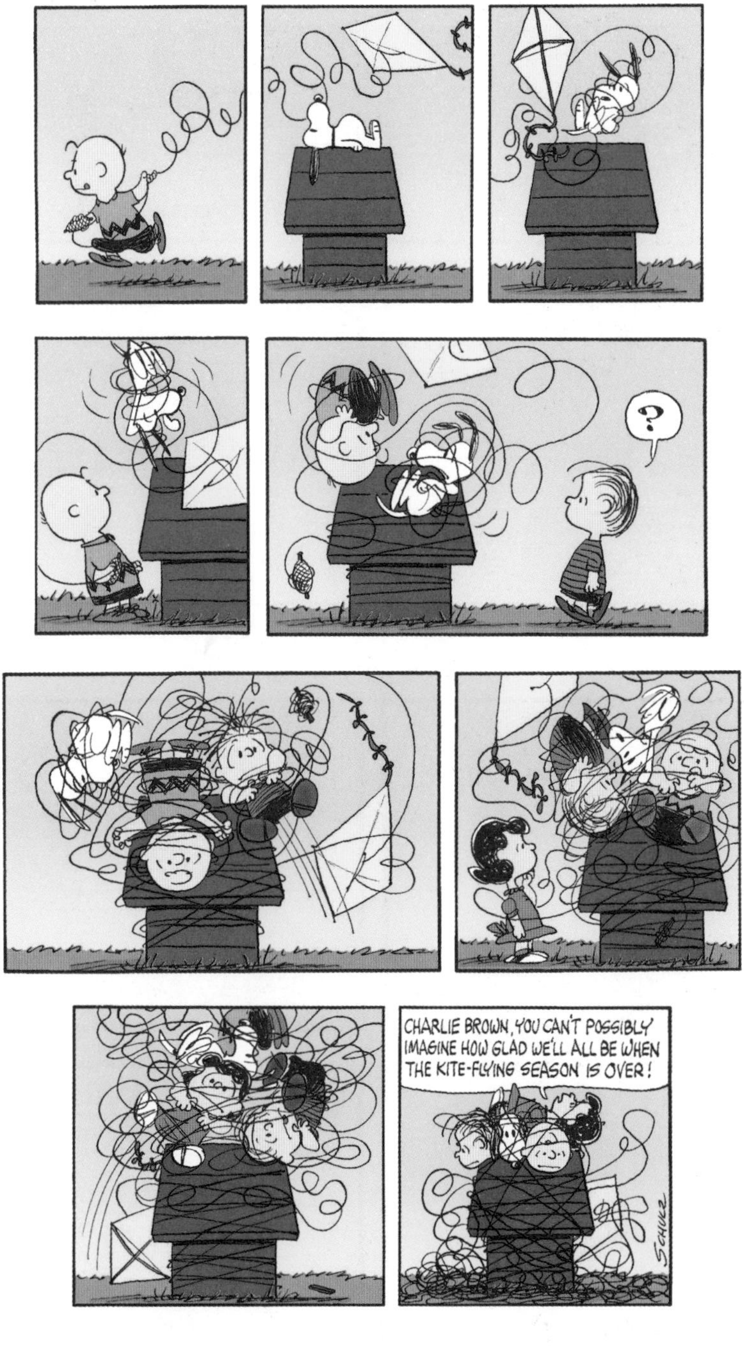
?
CHARLIE BROWN, YOU CAN'T POSSIBLY IMAGINE HOW GLAD WE'LL ALL BE WHEN THE KITE-FLYING SEASON IS OVER!
SCHULZ

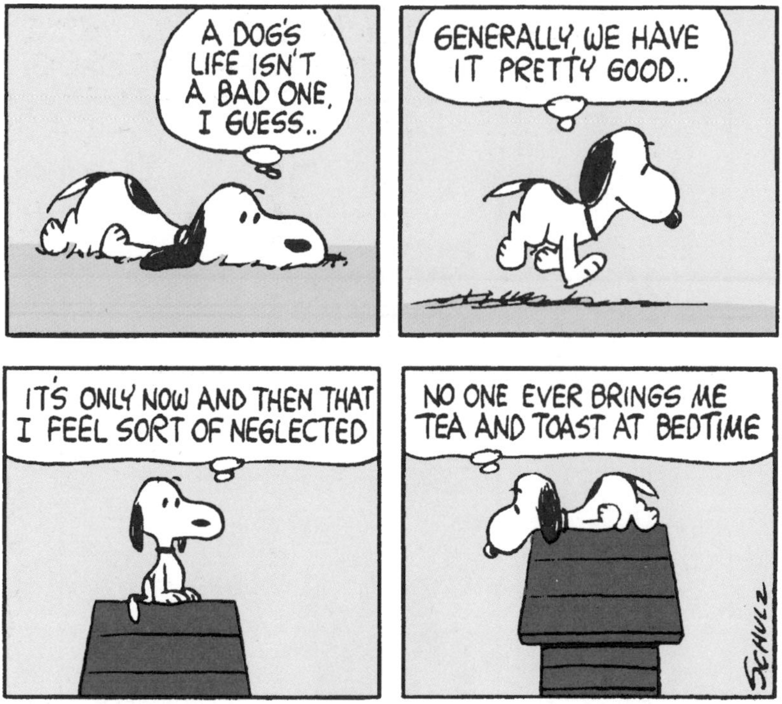
A DOG'S LIFE ISN'T A BAD ONE, I GUESS..
GENERALLY, WE HAVE IT PRETTY GOOD..
IT'S ONLY NOW AND THEN THAT I FEEL SORT OF NEGLECTED
NO ONE EVER BRINGS ME TEA AND TOAST AT BEDTIME
SCHULZ

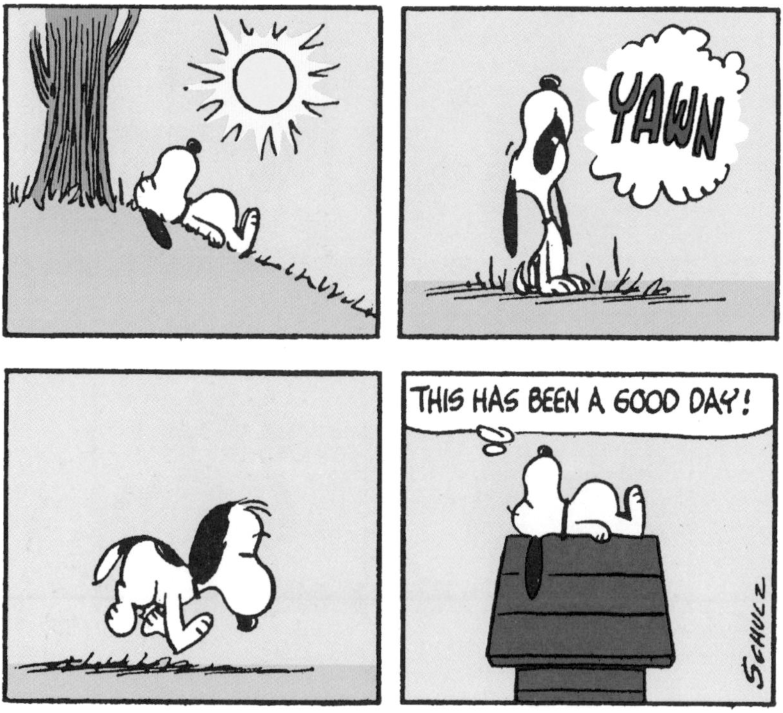
YAWN
THIS HAS BEEN A GOOD DAY!
SCHULZ

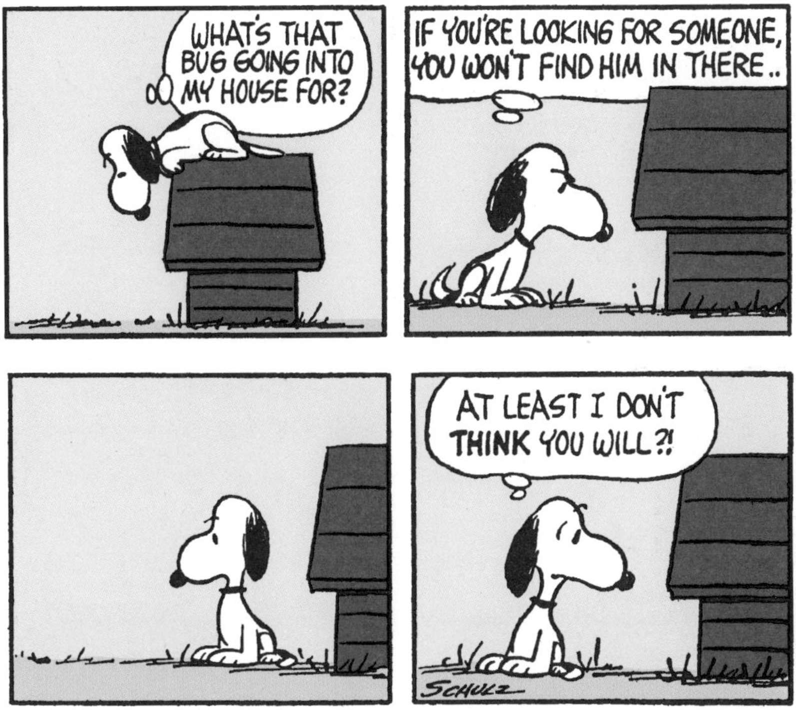
WHAT'S THAT BUG GOING INTO MY HOUSE FOR?
IF YOU'RE LOOKING FOR SOMEONE, YOU WON'T FIND HIM IN THERE..
AT LEAST I DON'T THINK YOU WILL?!
SCHULZ

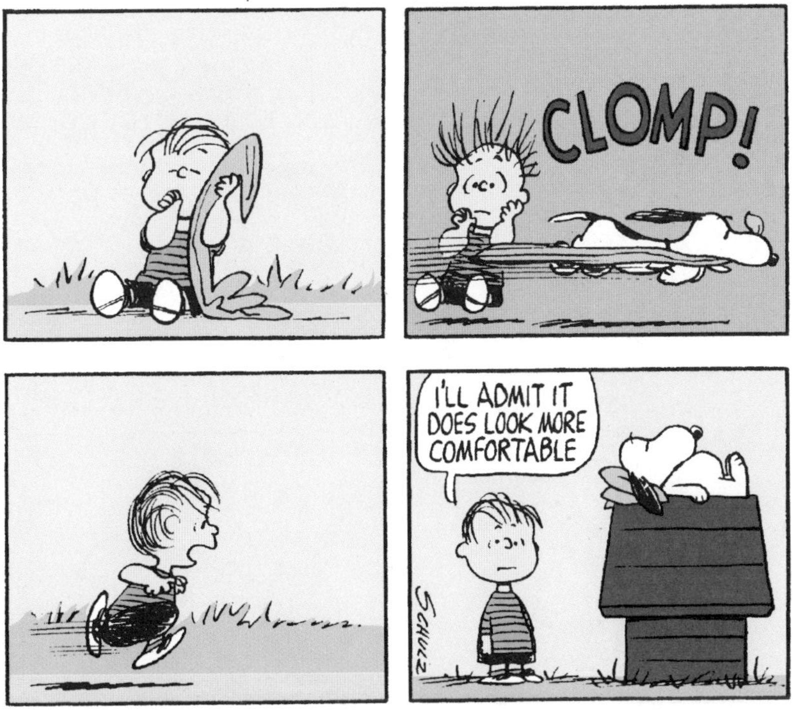
CLOMP!
I'LL ADMIT IT DOES LOOK MORE COMFORTABLE
SCHULZ

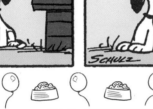

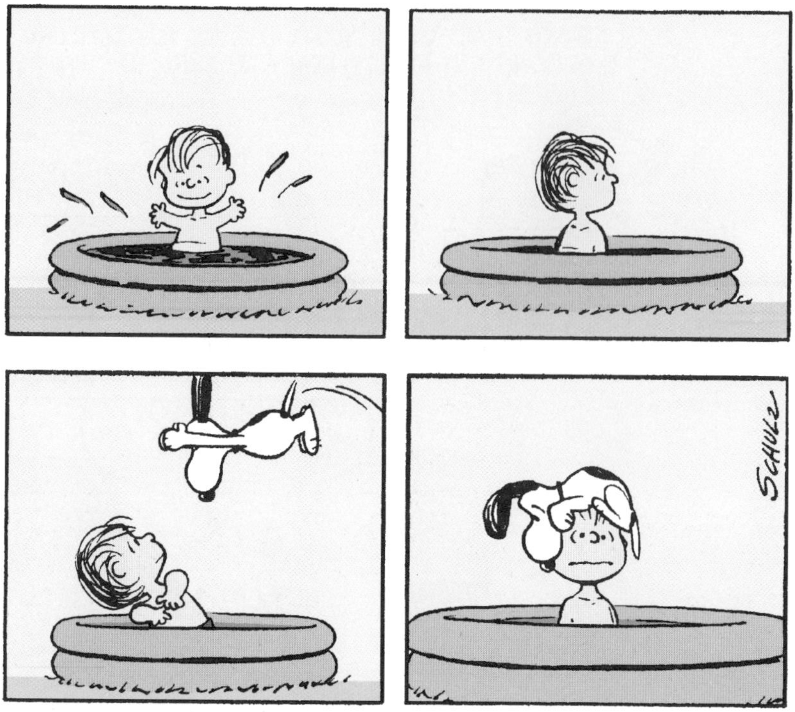

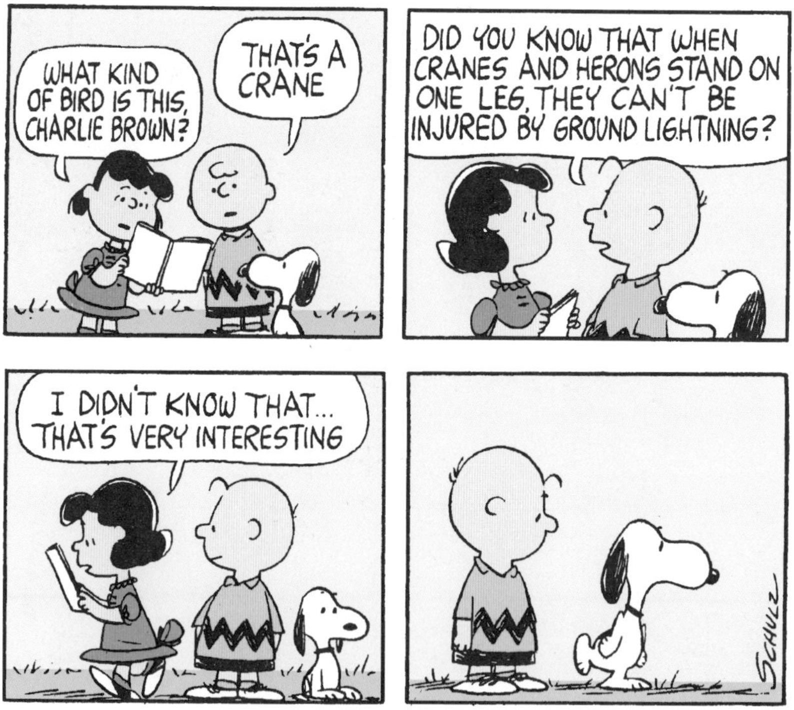
WHAT KIND OF BIRD IS THIS, CHARLIE BROWN?
THAT'S A CRANE
DID YOU KNOW THAT WHEN CRANES AND HERONS STAND ON ONE LEG, THEY CAN'T BE INJURED BY GROUND LIGHTNING?
I DIDN'T KNOW THAT... THAT'S VERY INTERESTING

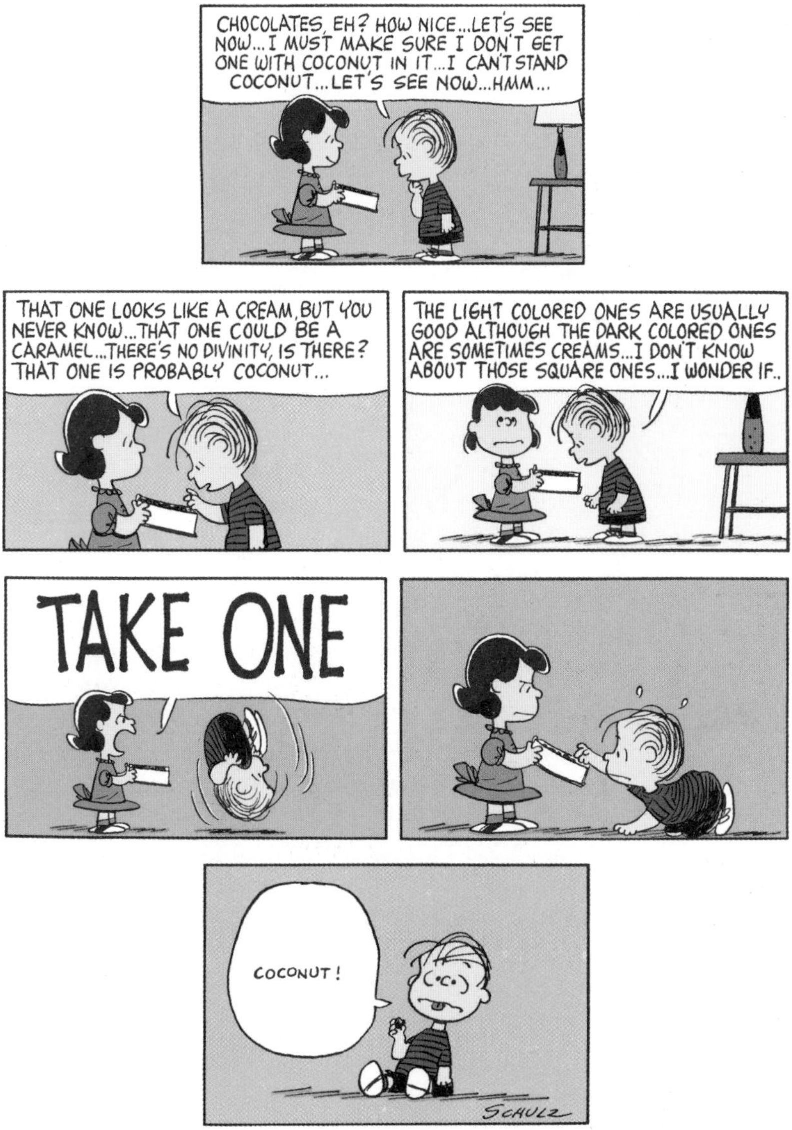
CHOCOLATES, EH? HOW NICE...LET'S SEE NOW...I MUST MAKE SURE I DON'T GET ONE WITH COCONUT IN IT...I CAN'T STAND COCONUT...LET'S SEE NOW...HMM...
THAT ONE LOOKS LIKE A CREAM, BUT YOU NEVER KNOW...THAT ONE COULD BE A CARAMEL...THERE'S NO DIVINITY, IS THERE? THAT ONE IS PROBABLY COCONUT...
THE LIGHT COLORED ONES ARE USUALLY GOOD ALTHOUGH THE DARK COLORED ONES ARE SOMETIMES CREAMS...I DON'T KNOW ABOUT THOSE SQUARE ONES...I WONDER IF..
TAKE ONE
COCONUT!
SCHULZ

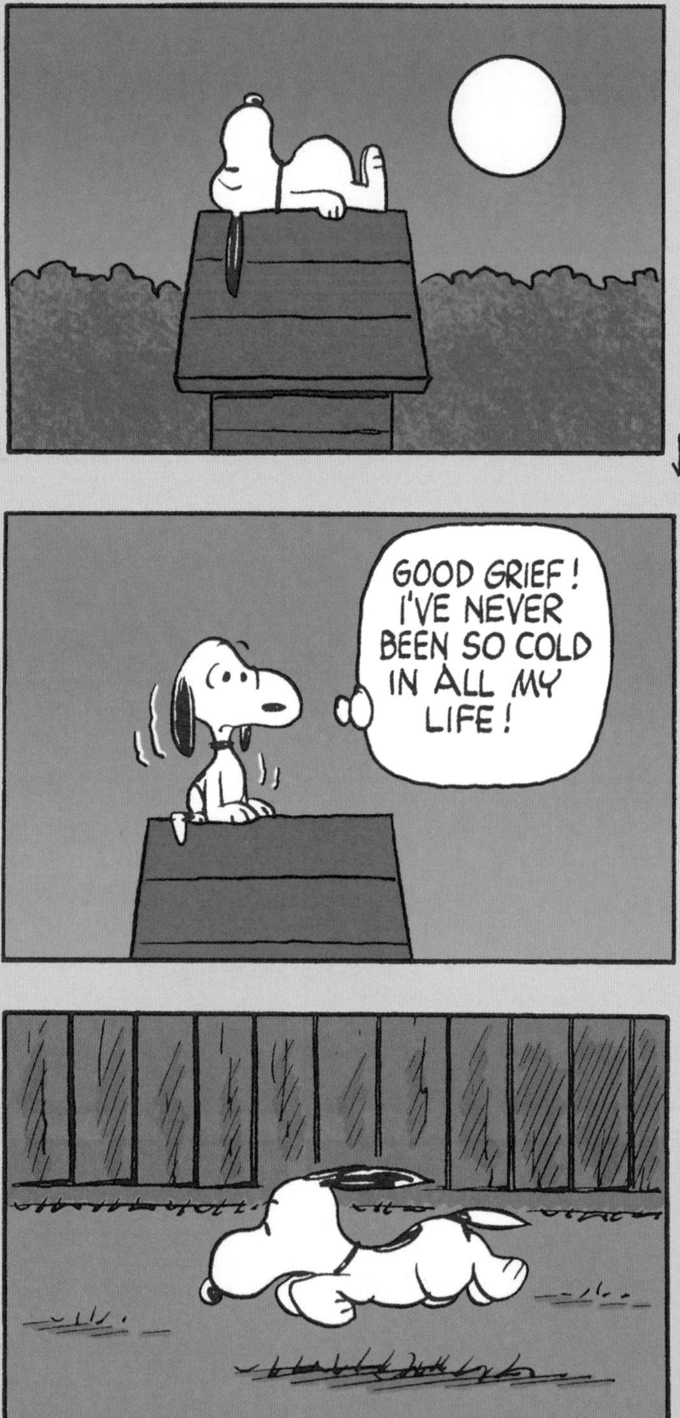
GOOD GRIEF! I'VE NEVER BEEN SO COLD IN ALL MY LIFE!

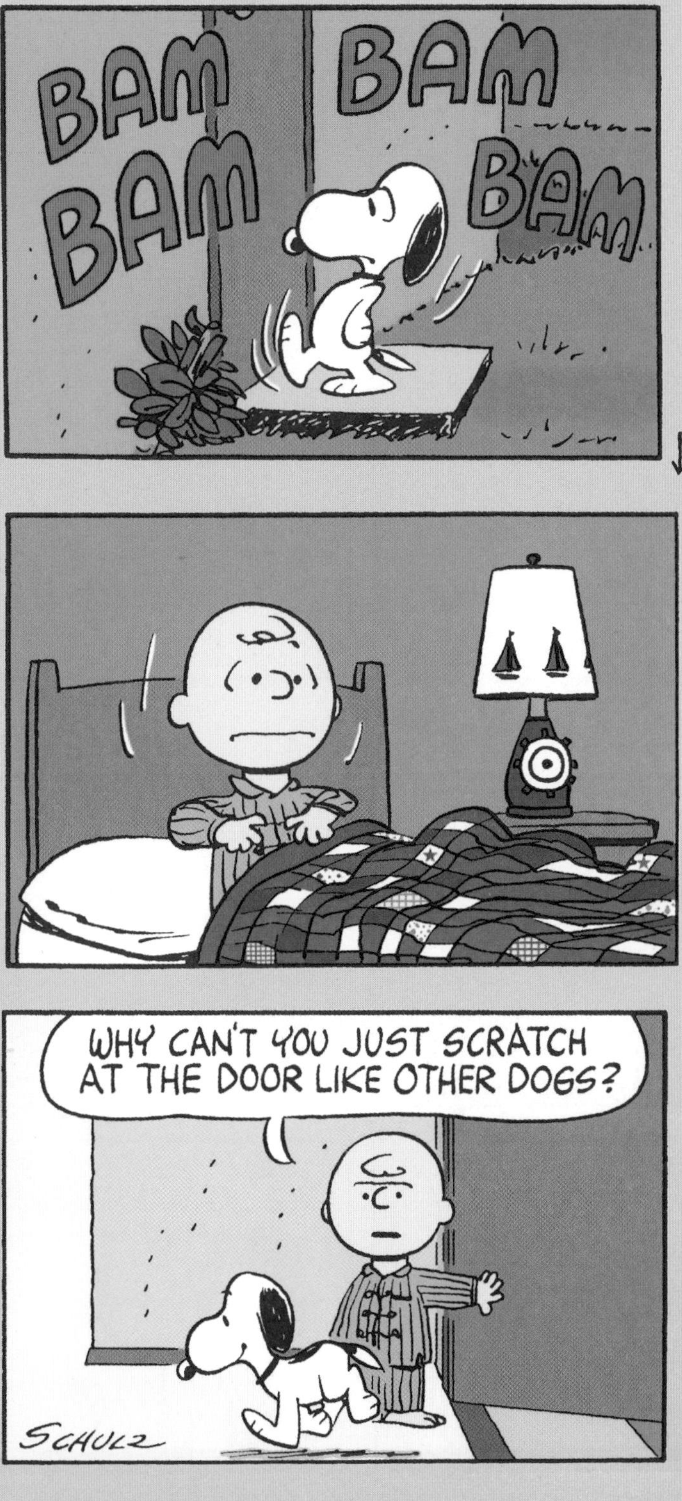
BAM
BAM
BAM
BAM
WHY CAN'T YOU JUST SCRATCH AT THE DOOR LIKE OTHER DOGS?
SCHULZ

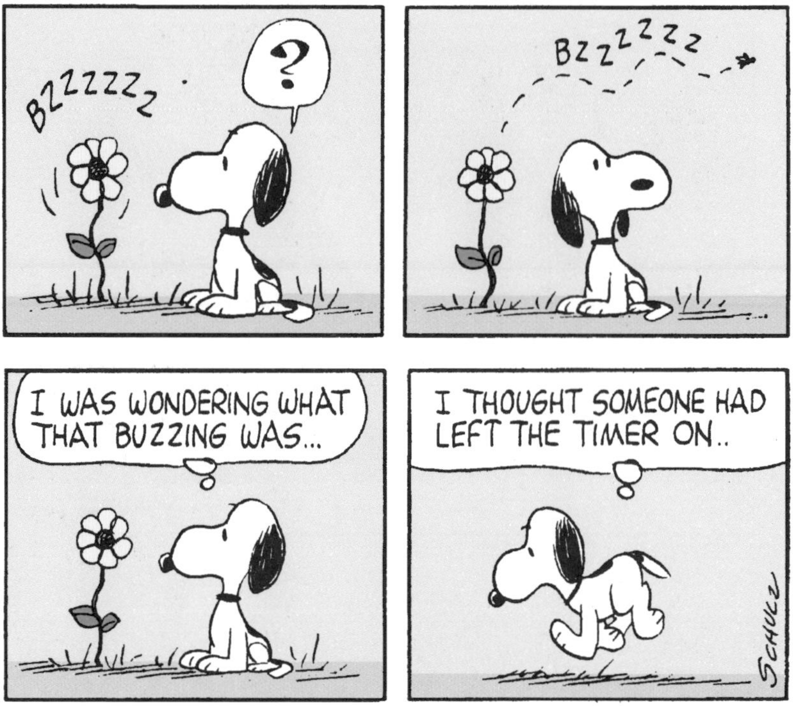
BZZZZZZ
?
BZZZZZZ
I WAS WONDERING WHAT THAT BUZZING WAS...
I THOUGHT SOMEONE HAD LEFT THE TIMER ON..
SCHULZ

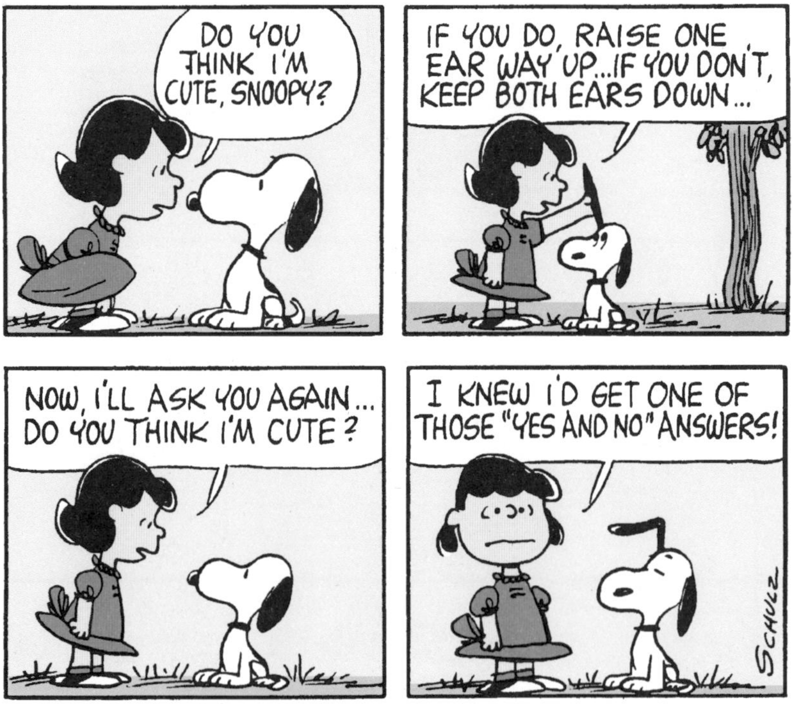
DO YOU THINK I'M CUTE, SNOOPY?
IF YOU DO, RAISE ONE EAR WAY UP...IF YOU DON'T, KEEP BOTH EARS DOWN...
NOW, I'LL ASK YOU AGAIN... DO YOU THINK I'M CUTE?
I KNEW I'D GET ONE OF THOSE "YES AND NO" ANSWERS!
SCHULZ

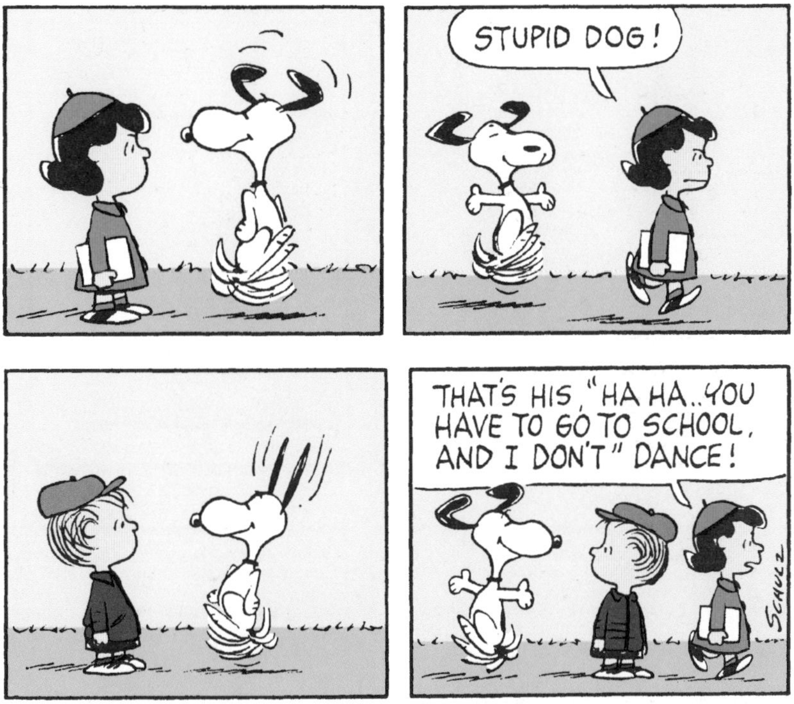
STUPID DOG!
THAT'S HIS, "HA HA.. YOU HAVE TO GO TO SCHOOL, AND I DON'T" DANCE!
SCHULZ

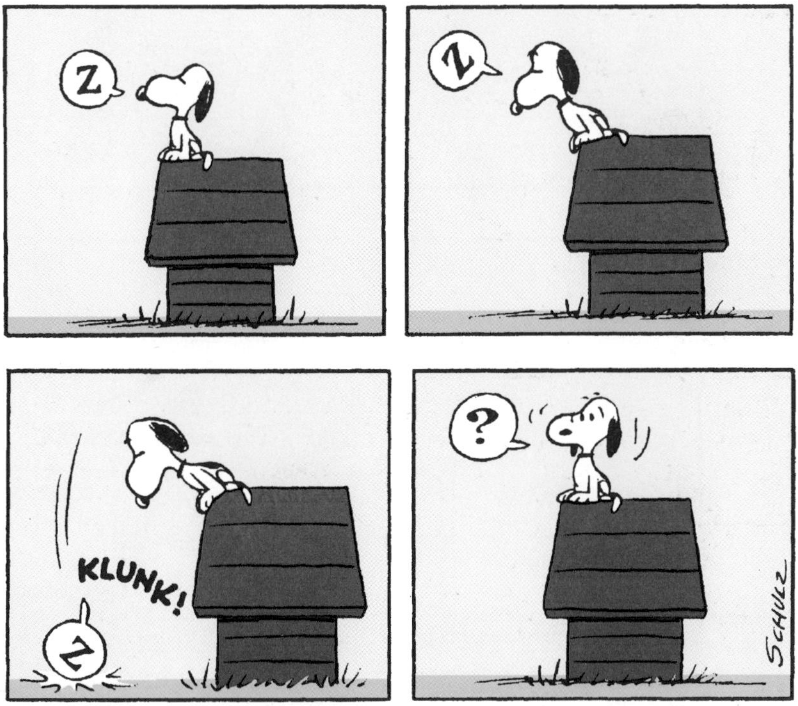
Z
Z
KLUNK!
Z
?
SCHULZ

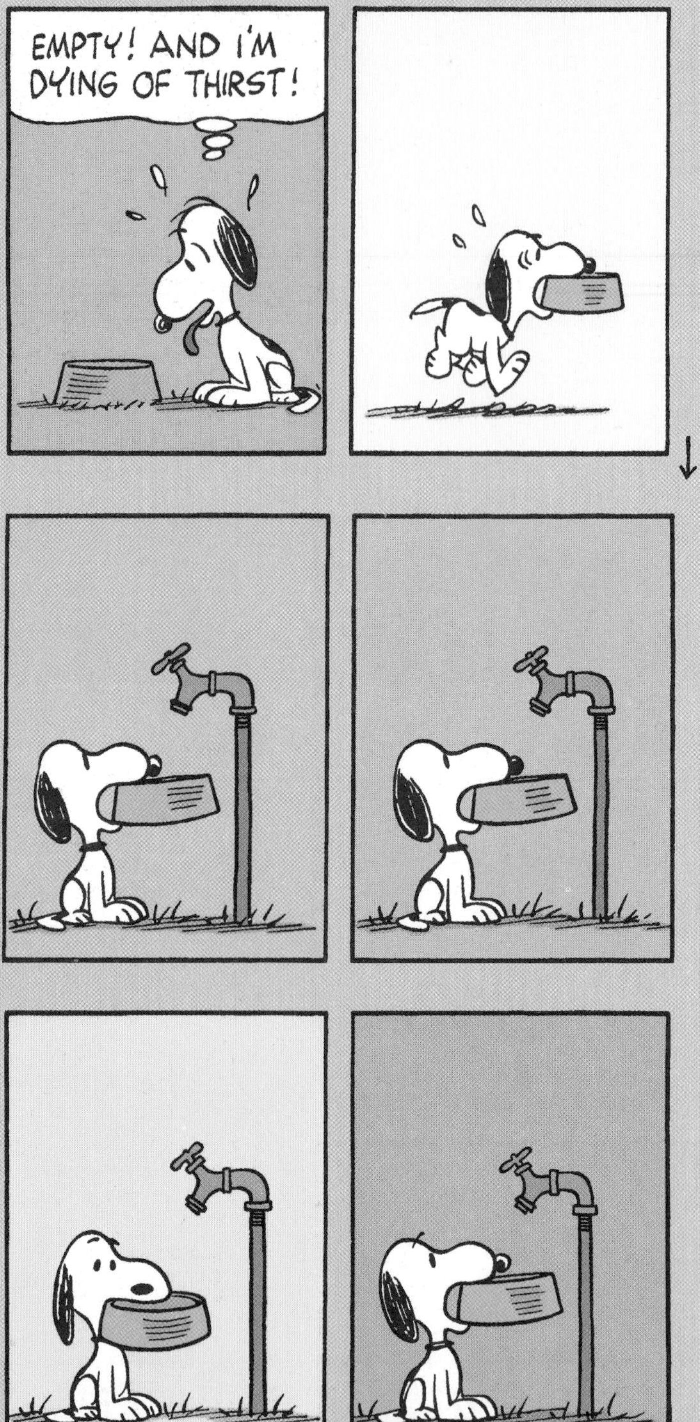
EMPTY! AND I'M DYING OF THIRST!

THAT'S ONE I'M GOING TO HAVE TO THINK ABOUT FOR AWHILE!
SCHULZ

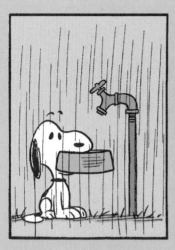

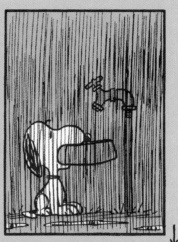

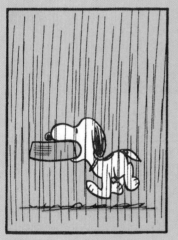

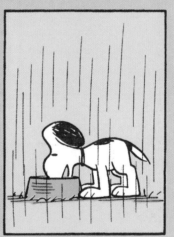

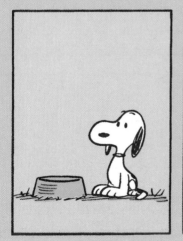

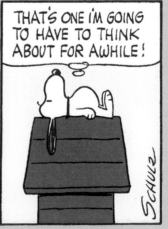

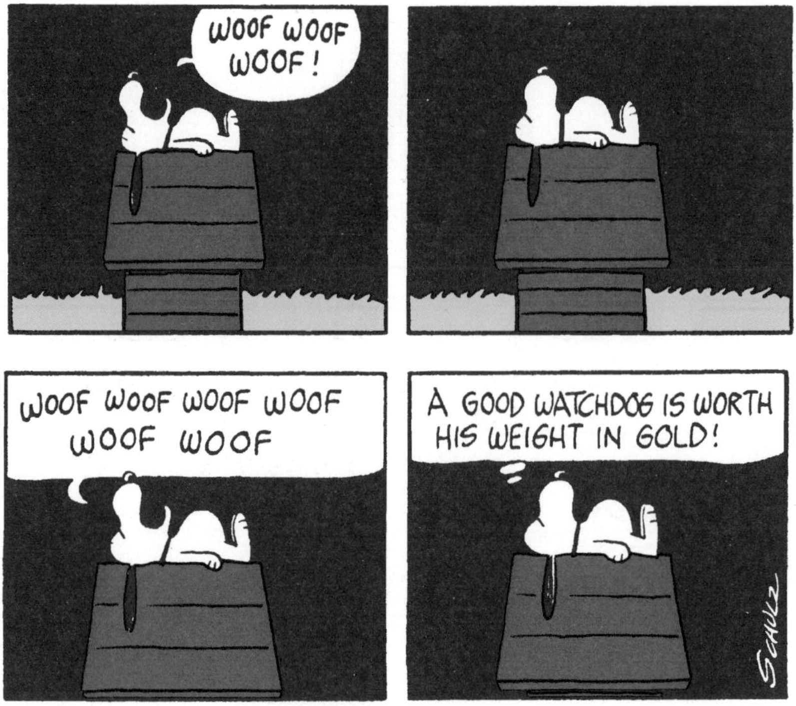
WOOF WOOF WOOF!
WOOF WOOF WOOF WOOF WOOF WOOF
A GOOD WATCHDOG IS WORTH HIS WEIGHT IN GOLD!
SCHULZ

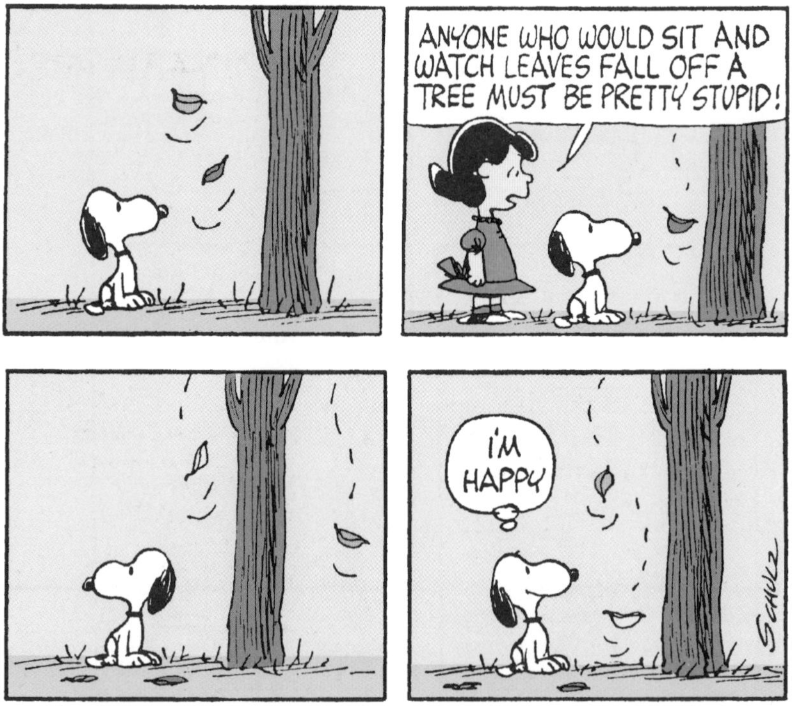
ANYONE WHO WOULD SIT AND WATCH LEAVES FALL OFF A TREE MUST BE PRETTY STUPID!
I'M HAPPY
SCHULZ

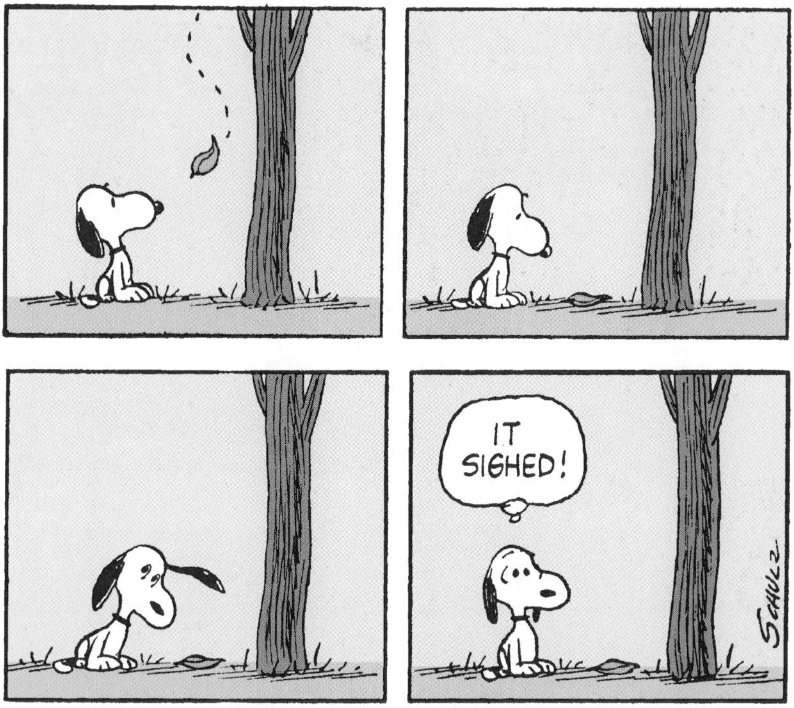
IT SIGHED!
SCHULZ

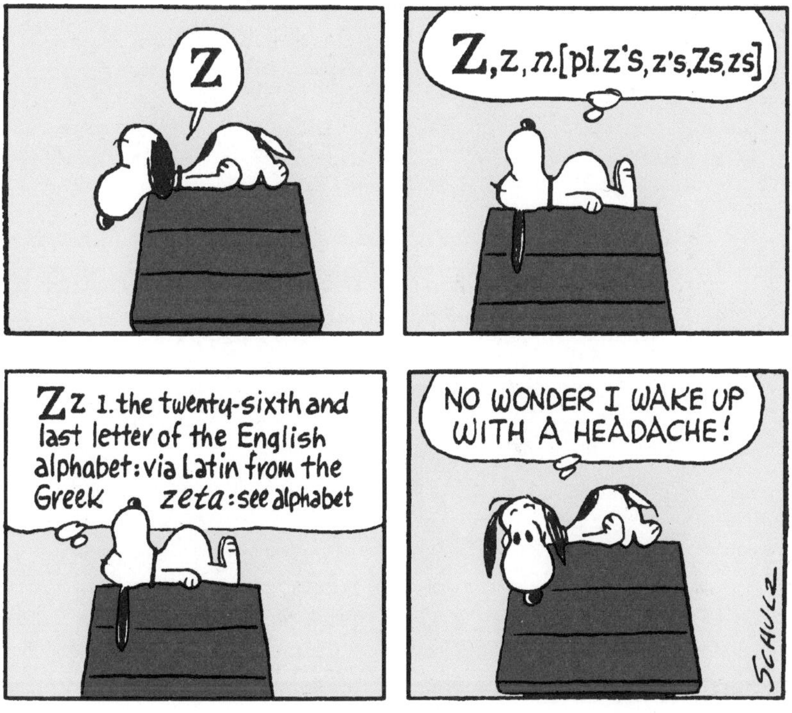
Z
Z, z, n. [pl. Z's, z's, Zs, zs]
Zz 1. the twenty-sixth and last letter of the English alphabet: via Latin from the Greek zeta: see alphabet
NO WONDER I WAKE UP WITH A HEADACHE!
SCHULZ

SEE THAT GROUP OF STARS, SALLY?
THAT'S CALLED THE "BIG DIPPER"
THE SHAPE OF THE "BIG DIPPER" CHANGES OVER THE YEARS BECAUSE OF AN UNEQUAL MOVEMENT AMONG ITS STARS...

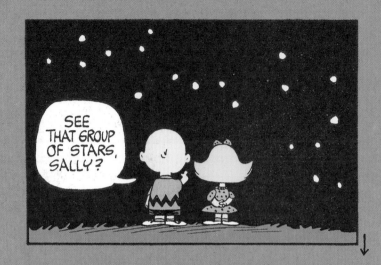

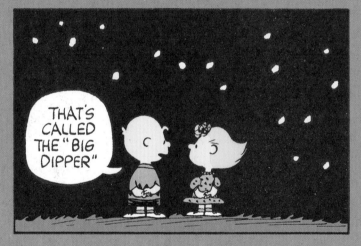

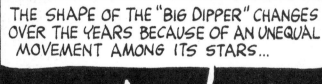

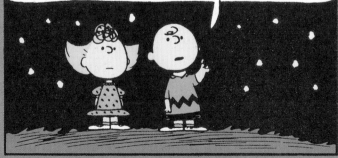

IN ANOTHER HUNDRED THOUSAND YEARS THE "BIG DIPPER" WILL BE GONE..
WAAH!
SCHULZ

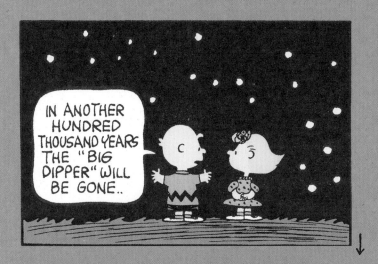

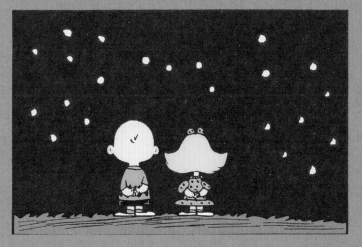

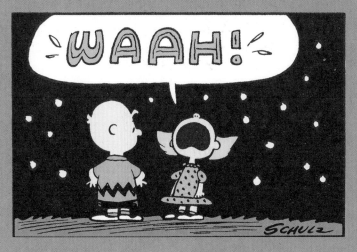

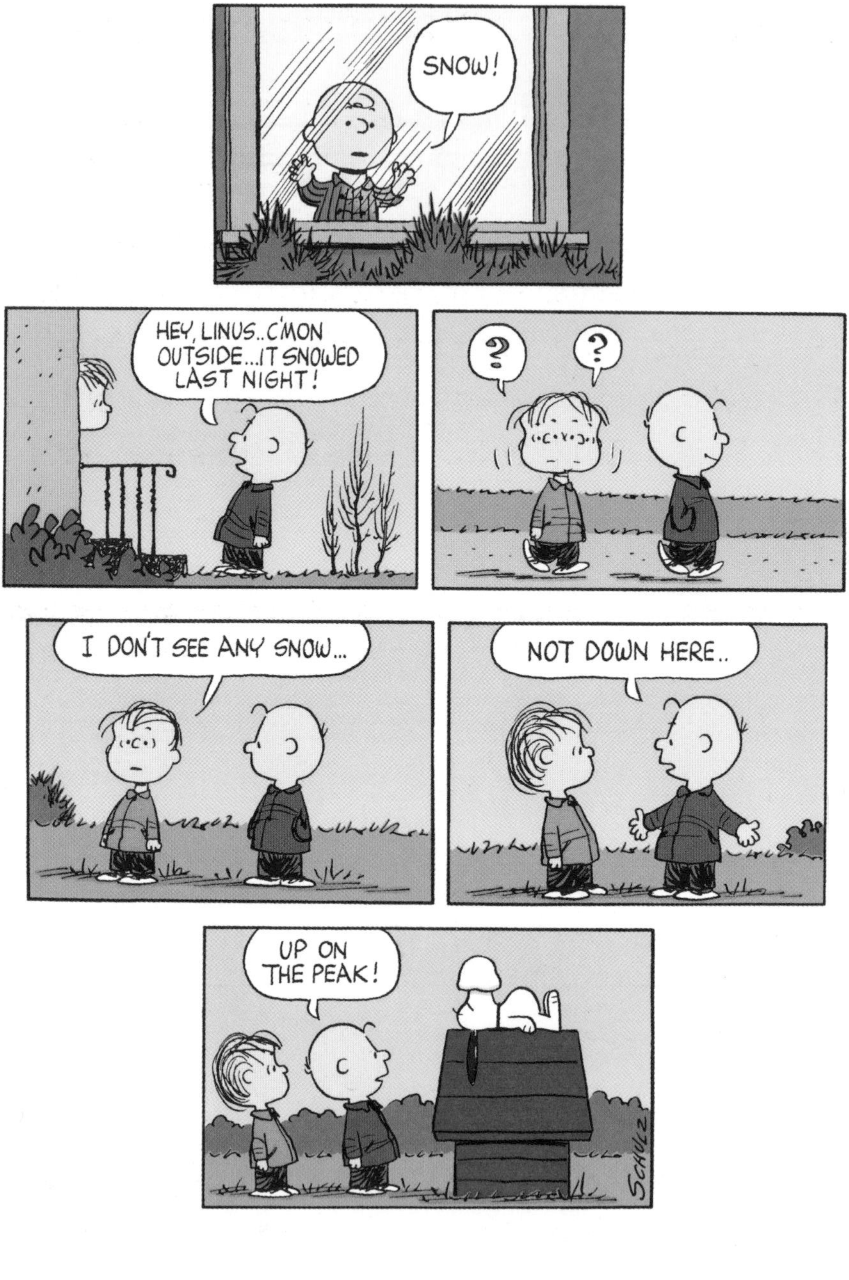
SNOW!
HEY, LINUS..C'MON OUTSIDE...IT SNOWED LAST NIGHT!
?
?
I DON'T SEE ANY SNOW...
NOT DOWN HERE..
UP ON THE PEAK!
SCHULZ

MORE TO EXPLORE! Featuring cool activities and fun facts!

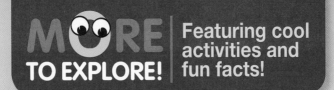

LET'S PARTY!

Here are some fun activities and things to make for your Snoopy party! Thanks to our friends at the Charles M. Schulz Museum and Research Center in Santa Rosa, California, for helping us out with these.

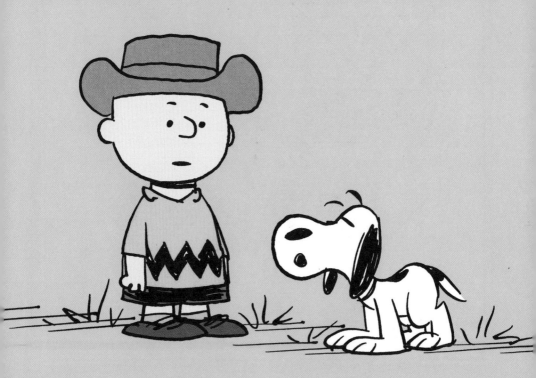

Orgami Party Hats

You can't have a party without party hats! These are fun to make and you can decorate them however you like when they're done.

INSTRUCTIONS:

First, make the Helmet Base.

1 Take a square piece of paper and fold it in half as shown.

2 Then fold it in half again.

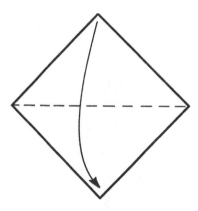

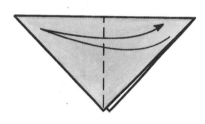

3 Fold left and right to center.

Helmet Base.

Then make the Party Hat.

4 Start with the Helmet Base.

5 Fold left and right to center.

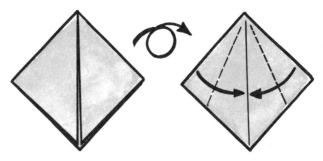

6 Fold bottom to indicated point.

7 Keep folding, as indicated.

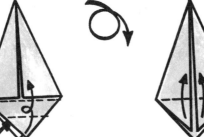
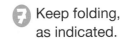

8

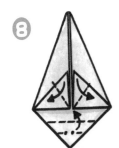

9

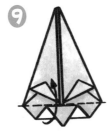

Party Hat.

Thanks to Jeff Cole, author of *Easy Origami Fold-a-Day Calendar 2016* (Accord Publishing, a division of Andrews McMeel Publishing) for the origami instructions.

Let's Make Pizzettes

These little pizzas are easy to assemble and fun for you and your friends to make, with the help of a grown-up.

INGREDIENTS:

1 tube refrigerated pizza dough

1 cup tomato pizza or pasta sauce

1 cup grated mozzarella cheese

(optional: pepperoni slices, green peppers, mushrooms, olives)

INSTRUCTIONS:

1 Preheat oven to 425. Unroll the pizza dough and cut it into 8 equal pieces. Form each piece into a rough ball. Place each ball on an ungreased baking sheet and press your fingertips to make it a 4-inch round.

2 Spoon sauce over each round, leaving a ½-inch border all around. Sprinkle the cheese evenly over the sauce. If using toppings, place them on the cheese.

3 Bake for 10 to 12 minutes or until the edges of the crusts are golden brown. Let the pizzettes cool slightly before cutting and serving.

Make Party Blowers

Let the merry-making begin! These make for a festive addition to the party. If you receive the Sunday comics, use that section for the paper part of these blowers to give them a real cartoony look.

MATERIALS: paper; scissors; straws; tape; pencil, pen, or marker; rubber band

INSTRUCTIONS:

1. Cut the straw in 6 1-inch pieces.

2. Cut a rectangle from the paper about 10 inches long by 2 inches wide.

3. Fold the rectangle together in the middle and tape the entire length of it closed and the top closed.

4. Roll the strip into a spiral and rubber band it together.

5. Tape the open end to the straw, making sure it is airtight.

6. Blow into the straw. If it's not completely airtight, use more tape to seal it.

Even More to Explore!

These sources will be helpful if you wish to learn more about Charles Schulz, the Charles M. Schulz Museum and Research Center, *Peanuts*, or the art of cartooning.

WEBSITES:

www.schulzmuseum.org
- Official website of the Charles M. Schulz Museum and Research Center.

www.peanuts.com
- Thirty days' worth of *Peanuts* strips. Character profiles. Timeline about the strip. Character print-outs for coloring. Info on fellow cartoonists' tributes to Charles Schulz after he passed away.

www.fivecentsplease.org
- Recent news articles and press releases on Charles Schulz and *Peanuts*. Links to other *Peanuts*-themed websites. Info on *Peanuts* products.

www.toonopedia.com
- Info on *Peanuts* and many, many other comics—it's an "encyclopedia of 'toons."

www.gocomics.com
- Access to popular and lesser-known comic strips, as well as editorial cartoons.

www.reuben.org
- Official website of the National Cartoonists Society. Info on how to become a professional cartoonist. Info on awards given for cartooning.

www.kingfeatures.com and www.amuniversal.com
- Newspaper syndicate websites. Learn more about the distribution of comics to newspapers.

Peanuts is distributed internationally by Universal Uclick.

Snoopy: Party Animal! copyright © 2016 by Peanuts Worldwide, LLC. All rights reserved. Printed in China. No part of this book may be used or reproduced in any manner whatsoever without written permission except in the case of reprints in the context of reviews.

Andrews McMeel Publishing
a division of Andrews McMeel Universal
1130 Walnut Street, Kansas City, Missouri 64106

www.andrewsmcmeel.com

www.peanuts.com

16 17 18 19 20 SDB 10 9 8 7 6 5 4 3 2 1

ISBN: 978-1-4494-7194-1

Library of Congress Control Number: 2015956192

Made by:
Shenzhen Donnelley Printing Company Ltd.
Address and location of manufacturer:
No. 47, Wuhe Nan Road, Bantian Ind. Zone,
Shenzhen China, 518129
1st Printing – 12/21/15

ATTENTION: SCHOOLS AND BUSINESSES
Andrews McMeel books are available at quantity discounts with bulk purchase for educational, business, or sales promotional use. For information, please e-mail the Andrews McMeel Publishing Special Sales Department:
specialsales@amuniversal.com.

WOODSTOCK
MASTER OF DISGUISE
A PEANUTS Collection

SNOOPY
CONTACT!
A PEANUTS Collection

the MUTTS Winter diaries
PATRICK McDONNELL

Unicorn on a Roll
Another Phoebe and Her Unicorn Adventure
Dana Simpson

big NATE
WELCOME TO MY WORLD
by LINCOLN PEIRCE

The Dreadful Fate of Jonathan York

ALIEN INVASION in my BACKYARD
by RUBEN BOLLING
AN EMU CLUB ADVENTURE!

THE G-MAN SUPER JOURNAL
Awesome Origins
Chris Giarrusso

MARK TATULLI
"A SUREFIRE HIT AND AN ABSOLUTE SCREAM!"
DESMOND PUCKET
AND THE Mountain Full of Monsters

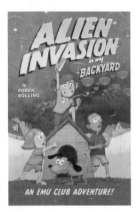